Thiefman's Oath

Rachel Pendley

CONTENTS

TRIGGER WARNINGS

Strong violence, gore and language. Brief mentions of child abuse/harm. Death by fire/housefire. Sexual content. Predatory villain.

DEDICATION

For my mother, who has loved this story from day one.
Thank you for always encouraging my art, even when it's really,
really weird.

SPRING

Through the ink black sky lightning crawled like a spider, a roar of thunder quick on its webbed heels. This night, on the cusp of a new spring, was to be a special one. Something significant was about to begin, and the tempests shook the earth with vicious applause, hungry for what came next.

Rain dripped in a steady bead from the end of her nose as she stared at the front doors of the inn. Clad in leather armor and an air of stark authority, it was clear that Francesca Draven was no common patron.

Steeped in her shadow were a dozen men. All quiet and dutiful, wearing the same styling of armor, and equipped with an array of well-crafted weapons. These weren't common sell swords, yet they flew no banners and wore no house crests or a shiny little placard of metal on their chests. Whatever powerful hand controlled their strings was carefully hidden from the public eye.

When Francesca opened The Tossed Tankard's front doors, she was greeted by the melody of a lively band and decadent scents weaving out of the kitchen. Almost every table was full of drunken parties, all smiling and laughing and telling stories of mirth. The bar maids were flitting between them, bringing out sloshing tankards, plates of food and swatting at hands eager for a palmful of their flesh.

The owner of the inn, Greglin, was behind the bar serving shots and talking with the locals, a smile plastered on his plump face. His demeanor changed once he spotted the party strolling in out of the rain, and his shift appeared to be contagious.

Everyone took notice all at once. The voices slowly died down to a hush, the band stopped mid tune, and Greglin's previously happy expression fell into one of concern. For a moment, no one spoke, and Francesca studied the room, sweeping a wet strand of copper hair from her face.

"Evening, miss! Can I help you?" Greglin asked.

A subtle motion of the hand was all it took to spread out her company behind her, effectively closing off the exit. "Just need to ask a few questions. By request of High Father Aolfrun." Francesca's smile was like honey, but the barkeep flinched as if struck. "So, if you would, please ask all present staff to join us here in the main room."

"Of course." Greglin relented quickly, gesturing to a maid. She slipped through a side door just next to the bar and when she returned, there were three cooks in tow.

"Is this everyone?" Francesca asked and the barmaid nodded, "Good. I will make this as quick as possible, I promise. And each and every person here will be paid for the disturbance. A gesture of gratitude, for your service to the church."

Riding spurs twinkled a song as she stepped deeper into the room, drinking in all of the faces who turned her way. Unfortunately, none were familiar.

"If you were here exactly two nights ago between the hours of dusk and dawn, please raise your hand." Four barmaids, Greglin, the three kitchen workers and six patrons all stretched a palm into the air. "Right, very good. All of you with me," she ordered before turning to Greglin, "Sir, is there a more intimate area where I can conduct an interview?"

He nodded and led the small group to an unoccupied private dining quarter in the left wing. Francesca left her accompanied men in the main room, to be eyeballed by the remaining customers.

As she shut the doors behind her, she heard the strum of a lute before the band resumed their set.

All of the patrons and bar staff seemed nervous, shuffled together like fowl, so she conveyed reassurance in her introduction. "I am Francesca Draven, personal emissary of the High Father. I am here at his request, so these are not my questions you'll be answering, but his.

"I'm going to need you all to think back roughly two days ago. Did you notice anyone who seemed suspicious? Particularly men." There came no immediate answer, just a few shared looks and tightly creased brows. "Any men who were wearing anything peculiar?" Francesca continued, "Perhaps, even... smelled peculiar. Like dirt?" Still, no one answered. "Perhaps they even paid with a strange tender. Old coins maybe?"

One of the barmaids suddenly cast her eyes at Greglin.

Gotcha.

Francesca stepped toward the young woman; one well-kept brow raised in question. Her height and authority consumed the poor girl, so Francesca leaned forward, leveling their stares.

"What is your name?" Francesca asked her gently.

The maid gulped down her unease. "It's Merrily, ma'am."

"Merrily. How lovely." Francesca smiled, her teeth clean and gleaming. "Well Merrily, you seem to have remembered something."

Merrily nodded, refusing to meet her eyes. "Yes ma'am. A gentleman that night, he paid us in gold saph, overpaid actually, and the coins... they were stamped weird." Through her choice of wording and the curl of an uneducated accent at the end of her words, Francesca thought her a simple girl.

"Stamped weird?" she mimicked with a little mockery, "How so?"

Greglin stammered into the conversation. "They were stamped with a symbol. One I haven't seen in a very long time, not since I was young."

Francesca tilted her head. "And what symbol is that?"

Greglin started fishing through his pockets and pulled out a dull coin, handing it over. It was heavy and had uneven edges; crafted by a family contracted smithie. In its center it bore the faint outline of a ship with waves breaking before it: The crest of a dynasty long since put into the ground.

"Please," Greglin said, "I don't run that kind of place here. I thought that maybe they were old family members, or perhaps he was gifted some sort of inheritance or dowry. But I want it known, we don't trade with thieves and robbers. Only respectable people do business with us. Stolen coin is useless here."

Francesca turned to him. "Stolen? Why do you think it's stolen?"

He fumbled in confusion, rapidly losing the color in his cheeks. "Well, that's why you're here, isn't it?" A swift point to the coin. "That's the J'harenmar crest. Those folks that came through, they were grave robbers weren't they? Stole the gold from the estate crypts?" When she didn't respond he almost sprinted to the doors. "I-I have the rest, in the lock box behind the bar. I can get you every piece they paid me. One moment." In a flash he was gone.

Francesca turned back to Merrily. "The man who paid with the coins, what did he look like?"

The maid shrugged sheepishly. "I don't know, he was wearing a hood the whole time."

"Can you tell me anything at all?"

Merrily thought for a moment and then blushed. "I just remember little things, ma'am. Things a woman would notice about a man."

Amused, Francesca encouraged her to continue. "What things?"

"Oh, you know. I could only see from the tip of his nose to the top of his collar but he had a nice jaw. A little stubbly from travel, and nice lips. And he was tall. Taller than the other man."

"Other man?" Francesca asked carefully.

Merrily nodded. "Yeah, the hooded man had come in with another fellow and a woman. The woman was of fair hair, average in body. Weren't missing no meals. Her eyes were pretty. The other man was tall and good looking but he had a cocky way about him, ya know? Although I will admit, he was funny." She giggled at a memory. "He had red hair, red as blood. Oh he was a womanizer, that one. You could just tell."

Merrily grinned and Francesca grinned back.

"Oh, I know the type. What happened while they were here? Did they mention anything to you about where they had come from? Maybe where they were headed?"

The maid took a moment to think back. "Well, they didn't talk much when I would come by the table, except the red head, but he just blathered on about the usual things. When they left out the next morning, they were definitely in a hurry. Left before most of the staff was even up and in the kitchen. I watched them from my window in the maid quarters on top of the barn."

"Which direction did they head out in?"

"West, down the main road."

"On horses or by foot?"

"Horses."

"Their colors?"

"A bay, a black and a rusty paint."

Francesca nodded slowly, taking a moment to think. "Which rooms did they stay in?"

Merrily gestured upwards. "The last room upstairs. They had to share one because all the others were booked. They were clean guests, and it looked like two took the bed and one slept on the floor." She leaned in a little. "Personally, I bet the redhead and woman took the bed. He was very flirty with her all night."

"And the woman?"

"She seemed a little fed up with his comings on," Merrily gossiped. "But I think it was in jest, because sometimes she'd look at him with that look. Never so he'd notice. Just another thing we women pick up on."

Francesca chuckled deep in her throat. "Nothing gets past us."

This time, when Merrily finally met her eye, the young maid's face fell a little just as Francesca looked away, addressing the rest of the witnesses.

"I thank you all for your patience, but I must ask for just a little more. Please remain here until I return." After, she exited the dining room and made her way up the staircase at the back of the main room.

A long hallway welcomed her to the top floor, and Francesca quickly made her way to the last door in line. When she stepped into the room it was cold and dark, thick with the scents of dryline sheets and food from the kitchens below.

Pulling the glove off of her right hand, she stretched and flexed her fingers in the chilled air. In her palm a light spread and grew beneath the skin, igniting a flame in the air just above it. The shadows were sent to the far corners of the room with the roll of her wrist, that conjured fire left to float in the air. It washed the room with golden light, illuminating quaint furniture. The bed sheets had been washed and made already, and the rocking chair cast a long shadow along the wall. Nothing remained in the dresser drawers nor along the dresser top. No sign of her quarry could be found but faintly, beneath the overall smell of the room, Francesca could detect the previous occupant's scents.

Inhaling, long and deep, she parted her lips, catching the taste on the tip of her tongue.

She sauntered around, drew her fingers along the mantle and checked under the bed. She wasn't expecting to find anything of significance but perhaps, if she were lucky, there would be some sort of clue as to where they were headed.

Francesca opened the two bedside night stands. The first drawer held nothing but an old and tattered holy book, which Francesca tossed away with a sneer. Within the other drawer however, there was a piece of parchment, creased by a crooked fold. When she plucked it out of the dark and laid it open, two words stared back, and she could feel the smug satisfaction of the writer in the sharp script.

'Hello Draven.'

Francesca studied the paper a moment longer, then left it on the bed as she snuffed the ball of fire and left out of the room.

Back downstairs in the dining hall, Greglin had returned with all of the J'harenmar coins in hand. Wavering a little, he held them out to her.

"Here, ma'am. Every piece is accounted for."

She spared him some strained kindness. "Keep it. Maybe... melt it down," she told him, then moved on to her cluster of witnesses, "Thank you so much for your cooperation this evening. The High Father and I appreciate your honesty and your time. Now, if you will wait here, I will be right back with your monetary compensation."

Greglin stepped up instantly, swinging his head side to side, making sure his decline was undeniable. "No no, that won't be necessary. Anything to help His Holiness and the Beacon Sect."

However, a patron protested. "Hold on, I'll take that compensation. City taxes me enough. Wouldn't turn my nose up at getting a little back."

Francesca nodded curtly and stepped out of the room with a bounce to her step. "Now that's the spirit! One moment, and I'll be right back." She gave them each a friendly smile and wrinkled her nose at Merrily, who flashed her crooked teeth brightly in return, and then closed the double doors.

Beneath her grip the ornate iron handles started to turn white from her conjured heat. Using little effort, she drew the softened metal together, fusing them as one.

With her men spaced out through the main room, Francesca moved to the entrance and then spoke to the watchful patrons who remained. "Thank you all for your patience this night. I truly appreciate your cooperation and understanding. Better yet, so does your High Father. He will hear of your compliance."

They stared back at her, still nervous but excited by the prospect of praise going all the way back to the cathedral.

Francesca inhaled deeply, basking in their eagerness. In their belief.

Her trained expression had been one of refinement and poise; a politician's facade that she had perfected over the years. But now, it changed. No longer did she wear that false mask. Instead, her eyes grew cold and her features rested into a stagnant repose.

The mood of the room shifted just as quickly as she did, the flock suddenly aware this wasn't a fellow sheep among them. She might have worn their wool, but there were teeth of a sharper cut inside that mouth.

Francesca took one final sweep of their increasingly fearful faces, savoring the moment like a fine liquor. "Tell your god who sent you."

These words released her men from their leash, and they hacked into their prey with vigor, severing limbs, taking heads from shoulders, gutting and cleaving people in two. There was no finesse, only carnage. Whichever diabolical way they saw fit to take a life, executed, painting themselves in washes of red.

Panicked screams filled the tavern and those still locked inside the dining room started to beat at the door.

Hands clasped in front of her, Francesca Draven watched the brutality unfold, unable to contain the enjoyment that had spread across her, toe tip to crown.

A man from the band tried to rush past her for the open door, still clutching his lute as fear had locked his thoughts on nothing more than escape. But Francesca was quicker than his instinct, and she reached out, taking him by the face with her damned right hand, all aglow with a hellish heat. She didn't even bother to look when the flesh boiled and popped, his brain flash-fried within the confines of his skull.

He crumbled to her feet without so much as a twitch, everything he ever was now pooling out of his nostrils as pink foam.

After their deed was done, her men returned to her side. Chests heaving, smattered in gore, they were sickly satisfied with their work. All about the room lay the dead or dying, their moans and gurgled cries mixing with the taps of rain on the roof. Some pleaded and others cried, but Francesca looked over them all with indifference before opening her palm and releasing a spray of white-hot fire across the floor. Engulfed, the wailing started again as a new wave of terror overtook those still clinging to life.

Francesca and her company took their leave, marching out into the storm to rejoin those who waited. All twenty were clad in the same unmarked armor as the rest, sitting on horses that shied from Francesca's approach.

Quietly, one footman handed her the reins of her mare and she swung up with ease, the sorrel charger knowing better than to flee from her master's cruel hand.

"We head west," Francesca commanded, raising her voice to combat the heavy rain, and then spurred her mount into the night.

Behind them, The Tossed Tankard burned brightly in the dark, the roof eventually collapsing on all of those still trapped inside.

ONE

S alt clung to the edges of dark brick, seeping through the cracks and pooling along seams of mortar. It dazzled in the afternoon sun; a shimmering cape of precious jewels. And a stark contrast to what laid beneath it.

Piercing into the heavens, the cathedral spire stretched its shadow over the city of Savhignos, chilling her people in its heavy gloom. The sea-drenched wind tore at the slabs of limestone, twisting and slithering through carved arms of granite saints that adorned the tiered ledges, like a malignant spirit seeking entrance into the holy sanctum. No weakness would be had, the craftsmanship sealed tight, but the tendrils of this pungent breeze did find something else. Something out of place along the finely chiseled edges of a high balcony. Something soft, moveable and intrusive.

"Don't look down," he muttered to himself in an attempt to conjure some rational courage. "Just keep your eyes straight ahead, yeah? No problem." But Callum wasn't looking straight ahead, he was looking down. Down at the crashing ocean waves and jagged rocks that awaited him a few hundred feet below the ledge on which he teetered.

"Shit." Another surge of nausea hit him, the salty breeze prickling his skin in an assault. Callum ran a hand through his dampening red hair and tried to calm those bone-rattling nerves with a chuckle.

Heights typically weren't an issue, all part of the whole professional thief gambit, but the water beneath him was like a fairy tale monster; roaring and gnashing and eager for a tumbling body, sent into the cold blue by a single careless step.

After a series of swift breaths in through the nose, it was time to move on. The daylight wouldn't last forever and the slice-happy guardsmen were particularly watchful at night.

Carefully, Callum shuffled along the ledge but the sandstone was slick with moss and under his scuffed boot a stone loosened, falling away to the lapping ocean. The waves sounded victorious as they devoured the broken piece in a violent rush of water and foam.

"Shit!" Callum righted himself and gave a broken little laugh into the clear sky. "And it's such a beautiful day to be on the verge of death."

His destination was a window that might have been within sight, but was not yet within reach. To get to it, he'd need to traverse this ledge and then up a thick ivy vine to the neighboring balcony. It wasn't going to be an easy task, but he'd faced worse before. At least that's what he was trying to convince himself of.

"Come on, you little tulip. Not much further now," Callum urged as he continued this slow travel along the cathedral wall. "You pull this off and you'll be set for life." He paused to reconsider, "Well, for a year. Maybe less if you go to Bravenya." His thoughts turned fondly to the sweet wine and the even sweeter pleasure district that usually took up every extra saph he had in his pockets. "Bravenya does sound nice right now..."

When on his own, Callum chatted to himself like a lonely bird to a mirror. The orphanage dean said it was because Callum couldn't stand not hearing the sound of his own voice. However, Six said it was probably a coping mechanism to deal with his crippling dependence on the presence of others.

Callum just thought it was because he was funny and enjoyed his own jokes.

When he finally reached the ivy vine, he grabbed a handful of the ropey greenery and started his upward climb, expertly choosing the strongest stems.

"Cathedral, cathedral, let down your shiny treasures," he said in singsong, wiping a little sweat from his brow. One last heave and he was on the small balcony, crouched like an alley cat while searching the sea and sky. No boats were headed in for port and no airships cruised the thickening clouds. All avenues barren of unwanted eyes to witness his sin and alert the holy guard.

Callum pulled a thin dagger from his belt and used the blade to open the lock on the double windows that led into a study. A quiet little click and then, he was in.

It was owned by one of the Beacon Sect; a branch of holy men who worked directly under High Father Aolfrun. They tried to portray themselves as nothing more than men of the cloth, but everyone knew their real purpose; church thugs. The group of five decided which houses to raid, which businesses to tax, which people to burn, who should give sacrifices and who the city guard should turn a blind eye to if caught at a brothel bed or placing bets at a fight house. They were the law in Savhignos, and the High Father was their god.

On the mahogany desk there were log books and papers scattered about, a well used quill and a still-warm cup of tea on the edge. Callum decided he didn't want to linger long. Besides, this room didn't hold the treasure he was after anyways. But, before he left, he decided a little mischief would do his soul some good, so he opened a ledger and took up the quill. Every so often Callum would add in a number here, or scratch one out there. It was mild chaos, but any displeasure he could cause these men was well worth it.

He then left the study, checking the hall thoroughly for any signs of life then headed down the carpeted hallway to an open wing. It was well lit, and plush with fine furnishings and marble pillars. To his left, a grand staircase descended to the next floor. To his right a massive stained glass window, depicting an angelic scion of war lofting a shining glaive above his double-haloed head.

Callum shushed the angel and looked around. "Avert your gaze, oh great defender," he whispered with a feline smile, "I'm stealing things."

Across the landing there were more doors, all shut up tightly, but luckily for Callum he knew the way. This was not his first time sneaking through the corridors of the cathedral, and so long as today went smoothly, he was sure it wouldn't be his last.

Not the first, not the second, but the third door was his aim and he gently pressed his ear against the cool wood, listening for any sign of life on the other side. When nothing seemed to stir he quietly slipped inside. Bookshelves filled the cramped space, the smell of old parchment and dust making his nose itch. Scrolls of every size were stuffed into any nook and cranny that would hold them, and there were open crates of empty ink bottles. Whoever kept this room wasn't too keen on organization.

Callum started scouring through the contents, not too concerned with leaving everything where he found it. In this mess, who would know? He rummaged high and low through three different standing bookshelves littered with piles of parchment and tattered holy books.

"Green knobs... green knobs...ah ha!" Finally, he spotted his mark. "There you are."

A tightly wound scroll, with knobs of polished green sea glass and a golden wax seal. A thin layer of dust covered the entire thing, seemingly untouched since the day it was stashed away.

"You, my little friend, just made me a rich man." He kissed the scroll, grimaced at the taste it left behind, then carefully tucked it away in the satchel concealed under the long fall of his coat.

Near the door, something glimmered in the corner of his expert vision. A very gold and very jewel-encrusted holy symbol, stuffed behind a small box of used quills. A solid brick of gold, molded to depict a marvelous tower. Its head was topped with an open circle, adorned with salt-water pearls and varying types of precious stones.

"Well, well... what have we here?" Reaching out, Callum took it in hand, impressed at the weight. "Now why do they have you stashed away back here in storage?" Such an ornate object with rich decoration would be on display for the public to be in awe of, yet here it sat, hidden away. After surveying the tower Callum discovered a few pearls were missing and he deduced that perhaps it was put aside for repairs.

"Tsk tsk, a shame to leave you here, love. Forgotten and unappreciated. You'd best come with me. We'll live a happy life together... until I sell you for a small fortune. You understand of course."

He placed it in the satchel and took one last greedy look around the room. "Anything else looking for a change of scenery?"

The door opened abruptly, a woman dressed in the garb of a church maid carrying a box of old log books striding inside. Callum froze, hoping dumbly that perhaps she just wouldn't see him; a tactic he often tried to employ, but often never worked.

She dropped the box and gasped, her hand grabbing at the collar of her dress. He raised a finger to his lips in a silent plea, putting a little sparkle into his mischievous eyes. She let out a horrible scream anyways, and ran from the room, abandoned log books scattered about the floor.

Callum sighed, "Shit."

It was time to run.

He slammed shut the door and engaged the lock, rushing to the nearest window. With some effort, he flung it open and jumped out onto the waiting ledge, closing the shutters behind him, giving its frame a good kick to wedge it into place. Just as he slid from view he heard voices in the room.

"You sure he was in here?"

"Yes sir, I'm sure."

"Well he isn't now."

There was a brief pause. "Maybe he ran downstairs after I left?"

"Maybe."

"Should I get the Beacon Sect, sir?"

"No!" He shouted quickly, fear causing his words to stumble. "They're in a meeting. My men will handle this. Come on."

The door slammed shut.

Callum was on the move, trying to jump ahead at least ten paces in his mind to figure out the best way not to get caught. Stealing in the streets was one thing. Might earn a beating, lose a finger or two depending on the merchant. But stealing from the church? A very certain, and very quiet death. And quiet deaths are the most brutal kind.

"Alright, keep calm. You've been through stickier situations," he reminded himself before taking a quick glance towards the sky, in search of nosy airships. "This isn't even in the top three."

There was another balcony within sight, so he decided that he would break in there and try to slip through the church. Maybe make his way through the kitchens and out into the back alley. Scuttling around the entire building would get him caught, or at least spotted by a local. And if he knew anything about the people of Savhignos, it's that they're not averse to snitching, especially if they thought it might earn them even a crumb of favor with the High Father.

Callum reached the railing and hopped over with ease behind a stone planter, but just as he made to move for the large double doors, they flew open. He hurried backward, squeezing himself between the window jamb and the planter with a grimace.

Fortune favored him in the form of a curtain, drawn just enough to keep him hidden from view and quietly he thanked every person who had ever wished good luck on his name. Which admittedly, probably wasn't a lot.

From inside the room Callum heard an old, familiar voice that made his skin prickle with sick memories.

"Thank you Marlan. Go fetch us all some tea."

"Yes sir," a young boy replies. There came the sound of footsteps and then a door closing.

The familiar voice belonged to Beacon Jonhas, one of the members of the Beacon Sect and a man who frequented the orphanage looking for children to come serve the church. He often clashed with Callum, who was a very outspoken child and made his hatred for the Sect well known. Often, orphans employed by the Sect were never seen again, and Callum and Six almost learned why.

"Let us not waste time," said Aolfrun, the High Father himself.

As carefully as he could, Callum rolled in his little corner, finding space between the open window and its frame to set a curious eye.

All the Beacons were present, each one shuffling their heavy robes as they took seats about an oak table. At its head sat Aolfrun, his back to the window. The skin of his bald head was pale, smattered with dark spots like bruised fruit. The high, flared collar of his robes cupped behind his ears, crisp and clean. Although withered, his spine still remained straight, setting his shoulders broad with pomp and dominance.

The sight of him made Callum tense.

Aolfrun addressed his esteemed force of brutes. "I've received word from Duke Welling, that his efforts have proven fruitful at the dig site south of Havnul. Another ritual slab has been unearthed."

This caused a ripple of excitement. "He'll be arriving by airship in a month's time."

"A month?" gawked Beacon Jory, "Why so long? Surely he has ships that are capable of faster travel?"

Jonhas scoffed at his colleague. "He said he wouldn't leave his township until after his daughter's return from Mar."

Across the table, Jory cleared his aged throat. "It may seem a crass suggestion, but could we kill the girl? Take her completely off of the board? This isn't the first time her schedule has hindered our plans."

"Killing the girl would cause the opposite effect. He'd become sullen and secluded, possibly even suicidal. We don't want that."

"No, we don't," Aolfrun agreed. "The girl stays alive for now. We just need to be patient a little longer. This is a slow, steady game gentlemen."

Another Beacon posed a question, one who Callum knew as Aisehp. He controlled the, often violent, tax collection force for the city. "Could we send your envoy to retrieve it for us?"

Sighing with annoyance, Aolfrun replied, "No."

Jonhas sniffed, dabbing at his short nose with a cloth. "Has this new slab been translated yet?"

"Just a few more requirements." Beacon Trebor shuffled through his stack of creased parchment until he found a letter. Callum could barely make out the seal stamped to its outer hide but it looked royal, and official. "On the day of sacrifice there must be the quartering of a yearling babe; A promise of new life for the days ahead. No older, although younger would surely suffice."

"A yearling? Won't be hard to find. I'll contact Bruznik soon enough, see what he has in stock."

Hearing the Beacon mention his old tormentor at the orphanage made Callum sick, but how he spoke of the children turned him downright green.

Trebor continued, reading from the list as if it were meant for the market. "We still need the blood of a dying star to complete the ritual."

Aolfrun flicked his thin fingers in dismissal. "That is being handled."

"How many slabs are now accounted for?" asked Jonhas.

Old Trebor rattled off a cough. "Five. And with still four more dig sites to search, but Havnul has been lucrative. Perhaps it hides more."

Jonhas sighed. "So close and yet so far."

There was a shift in Aisehp's tone. "Have we considered searching the estate again? Perhaps we're missing something."

Jonhas hissed his words like a snake curled before the strike. "There is nothing there to be missed! Crumbling walls and bones in coffins. Nothing more."

Countering, Trebor was on the cusp of sounding combative. "But what about the under crypt? With Tytian? Perhaps he took something with him or hid it away. Some treasure of his mother's maybe? She was a Carmine after all. And Khaladhuun seems fond of him-"

The High Father slammed his hands against the tabletop, rising to stand. "Enough! Tytian J'harenmar took nothing with him but the clothes on his back and a blade through the heart."

Trebor spoke then, softer than before, his watery eyes turning down to his palms. "Forgive me. I just thought, perhaps-"

An angry scoff from Aolfrun was enough to quiet him and Trebor spoke no more.

Rubbing his temples, the High Father slumped into his chair, groaning malicious words beneath a breath. "We will remain patient and wait for Welling's scholars," Aolfrun reminded them with a sharp tone. "Patience is required of us still, gentlemen."

The silence that overtook the room was short-lived as Marlan returned, bringing with him the sound of creaky wheel spokes.

"Tea, sirs," said the boy from before, setting down a polished tray of cups and cubed sugar at the end of the table.

Jonhas offered an alternative. "Perhaps we should take our tea in the parlor?"

There was a unified murmur of agreement, followed by the sliding of chairs. As Trebor tousled the hem of his robes from around his feet, a coy smile split his mouth. "Marlan! Send for one of the orphan girls. A pretty one! These old hands need a good massage."

Cowering from his gaze but too afraid to deny the Beacon's request, the young tea boy nodded, carrying out the trays with shaking hands.

The double doors fell shut with a gentle click and Callum was finally alone. At first he didn't move, still trying to wrap his brain around what he had just heard. Slabs, a ritual, the Duke, summoning.

"The blood of a dying star..."

In a sweeping flush his skin grew hot as something remembered, and something feared, entered his mind. At his back the wind clawed again, only this time it brought urgency, spurring him to act.

Cautiously, Callum looked around the window and was relieved to find the room empty. As he darted through, he looked the long table over for anything that may be of use to him. A letter or note, maybe even a scribble of a map. Sometimes information was worth far more than diamonds and gold, but the table was bare.

"Shit." Callum stared around the empty room, his mind moving so quickly he couldn't process what to do next. When he looked down at his hands, they were shaking.

"Can't do this," he whispered to himself, "Not here."

He eased the door open, the hinges silenced by a coating of oil, and looked out across the wing. There wasn't a soul in sight, only the methodical tick of a grand clock. Callum rushed across the landing and made his way down the seemingly miles of staircase at a jog.

Cat quiet and fox quick, there wasn't a soldier alive who could hear his fleeting steps. Trained well in the city streets, no other thief for leagues was as slick, or as experienced, as he was when it came to a clean escape. When you're a natural pacifist with a face too pretty for prison, you learn very quickly to hone the art of stealth.

As he came to the second floor of the cathedral there was the unmistakable jingle of men in fair armor headed his way, so Callum darted into a nearby stairwell and tip-toed down into the dark. From the shadows he could see the guards trot by, swords already in hand.

All of this for me? he thought with a grin. *How complementary.*

With the threat of capture now landing on the upper floor, Callum descended the dark stairway, whispering under his panting breath. "Please don't lead to the dungeons. Please don't lead to the dungeons."

A common thiefman's plea.

He was met by another door, this one far shabbier than the rest, and when he opened it he had to hold back the relieved laughter in his throat. Not the dungeons but the kitchens, thick with scents of hanging meat and imported spices. And, best of all, it appeared to be empty.

Across the room was an open archway, beyond it, the narrow space of a side alley. "There you are," Callum huffed. His feet carried him through the room quickly, and for the inconvenience of being spotted by cathedral staff, he plucked a fat roll off of a platter as he went. But just before he reached his freedom, there came a curt little sound behind him.

Wincing, Callum turned slowly on his heel to find a portly cook staring at him, her hands on her round hips and a toe tapping the floor.

He raised his hands and then shrugged with a chuckle. "Hew-wo," the word muffled by the mouth full of bread, the roll puffing out his cheeks like a chipmunk. "Wunnerful food. Jus dewicious."

The woman threw a shout over her shoulder and called the guard.

"Oh, you snitc-h!" Callum shook a finger at her and then dashed out of the door, crashing into the alley.

He held the satchel up to his chest and ran as hard as his legs could carry him. Tall and lean but well muscled, like an athletic horse, he could just about outrun and outmaneuver any city guardsmen. However, that same city guard outnumbered him one hundred to one so if he were to be cornered, the odds would be stacked against him. His best bet would be to try and find a crowd and blend in for a while until he could make it to a safer location.

"Need some bodies, need some bodies..." he murmured to himself as he slid out of the cathedral's hungry shadow and headfirst into the dying afternoon light.

"Whoa!" Almost striking a passing carriage, Callum came to a halt, face twisted in a flinch. The wheel narrowly missed him and the cabby cried out a quick obscenity, shaking a whip at frazzled Callum but there was no time to recover.

Dashing down the cobblestone street, trying not to knock anyone over, he wove his way under the many ivy-dripped shop and business eaves at a sprint, a long string of pardons tumbling out of his mouth. A quick left down an alley and then another left. Run, run, run this rat maze until finally he was brought back out onto the street in the middle of the bustling square.

Washed in the reddish shades of sandstone, Savhignos's market street was a golden haven in the setting sunrays, her people just as yellow in their typical tones of warm beige and browns. The smells of spring fruits and dried spices were thick as fog, laying so heavily on the back of the tongue you could practically taste the fruits imported in from the far islands. Overhead, the hum of an airship engine caused a buzz in the bones, briefly drowning out the overlapping voices of the crowd.

Callum flipped up the hood on his duster, hoping to hide his vivid hair and blend into the shuffling activity. A few more strides and then he slowed, coming into the main stretch of vendor carts and stalls. Callum waded into the rolling sea of people, casually glancing around to take stock. A group of three guardsmen entered the market as well, pushing through the throng of grumpy, late afternoon shoppers. Ahead of him were two more guards, closing in.

He couldn't fight them off if they spotted him. Five against one weren't impossible odds but he was a thief, not a brawler. And should some upstanding citizens in the crowd try to help out, it may get hairier than he wanted.

Really missing Six right about now.

Callum looked around, trying to form a plan when he spotted a woman standing alone at a cart. She wasn't much younger than he was, with blonde hair in a well crafted bun and wearing a plain looking gown. There were faint handprints of flour on her hips, dusted by working hands, and a stain of blueberry jam on her sleeve. A worker or shop wife no doubt. Should he be seen with her, they would match as well as any couple to those who knew no better.

He swooped in beside her and smiled brightly with weaponized charm, hoping to the heavens that she wouldn't sell him out.

"Hello darling, I have been looking all over for you."

The woman was clearly surprised, fumbling over an exclamation. Callum threw a pointed look towards the approaching guards, and she followed his attention, then came back around to him and his pleading eyes.

"Oh... so sorry dear. I was uh..." She briefly took pause, thinking of her next line while looking over the open display cases and their contents. "Just trying to... pick out my present."

Callum's smile grew tighter around the edges. "Your present?"

The woman nodded, her eyes sparkling with mischief at her lucrative and well-crafted lie. "Yes, the one you promised me, remember? For my birthday?"

Of course I picked an extortionist.

The cart vendor had paid no mind to the guard, focused solely on his potential sale. "Did you see something you like?" he asked, hopeful.

"Yes!" The woman replied, sealing the deal. "That is, if my husband here is willing to make the purchase. To keep me happy." Her tone was dripping with sticky, fake sentiment as she stared into Callum's bemused face. "To keep me from... making a scene?" She turned back to the vendor, "I swear if he doesn't get me a birthday present for the fourth year in a row I am going to scream."

Your move, pretty boy.

"Alright." Callum agreed, giving her a look that could cut. "Since it's your birthday and all, dear," he said through clenched teeth, throwing another look towards the guard.

"Wonderful!" The vendor spoke with obvious relief. "Do you have anything in mind?"

Nodding, the young woman pointed to a bracelet made of golden chain adorned with amber and blue beading.

"That one, please."

His hands clapped together with a nod. "Perfect! I think this would make a marvelous addition to your wardrobe."

Behind them the guards shoved through shoppers, swords drawn and heavy armor singing with each step.

"How much?" asked Callum, trying to ease the addictive tension in his shoulders.

"It'll be eighty," said the vendor.

"Eighty? Eighty saphs?" Callum questioned and when the vendor nodded he suppressed an angry sigh and rummaged through his coin pouch. "I only have sixty... "

The vendor looked between them and waved his hand. "I'll take sixty." He then smiled at the woman, "Since it's your birthday."

She placed her hand over her heart in a genuine show of appreciation. "Thank you so much for your kindness."

Callum, quietly mimicking their exchange with a hush of mockery, handed over the coins and once he was paid, the vendor delicately placed the bracelet around the woman's wrist.

"Just lovely," he complimented with warmth.

Looking over his shoulder Callum spotted the guardsmen wading through the thinning throng, snatching hats off of heads. Trying to contain his building tension, Callum turned back to the woman and wrapped his arm around her waist with a smile.

"Well dear, let's head home."

He thanked the vendor and before she could protest, had led the woman into a neighboring side alley. Once they were alone, Callum pulled the dagger from his belt and touched the end against the woman's ribs.

"Take me somewhere to lay low," he whispered in her ear.

She grew stiff at the feel of the blade, all former levity gone.

"I could still scream... " she warned.

But Callum shook his head. "You wouldn't even have the time to breathe in before this blade punctured your lung. I paid for protection, now provide it." His tone was dripping with promised threat.

She appeared to weigh her options for a moment before giving in. "Fine. When we get to the end of this alley, take a right, then the first left."

TWO

Together they traveled through the darkening city, steering clear of the main road as much as possible and trekking through a few ill-kept courtyards. After almost a half hour of winding back streets, they finally came into one of the many housing districts in the Western Lows, and the woman led Callum to a very small home at the end of a row. They never spoke a word until safely inside.

"Leave the lights off," he commanded and she complied quietly, although the look in her eyes screamed rebellion. "Sit in that chair and don't make a sound." Once more she did as she was told and sat down in an armchair in the corner of the sitting room. He perched on the sofa arm, peeking out the curtain for any signs of city guards, or worse; The Beacon Sect's authority.

"So, what'd you do?"

He cut her a glance. "I thought I told you not to make a sound?"

She shrugged. "Never been great at taking commands. So, what did you do?"

Callum wrestled with a grin. Amused, but trying to keep up the gruff kidnapper charade. "Maybe I'm innocent."

Out of that he got a laugh. "Oh, I doubt that. C'mon, spill."

With no sign of guards patrolling the streets he pivoted to her, glaring from beneath his brow like some devilish brute, trying not to laugh at the absurdity of his acting skills. "I butchered a family of four upper crust primps. They weren't my first, won't be my last."

She squinted into his frivolous claim. "Hmm, that so?"

He tilted his head, "What? Don't believe me?" and then wagged the dagger at her, slowly rising to his feet. "Perhaps you're next."

Old springs creaked as she leaned back in the seat, folding her arms across her chest and drawing her tongue over clean teeth.

"Actually no, I don't believe you."

Callum faltered. "I-... you don't?"

"Nope," she said with a grin. "See, your clothes, your gloves, your boots- they're awfully clean for a man who butchered a family of four just this afternoon."

A quick study of his attire revealed the coat and pants had a few dirt stains, his shirt a streak or two of green from the vines on the cathedral walls, but other than that he was as clean as a whistle. No sign of blood or gore splattered about his person.

"Uh. I'm just that good?"

The woman laughed again, the texture of it like smooth music. "You're really not. So drop the tough guy act." She stood, motioning to the satchel on his side. "My guess is that your run-in with the guard has something to do with that very sparkly monolith sticking out of your bag there."

Callum looked down and sure enough, one arch of the holy piece was staring up at him like a bad joke.

"Traitor," he told it. "We're supposed to be in this together."

Another lyrical laugh. "Look, what happened between you and the guard is between you and them, I won't rat you out.

However, I won't be treated like a prisoner inside of my home either, so I'm going to fix a cup of tea. You're free to join me, or free to leave." With that she turned and stepped into the kitchen, flicking on the light as she went.

A quick look out of the window once again determined there were no guards on the dimming streets, but Callum still didn't want to risk roaming around while a little daylight lingered. He double checked the locks on the front door and followed her footsteps.

It was a tidy little room, painted in a shade of mustard yellow and well decorated. Houseplants in colorful pots hung from the ceiling, kettles and drying bundles of varying herbs hung from wood woven racks. Bottles of oil stood like soldiers in line near the pot bellied stove, with bowls of fruits and brown eggs on the countertop. Large sacks of flour and rice were piled near the back door, in crates he recognized as cast-offs at the port docks.

This was the kitchen of a cook.

Filling a pot with water from the copper tap, the lady of the house passed a look over her shoulder. "Decided on tea then?"

Callum leaned against the door frame, soaking in the details of the space, learning more and more about his hired covered in every minute detail. "For the moment." He eyeballed the cheap sconces on the wall that hummed with light, powered by the giant, earthen crystal under the city's belly. "Didn't know this part of the residential quarter had access to the lightstone."

"Had this all installed last year. A donation in funds for expansion from King Fahrlo."

"Hmph. I'm surprised the High Father didn't just add it to the church's purse."

"Keeping us in the dark would have been counterproductive to the city's image. And we both know the High Father is a man that thrives on image." She placed the pot on the stove, a newly built fire rumbling in its cast iron oven. "But he'll still tax you straight into poverty and then wonder why you died. Who cares if there's no bread on the table so long as the lights are still on?"

There was no arguing with her there.

Rubbing the heel of his boot against the floor, Callum eyed the grooves with educated unease. "It ever make you nervous, living right above a lightstone? Those things are volatile, ya know. One crack in 'em and-" he pulled his hands apart while imitating an explosion, "pow, everything's gone."

Her shoulder shrugged as she pulled an old tin from the overhead shelf, sniffing at the loose-leaf tea inside. "Only makes me nervous when I think about it." Her nose twitched like a rabbits' at the scent. "So, I don't think about it."

"A healthy approach," he chuckled. "So, what's your name? I don't think I ever asked."

"Not asking a woman her name seems like common practice with you."

His hands flew to his chest, an exaggerated expression of mock hurt on his face. "Madam, are you calling me unchivalrous?"

"Well, you did hold me at knifepoint until I brought you home."

"I bought you jewelry at least," he said, wagging his finger.

"That's true," grinning as she examined the smooth beads of amber. "My name is Fenella."

Callum quirked a confused brow. "V-vanilla?" It was an odd name but then again she was rather pale.

"No, FEN. FENella... with an F." When she laughed in earnest Callum felt a devilish warmth in his face.

"I'm Callum."

Fenella stared at him for a beat before replying, "Well, it's nice to meet you."

"Eh, just wait." His face scrunched with a wink.

From a small overhead cupboard, she took two teacups and their serving saucers. They were made of fine porcelain, not something often found here in the Lows.

"You're a thief, huh? Professional or petty?"

Callum smirked then took a seat at the small dining table, picking at the hem of a hand knit placemat. "Oh always petty. But uh yeah, professional. In a sense at least. I'm good at it, it pays the bills and it's one of the few things I like to do."

"Do you steal from everyone?"

"No, only those who deserve it. Fat cats." A double slap to his stomach.

"So, the rich?"

"Rich enough."

"Right." Fenella drew out the sound of the vowel.

"What?" asked Callum, amused by the thought of a challenge.

"Well it's the typical line isn't it? You big time fellas always claim to only steal from the rich, like it makes you noble in your efforts, but in the harsh light of day it's still stealing. Doesn't matter if it's from a king or a peasant, you're still taking what isn't yours to take. All the while hiding behind some ill conceived belief that you're actually not a bad guy. It's the lie you tell yourself at night so you can actually get some sleep."

Callum leaned back in his chair, a playful smile on his lips. "Someone stole your puppy as a child, didn't they?"

Fenella scoffed and waved off his assumption before grabbing a bottle of tea leaves. The kettle was bubbling heavily now.

"No you're right. It is a bit of a lie," he admitted. "An excuse we give our actions, so we don't feel like total pieces of shit. But I've stolen from some real bad people in these last few years so, I don't need the lie to fall asleep at night. I actually sleep like a baby."

The water on the stove was starting to boil, and Fenella spooned out the tea leaves into the sifter atop a chipped teapot.

"Will you sleep like a baby tonight? Knowing the church is after you?"

"Of course! This was actually a good day. Got what I was after and made a new friend."

Fenella chuckled. "Oh yes. It was a fated encounter!" She said with theatrical mirth, "The prophecies all foretold of our untimely meeting and the life stories we would share over cups of poor-quality tea."

As she chuckled again, she looked over her shoulder at Callum but was surprised to find him wearing an expression of dismay.

No, not dismay. He looked terrified.

"Tea..." he said under his breath. In the back of his mind rang the voice of the Beacon's errand boy and the sound of a serving tray against the table.

He'd almost forgotten, and that scared him more than anything.

"Hey, what is it?" Fenella asked.

Callum shook his head a little, half hoping it would knock the memory clean out of his skull. "I heard something strange today when I was in the cathedral. Some kind of plot from old Aolfrun."

This surprised her. "You know the High Father?"

"No, no. This was something I overheard when I was running. I was on the balcony of his study and he and the Beacon's were having a meeting. They spoke about some terrible stuff."

Fenella sat down opposite of him, her hands folded in her lap. "What stuff?"

Callum tried to think back and get the details right. "Something about a ritual? And a slab? Apparently the Duke is backing their endeavors."

"A Duke?"

"Yeah. Duke Welling, youngest brother to the king. He runs a city to the northwest."

"Welling," she said the name as if she were afraid it would cut her. "He was at the church this past winter, talking with the Beacons."

"How do you know that?"

"Because I was there," she sighed. "I had a meeting with Beacon Jonhas about getting a loan from the church. Welling was there, Jonhas introduced me. I think he was trying to prove how important he was while also showing the Duke how kindly he treated the locals."

Callum leaned forward, staring at her with wide eyes. "You got a loan from the church?"

Fenella stiffened with frustration and looked away. "Yes."

"Oh Vanilla, what have you done?"

"I know! Okay? I know I messed up. But I was new to this city and the only places that wanted to hire me were brothels and-"

He interrupted her with mild judgement. "And you're too good for that?"

"Well, yes and no. I didn't want to feel used. Owned." She absentmindedly pulled at the collar of her dress.

Callum gave a small smile and then gently said, "Go on."

Fenella's newfound tension faded. "I decided to ask the church for a loan to start a bakery. There was an open storefront in the upper part of town but I didn't have enough for the first rent so, I asked the Beacon Sect. Jonhas met with me and it was awful. I could feel that man's eyes looking clean through to my bones." A quick shiver. "Anyways, Welling was there that day. I didn't see him but for a moment. Perhaps he was there about these- what did you call them? Slabs?"

"It's quite possible," Callum said distantly, falling into deep thought.

Fenella stood and took the steaming pot of water off of the stove, slowly pouring it into the top of the teapot. "Why do you seem so scared by this? If the church discovered a summoning stone or something, of course they would want to find it. They destroy any and all Carmine artifacts."

Callum shook his head. "I don't think they plan on destroying it. I think they plan on using it."

Fenella turned to him. "Wait, what? Using it?" A dismissive laugh. "That's absurd."

"Why? You know yourself how corrupt they are."

"Corrupt, yes. But you can't summon demons. The artifacts were just made by heretic extremists." But the look in his eyes said something different and all of a sudden Fenella seemed uneasy. "Callum, summoning can't be real or every pauper from this coast to the next would be calling upon the dark to fill their pockets."

Callum held his head in his hands. "Demons tend to ask for too much in return," he mumbled but when Fenella asked him what he meant by that, he looked at her with momentary confusion, and then it clicked. "Wait a minute... you're a primp, aren't you? Grew up in a wealthy household."

Her cheeks flushed red and she glanced around. "Well, yes. But what does that have to do with anything?"

"Oh my dear Vanilla, a lot." His mirth faltered a little. "It explains why you don't believe. You've never seen folks at their worst."

"I have seen plenty of bad in this world, thank you," she huffed. "Just because my family had money doesn't mean I'm ignorant. I live here, don't I? I've seen the slums."

"Ah yes," Callum said with a raise of his finger. "Savhignos has slums and beggars, but there are some things out there more important to the truly desperate, and when they reach that point there's no calling them back. But summoning isn't an easy practice. It calls for hard to obtain ingredients and unspeakable actions. Most folks, no matter how downtrodden, don't have the stomach to do a spell, or they fear for their souls. But you get someone at the very bottom of life's ladder and they become unhinged."

Two cups and a sugar dish were set on the table before she poured the tea. "What could drive a person to fall to such a low level?"

Callum dragged a finger around the rim of the warming cup. "Says the woman who took a loan from a crooked church. If you grew up wealthy, why ask the Beacons for a loan? Why not get your family to pay for your shop?"

Fenella sat down with a scowl and angrily scooped a spoon through the sugar. "Not that it's any of your business, but when I walked out of that life I made a promise to myself that I would never ask my father for anything ever again."

"So, you came here and asked the church. Out of one man's house and into another."

When he heard her slam down her spoon he flinched and replayed his statement in his mind. "Oh. Ah... that came out far meaner than I had intended. I'm sorry."

"You're not wrong but it's not something I like to think about."

Instantly he felt bad. More times than he could count his mouth had gotten him into trouble. It was almost his trademark. "Well, this new house is run by a man summoning demons so one point for old dad, eh?"

He was rewarded with a small laugh.

For a while they sat in silence, the open air healing the sudden tension until finally Callum spoke up.

"You were right, ya know."

Fenella cocked her head. "About what?"

"This really is low quality tea."

She stifled a smile. "So, what will you do now?"

That was a good question, and he didn't have a complete answer for her yet, but he knew one thing. "Guess I'll start by rounding up the old team, get everyone together and devise a plan. Maybe stall the Duke or possibly steal his airship. Aldan might have some ideas for that one-"

"Wait, what?" she asked with surprise.

"Hmm?"

"I-I just meant, are you planning on leaving now or... " Abruptly her cheeks flushed.

Callum grinned a sly grin and slowly leaned forward. "Or? Stay?"

"No."

"Were you going to ask me to stay?"

"Nope. No." Clearly flustered, she tried to hide behind a long sip of tea.

"Yeah... " Now he was playful, biting at his lip as she grappled for stable ground.

"No, I wasn't."

"Ooo, primpy miss Vanilla, I have to admit I'm a little surprised."

In a rush she grabbed her tea cup and went to the sink, stammering to come up with some way to steer the conversation back onto a subject less embarrassing.

"You wanna come?" he asked with a low, smooth tone.

"W-what?" Those big eyes of hers were like saucers when she turned around.

He was laughing at her now, admiring the blush in her cheeks. "Do you want to join the team? Come with us to try and intercept the Duke?"

Out of all the things he could have asked her, that particular question clearly had never crossed her mind and she must've thought him mad.

"Why would I want to? Why would YOU want to?"

A baffled sort of confusion was written all over his face. "Uhm ... to stop them? From whatever nefarious plot they're planning?"

"Yes, but *why*?"

Callum squinted. "Because clearly, they're up to something? I have to admit Vanilla, I thought you were quicker than this."

"No, I mean, why you? Go tell the city commander or something. Maybe tell the king. What are you expected to do about it?"

"The commander is owned by the Beacons, and whether he knows it or not the king himself is owned by the High Father. If we tell anyone under his cloth, then we'd be dead on the spot." When she didn't respond he spoke with a softer sentiment. "What am I supposed to do? Just sit back and let it happen?"

"You don't even have all of the information. You don't even have proof!"

He shrugged. "I've started adventures with less."

Fenella stepped toward him, hands rising up to rest on her hips. "There's something you're not telling me."

He mimicked her. "There's something you're not telling me either, but unlike you I wasn't going to be rude and bring it up. Not many people are so comfortable with knife wielding strangers in their home, Vanilla."

When she stuttered at his assessment, Callum chuckled. "So, what'll it be?"

"Why me?"

"Honestly? I like lookin' at you," Callum said and was rewarded with a level glare. "Plus, you've got sharp wits, which is a component sometimes lacking with my group, and I think there's more to you than you're letting on. I want to find out what that is." He started out of the kitchen door but stopped. "So I ask again, wanna come?"

Fenella stood there like a statue. "We've only just met each other," she said out loud, although it was more to quell the storm in her chest than a retort to Callum.

When he looked at her this time, something different flashed in his sea green eyes. "Some of the best stories begin with a chance encounter." And then he slipped into the darkness of the living room.

THREE

Fenella stood frozen in the kitchen, battling with the choices set before her. One sounded so stupid it was almost comical. Follow the handsome stranger into the unknown to join his ragtag group of sketchy adventurers, or stay behind and live out her life as she'd planned. There was no guarantee that he was even right, or that he had even overheard what he did, but something in her bones was pushing her towards the living room, towards the front door and out into the fresh night. She stood on a cliff now, with only the option to leap and she knew that the decision she made right here and right now would completely change the course of her life.

Sometimes, she would get feelings she couldn't explain, but they always served her well. Warning her against taking a certain side street home, when to bring a parasol when there wasn't even a cloud in the sky, or telling her not to do business with a particular merchant. Her mother called it intuition but her father claimed it was all made up in her head and that she idolized witches and seers. He said her spirit was sick for believing such things, but it had never steered her wrong before and right now it was screaming danger, and not about Callum but his words. She didn't want to believe it, yet there was truth in his eyes.

"This is madness," she whispered, "Absolute madness." But she couldn't seem to turn herself around and go back to the table, to let that man take his heroics and slip away, leaving her to do the same thing she'd done day in and day out for over a year.

She tried racking her brain for all logical reasons to say no, and there were plenty. However, her intuition was drowning out her thoughts, screaming at her from the pits of her soul to follow him, that staying would be a mistake. That staying meant-

"Death."

Suddenly, a warm sensation spread across her feet and a deep meat kind of pressure that, for only a second, threatened to crack her skull.

Before she even realized what was happening, Fenella crashed into the living room after Callum, catching him just as he placed his hand on the door.

"Wait!" she pleaded, almost breathless, "I'm coming with you."

The way he turned around, with that expression of surprise, was almost familiar. His lopsided smile oozed obnoxiously with confidence, as if he had expected her to say yes this whole time.

Cheeky asshole, she thought.

"Let me pack a bag." Once satisfied that he wouldn't walk out and leave her, Fenella sprinted up the narrow staircase to her bedroom.

Light sprang to life with a flick of a switch. From the trunk at the foot of her bed she grabbed a deep traveling bag. Hastily, she stuffed it full of clothes, a brush and some wool socks. Her flat-soled town shoes were replaced with a pair of practical boots, and around her waist she wrapped a belt, sliding a small but lethal dagger into a calf skin sheath after inspection. There was the fleeting thought of having to use that dagger for more than just carving apples.

Her hands started to shake.

Wringing out her nerves, Fenella scooped up the satchel and took a second to look at her reflection in the mirror, dusting the remnants of flour from the front of her dress. She was as travel ready as any adventurer. But when Fenella looked up to her face she frowned. There was terror in her eyes.

"What am I doing?"

A tingle blossomed in her chest, spreading out to her fingers with an electric touch. It was a common reaction to indecision. Her body's way, as she understood it, of urging her into action when self doubt seemed to block her path.

Her hands settled over her stomach. "This is ridiculous," she told the flutter of butterflies. "I don't even know him. What if this is wrong? What if I'm wrong?"

It was frivolous is what it was, and Fenella was anything but frivolous. She was well measured, precise. But something was happening here, something she couldn't deny. She could feel it the moment she opened her eyes that morning, that something strange was on its way. Now it was here, standing in her living room with a crooked smile.

She lifted her head towards the ceiling and closed her eyes, surrendering to that feeling of pressure against her shoulders telling her to move to her feet.

"Okay," she whispered, "I'll go."

Fenella pulled away from the mirror and untied the ribbon on her head. Fluffy, blonde hair tumbled into curls down her back and she shook it out before dragging it around in front to weave into a single, fat braid. With this final act, she flicked off the lights.

Callum was leaned against the front door, head bowed and arms crossed over his chest. When she descended the stairs he looked up and gave a nod. "Ready?"

With more certainty than before Fenella nodded in return. "Ready."

Outside the street was quiet and mostly barren, washed in shadows, the sun gone behind the sea. Once he was sure there were no guards or goons lurking about, Callum gave Fenella a signal and they rushed down her stoop and across the street like ghosts.

Very few people were mingling about, but there were many windows open or doors hung ajar, voices and smells of cooking foods filled the humid air. This end of Savhignos was one of the many housing districts, and although it wasn't exactly the slums, most families here had to make due with the lesser things in life. While they may not have a lot of coin in their pockets, life was made richer by those around them.

Often, as children, Callum and his friend Six would sneak off from the orphanage and come to this neighborhood, quietly sitting on roof tops so they could listen to all the conversations, the fights, the singing and music. The wealthier end of the city never had much life, and the slums were dangerous, especially for children. But here, this was the sweet spot.

Callum hit the main avenue, just within view of the massive front gates. Instead of making his way out of town, he led Fenella to another side street, heading for the far eastern edge of town.

They crouched by a closed fish cart, away from the humming glow of street lamps.

"Where are you going?" Fenella asked, "The gate is back that way."

"We're not going for the gates," Callum whispered as he surveyed the upper street.

Fenella groaned. "Oh no, we're not going to go through the sewers, are we?"

And Callum made a face. "Oh, gods no, that's disgusting. But, not a bad idea, Vanilla. See what I mean about quick wits?" He tapped her on the nose and then dashed up the street, Fenella following close behind.

"Then where are we going?" she whispered urgently.

Just as he was about to reply he grabbed her arm and shuffled them both behind the front pillar of a shop. A night watchman strolled by, carrying a torch and dragging his feet, sleep heavier on his mind than the job at hand. After his footsteps faded, the pair slithered out onto the sidewalk and through the darkness for the next row of buildings. They found safety in a narrow alleyway and Callum slowed his pace.

"Do you know anything about the J'harenmar estate?"

There was a slight wrinkling to her nose as she rummaged her thoughts. "The ruins on the backside of the city? Past the cemetery?"

Callum confirmed, "That's the one."

"I don't know much, just what I've heard from locals."

"Ever been there?"

"Just to the cemetery. It's quiet. Why?"

"Because that's where we're going."

Fenella tilted her head like an inquisitive dog. "Why there?"

"Because, when I... overheard what I overheard, they mentioned the J'harenmar. More importantly, Tytian J'harenmar, the last heir, and someone in particular was not too happy at the mention of his name. A Beacon had brought up raiding his crypt but ol' bubbleheaded Aolfrun shot that plan right down and I want to know why. What's in that family mausoleum that he's so scared of? Maybe there's something there we can use."

Fenella quirked her mouth. "Or maybe it's all just dusty bones and broken stones."

Callum grinned. "Vanilla, you're a poet."

One alley led to another, and then another. They kept their heads down as they passed by an active bar, lit up like a drop of sunlight in the dark, and then creeped down another side street until they finally came to the open cemetery gates.

There were no grave keepers wandering the grounds, the Beacon Sect having eradicated the job position two years prior as a way to cut city spendings. There were also no lingering mourners, the place just as dead as the bodies it encased.

Headstones and monuments carved like winged specters were eerily illuminated in a wash of silver light, the rising moon turning the world blue.

Callum put his hands together as if in prayer and looked up. "Thanks for that, gorgeous."

"Did you just talk to the moon?" Fenella asked with a twitch of her brow.

"Yeah, don't you?"

"Can't say that I do."

"Well, you should try it sometime," Callum advised. "She's a great listener."

Alongside them the cemetery curved and rolled with knolls, eventually lost from sight behind the rise of stone walls as they followed the sidewalk deeper into the Eastern Greens; the only part of the city to still have natural, locally grown trees. Even the park on the upper end of Savignos was lacking in fauna. The only plant life one could find was the huge rose gardens near the cathedral, used to mask the stench of salt water, fish and piss that permeated every other street in the city, and off-limits to anyone who didn't live in the Uppers.

"So, who were the J'harenmar's?" Fenella asked as the trees began to thicken, the sidewalk tapering off to an unpaved dirt path.

Callum shrugged. "Old money that came from across the sea. Apparently, their wealth was made with cargo ships. Hauled a lot in and out of this place. Dabbled in airship components as well, near the end. Built the monument to their grandeur out here, away from the church.

"Word about town is that when the crown established the cathedral here, the J'harenmar didn't contribute any funds or labor, preferring not to have a hand in its construction. That immediately put a kink in their relationship with the city. Folks said after a while the family became secluded," he wiggled his fingers for emphasis, "mythical, in a way. So many wacky stories came out about them, mostly from the poor folks who didn't know any better. Then, one night a little over forty years ago the house caught fire and everyone inside died. At least that's what everyone was told."

"You believe something different?" Fenella asked.

"I mean, I wasn't alive at the time so all I got are old rumors. But, when I overheard the High Father he said something about the last heir, Tytian, lying in his crypt with a dagger in his chest."

Around a corner they could start to see the outline of crumbling walls in the distance. "How do you know all of this?" she asked.

"Worked on the street a lot as a kid, trying to make money for the orphanage. Folks like to chit chat about town gossip, no matter how old it is." He shrugged, "There's probably nothing here, but it doesn't hurt to check it out."

"It hurts if we get caught."

"Then let's not get caught."

At the top of a rain-washed rise they were greeted by the estate's main gates, which were in shambles, bent and twisted as if hit by a battering ram. After Callum hopped over them, he helped Fenella across and she took a moment to ponder over the wreckage.

"They look melted..." remarked Fenella, and as she touched her fingers to the iron she suddenly felt sick.

"You okay?"

She nodded away his concern, hiding the twist of her gut behind a brief smile.

Past the gates and up the hill, the tattered remains of a house rose into view. It was barely even three standing walls but at one time, it had been a grand house. The foundation was still intact, but the internal structures were either crumbled or just gone, overgrown with thick ivy. What was left standing was painted by moonlight in such a way that it looked like the bones breaking out of the ground. A risen body, bleached by time and sun.

Fenella halted, staring at the empty shell, one hand kneading at her dress. "Something about this place feels wrong."

Callum looked at her and then the house. "Yeah, I imagine it does."

Nothing moved on the hilltop, not even so much as a rat rustled the leaves, and the stillness of it made him shiver. The trees themselves seemed suspended in time, but Fenella knew this forgotten patch of dirt was hiding something, she could feel it.

Together, they walked shoulder to shoulder through the overgrown front courtyard, then around the house, heading for a lone standing mausoleum at the center of a private garden. A few yards behind it was a strange row of what looked like a dome of glass windows planted in the ground.

If the High Father was so against this place, why not board it up or knock it in? Was it arrogance? Or was he afraid to disturb the estate?

As expected, the doors were locked. Callum dropped to one knee and fished a set of small files from his satchel and set to work while Fenella watched the area anxiously. The old fashioned lock was easy enough to pick, and the mausoleum doors opened up with a noisy creak, revealing a narrow set of stairs that disappeared into a void of shadows.

"So much for the full moon." Fenella sighed.

Callum looked around and found an old torch hung on its ring just inside the doors, "Perfect." He then crouched down and started to sift through his bag. "Tear off a part of your skirts."

Affronted, she put her hands on her hips. "Why do I have to tear up mine?"

Callum swept a hand down the front of him, emphasizing his lack of skirt. "Well I'm not going to rip up mine."

They held each other's gaze for a beat until finally Fenella gave in. "Fine," she snapped and started to rip off the bottom hem.

"Atta girl."

When she handed him the fabric, he wrapped it around the torch head and popped the cork on a small bottle from his satchel, splashing the greasy contents over the rags. After a few strikes of a flint, the old torch blazed with fire.

"Alright, let's go."

Carefully, they followed the stairs down into the crypts. Despite the darkness of the steps, the inner chamber itself was slightly illuminated. Callum looked up and discovered that the glass structure topside was a skylight. Time and weather had loosen a few of the panels, so broken glass lay scattered about the floor. Skeletons wrapped in rotten cloth laid peacefully in the rows of pockets carved into the walls, some overtaken by invasive ivy that dripped down from the skylight. Directly in front of them was a closed door, an iron bar set across its middle.

Callum took in the room and looked for anything that may stand out. Fenella however, stepped past him into the middle of the room, hands held out in front of her as if in surrender.

"Please know," her voice was steady and gentle, "that we mean no harm, and we won't be long."

Stepping up beside her, Callum set his hand on her shoulder. "Vanilla, they're just bones. They don't care if we're here." He gave her a reassuring smile, but she shook her head.

"Bones have power, Fenny," she whispered.

"What?"

Fenella blinked, then shook her thoughts clear. "My mother told me that."

"Huh..." he huffed, "Alright then, play with your skeletons. I'm going to look for anything unusual."

She gestured in front of them with the twist of her hand. "More unusual than the barred room in a place meant for the dead?"

Callum sighed and held the torch aloft, illuminating the door. "Yeah well, I was kind of hoping it'd be easier than that. Maybe something useful just sitting out here, in the open."

She clucked her tongue and said mockingly, "No such luck, fearless adventurer."

"Mm," he responded.

"Mm," she repeated.

Callum heaved a sigh and threw back his head. "Fine. We'll open the barred iron door in the center of a forgotten crypt. What could possibly go wrong?"

The torch was dropped in a wall-mounted ring and the two of them lifted the heavy beam from its cradle, setting it aside before slowly drawing open the door.

Stale air wafted past them as light spilled over the threshold, displaying a much smaller room than the one they were in. It was bare except for a single pile of rubble in the center.

Fenella clucked again and pointed at the rocks. "Now, if I have learned anything from bedtime stories, that is where you'll find what you're looking for. So, good luck."

Callum slowly glared at her before putting his hand against her back and shoving her into the room.

"Oi!" she cried before turning on him.

He strolled in casually behind, looking around with a grin. "Oh good, no booby traps."

Fenella's eyes widened with rage. "You bastard, there really could have been booby traps!"

"Who booby traps a crypt?" Callum scoffed.

"WHO BARS THE DOOR TO A CRYPT!?"

Callum opened his mouth to deliver a rebuttal but then discovered he didn't have one. "Yeah, well. How about this, you can shove me into the next room, yeah?"

"I'm going to shove you off a cliff!"

"Deal, but first help me move these rocks."

Fenella made a sort of muffled growling noise that reminded Callum of an angry horse and then stamped her foot, her hands balled into fists at her side. After a moment she rolled up her sleeves and started sifting through the stones.

"They're scorched," she remarked while wiping black soot from her hands.

"Maybe they tried to burn something."

"Yeah, but what?"

"Dunno, guess we'll find out." A few more rocks moved and Callum started to see a smooth slab emerge and once the last piece was slid away they discovered a simple, granite coffin.

"Oh..." Fenella said sheepishly.

Callum stared at it for a moment, trying to decide if it was worth opening.

It was a coffin after all, one that had burned stones on top of it, locked behind a barred door. Nothing about it seemed like a good idea, but he'd never been one to walk away from a possibility.

"C'mon, help me with the lid."

Fenella hesitated. "Callum..."

He touched her wrist. "Look, if it's just some bones then we'll cover them up and leave them to their sleep. No harm done. We can even come back later with some flowers or something, for the disturbance."

Her gaze on him softened. "Really?"

"Really," he said with a gentle squeeze of his fingers.

Together they stood on the left side of the coffin and after a short count down, shoved against the lid. Being far heavier than they thought it would be, it took several heaves for it to fall off the other side. It shattered on impact and Fenella flinched, throwing a look at Callum, who gave an apologetic frown and shrug before retrieving the torch from its hook. When the golden light fell into the coffin the pair discovered the remains had been haphazardly covered in an old blanket, and not wrapped in traditional threads.

At the body's center, the blanket peaked.

"What is that?" asked Fenella.

Callum handed her the torch and then took up one corner of the mildew speckled sheet and pulled.

The object causing the raise in the fabric was the handle of a dagger, twisted and caked in something dark. It rested right in the center of the skeleton's chest, although it wasn't a skeleton at all.

Fenella gasped and almost dropped the torch when they saw the body beneath the sheet, perfectly preserved from the ravages of decay.

"What the hells...?" Callum took a step back.

The man in the coffin lay there as a child carelessly plopped in bed. His head turned to the right and his limbs limp. Bruises splashed his face and the elegant clothing he wore was slashed, the hems of his trousers blackened. The thick hair on his head was as silver as deep winter snow and trimmed to just above his collar bones, but despite its color he wasn't an old man. Maybe in the twilight of his thirties, not too much older than Callum. His skin held an ashen pallor and his lips were blue, but he had no smell of rot about him. Only smoke.

"How is this possible?" Fenella asked. "He's clearly dead, but there's no sign of decomposition."

Callum ran through a list of scenarios. "Maybe the rubble? Could have locked down the lid tight and kept air from getting in to him?"

Fenella shook her head. "He'd still...bust though, wouldn't he? Gases and all that?" She tentatively reached out and lifted his shirt to show a taut stomach that was still very much intact, although it was damaged with unhealed bruises, cuts and burns. "Whoever he is, someone beat him all to hell."

"It has to be Tytian J'harenmar. The High Father mentioned the dagger in his chest, but that doesn't make any sense either. He died forty years ago."

The dagger.

Callum leaned closer and examined the weapon, how its handle was twisted in a spiral and as black as coal. Its surface was not polished but cracked, like dried mud and the open seams glowed with a dull, dancing light.

"Maybe this is what the old bastard is scared of. It definitely doesn't look like a holy artifact."

Fenella studied the body again. "Maybe the dagger is what's kept him preserved." Her eyes grew wide. "Maybe it steals souls."

The possibilities were endless and Callum's hands were starting to itch with the need to take. "Maybe. Lucky for me, I steal treasure." He grinned at the dagger, addressing it as if it were listening. "Look at us, two thieves. It's like it was meant to be."

Rummaging through his satchel he found a rag and palmed it, not wanting to touch flesh to this dagger should Fenella be right and it suck the soul right out of him. The logic that a slip of an old shirt would save him from that was flawed, but he didn't have any better ideas.

Callum was a little disappointed to find there wasn't a rush of power or a sudden howling of wind once the blade slid out of the flesh.

"Oh," he told Fenella with a frown. "I was kind of expecting something dramatic."

They looked at the dagger in awe, its edges pulsing with a molten glow.

"Think this is it?" asked Fenella.

Callum smiled. "Certainly looks like something. Perhaps it's the only thing that can destroy those slabs he talked about. Or maybe it was forged to slay the High Father."

Fenella, excited, "Maybe he's a demon."

"Oooh that would make so much sense," Callum agreed. "Whatever it's use, it's important...you can just tell, ya know?"

"Yeah."

Without warning, the dagger crumbled into dust.

"Uuuhhh..."

Fenella's expression changed from wonderment to deep confusion. "Wait. What happ-"

Something flashed in the corner of Callum's eyeline, and before he had a chance to even comprehend what it was, Fenella was being dragged through the crypt and up the stairs, her screams echoing around the chamber.

"CALLUM!"

"Shit!" He dropped the torch and ran after her, his heart pounding in his throat. Through the main room, up the stairs and out into the open air. Once topside he could see a man standing at the edge of the cemetery, holding Fenella up by her throat.

"Let her go!" Callum shouted as he closed the distance, and the man complied, throwing Fenella with force. She struck Callum square in the chest, taking the air from his lungs. They both tumbled backwards over a stone bench. Dazed and coughing, Callum blinked rapidly as he tried to clear the stars from his vision. Beside him, he heard Fenella groan and could make out her legs moving. She muttered something, unable to catch her breath, but Callum couldn't focus long enough to understand her, the sky above him swimming about. He tried to stand, to find his footing, grab the girl and run, but strong hands gripped the front of his jacket and lifted him off the ground.

Adrenaline and something akin to sea sickness hit Callum in a rush, and with it his focus returned. After a few blinks he found himself staring into the unusual eyes of the dead man from the coffin. Wide with rage, they were a molten gold in color, and while the iris was perfectly intact, the pupils were absent, only a faint ring of pale yellow remained in their stead. Callum might have thought him blind if it hadn't been for all the well aimed, rough handling.

The man snarled, flashing sharp canines and lateral incisors, readying himself to throw Callum into the weathered planters, but suddenly Fenella was there, her hand grasping the undead's thick forearm.

"Don't!" she pleaded, "We are not here to hurt you!"

The man dropped an angry hand from Callum's jacket and grabbed the collar of her dress, snatching her up and off her feet.

Say his name. Call out to him.

She couldn't say for sure where that idea came from, but Fenella took the advice.

"Tytian!" she shouted with authority. "Tytian J'harenmar, set us down!"

The yellow-eyed assailant faltered for a moment at the use of his name and the snarl fell from his damaged face. The beast was slowly put to slumber and the man retook control.

In a blink he released them. Fenella hit the ground, but Callum landed on his feet and immediately grabbed her up by the arm, ready to run.

She shook her head. "No. Stay." She never took her eyes off of their attacker. "Give him a minute."

Callum stared at her. "Uhm, no? He just tried to kill us!"

"He just woke up," she countered, sharply.

"And he's volatile as shit."

"He's not going to hurt us."

Callum's face twisted. "How do you know, huh?"

There was no explainable reason for it, she just knew. Somewhere in the depths of her mind, he was no longer a threat, only lost.

The previously dead man stood there quietly, his head bowed as he stared at his trembling hands. Very slowly he started to look up, his brow furrowed, silver hair plastered to his sweaty brow. After a pause, he spoke with a voice that was accented and deep, although tight from lack of use.

"W-where am I?"

Fenella took a step toward him, her hands held palms out in front of her. "You're in Savhignos. You just woke up, in the J'harenmar family crypt." Another step, "You are Tytian, right?"

Her words were absorbed but there was no immediate answer. He had the forlorn look about him as he peered around the gardens and then out to the hollowed remnants of the house.

His broad shoulders trembled with an uneven exhale. "Yes."

Callum glanced back at the crypt, trying to put together all of the jagged little pieces to this mystery. "How did you wind up in that coffin? What was with that dagger in your chest?"

Tytian looked down and touched the stained hole in his shirt. "Ches..." he whispered.

Callum sighed and put his fingers on the bridge of his nose. "Yes, you were stabbed in the chest." His patience was beginning to thin. "But by WHO? And when for that matter. And why are you not a bag of bones?"

Fenella shushed him.

Tytian shook his head. "No, Ches- Francesca. She's the one who stabbed me." Once again, he grew distant. "My apologies for attacking you." He dipped in a rusty sort of bow and then started to leave.

"Oi! No no," Callum called, and then jogged after him, Fenella falling in behind. "You're not going anywhere."

A dangerous light flashed in Tytian's eyes as he spun on the pair, and Callum grimaced.

"Could you not do that? It's off putting."

Fenella's delicate hand smacked Callum on the arm before she shoo'd him out of the way. "We need to ask you some questions, Mister J'harenmar."

"And who are you, exactly?"

"This is Callum, and I'm Fenella. Fenella Burberry."

Callum's face pinched. "Burberry? Like a cold fruit?"

Immediately he was shushed again.

They trailed after the freshly risen Tytian to the front of the mansion and after a pause he climbed the cracked stairs, ripped his way through the vines over the rotten threshold and entered the ruins, leaving them behind.

Callum put his hands on his hips. "Pulled him out of his own coffin and he still won't talk to us. Typical man."

Fenella grabbed his arm and tugged him up the stairs.

Very little was left of the home except for the marble flooring and a few back rooms, although the ceilings were caved in and foliage had crawled over every available surface, turning the structure into a jungle. Tytian had made his way across the broken floor and piled beams, slipping into a barely standing distant room.

Fenella started to follow but Callum stopped her.

After a while Tytian emerged, a soiled coin purse and tattered cloak in hand. Little holes littered the bottom hem, eaten away by moths. With all of the grace of sea fog, he traversed the rubble, never once stumbling or causing the debris to shift. After tying the purse to his belt and the old cloak around his shoulders, he finally acknowledged the pair that waited for him.

"I have a few questions," He stated heavily.

Callum agreed. "Yeah pal, so do we. Quite a few actually."

Tytian looked him over. "Go on."

"Okay first off, what the hell are you?"

There was a notable pause. "I'm a vampire."

Callum gave a suspicious squint. "Look, if you're not going to take this seriously-"

"Next question."

Fenella cut in front of Callum's annoyed inhale. "What was that dagger in your chest?"

"A demonic conjuring."

She paled. "How did it work?"

"I don't know."

His short snip answering made Callum quirk a brow. "How do you not know?"

"It killed me. I wasn't exactly able to do research studies."

"Ah, but it didn't kill you."

"What?"

"Why is the High Father scared of you?"

This made Tytian hesitate. "Ask another."

But Callum crossed his arms, a toothy grin spreading on his face. "Ooo, no. Let's stay on this one."

"Why are you asking about the High Father?"

"Why are you now asking the questions? I wasn't finished."

"Alright, enough!" Fenella cut in, stepping in between the two men. "Mister J'harenmar, there's a situation happening and we could really use some insight." She gestured behind her to Callum. "My friend here overheard a meeting between the Beacon Sect and the High Father this afternoon. They talked about some very ominous things. There was mention of some kind of slabs? And what sounded like a ritual? Would you happen to know what they were referring to?"

Tytian's brow tightened. "Do they have all of the stones?"

Callum shook his head. "Just five so far."

The other man stepped toward him, his shoulders raised with tension. "And you're sure they said only five?"

"Yeah."

Tytian's gaze swept them both, his mouth chewing on his words before speaking them. "Leave. Get out of the city while you still can."

"What are they up to?" Fenella asked with concern.

A quick flick of the wrist and Tytian pulled the hood on his cloak over his head. "Those bastards are going to summon Khaladhuun." He then marched down the steps.

The two of them exchanged looks of budding dread.

"Oh, yep. That sounds like a big name." muttered Callum before following.

Fenella had to almost jog to keep up with Tytian's long, determined stride. "Khaladhuun? Who is that?"

"He is malice in a physical form. A demon lord, very old and very powerful."

"Oh he sounds lovely," Callum snarked.

"Why would they want to summon something like that?" questioned Fenella, only to receive no reply. "Hey, where are you going?"

After a few more steps Tytian began to slow until he came to a halt. "I don't know." He turned and looked back at the house, an aching pain visible on his face. Born not from a blade, but loss.

Across his brow and cheekbones, the bruises were beginning to fade.

With an almost motherly ease in her voice, Fenella tried her best to soothe him. "It's a lot to take in at once."

"How long has it been?" Tytian asked with a wavering tone.

Callum answered. "Forty three years since the estate burned down, according to the old timers."

Sorrow swam in their depths as his eyes traced every moon-soaked remain of the mansion. "Why are you here then?" he asked them, Callum the first to speak up.

"One of the Beacon's mentioned your name and the tomb, and it put Aolfrun on edge. Like he was scared of a ghost or something. I figured, if he were afraid then this would be the best place to look."

"For what?"

Callum shrugged. "For a way to stop him. I wasn't quite expecting to find a reanimated *vampire* corpse but sometimes you just have to use the tools you were given."

Tytian shook his head. "But why? Who are you?"

Callum grunted and threw his arms in the air. "Why does everyone seem to have difficulty understanding this? You don't just lie about and wait for death to come shake you out of your bones. You live, and you fight. I may just be a humble thief but if there were a dam to break and destroy the city, I wouldn't just stand there and watch the cracks grow. I'd get my ass up there and start working on a fix."

Tytian's lips twitched in a small smile. "Hmm."

Callum glared. "What?"

"Most men would just watch the cracks grow." He threw a glance over to the glow of the city in the distance, lingering on the towering cathedral spire. "Alright, so you're going to stop this. How? Do you have a plan?"

"Part of one. The first step at least."

"Wait," Fenella spoke up, "Tytian you're very fast and strong, couldn't you just...kill the High Father?"

Callum snapped his fingers. "I'm not a killing sort of man, but I like that plan better."

But Tytian shook his head. "No. I cannot step foot on holy ground."

She looked at him with mild confusion. "How come?"

"Because of what I am. If I did, it would be mere seconds before I was dead."

Callum tapped his temple. "Filing that away for later."

"What about out on the street?" offered Fenella. "He's out and about sometimes."

"That won't work either, he's too-" Tytian grew rigid, "heavily protected."

She crossed her arms. "You nearly snapped us like twigs; a few guards shouldn't be an issue. What about an arrow from a rooftop?"

"It isn't the guards you should be concerned with. He's protected by something else."

Fenella cast her eyes to the ground, confused, but Callum made a little groan and dragged his hand down his face. "Son of a bitch. He's protected by demons, isn't he?"

Tytian nodded. "He has his own personal hell hound of sorts."

"And you can't just kill it?" Fenella asked.

Callum chuckled. "You're awfully homicidal, Vanilla."

Tytian's bitter grin never reached his eyes. "The last time he sent his bitch to my door she put a dagger in my heart, burned down my home and killed my family. Humans I can butcher with ease, but her?" He shook his head. "Plus, I've been trapped in a standstill for forty odd years. I'm weak and tired. She'll be well oiled and ready."

Crestfallen, Fenella stepped back from the group, losing herself in her thoughts.

Things were starting to steadily tilt uphill, and Callum was beginning to realize the size of the mountain they would have to climb. "Alright, so we stick to my plan."

"Which is?" Tytian asked.

"First, get out of the city and head west to Havnul, see if we can get the jump on this stone before it can be delivered. Along the way, we pick up as many of my friends as possible. We're going to need them."

"We're going to need an army."

Callum smirked. "Trust me, this lot could punch straight through a wall made of men and demons. These folks we're going after? They're the only people in the world you need at your back."

Tytian looked up to the sky, his face full of moonlight for the first time in decades. "I hope you're right. Because most of us are probably going to die." Without another word he turned and started down the pathway.

Callum huffed. "Well, guess he's with us." Then he turned to Fenella, who was still submerged in her mind. "Hey," he said gently before brushing his fingertips across her arm. "You still here?"

She nodded, "Yeah. Let's go," and together they followed Tytian into the sleeping heart of the city.

FOUR

Set within the looming front gates of Savignos was a single man door, to allow easy in and out access to the city guard. That was their objective, and after winding through the city's back alleys for hours, it was a welcomed sight for the trio.

Callum and his two new strays kept their distance while surveying the scene, relieved to see only one footman on duty. A typical sight for the early morning hours, between the shift change of the nightmen to the day.

A few yards from him was a guard station, yellow light illuminating the slick cobblestones from the open doorway. With ease, the group of three managed to keep low enough in the shadows between varying lamp posts and made it to the shack unseen. They peered around the corner at the nightman, who stood at languid attention in front of the one-man door.

Callum looked at the others and put two fingers to his eyes then away at the guard, signaling to keep him within sight. Once there was a nod of recognition, Callum took in a quick breath and half-jogged for the door, Fenella hot on his heels. Tytian however, pulled ahead, sprinting toward the guardsman who was just starting to stiffen at the sound of approaching boot heels. He placed his large hands on either side of the man's face and with little effort, snapped his neck with a sickening sound.

The man crumbled to the ground.

Callum and Fenella came to a halt, shock and dismay openly displayed on their faces.

"Welp, that man is dead," Callum grimaced.

Unbothered by their horror, Tytian opened the door and motioned to them to follow. "Come on, the sun is rising."

After an exchange of glances, Callum and Fenella reluctantly followed their murder-happy comrade out of the city and hung a hard left, getting as close to the wall as possible. They followed the subtle curve until the forest was thick enough for them to slip into undetected.

Savhignos was set against the base of a high, red rock shelf that tucked the city's back right against the sea. Beyond her front gates the expanse was mostly thick forests, with pockets of homesteads and villages. Easy enough to mingle through and look natural enough to those might be watching from the high guard towers along the city walls, or an eagle-eyed airship sent to scour the area for thieves, murderers and a rogue pastry chef.

The three of them weaved their way through the trees, Callum and Fenella picking their route carefully through the underbrush while Tytian traversed with little effort, his eyesight accurate in the waning dark.

"This way," Callum whispered near the edge of the forest. When their boots hit the soft sands of a well-worn road, all three looked back to the city, which was nothing more than a faint outline in the distance.

"It should be smooth travels from here to Rodenburg." Callum gave his tallest companion a passive aggressive glance. "Although, should there be any more instances of senseless murder, that could all change."

Tytian's moth-eaten cloak hood was pulled low enough to cover his eyes, but Callum could sense them rolling.

"Yeah, can you not do that again?" Fenella's nose was slightly scrunched at the memory of snapping bones. "I'm a little nervous now about the speed at which you killed an innocent man."

One shoulder rose in a shrug. "He was a city guard. They're anything but innocent."

Callum chimed in. "Not all are bad folks. Some are just collectin' a salary."

This made Fenella curious. "Didn't think you were the type to defend the law."

"I'm not." Callum crossed his arms, the posture only slightly defensive. "I've known one not to be too bad, that's all."

"Just because one wasp didn't sting you doesn't mean the rest won't swarm," Tytian warned with a firm conviction. "We were too close, he would have heard us and surely called on the rest. Word would have spread to the cathedral and then Francesca would be at our throats as we speak. His death was necessary. Unfortunate for him, but necessary nonetheless."

When he saw the way Fenella had begun to shrink from him, his tone softened and Tytian spoke again to calm her worries. "You have nothing to fear from me, Fenella." He offered her a small, tight smile. "I like you. You've been kind."

This seemed to put her at ease.

Behind her, once he realized that he was not included in that declaration of safety, Callum moved in an animated gesture of *what about me?*

Tytian never extended his assurance, instead choosing to walk on down the sandy road.

Left to wallow in rejection, Callum looked to Fenella, who was grinning at him smugly.

"He likes me," she cooed, "I'm nice."

"Oh, shut up." Callum gave her a slight shove to the shoulder and followed behind their toothy confidant, with Fenella cackling like a hag.

"Don't worry, I won't let him kill you."

"Promise?"

"No."

Callum squinted at her laughter, which only made her laugh more.

The two of them bickered for most of the morning, throwing banter back and forth like a game of hot stone, enjoying the long walk on the highway. It was nice, the distraction of it, keeping her thoughts occupied by the next quip and not the grander scheme.

Fenella tried to ooze with confidence, because inside she was waging a war. No matter how much her instincts told her that she was exactly on the path she was meant for, her logic couldn't help but to issue a challenge. She looked towards the dawn slowly creeping up the horizon, and played through her usual routine. By now she'd be in the shop kitchen, tying on an apron and starting up the stove fires. Then she'd haul the bags of flour and sugar from the pantry, and the butter, milk and eggs from cold storage. She would eat a single strawberry before finely chopping the rest, and then bust her ass for hours, baking breads, pies and pastries. Just as the sun found its way into her shop windows, she would prop open the door and let the scent of her work flood the streets. After a day of sales, if there were sales, came the cleanup, the lock up and the long walk home, where she would eat her meager dinner, bathe and then go to bed only to wake up the next morning and do it all again. It hadn't even been a full day since she had closed her bakery doors for the night, and yet that life seemed to fade from her, almost as if it were a dream. Her existence felt as though the only reason she was alive was to continue that same routine until she was old and gray, but now something new had taken its place. For the first time in her life, Fenella felt as though she were on the right path, despite her fight against it.

It was too late now for anything else, and it was pointless to torture herself with the never-ending carousel of what-ifs. Acceptance was the only choice she had if she wished to remain sane, and if Fenella Burberry was anything, it was pragmatic.

She smiled as the breeze touched her skin, stirring the sweet scent of wildflowers that grew unchecked between patches of farmland.

Callum watched her with piqued interest. "You seem eager."

"It's the morning air, that's all."

A lie, and he knew it.

"I don't think it is. I think you're having fun. Finally out of that rut."

"I beg your pardon, what makes you think I was in a rut?" she asked with false agitation, not wanting him to grow cocky about the fact he was right.

"Oh Vanilla, it was written all over that pretty face. You needed this." He winked and then picked up his pace as hers slowed.

This man was more than she had bargained for, and she scoffed at his perception, heat flushing her cheeks.

Among the homesteads that dotted the countryside, one in particular sat deep in the forest just off the main road, a wooden fence stretched in front of the tree line. The shale drive was well worn with cart wear and buckets of flowers sat next to the open gates.

Callum motioned for the others to follow. "Come on, this way."

Chickens of varying breed and size strutted about a tidy yard, excited and vocal for their morning scratch. In a shed, adjacent to the farmhouse, a little girl was scooping crushed corn into a bucket, fending off the hungry thievery of a yearling goat. So preoccupied by her duties, the child didn't notice the strangers who came striding up the drive, but her guardian sure did.

Lying just outside the shed door was a sizable dog, his naturally white coat dirty from the dust of the field. When he saw them approach he raised his head and growled low in his throat, lips twitching just enough to show the tips of his teeth.

"Easy boy," Callum said with an outstretched hand.

The farmhouse door swung open on talkative hinges and a man stepped out on the porch, wiping water from his freshly washed hands. He was portly in size and short in stature, but with the cheery face of a cherub.

"Better pick those peppers today before they blister!" He called over his shoulder to someone in the house, wearing the expression of a man happy to simply be alive. He nearly jumped out of his skin as soon as he noticed there were people standing at his steps.

"Oi!" he shouted, then rolled his eyes with a chuckle. "Callum!" After marching off of the covered porch the two of them shook hands. "You spooked the shit out of me."

Callum grinned. "Knew I smelled something."

"Shut up." He looked at the others and smiled brightly, although it dimmed at the sight of Tytian, clothed in a wardrobe best described as a corpse found in the gutter. "Hello! I'm Bo."

Fenella stepped forward with a small wave. "Hi, I'm Fenella. And this is...Ty."

Tytian gave a sharp little nod of his head.

Bo hid his scrutiny well enough. "It's nice to meet you both! What brings you to my humble little farm?"

Fenella lightly punched Callum in the arm. "This thing."

Behind him, a dark-haired woman stepped through the front door, drying her hands on her apron. "Everything alright?" she asked, but once she saw Callum, she placed her fists on her hips. "Oh."

"Oh." Mimicked Callum before he hopped up the stairs and gave her a hug.

She patted his back and then hit him with a rag when he pulled away. "Where have you been?" she asked, and he rubbed the back of his neck with a small shrug.

"Around."

"Just 'around', huh?" Her arms crossed. "Been to see Six lately?"

Bo turned to her, his words fumbling around a nervous chuckle as he tried to interject. "Laurel, got any of that coffee left?"

She gave him a look that could cut, but surrendered with a flash of her palms as she dipped back inside the house.

"Laurel, my wife," he told Fenella and Tytian. "She makes the best coffee."

Callum agreed, coming down the steps with the shrug of a scolded dog. "As much as I would love for this to just be a social visit, I'm afraid we're here on business."

He watched the front door with trepidation, then dipped his head toward a large barn outside of the yard. "Let's talk there. Laurel loves ya Callum, but she doesn't love my involvement with some of your escapades."

Callum nodded. "Fair enough. I'd like to be far away from any rolling pins and iron pots."

Bo laughed and then addressed the others, waving a hand at the porch. "She'll be right out with that coffee, if you two want to have a seat and rest up a bit." He glanced at Tytian's shoes before heading out to the barn.

Fenella started to follow, prompting Callum to hold up his hand. "It's fine, this won't take long. Go get some coffee."

With her hands on her hips she watched him leave, suspicion narrowing her face until Tytian moved, heading up the steps as instructed. Defeated, she decided to do the same.

On one side of the covered porch there were all kinds of buggy tack for horses piled in barrels, and bridles equipped with various types of bits were hung along the wall. On the other side was a comfortable little sitting area, with a cushion lined couch, two iron chairs and a wooden crate for a center table. All around the chairs, couch and railings were pots filled with brightly colored flowers. Bees and butterflies flitted through the sun beams and landed among the open petals, greedy tongues seeking the nectar inside. A light breeze tickled the chimes and filled the morning with a gentle tune, matching the sparkle of dew that coated the vegetable plants and flower bushes encircling the home's small front courtyard. The chickens clucked peacefully. A foal whinnied somewhere in the distance, and Fenella marveled at it all.

It was obvious that this place was nurtured with so much love and care, but somewhere, just a few leagues away, there was a man who would burn it all down and not even think twice.

Evil has no place in this world. The words were thought with so much hostility that this level of hatred she felt was downright alien.

For a moment she was lost to dark, hideous thoughts. It was the sounds of a bucket being dragged through dirt that brought her back to the world. The young girl who had been gathering corn for the chickens was now attempting to carry a pail heavy with water to a shallow trough. She had successfully distributed the corn among the hens and goat, but now she was determined to water the animals as well, although her little arms defied her efforts. Water sloshed every step she made, leaving stains of mud in the dust behind her. With her tongue stuck out and her eyes clamped shut, she tried her best to keep the bucket as steady as possible, but once she reached the trough and turned it over, only a tiny sip came spilling out. Without fuss, the little girl waddled herself back over to the well pump and started again.

Amused, Fenella was about to go help the child when she noticed Tytian was already coming to her aid. For a moment, the memory of a snapped-neck nightwatchman flashed inside her mind, and her stomach free fell into her boots. But, when he reached the little girl, he laid his hand on the end of the rusted lever and filled the bucket for her in three solid pumps. The little one stepped out of his way and blotted the sweat from her brow. Her ever watchful guardian was laying a few steps away in the shade of a tree, studying the pair with dark eyes. Should she so much as yelp, there was no doubt the dog would be on Tytian in an instant.

Once the bucket was full, he carried it to the trough and filled it to the brim with a single pour. The child retrieved the bucket from her intimidating helper and looked up to him, squinting against the bright sky.

"Thank you," she said in a tiny voice, and he bowed his head in kind. She then tottered back to the shed to put the pail away, and took up a tiny broom, which looked as though it had been handcrafted just for her. Tytian was dismissed with the small wave of her hand, and she began her task of sweeping the shed floor.

When Tytian rejoined Fenella on the porch, she didn't even try to hide her smile.

Laurel emerged soon after, serving tray in hand. "Oh," she said, a little startled to find that it was only going to be the two strangers she would have to entertain. "Bo and Callum?"

Fenella pointed towards the tree line. "The barn I believe."

Clearly annoyed but trying to hide it, Laurel moved between them to the seating area. "Oh, guess it's just us then." She set the tray on the crate, gesturing for them to take a seat. The mugs offered were well kept, not a chip to be seen, while the percolator had a noticeable dent to the side and a bit of rust beginning near the handle base. There were two dishes of cream and sugar, with a small blue glass filled with apple juice set to the side.

"Del, honey? Come on," Laurel beckoned, holding out a hand.

At the call of her mother, the child set her broom against the door frame and ran up to the porch, taking her time climbing the stairs. On her heels, the big dog followed.

"That's enough chores for today, come get some juice." Laurel smoothed her daughter's hair once Del was perched on her knee.

"She's beautiful," Fenella told her, stirring a swirl of cream into her coffee.

Laurel swept the dark bangs from her daughter's eyes. "Thank you. Her name is Delilah."

Fenella displayed exaggerated surprise. "Delilah? That's such a nice name," she told the child, and the little girl lowered the cup, swallowed her big gulp of juice and then wiped her mouth with the back of her hand.

"Thank you."

Her mother smiled at her and batted some dust from her dress. "So, how long have you known Callum?"

"Since yesterday."

Laurel's brow furrowed in confusion. "Huh..." She then looked to Tytian, "And you?"

"Since yesterday," he repeated, tone flat.

She nodded slowly, kneading at her lower lip with her teeth. "Okay." Her arms grew a little tighter around her daughter. "Are you two colleagues of his? Are you all in the same profession?"

Fenella registered her change in body language and held up a hand, shaking her head. "Oh no. I'm a baker, from Savhignos. And Ty-" She hesitated, gesturing to her companion who looked like a body you'd find murdered in the forest. "Is... a... groundskeeper. For the cemetery!"

Subtly, he turned to her, and she could tell he was wondering where she pulled that lie from.

Laurel looked Tytian over, evaluating. "Custodial work never pays well. If you'd like, I could see if I can find you some of my brother's old clothes. He was tall like you, they should fit."

Tytian declined. "There's no need, I'll make due with what I have."

But she was already shaking her head. "Nonsense." She patted Del on the leg and the child slid out of her lap. "I've just been using them for the odd patch in Bo's clothes when he needs them. I can spare a few pieces."

"Your brother won't mind?" asked Fenella.

Laurel's grin was slight. "He's been dead for about fifteen years, I don't think he'll be missing them." In a blink she was gone inside the house.

Fenella leaned in and whispered, "You could use a change of clothes."

Del set her little cup very carefully on the tray and then climbed up onto the couch next to Tytian, plopping herself down in a cluster of pillows to curl up like a cat, her little feet flat against his leg. Quietly, she batted a tassel on one corner of a cushion, watching the threads swing with mild fascination.

"I think you made a friend," Fenella said with amusement.

Tytian watched the little girl for a moment, then turned away, his chest noticeably tight. When Fenella saw the clench of his jaw, she didn't remark on it. Instead, she leaned back and spoke to the girl.

"Hey, Del?" A quick motion across the porch, "What's your dog's name?"

The girl never took her eyes from the tassel. "Baabaa."

"Baabaa?" asked Fenella and the dog tilted his head, ears perked. "That's a great name. Did you name him?"

Del nodded. "Mhm."

"Why Baabaa?"

"Hims white, like the sheeps." She looked up from her pillow pile and then mimicked a sheep's bleat. *Baabaa.* The dog rose and came to her, lapping a big tongue up her knee. She gently patted his head. "Good Baabaa."

Despite the draw of his hood, Fenella saw the hint of a smile on Tytian's stern mouth.

The door hinges creaked as Laurel came out of the house, arms full of clothing. When she saw Del giggling next to Tytian she paused a moment before putting on a friendly face. "Here ya go. One of the socks has a patch in the heel but it's a tight stitch. I didn't have any of his traveling clothes still in one piece. These may be a little glitzy." When he stood and retrieved the clothing she pointed towards the door. "You can change in the house. First door on the right. I also filled the basin for you."

After quietly expressing his gratitude, Tytian entered the farmhouse.

There were almost as many plants inside as out, at least some sort of greenery on over half the shelves in the small living room and connecting kitchen. All the curtains were open so light spilled in every direction. Down the hallway he spotted his destination, and quietly shut the door behind him.

Inside he found a sewing room. There was a sewing machine, a tall wardrobe and multiple bolts of fabric scattered about the room. On a desk he set down the new clothes and stripped of the old. He really did look like some sort of beggar. His pants were new the night he first pulled them on, now they were shredded almost up to the knees, spots of mildew blooming along the seams. His shirt, once a birthday gift, had scorch marks and dried blood infused into the fabric, the smell of him only overpowered by the smokey scent of his cloak. If his attire looked this bad, he could only imagine the rest.

Tytian moved to the basin and scooped up the soap and rag that were provided. He washed his skin, examining the old injuries to his body as he went. What once was a horrific burn was now pink skin, slowly darkening to his natural tone by the hour. Broken bones were fused back in place and even the deepest of bruises no longer held their shade. Accelerated healing was probably the only thing his body could do that he was grateful for.

While he slept, whatever magic was in that dagger kept everything in suspended repose. He hadn't aged, nor had his muscle mass deteriorated over the last forty years, although Tytian had stopped aging long before that night with Francesca. Built like a brawler, thick and powerful, his height added balance to his stature. With the enhancement of his affliction, Tytian J'harenmar was truly a dangerous man, and yet she was able to put him in the ground for decades.

"Ches..." he whispered without meaning to. His sharp nails traced along the scar left behind by the dagger.

Unlike the rest, this wound would not fade away.

Once the water was murky and his skin clean, Tytian dressed in the gifted clothes. The trousers were plain enough, but the shirt was finely made. Thick, maroon fabric with silver pattern stitching on the collar. It had a deep neckline that could be cinched with a braided string, but he left it untouched. The boots were comfortable and broken in, polished gold buckles adorning the sides. There was even a full-length cloak made of gray wool, the hood and borders stitched with white yarn embellishments. He tied it over his shoulders and then raised the hood, hiding his white hair and pupil-less eyes. His tattered clothing were tossed in the dustbin by the door.

When Tytian rejoined the women on the porch, they both stood. Laurel looked him over and gave an approving nod of her head.

"Told you they would fit."

Fenella gave him a thumbs up. "Much better!"

"Thank you." Tytian tried to hand Laurel a few coins for her generosity, but she waved them away.

Callum and Bo's return was signaled by the sound of hooves on sandy shale, the pair leading three horses behind them by long split reins.

"Holy shit, you're clean," Callum called out to Tytian. "Won't have to ride up-wind from you now."

Laurel put her fists on her hips. "Hey, watch the language. There are little ears present, you ass."

Callum started to argue, only to be cut short by Fenella's well timed interjection.

"Are those for us?" She jogged out to meet the horses, immediately drawn to a glossy, black gelding.

"Yep!" Bo patted a bay horse's neck. "Fine animals, all three."

Callum spoke up, pointing out each horse. "Their names are Bought, And, Paid For."

Laurel squinted at her husband. "With legal tender this time?"

Bo gave a weak flick of his hand, suddenly unable to look his wife in the eye. "Yeah yeah, no worries love."

Fenella saw him pull his shirt down over the bejeweled holy relic stuck in the waistband of his pants.

The leggy bay mare was Tytian's pick, her height perfectly matched for his own, and he pulled himself up into the saddle, ready for the road.

"Leaving already?" Bo asked, crestfallen, and Callum confirmed his fears.

"Yeah, sorry buddy. We can catch up next time." He leaned in closer and whispered, "Remember, take that relic to Fletcher in Tarandale. He'll melt it right down for you." When Bo nodded, Callum offered Laurel a wave. "Wonderful to see you again, Laurel my dear. And you too, Del."

Delilah wandered over to her mother and waved her little hand. "Bye, uncle Cal."

Suddenly stern, Laurel hoisted her daughter on to her hip. "Callum? Go see Six, will ya?"

Fidgeting with the paint gelding's reins, Callum's nod was brisk enough, but the words were slow to come. "Wouldn't you know it but uh, we're actually headed that way now."

Bo's chubby face lit up. "Hey, send her our love, yeah?"

"Mhm. Sure thing."

Callum never looked him in the eye.

The three of them headed down the drive and pointed their horses west on the main road, dodging a small caravan of vegetable merchants making their way toward the city.

After adjusting her skirts for comfort and modesty, Fenella reached out and stroked her gelding's neck. "Do they actually have names?"

Callum shrugged. "I don't know, but they're ours now so I guess it's up to us." He leaned forward. "What do you wanna be called, boy? You need something dashing and heroic- like your owner."

"Oh boy," muttered Fenella.

"Hmm, let's see." He thought for a moment and then snapped his fingers. "How about Red Widow-maker? The Painted Blight? Death Splotch?"

Fenella laughed. "You're really bad at this."

He slowly looked back at her, his expression unimpressed. "If you're so creative, Vanilla, why don't you show us how it's done, hmm? What are you naming yours?"

Being put on the spot made her sit a little straighter in the saddle. "Well, I was considering calling him Apple."

Both men stared at her in judgmental silence until she became self-conscious. "What? Horses like apples." Her voice was small at first, then she gestured wildly at Callum. "Oh, come on, it's far better than something ridiculous like Death Splotch!" She turned on Tytian. "What about you, huh?!"

He shrugged. "Outstrider, after my fastest cargo ship."

The other two now stared at him, eyes narrowed in mild jealousy.

"Okay, that name is cool," Callum admitted tightly.

"Yeah." Fenella gave her gelding another pat. "I still like Apple, though."

He snorted in response.

"Well fella, guess I'll just call you Red," Callum told his own steed, but behind him he heard a scoff.

"Red? That's so lackluster!" claimed Fenella.

"So, the others were too ridiculous, and this one is too plain? Make up your mind, woman!"

"Find something in the middle! Red sounds like you don't care about him at all!"

"We just met!"

"He still deserves something impressive!"

"How am I, a simple man, expected to compete with the grand genius of *Apple*?"

"Horses like apples!"

Tytian, head hung in annoyance, rubbed at his temples. "This is going to be a very long journey."

FIVE

In the early morning, a shrill whistle sounded in three bursts. Guards came pouring in from every bunk house and tower stairwell, crowding the area like ants to witness their fallen comrade, left crumpled by the city gates. The state of him was grotesque. Bluing skin and head snapped at an unnatural angle. Bones had broken and pierced the skin, leaving blood to cover the ground beneath his cold body.

A captain beckoned over the closest footman, never taking his eyes from the twisted corpse at his feet while giving instruction to fetch the Beacon Sect.

"Go straight to the cathedral, do not stop, and inform the first Beacon you see that a guardsman has been murdered."

The footman hopped on a horse and spurred the animal on, the sound of shod hooves crackling through the morning silence.

It was a long ride, snaking through the city streets, dodging those milling about the new day, but soon the grand church appeared around a corner stretch, and the footman abandoned his horse in the courtyard. He stormed the entryway and grabbed the collar of the first person he came to, which happened to be a custodian.

"Get the Beacons, now!" he barked between heaved breaths.

Beacon Trebor was already walking through the nave when he heard the guard's frantic request.

"What is it?" he croaked.

The man took a few more deep swallows of air, close to vomiting with nerves. "A nightwatchman, Beacon. He's dead."

Trebor waited, then shrugged. "And?"

"His head was almost ripped completely off, and the man door in the main gate was open."

Trebor's interest was piqued. "Did someone come in or go out?"

The footman shook his head. "I don't know sir. But why would someone kill him just to go out?"

The Beacon's face twisted. "To go unnoticed," he murmured more to himself than anyone else, a million thoughts racing through his mind. "Go back to your post, tell the other men to move the body into the barracks and wait for my associate. Say nothing to the citizens."

Trebor immediately rushed through the sanctuary, to a door behind the high standing pulpit. His robes billowed like waves behind him, slippers shuffling along the polished floor. Through the entry he sprinted for an ornate elevator, reserved for Beacons and the High Father only.

"Out of my way," he snarled at the armed guard, swinging into the open pod and smashing the highest button on the list. Ropes groaned as they began their hoist, moving floor to floor until finally reaching the top.

The doors opened at the signal of a bell.

Dedicated solely to the High Father, this wing was large enough to fill with two houses, the high ceiling echoing his footsteps as he crossed the marble foyer and through the archway of a long corridor. A pair of carved doors stood shut at the end, but this wasn't his destination, and Trebor instead swung himself through the pulled curtains of a sitting room just adjacent to the High Father's own bed chambers.

Flames crackled in a broad fireplace, seating shadows in the two plush armchairs stationed nearby. Full bookshelves and polished mahogany chest of drawers lined around the spacious room, the etched glass doors of a liquor cabinet sparkled as firelight hit its prismed cut.

For all of his rushing, Trebor now moved with caution. He glanced around the empty room before speaking aloud, his hands wringing about themselves.

"I need to speak with you." He kept his voice low.

Not even the air stirred, and for some time Trebor started to wonder if she was even there.

He tried again. "The matter is an urgent one."

From the far corner, where the shadows painted the deepest gloom, Francesca Draven bled into the room like a smog.

"What do you want, Beacon?" Rabid, she bit the last word between her teeth.

Trebor flinched and bowed his sweaty head. "I need to speak with you."

"About?"

"A foot just came crashing in downstairs. Apparently, there's been an incident with a nightwatchman."

Subtle, the tilt of her head indicated a thinning patience. "And what do I care for nightwatchmen?"

Trebor's next statement came spilling out with haste. "He was murdered early this morning, and his death was odd. The guard who reported it said his head had almost been torn from his body, and the man door was open." Suddenly, he found himself backed against the liquor cabinet, but he couldn't recall ever taking a step.

Francesca's merlot eyes leveled with his as she leaned down, the circle of hellfire around her slit pupils pulsing on beat with her heart. "Get to the fucking point, Trebor."

His chin dimpled, hands raised up to his chest in a pathetic, uncontrollable display of fear. "I think it might have been J'haren-mar. Who else has that kind of... *force*, besides you?"

"It's been forty years, you little worm. He still sleeps." A mani-cured brow then arched, and she gripped the front of his robes. "Is this a pathetic attempt to undermine the High Father? Didn't he shoot down your previous proposal of exhuming Tytian's body?" The scent of burning fabric started to grow stronger, wisps of smoke slipping between her clenched fingers. "Did you think you could use me to get your way?"

Sweat trickled down Trebor's face and he shook his head in panic. "No! No Francesca, I swear!" He pointed a shaky finger. "Go look at the body. M-maybe he was exaggerating, but you should've seen the boy. He was spooked and pale-"

"I am not your pawn." Francesca pulled Trebor off of his feet, dragged him out of the sitting room and into the High Father's chamber. The doors opened without touch, and she cast the Beacon at Aolfrun's slippered feet.

The High Father stood there in mild confusion, one arm already sliding into a silk robe. "Francesca?"

She looked down her nose at Trebor. "Tell him what you told me. What you came to me in secret about." When the Beacon stammered, tears in his eyes, she kicked him hard in the ribs.

"Please! Aolfrun-" He shuffled closer on his knees. "A night-watchman was killed, viciously, and they found the gate door open."

The High Father shrugged, unbothered. "And? There's mur-der in these streets almost every day, how is this any different?"

Trebor gulped before he looked down to the floor, shoulders trembling. "There was a man yesterday, a thief, in the old scroll room on the third level. A maid walked in on him and ran out to get the church sentry, when they returned they found him gone."

Aolfrun's nostrils flared. "A thief? In my house? And not a soul told me of this?!"

Trebor sniffed. "The Beacon's were only made aware of it late yesterday evening."

"The Beacons...or just you?" asked Aolfrun.

The man at his feet squeaked out an answer. "Just me."

"What did this man take? And what does this have to do with the dead guard?"

Trebor wiped his nose on the back of his sleeve. "He didn't steal anything of worth, I don't think. The only thing the maid noticed missing was an old relic with loose gems."

The High Father's voice rose. "Then what does this have to do with anything?! Get to the point, Trebor!"

A different kind of fear found its way into the Beacon's gut, a kind that seems to tingle the whole body as if the soul itself was detaching from the meat. "My tea boy, Marlan...when he left us in the parlor after our meeting, he said he saw a man dash from the room and head down the stairs. He fit the description the maid gave." He turned wide, fevered eyes up to the High Father, a sob clogging his throat. "What if he overheard us?"

Aolfrun gestured broadly. "What if he did?! Why should I fear an eavesdropping pickpocket? Let him try and alert the masses." He rolled his shoulders back into a proud pose, "Who would believe him?" and leaned over Trebor, hands clasped behind his back. "I fear no man."

"Tytian J'harenmar is not a man," The Beacon whispered.

The High Father's eyes bulged. "What did you say?" he asked with controlled rage.

"Please," Trebor begged, placing shaking hands on the golden stitched slippers in front of him. "A brutally murdered night-watch, an open door to and from the city, a sneak thief with an ear to the door of our secret plots- something is afoot, your holiness. I can feel it."

A violent scoff and suddenly the slippers were snatched away. "You can *feel it*," Aolfrun mocked. He strode toward a grand dresser, shaking his head. "You've set this up, haven't you?"

Trebor frowned. "No! No, why woul-"

"Because!" Aolfrun swung around to face him, hands clenched into bony fists at his sides, "You have been pushing for us to check the tombs. Every time, *'Maybe we should check the crypts, check the crypts, maybe something was left behind'*. Why is that?! Were you planning something, Trebor? An ambush for my men, perhaps? Or a trap for Francesca? Hmm?!" He rushed Trebor then, pulling the other man up to his feet roughly. "Answer me!" he barked, spittle flying from his yellowing teeth.

"No plot, High Father, I would never!"

"You have been downright begging for our return to the J'harenmar estates! Why? Have I been harboring a loyalist all these years?"

Bloodshot and rimmed in panic, Trebor's eyes were feverish as he shook his head, jowls rattling with the effort. "No! Never. I just thought perhaps there was something more there, something of Tytian's mothers, or even of his! He always was Khaladhuun's favored and your rage, while justified, was so swift, High Father. There is a chance-"

Aolfrun raised a bony hand. "Enough."

Tears were running down Trebor's face and for a split second, that mask of fear shifted to shame once the pungent stench of urine wafted through the air.

Aolfrun looked down to see a wet stain on the front of the Beacon's robes and slowly he released the sobbing man. "Shh shh, alright," he said gently, patting the back of Trebor's balding head before striding around him to a tall bookshelf. He studied the titles of all of the spines, falling into his thoughts.

Trebor sniffed and again wiped snot from his nose. He glanced at Francesca who stood nearby; her shoulders set square, hands cupped behind her back. Dutiful as any sentry, but the way she watched him belied her calm exterior.

Trebor was treading water, and Francesca was a shadow in the surf.

"Where is the dead man?" Aolfrun questioned, breaking the tension.

"I ordered him taken to the barracks."

The High Father nodded slowly then addressed Francesca. "Go to the barracks. Look the body over. If you think the murder was committed by anything not human, then check the tombs. If J'harenmar is still bound within, crumble that mausoleum down around him and let that be the end of it." He surveyed his polished nails. "Perhaps the petty thief killed the nightwatchman and fled the city, afraid of what punishment awaited him should he be caught with stolen church property." He then looked up to her from beneath hooded lids. "I trust your judgment, Draven. Make your assessment and we'll proceed from there."

Francesca inclined her head. "And him?" she asked, glancing at Trebor.

Aolfrun's smile was slow and deliberate. "I trust your judgment."

By the time Trebor realized what the High Father meant, Francesca was already on him. A plea rose in his throat but never made it to the air. As soon as he opened his mouth her palm was smashed against his teeth, her index and middle finger shoved deep into his nostrils as she hoisted him above her head. An incredible heat filled his frontal lobe and spread like smoke, melting out his eye sockets, cooking his brain within his skull. Blood boiled out of his ears and nose in a delicate stream, leaving his extremities to flail for a few final beats of his heart before falling limp.

The High Father made a face and wiggled his fingers. "Ugh, get rid of him before he shits himself. This rug is freshly shampooed."

Francesca carried Trebor's body to the window, opened the pane, then flung the pudgy carcass down to the ocean below. When he finally hit the rocks, it wasn't long until the waves rose and took him away, happy with the offering of decaying bones and flash-cooked brain matter.

As she rinsed off her hand in the basin, Aolfrun began laying out his robes for the day. "If Tytian's tomb is empty, I want him hunted down and slaughtered, you understand me? I'll deal with whatever repercussions that comes with later." He turned to her, a snarl on his gaunt face. "I want that bastard dead."

Francesca closed the space between them, raising her fingers to his face. It brought her such pleasure, the way he flinched then leaned into the warmth of her palm. "Of course, High Father."

Shaking, Aolfrun's own hands took hold of hers and he placed a kiss along her knuckles.

Without another word Francesca left his chambers and took the elevator down to the ground floor of the cathedral. When the doors opened, and the working staff saw who was inside, they scattered like insects caught in the light. From there she crossed the hall out into the nave, where the rising sun started to bleed through the stained-glass windows that fanned behind the head of a towering statue near the pulpit. The multicolored light speckled her skin, and she stopped a moment to look up into the carved face of the angel. Candles were lit at his feet, flickering shadows along the underside of his face, those judgmental eyes hidden by rings of gold and pearls.

Francesca stared not in awe, but in loathing. "You stand inside a house that is no longer yours," she whispered to the angel, the smile that followed putting every sharp tooth on display. "You'll burn soon enough."

Silence followed, as always. That harsh, silent inaction that made her insides twist.

She left the nave and moved on to the stables, tacking her red mare in nothing more than a bit and bridle. Bareback, Francesca rode for the gates at a brisk run, her mount well attuned to the subtle heel and seat pressures from her often heavy-handed rider.

It wasn't long until the gates rose into view, a gaggle of watchmen and city guards all milling about like bugs under a log. Judging by the looks on their faces, none of them expected the church to send her, and all at once, they found how rigid their spines could get.

"Ma'am," the captain said in brisk greeting, removing the cowl from his head.

She sneered at his weak attempts of submission. The man should have been on his knees.

"Good morning." Her voice was sticky sweet. "High Father Aolfrun has sent me to investigate the incident that happened here in the early hours. Show me the body."

The captain nodded, motioning for someone to hold her horse while he led her to the barrack station nearby.

Inside were small dining tables and rows of cots for naps between shift changes. He apologized for the mess but Francesca's nose was not curled at the stray clothes or unemptied wastebaskets. It was the concentrated stink of human flesh.

In the back room was a door that opened to a spiral stairwell, leading into the underground provision stores.

"We moved him down here where it's cooler," explained the captain. "We were unsure of when the church could send someone."

An old cot had been placed between crates of root vegetables and rice sacks, a sheet draped with care over the body. A few blots of red blossomed like roses around his mouth and nose. Francesca drew back the fabric, exposing the body. He was handsome, young in years but with an age to his body that would make a girl look twice at him on the street. Beneath the smell of death, she detected hints of shampoo and body soap, with a bit of cologne about his collar.

Some might think it a shame, this poor soul struck down in his prime. Francesca couldn't have been more thrilled.

Her fingers traveled around his neck, feeling the bones that were so forcefully snapped that they had protruded through the skin. No mortal man was capable of such strength.

"What do you think, ma'am? Could he have been hit with something? Maybe some sort of cleaver?" asked the captain.

Francesca never answered him. "Have the body wrapped up and prepared for transport." When he hesitated, she gave him a kind, reassuring smile. "I will take him to the church myself, so they can get him prepped for burial. He died valiantly and will be treated to a funeral with full honors. You have my word."

Back outside, she questioned the others, mostly the wallmen. No one had seen or heard anything suspicious. They didn't even know the murder had happened until the man's replacement clocked in for duty. There had been twenty souls within earshot of the nightwatchman and yet not a single one heard a dispute.

The man's body was eventually brought out of the barracks, expertly wrapped. Francesca had already mounted her mare when two officers hoisted the cargo over the animal's shoulders, exchanging looks between themselves but not stupid enough to question. They had all heard the rumors about the High Father's personal envoy, and none of them dared find out if they were true.

Without another word, Francesca set her heels into the mare and steered her onward. Not for the cathedral, but east, toward the cemetery and the estate beyond. The last time she had ridden up to this house it was still standing, tall and elegant against the forest backdrop, with well-tailored gardens and trickling fountains. After she was finished with it, all of that beauty and wealth had been stripped away, eaten by the flame from her hands.

She cut through the courtyard and across the family cemetery, reining in her horse at the mausoleum's open door. A door that had been chained shut decades ago.

With a shove she dropped the nightwatchman's bound body to the ground and dismounted, allowing the mare to wander as she pleased.

The mausoleum yawned in front of her, its throat black despite the sunlight. With a flex of her left hand, a dark colored sword formed in her clutch, rivers of orange firelight pulsing like blood through a vein along handle and hilt. She descended the stairs with caution, dipping her head under the curtain of ivy. In the belly of the crypt, nothing moved. Not even a rat was here to breathe in the stale air but there were footprints along the floor. And, across the chamber, Francesca stared at the once-barred door, now standing ajar, the coffin inside open and emptied.

He was gone. Forty years of silence. Forty years of some presumed peace, gone.

Tytian J'harenmar was awake.

Took you long enough.

Francesca clenched her fist, crumbling her summoned sword back into dust. Around the chamber, her laugh echoed. Sick with joy and excitement. Her biggest rival was on the loose, the only thing topside that could give her a real challenge, and she couldn't wait to stretch her claws again. Like a feral cat brought in from the cold, she had grown idle and bored in her duties. Now she had a reason to hunt again.

Lifting her right hand, she released a serpentine flame over the floor. It crawled up the walls in a violent wave and began to drain of color. The white fire wailed, engulfing all that it touched with a melting heat. Above, the remaining glass from the skylight shattered and rained, releasing licking tongues to scorch the topside soil.

Francesca emerged from the smoke and embers that billowed out the mausoleum doors, tipping her face to the sun. "Tytian," she whispered, nearly breathless, itching and eager to see him again.

To take from him again.

Behind her, the interior of the crypt collapsed, rolling smoke through the surrounding headstones.

After admiring her handiwork, Francesca turned her feline attention to the swathed body still lying in the tall grass. Slowly, with intent, she unwrapped the young man, stripped him bare of his uniform then dropped straddle of him.

"I am going to eat you now," she told the corpse with a subtle roll of her hips over his own, tingling as his cold skin met hers that burned. "Slurp your bones clean all while He watches. His most favored creation, desecrated beneath His high eye." She smiled against the skin of his broken neck, inhaling the scent, turning her face towards the witnessing sky. "And He will not stop me."

Francesca's teeth sunk deep into the flesh.

SIX

"I'm hungry," Fenella said with a hand against her growling stomach. She realized it had been a whole day since her last meal, which wasn't much of one to begin with.

Tytian agreed with her. "I could eat."

She gave him an inquisitive glance. "What *exactly* do you eat? You know, given that you're a..." She didn't want to pry but curiosity had gotten the better of her.

Reading between the thin lines of her curiosity, Tytian couldn't fight back the smile that put his sharp canines on display. "Actually. I'm quite fond of roasted chicken."

"Really? Good! That's good, I can make that." Fenella had been bursting with questions since the cemetery, yet decided to hold her tongue, mostly due to not wanting to stick her nose into business that wasn't her own. But one mystery in particular had been at the forefront of her thoughts, and now that one question was answered, the rest were harder to hold back.

"So, were you born as you are? Or, were you...uh, bitten? I'm sorry, I don't know how this works." She winced faintly, hoping not to offend him. The fact that she was even asking in earnest was somewhat comedic when just two days before she would have called someone mad had they told her that vampires and demon deals were real. Now, however, she found herself checking for dragons in the sky.

He took his time replying. "I don't know. My memory is still a little fuzzy."

Callum, having been a few paces ahead, reined in his horse so that he was sandwiched between the others. "That's it, I'm calling bullshit on the whole vampire thing."

Tytian sighed. "Of course you are."

"Well, yeah. Mostly, because they aren't real, but also-" Callum said very matter of fact before he reached out and drew back Tytian's hood, exposing him to the sun with an animated gasp. "Wow, would you look at that, you didn't explode. Not even a single singe!"

Annoyed but unharmed, Tytian's slid the hood back over his face.

Callum grew cockier by the second. "Ya know, this whole *mysterious stranger* thing is going to get old eventually. We should all get to know each other!"

"Alright then Callum, let's talk about what you were doing breaking into the church." Tytian said smoothly.

"I'm a thief...?" Callum asked with feigned confusion.

"What did you take? And for whom?"

Callum shrugged, the horizon suddenly very interesting. "Just a meager bauble for an eager client."

"Must have some deep pockets, this client of yours, given how dangerous it is to steal from the High Father."

Callum chuckled, weaponized confidence hiding the fact he was getting nervous. "Skills like mine? Those don't come cheap."

"Uh huh." Tytian watched the artery in Callum's neck, noting the increased speed of his pulse. "Who's Six?"

He made a subtle little shift in the saddle to hide the clench of his jaw. "You're askin' a lot of questions, J'harenmar."

"You wanted to play this game, Callum."

"Alright then. Why is the High Father scared of you?" When Tytian didn't respond, Callum knew he had strummed the right nerve. "Suddenly so quiet. Don't want to play anymore?"

"Some things are none of your business."

But Callum disagreed. "Nah, I'm making it my business now."

Storm clouds were brewing between them and Fenella grappled over how to quell the rapidly building tension.

"My gut tells me to do things sometimes and I listen to it," she interjected quickly, voice raised enough to break through their posturing.

Both men looked at her in unified confusion.

She fiddled with her reins nervously.

Tytian spoke first. "Your intestines tell you things?"

"No, not my intestines themselves. It's like an intuitive thing."

Callum's face was pinched in confusion. "So, instinct? You're telling us you have instinct?"

Out loud she could hear just how silly it must have seemed and tried desperately to explain it in a way that didn't sound like school anatomy studies. "No- I mean yes, I have instincts- but this is like, my gut. A gut feeling? It'll tell me what to do, and if I listen, good things happen."

Around his crown, Callum waved a hand. "Do you hear voices, Vanilla? Are they the ones who crave the murders?"

She rolled her eyes at him, fully aware he was making fun of her. "Shut up."

"Do all your organs talk or just the bowels?"

"I'm going to push you off your horse."

Callum raised his hands in front of him as if in prayer. "Don't do it Vanilla, fight the voices!"

Fenella reached out to smack the side of his head, but he was too quick and dodged, laughing victoriously.

By midafternoon the forests had fallen away, and lush, rolling hills had taken their place. Wild flowers perfumed the air, channels of low wind rustling them in the sea of green. Every so often a homestead was planted in the knolls, each one charming and picturesque against the backdrop. Some had impressive paddocks filled with horses, others had gardens of varying size and options. Corn, soybean and bean crops were the most common, then there were some that focused solely on cabbages, lettuce, collards and carrots. Comically crafted scarecrows waved to them from their perches, hay-stuffed sleeves swaying gently.

Tytian surveyed these sites quietly. The older ones he recognized, while others had been erected in his time of repose. Even some of the side roads had only been sanded and graveled in the last decade. This place was now unfamiliar, and he was having to learn his homeland all over again.

As he watched the scenery, Fenella watched him, silently wondering what he must be feeling. She thought back to what he had said the night before, about being forced into his preservative slumber. For the rest of the world, it had been decades. For him it must feel like a blink, a wound that was still open. And even though he seemed okay on the surface, Fenella could feel a sorrow radiating from him that nearly took her breath.

Over the next few hours they rode in silence, only speaking to warn the rest of an oncoming airship. Most hummed high among the clouds, nothing more than a fleck of black in the blue. Those that cruised lower, were watched with apprehension. An acquisition crew they could out maneuver, but a cannon ship would turn them into pink smears on the highway.

Pointing ahead of them, Callum offered a sliver of good news. "Just over that rise is our first destination. A nice little tavern and inn. We can sleep there for the night."

"What about supplies?" asked Fenella but he shook his head.

"Not a grocer, dear. Just booze and food. We'll get supplies in Rodenburg, after we pick up Six."

Tytian had a golden eye trained on the sky. "How long before we reach Rodenburg?"

Callum shrugged. "If we leave out from the inn at a reasonable hour then we should get in around this time tomorrow, maybe a little later."

"Just the one associate in Roden?"

"Yep."

"How many others will we be recruiting after?"

Callum held up three fingers and Fenella slumped in disappointment.

"That's not a whole lot of people."

"No, it isn't," Tytian agreed tightly.

Callum tweaked a sly little grin and shrugged. "Just wait until you meet them. Might change your mind then."

Rising above the folded knolls was a shingled roof and high chimney stacks, smoke curling around its crown. Inside, the double-decker tavern was already noisy with regulars, and outside the staff worked to meet their patron's needs.

With a bundle of firewood cradled in her arms, a barmaid was making her way up the front steps when she spotted the trio stroll down the drive.

"Hi folks! Welcome to The Tossed Tankard." Her tone was friendly, years of working in a hospitality industry crafting a muscle memory of polite greeting. "Just here for the evening, or staying the night?"

"We're here for the night," replied Fenella as she carefully lowered herself from the saddle, legs sore after riding most of the day.

"Okay, no problem at all. Here, you take this-" Before he could protest, Callum was passed the armful of firewood while the maid collected the horses. "And I'll take these. Head on in and make yourselves comfortable! Speak with Greglin about booking rooms."

Callum opened his mouth to ask for further instruction on what to do with the firewood, but the maid was already around the corner and headed for the barn.

Compared to other taverns inside the city, The Tossed Tankard was downright elegant. Spacious and well laid out, with round tables big enough for at least four dotted across the well polished floor. An iron wagon wheel served as a chandelier, and ornate sconces were placed on each thick support pillar. A small stage was built along the right hand wall, with a lanky bard and his band mid performance. At the back of the room was the bar, and behind it, an impressive array of liquor bottles, each shining like a jewel.

"This place is really nice." Fenella soaked in the room with awe. "How are we supposed to afford this?" she asked, thinking of the few silver saphs she had in her possession.

Callum nudged her with his elbow, careful not to drop the firewood. "No worries, I've got some coin on me."

She passed him a confused look. "But, you told the vendor you only had sixty saph on you yesterday."

"Oh I lied," he admitted with ease, "There was no way I was paying full price, he was trying to swindle us."

"He was?" she asked before holding up her wrist to examine the bracelet. "I thought it was a good price. It is amber, after all."

"If you learn anything from me Vanilla it's that you never, ever pay full price for anything if you don't have to, no matter how valuable."

She took in his words with a slow nod and then headed for the bar.

Tytian leaned in close to Callum's ear. "You didn't tell her that wasn't real amber."

Callum cut him a sharp look. "Nope. And neither will you."

As the three of them approached the bar they spotted a man filling a tankard full of ale. He glanced up at them and then spoke to Callum with a wag of his finger. "You, take that to the kitchens." When Callum opened his mouth to decline, the man pointed again. "Be quick about it!"

Callum snapped his jaw shut in a pout but relented anyways, taking the firewood behind the swinging door next to the bar.

One more drink was poured before the keep turned to Tytian and Fenella, plastering a smile on his plush face. "Welcome! I'm Greglin. What can I do for you folks this evening?"

Fenella smiled back. "Hello! We'd like three rooms please, and some food and drink."

His mouth dipped in a brief frown. "Sorry lass, we only have the one room available. Got a nice double mattress in it though. All the other rooms are booked."

"Oh," she said with disappointment.

"That will be fine, we'll take the room." Tytian reached around to his purse and pulled out three golden coins. They hit the counter with a heavy sound. "Will this cover it?"

Greglin stared at the gold for a moment, then nodded. "Y-yes, this should be fine."

Tytian dropped another. "For the food."

The inn keep swept the coins into his palm and pulled a lock box from the shelf beneath the bar. He deposited the money and then produced a key, handing it to Fenella. "Here you go, she's yours for the night. Up the stairs to the second landing, it'll be the last door on your right." His eyebrows raised then, and he waved a hand above his head, catching the attention of a passing barmaid. "Merrily!" he called out to her, "Find these folks an open table, yeah?"

The young maid nodded. "Yeah, sure! You can follow me."

About that time Callum backed quickly out of the kitchen, riled as a stepped-on cat. "I told you, I don't work here, you old goon! Get your own damn cabbages!" An angry voice rang from the back and Callum flashed the cook a middle finger just as the door fell shut.

He wiped a sling of gravy off his coat sleeve with a mumble.

Reunited, the three of them followed their hostess through the boisterous patrons and found a clean table. It was against the west wall and just far enough from the others that they felt comfortably secluded. Callum sat with his back against the oak panels, Fenella and Tytian claiming the chairs either side of him.

"What'll be for drinks?" asked Merrily. "We've got ale, berry mead, dark liquors, honeyed liquors, pepper liquors, wine..." The trio ordered a round of berry mead and with a smile she left.

Callum stretched, resting his hands behind his head. "Ah, this is the place to be, isn't it?" He looked around with a smug grin.

Fenella took in the sights and sounds. "It is a lively atmosphere. Oh, Tytian took care of the bill."

"He did?" asked Callum with mild shock. "Well, thanks for that, old man."

Tytian shook his head and turned his attention to the band, mumbling under his breath. "Old man."

In truth he wasn't much older than Callum was, having been just a few months shy of his thirty eighth birthday when Francesca stormed his home and planted him in the ground, although he looked even younger than that. His aging had come to a halt in his early thirties, his condition ensuring that he didn't deteriorate past his physical prime. It was the blessing within the curse.

Fenella explained they only had one room available, prompting Callum's crooked grin to widen. "We've only just met and already you're trying to get me into bed. Tsk tsk. I will have you know that I am a lady, Vanilla, and I will not be at the mercy of your depravity!"

Fenella rolled her eyes in amusement. "As if my depravity would ever involve you."

He gasped and grabbed at his heart. "You should be so lucky! I am an absolute dream."

"More like a nightmare," muttered Tytian.

When the barmaid returned with drinks and a plate of house bread in hand, Fenella put in a request. "Will you do me a favor and slip a little poison into his next drink?"

The barmaid chuckled, then winked at her. "Think I still have some poison behind the bar."

Callum turned to Fenella with theatrical hurt. "You are so rude to me, Vanilla. It hurts my heart, it truly does."

She grinned and leaned in. "What heart?"

He grinned as well, squinting his eyes. "Touché." He then clanked his tankard against hers and took a long swig. "Alright Merrily, what's on the menu?"

"The house special."

A pause.

"And?" asked Callum but she just shrugged.

"That's it. We don't get too fancy here."

"Ah. Alright, well, three house specials please."

"Comin' right up."

Fenella took one of the slices of sourdough Merrily had provided and took a bite, savoring the flavor. "This is amazing." As a baker herself she could appreciate a good loaf and this one was well crafted.

The smell reminded her of home and cooking with her mother every morning. It was really the only time in her childhood that she could remember being truly content, and the memory carried with it a confusing sort of homesickness. She didn't want to go back, not really, but she wondered if it would clear away some of the guilt.

"Hey," Callum said gently, "Where'd you go?"

Fenella blinked away her thoughts. "Sorry, just tired I guess."

Merrily returned with three plates and scattered them about. Each platter contained the same slices of smoked pork loin, red potatoes and cabbage topped with butter, long cuts of green beans and a miniature boat of brown gravy on the side.

"Enjoy!" Merrily departed with a bounce.

Callum inhaled deeply. "This place is heaven... I'm telling you, when I die, just stuff me and stand me up in the corner."

Fenella stuck a fork in a potato. "How's it look, Tytian?"

He gave her a toothy little grin. "Well, it's no roasted chicken. But, I suppose it'll do."

They each ate their fill and ordered another round of mead for the table just as the band started on a particularly upbeat set, luring patrons to their feet for swinging dances and shouting along with the lyrics.

This was the moment Callum suggested they retire for the evening, claiming it would be best to slip away unnoticed should there be any off duty city guard among the crowd. In reality, it was the perfect chance to plunge a sticky finger or two into coin purses as the three of them slithered through the gaggle of bodies. No one noticed the thief and his plundering, years of practice giving him a feather-light touch, so they made it up the stairs without issue.

Down the hall and to the right, Fenella led them into their rented room. One double mattress bed flanked by nightstands, a rocking chair and a chest of drawers were the only furnishings. In the short fireplace, flames twisted smoothly, working with the lamp on the nightstand to flood the space in shades of gold. At the foot of the mattress were extra covers and a pillow, which Callum scooped up and dropped into the rocking chair before falling backwards onto the bed. He gave a sigh of relief, kicked off his boots and put one arm behind his head.

Tytian shot him a glare as he removed his cloak. "You're really going to take the bed? What about Fenella?"

Callum swept his arm across the mattress. "There's plenty of room. You could even curl up at the foot like a loyal hound."

"I see chivalry isn't a trait you possess."

Sighing, Callum leaned up on his elbows. "Look, I may be a shameless flirt but I'm not some disgusting asshole. She has nothing to fear from me. But I ain't taking the floor. I have no plans on riding all day tomorrow with a catch in my back from sleeping on hardwood, alright?"

Tytian opened his mouth to counter when Fenella held out her hand and stopped him.

"It's fine, really. I don't mind."

He relented, then grabbed the spare bedding from the rocking chair and spread it out on the floor at the foot of the bed. "We should try and be headed out in the morning before sunup."

Callum groaned, throwing an arm over his eyes. "Why are you so eager to ruin my beauty sleep, J'harenmar?"

Tytian sat down on his makeshift palette and stirred the mellow flames swaying in the fireplace with a poker. "We need to put as much distance between us and Savhignos as possible. It isn't going to be long before they figure out that I'm no longer asleep."

"A half-decapitated guard might be their first clue," snarked Callum.

Fenella pulled off her boots and set them by the door. "So, what if they do figure it out? We've got a head start and they'll have no idea where you're going or who you're with. You could be headed straight for Mar as far as they know."

Tytian shook his head. "If they search the tomb and find me gone, the High Father will send Ches. She is clever and skilled and ruthless. It won't take her long to map out our exact path, and should she catch us, I don't know that I'll be able to protect you."

Callum sat on the edge of the bed deep in thought for a moment, then got up and grabbed his satchel off of the chest of drawers. "What did you say her name was again?"

"Francesca Draven."

From the bottom folds of the satchel Callum produced a pen, then went to the nightstand, retrieved a holy book from the drawer, ripped out a small shred from a blank back page and began to scribble.

"What are you doing?" asked Fenella, tilting herself to see over his shoulder.

"Leaving our friend Franny a little love letter." He turned the paper piece over to show the words 'Hello Draven' inked into the parchment. "If she tracks our path and comes through the tavern then maybe she'll find this, and then she'll know she isn't as smart as she thinks she is. We won't give her the satisfaction of thinking she has the upper hand."

Tytian didn't protest, but the scoff that jerked his stomach made his feelings clear. "Francesca Draven will always have the upper hand."

Fenella made a face. "Are you sure leaving breadcrumbs is a smart idea?"

Callum folded the paper and set it inside of the opposing nightstand, "Have you seen my hair? Darlin', I am a walking breadcrumb."

A few more quips finally led to the light being extinguished and the two of them settling in to sleep. Callum might not have relinquished the bed, but he did sleep on top of the covers, giving Fenella a layer of comfort and privacy.

It wasn't long until both were softly snoring, leaving Tytian to spend the rest of the night with his thoughts. His smoke-filled, screaming thoughts.

He pressed cold palms into his eyes, trying desperately to wring his mind free of his torments. He tried shifting to evasive strategies, and even ritual stone locations, instead of the faces of those he missed terribly.

Just before the first splash of color started to lighten the sky, he woke the others, laying a gentle hand on Fenella's shoulder and whispering her name. For Callum however, he struck him in the head with the spare pillow, causing the other man to come up swinging. It didn't take long for them to don their boots and grab their things, and once everything was collected Callum smothered the fire and the three of them quietly left.

Downstairs, the main room was empty. Except for Greglin, who was wiping down a table.

"Leavin' so soon? Is something wrong?" he asked with a concerned brow.

"We're early risers is all," fibbed Callum. "Thank you for the accommodation though. This place is great."

Fenella and Tytian swept past them and out the front door, hoods raised against the morning chill and nosy eyes.

Callum caught up to them outside and joined them in the barn. While the two men outfitted the animals in their rigging, Fenella stepped into an empty stall and changed out of her dress and into some trousers and a plainly embellished cotton shirt. Her legs ached from the long ride the day before but her hips particularly from having to sit on her skirts. Plus, it just felt nice to be in clean clothes again.

By the time she exited the stall, Callum had her horse ready for her. She noticed that he gave her a quick up and down glance before grinning to himself.

"Ready?"

Fenella took Apple's reins. "Lead the way."

On the waking horizon, clouds were beginning to bank, their belly full of rain.

"Oh, joyous. A storm." Callum sneered into the rough breeze.

"Think we should stay another night?"

Both men said no in unison. One worried about the woman at their back, while the other was desperate to reach the woman ahead.

Callum popped the collar of his coat, his eyes trailing west to the approaching storm. "We need to get Six. And we need to get her today."

SEVEN

Throughout the day the scenic landscape of rolling hills and quaint farms turned barren, life thinning the further they moved out from the city. Side roads snaked off and disappeared into terrain that looked like it had been exclusively designed for mountain goats. Rocky inclines and large boulders pocked the area- All signs of mining efforts, long abandoned after the earth was scraped of her riches.

The horses stumbled a few times in the loose gravel and on a particularly steep incline Outsrider fell to her knees. It was decided to walk the horses through on foot, until the ground evened out once more.

"Wouldn't mind having an air ship right now," remarked Callum, adjusting his gait to accommodate for the pebble in his boot. He had a thought then, one that didn't bring him an ounce of joy, but the irony could have proved humorous. "Please don't tell me you have one stationed back in Savhignos."

Tytian shook his head. "Burned down in the city hangars two nights before my estate was attacked. Seems the High Father didn't want any trace of the J'harenmars left in his city."

"Seems he doesn't want anything left in his city." Fenella's expression was sour.

 Callum halted on the spot, grit crunching under his heel as he turned on them. "Hey, that isn't his city. It's ours. Aolfrun might sit at the head of the table, but he can sure as shit choke on the food for all I care." He raised a head to his chest. "That is our blood and sweat in those streets. I might not live there anymore but it's still home, and he can't have her."

Blinking, as though stunned by his own words, Callum cleared his throat and clucked to Red, carrying on.

Fenella swiped a quick look at Tytian and muttered, "That was actually kind of inspiring."

In spite of himself, Tytian agreed. "True, but for our sake, don't tell him that. His ego is big enough as it is."

They marched on through the remains of spoil piles, little patches of grass trying desperately to grow along the overturned earth. Those that did were brittle and eager for water, waving their arms at the darkening overcast in anticipation.

"Maybe the rain will hold off until Rodenburg," hoped Fenella, watching the ominous skyline.

The heavens never opened up on them, but they certainly churned and tumbled through the sky like the waves of the sea, making the air around them damp and sticky. Around mid afternoon the knolls and outcrops leveled, putting them at the mercy of the winds.

Beneath the flat limbs of a crossroads sign, the three of them decided to stop for a quick rest before the last push.

Fenella read the township names on the signage out loud. "Savignos... Talonwood... Rodenburg." She put a hand to her brow, squinting into the north. "I've never been to Rodenburg. What's it like?"

Callum, bent over and picking a rock out of Red's hoof, answered with a mild bite. "You'll find out soon enough I suppose. We'll be there in an hour."

Fenella dropped her hands to her hips. "Wow, your mood swung faster than a weathervane. Is there something about the town you're not telling us? Or about your 'associate'?"

He dropped the horse's hoof with a sigh, smacking dust from his hands. "No, Six is great, you're gonna love her." A quick tightening of the saddle cinch, then he hopped up on Red's back, steering him up the roadway. "Let's get a move on before we find ourselves in a deluge."

Tone, body language, everything was dismissive, and Fenella wanted to challenge him on it.

Tytian stayed her with a shake of his head. "Leave him be. I want to see how this plays out."

"Something is bothering him," she said under her breath as the two of them mounted their horses. "Think it's dangerous?"

"I don't know yet." He looked at her over his shoulder. "What are your intestines telling you?"

Fenella made a face. "My gut, not my intestines."

"It's the same thing."

"It really isn't." Out of habit, her hand rested against her core. "But, it's been quiet. No alarm bells that I can tell."

"Let me know if they start ringing."

The last leg of travel was smooth, aided by the hard packed cart road that gradually bowed and dipped into the sleepy town of Rodenburg. Big enough for a hundred people or so, houses and shops were all built among each other, the only way to tell them apart were the hanging signs bearing store names and hand carved Welcome plaques in the windows. Every structure appeared to have been crafted by the same man with the same plans he'd used to build everything else. Ashy gray wood, each shingle an identical cut, each doorframe the same height. Even the wooden fences were laid out just like the next. Cut and molded for strict functionality, like the kind of place you dreamed of leaving as a kid.

"Not exactly glamorous, is it?" remarked Fenella.

"No," replied Callum. "But it's quiet. And safe. Not a whole lot of crime in this place."

Matched to their surroundings, the people were just as listless as the environment around them. Grays and browns were the predominant color choice, pairing well with the expressions of dull intrigue at the strangers who rode into town. Callum weaved Red in and out of the slow foot traffic, leading the others deeper into the shopping district until he paused just outside of a two-story general store. Through the foggy windows there was a cast of light, pooling lily pads across the covered front porch. Quietly, he searched these portals for any signs of life, then urged Red onward, down the adjoining alleyway. On this side of the shop was a staircase, leading to the upper level, and Callum hopped from the saddle, hitching his horse to the railing.

When Fenella's feet hit the ground, she looked around expectantly. "Okay, where to?"

Callum swallowed down his nerves, trying to steady the tremor in his hands by shoving them in his pockets. "You two wait here." Coattails billowing, he made a quick exit, although Tytian's confused voice followed along in an echo.

"Callum-"

He repeated his command to wait, then slipped around the edge of the shop, hopping up onto the shallow porch. His march up to the door was confident, but as he reached for the handle Callum froze, fingers lingering just on the edge of touch.

"Get it together," he whispered to himself. "Just open the damn door." His stomach felt infested, housing angry eels.

Exhaling slowly, he entered the shop.

Along one wall hung iron pots and pans of varying size, fire pokers, shovel heads, hammers, chisels, scythes and pitchforks. Lining the two standalone center aisles were fire treated jugs and dining ware, intricately designed silverware and coffee mugs made of thinly worked metals. On the other wall, were rows of cabinets and shelves holding tins of teas, herbs and various dried goods.

A woman, both short and thick, stood in front of the herbs, counting boxes and containers, writing down how many of each in a ledger. Her dark hair was pulled back in a neatly crafted braid, the few loose strands obscuring faded scars on her face. When she heard the door open, she called out a greeting to Callum, never pulling her gray eyes from her work.

"Hello," she said in a welcoming manner. "Please let me know if you need any assistance."

Callum lingered at the end of the aisle, fiddling with the hem of his jacket sleeve until he could will his words into existence. "Hey, Six."

Immediately the pen stopped, and he could see the subtle shift in her shoulders, a shift only noticed if someone knew where to look. And Callum knew, all too well.

He persisted. "It's been a long time." Surprisingly, his voice didn't waver.

And neither did hers. "What are you doing here?

"I can't just stop by and see an old friend?"

"What do you want, Callum?" she snapped at him softly, her rage kept in check. Six was never one to cause a scene, because a scene meant attention, and in the line of work they did together, attention was the enemy. It made her wrath quiet, seething, with the kind of sharp cut that he never realized was there until he was left to bleed out.

He opened his mouth, all of his prepared speech gone in the instant the door behind the counter creaked open. Out stepped an old man, hunched and haggard by time. Thick glasses were perched precariously on top of his nostrils, and his white hair was frazzled. His lips were sucked into a mouth that no longer housed teeth, so when he smiled, it was nothing but a cavern of gums.

"Ah, a customer!" He wobbled around the counter and came over to greet him, shrinking in size the closer he got. "Welcome to the shop! I'm Popp." The old man shook Callum's hand with enthusiasm, his skin warmed by a stove in the backroom. "Please please, take a look around. Are you in the market for anything in particular? If I don't have it here in the shop then I can certainly have it delivered within the month!"

Callum looked between the two of them, watching Six as she stared at the floor. "I'll keep that in mind, thanks."

Popp dipped his head. "Of course! If you need any help, then ask my assistant here. She'll get you squared away." He gave Callum's arm a friendly series of pats then shuffled his way to the other side of the room, taking count of his cast irons.

Once he was out of earshot Six resumed her hostility. "Answer the question." Callum barely opened his mouth before she cut him off. "No, you know what, don't bother. The answer is no."

"Six." He searched for the right words, but nothing was sticking, his thoughts moving too fast. "I need to talk to you, and it's important."

"It's always important, isn't it?"

"Five minutes," he pleaded.

"We're not doing this." She glanced at Popp, still happily surveying his inventory. "Leave."

"Five minutes," he repeated with urgency. "I am not riding out of this town until we talk. Something's coming, Six. Something real bad." When she didn't immediately shoot him down again he reached out for her. "Please."

Six flinched away from him like a cornered dog and Callum dropped his hand to his side, stung. For the next few moments she held his gaze and he expected her to tear into him with every hurtful word she could muster.

"Please," he begged, desperation prickling his eyes.

Seeing the look on her face, that expression that was caught somewhere between grief and loathing, caused the ache in his chest to deepen. It had been a long time since they had last seen each other, and he knew to expect her wrath. But standing in front of her now, seeing that pain in her eyes, was pure hell.

Six drew in a long, uneven breath, then flicked her chin at the door. "Fine. Five minutes, but not here."

The relief that swept through him almost made him buckle. "Thank you." Callum jabbed a thumb over his shoulder and whispered, "In the alley."

His body felt numb walking out of the shop, the ringing in his ears almost too loud.

Fenella and Tytian were still where he left them, and when he approached, Fenella looked nervous.

"What's going on?" she asked in a lowered tone. "You look spooked."

"Just... hang on."

Together, the three of them gaggled together in tension-filled silence, until finally Six came around the corner. An old injury un-evened her gait, the damage done to her right knee years ago causing a noticeable limp. Callum tried to keep his expression neutral.

She paused a few paces away, crossing her arms over her chest, automatically shifting weight off the offending limb. "Speak." Her tone was already sharp.

Fenella stepped up beside Callum and gave a small wave of her hand. "Hi, I'm Fenella. A-are you Six?"

A curt nod. "I am. And I don't have all day."

"Right." Callum swallowed his nerves. "So uh, something bad is happening. Something real bad. When it comes to the details, well-" He looked around the alley, barren of life except for them but still, he didn't trust this information being shared out in the open. "I'd rather not discuss them here. But I need-" a quick motion to the others, "*We* need your help."

Her eyes narrowed. "Really? That's your angle? You had five minutes."

"Six-"

"Five minutes, Callum, and so far you've told me nothing. Something bad is coming? Everything is bad with you."

His patience was waning, and he fought the urge to shake her shoulders, knowing it would only result in him getting a bloody lip. "I overheard a plot, okay? A big one- a *big*, big one. Like, grand-scale-holy-shit-big."

"Okay." She raised and dropped her hand in annoyance. "Where did you overhear this plot?"

He glanced around, eyeing the windows of the building next door. "That's kind of the part I don't want to talk about on the street."

"Well good thing we're not in the street then." She tilted her head. "Where?"

Callum sighed and his shoulders hunched slightly, feeling the thread of their thin civility start to fray. "The cathedral, back home."

Fenella tried to offer up a solution, "Maybe we could go somewhere a little more pri-" but Six cut her off.

"Why the fuck were you at the church? That close to the Beacons?" The answer was discovered in the same breath. "Oh."

Callum sighed, knowing that in that moment he had lost her, and scrambled to hold on. "Six-"

"You get what you were after?"

He glanced at his satchel and then away from her, not wanting to meet her gaze.

She barked a mirthless laugh, "Gods, I should have known," and passed a look between Fenella and Tytian. "Are they with The Den? Langdon's newest lap dogs?"

Callum shook his head, tripping over his words. "N-no, they have nothing to do with that."

"Okay, sure."

For the first time he was becoming angry with her. "You are not listening-"

"No, I am listening, Callum. And all I ever hear from you are empty words, like always."

A scalding tingle rippled under his skin, shame cooking him on the spot. "We don't have time for this now."

"We never do."

"Six, I am telling you-"

She looked past him at Tytian and Fenella, wagging a finger. "If you two are smart, you'll go home right now." She then turned and walked away, leaving Callum to beg in her shadow.

"Six!" he called, but she kept walking. He started after her, Tytian and Fenella falling in behind. "Six! Please talk to me. Six?" When she was almost gone around the corner, Callum shouted, "Lucia!"

Despite the limp she spun on him, quick as a viper. "No!" Her voice ricocheted, storm cloud eyes alight with wounded anger. Everyone stared at each other in silence, rooted to the spot, witnesses to her fury.

Without another word, Six climbed the porch and disappeared inside the shop.

A few drops of rain splashed against his skin, warning him of the pending downpour, but he didn't feel them. Numbed, fighting quietly for breath, Callum's mind was swimming in the past, and the current was a violent one.

Tytian and Fenella stood behind him, exchanging looks of concern, neither one of them knowing exactly what to say or what to ask next. After what felt like an eternity, it was Tytian who broke the heavy tension.

"Seems we have some things to discuss."

Callum agreed, slowly coming back around to the moment. "Yeah, we do."

Deeper into the heart of town, the three of them found shelter from the rain at the local bar. It was a rickety looking establishment, every pillar and post just slightly crooked. Unlike The Tossed Tankard, this place wasn't richly embellished or furnished. A low-hung ceiling, tables small and huddled together. The bar was lined with folks who were either crying into their tankards or on the verge of a fight.

Fenella tucked herself in between her companions, one hand clutched to her meager coin purse.

In the furthest corner of the room they found a table, still dirty from its previous occupants, and called over a maid. She wasn't as peppy as Merrily, but she wasn't unfriendly either, just worn down from a long day in a dreary mark on the map.

"What'll ya have?" she asked with seasoned haste and Callum ordered an ale and a shot of dark liquor. The others declined. After the drinks were delivered, Tytian decided to start asking some questions.

"What the hell happened back there?"

Callum downed the shot, staring into the bottom of the water-stained glass. "That..." His brow furrowed. "That was a lot of history." He set the tumbler down on its top.

Tytian agreed. "Who is Langdon?"

Sighing, Callum hung his head, pressing his palms into his eyeballs until they hurt. "He's the big boss of the syndicate I work for. He and Six- they don't get along so well."

"The Den?"

"That's the one."

"Is this something that's going to be a problem?" Tytian asked with an edge and when Callum shook his head and assured him that it wouldn't, he didn't quite believe him. Men like Callum were tricky, and the kind that made Tytian uneasy. It was hard to know where their true intentions aligned and their concept of loyalty was often muddy. For a moment he wondered if this man was really the kind of person he wanted next to him should things take a turn for the worse. Was he following a fool? Tytian knew he wasn't lying about the plot. That had already been in the works long before Aolfrun even took up the High Father mantle. But Callum was a difficult read, and Tytian worried about his tethers to well organized crime.

He might not be an evil man, but it was clear that Callum had more than dirt on his hands.

"Are these other associates of yours affiliated with The Den?"

Callum was quick to shake his head. "No, not them. They'd help me out with a few jobs, but they were never part of the company."

With a careful choice of words, Fenella proposed they move on. "We should head out then, for the next name on your list."

"No," Callum said with sudden force, planting a palm against the table. "We will not leave this town without her."

"She seemed pretty set in her answer."

He grinned bitterly. "Talked you into it, didn't I?"

Fenella rolled the empty liquor glass between her fingers. "Why is she so mad at you?"

In two swigs, Callum drained the rest of his ale. "We had a fallin' out is all. When you spend your whole life with someone, you tend to do that. Fight, make up. Fight, make up. And Six and I ...well we haven't made it to the make up part just yet."

They sat in silence for three more rounds. Fenella and Tytian still refused beverages, allowing their companion to drown some of his sorrows in the bottom of a glass. Callum looked sick, sitting there picking apart every decision he'd ever made. It had been a few years since he'd last seen Six and he'd hoped maybe the passage of time would have eased some of her pain and anger, but clearly that wasn't the case.

Some things can't be washed away so easily.

Callum stared into his mead for a moment longer before he stood, swaying slightly. He dropped a few saph on the table then perked his jacket collar. "The inn is across the way. Let's get some rest."

The three of them jogged out into the rain, to a long, single story building directly opposite the tavern. Inside, they were greeted by a bored hostess, who barely looked at them as she accepted their payment and grabbed three keys from the hooks behind her. "Down the hallway, last three doors on the left."

Callum offered his thanks in a gesture, then shuffled the corridor, drunkenly sticking the key into every door until he found the one that fit. "Shu-cess," he whispered in triumph, then slipped into the room.

Tytian and Fenella stood in the lobby, sharing quick glances of concern. When Tytian broke away and asked the woman behind the desk if the inn had a barn she said no, but that there were a few single horse stalls under a porch just outside. He told Fenella to get settled in, and left.

Outside, the rain smelled warm. Rolling back his sleeve, Tytian stuck his hand into the stream running off of the roof, working the water around his palm. He had always loved storms, but the rain in particular. It was peaceful. The pause it evoked allowing life a moment of respite to be nourished, cleaned.

It had rained that night, forty years ago. But it wasn't enough to stop her fire.

"Francesca." Tytian was unsure if he had said her name out loud or simply thought it. The presence of her name alone so fresh in his thoughts made him shiver, and urged him out into the soft sheets of rainfall

Hitched at the tavern, it didn't take him long to fetch the animals and lead them to shelter beneath the inn's connected porch eave. He untacked each one and forked a few piles of loose hay into their stalls, their gratitude expressed through contented sighs and the sounds of chewing.

"I have an idea."

Tytian felt his skeleton jump inside the meat when Fenella suddenly appeared, her words spoken in haste.

She grimaced apologetically. "Sorry."

"It's fine," he told her. "Just briefly died and came back again."

Fenella rolled her eyes then grabbed his sleeve, tugging him out to the road. "Come on."

"What are we doing?" he asked while they made their way through the sloppy streets.

"I don't think Six is going to listen to Callum, even if he were able to tell her every single detail he overheard. Her anger is too strong. You saw how she looked at him. And he's scared of her or at least scared of her words. But I thought that maybe if *we* talked to her and got right to the heart of it, we could change her mind."

Tytian slowed. "Perhaps we should just leave this woman alone."

"Callum said he wasn't leaving her without her. We need to collect this group of his. We're going to need allies for this, right?"

A gentle grip of his hand drew her to a halt. "What are we doing, Fenella? Why are we following his lead? He hasn't exactly been very forthcoming."

Her head cocked to the side as she crossed her arms over her chest. "Like you have?"

Tytian looked away from her and tried to build an argument, but she never gave him the chance.

"Look, we don't have to know each other inside and out. We can have secrets; those are ours to keep. But we have the same goal and right now we're in this together. Find a few things, destroy those things, keep everyone safe- that's what we're striving for here." She reached up and placed a hand on his shoulder, "I'm not asking you to trust him completely, or to trust me for that matter. All I'm asking for is your help. And help is all he's asking for as well. I know that, much like myself, you want to kill him a little sometimes, but we're in this together." With conviction, she gestured toward the inn. "Like it or not this group was destined."

Tytian saw the belief in her eyes, saw how committed she was to her own declaration, and inclined his head. "Destined, huh?" he asked, interest piqued. "How do you know?"

She flashed a smile and patted her stomach. "My intestines told me so."

"Maybe you should start listening to different body parts."

"Oh, shut up."

Together they sloshed down the muddy road until they arrived back at the shop. The entrance had been locked and the lights extinguished, but the windows in the little home next door were ablaze so Fenella jogged over and gave a swift triple clack of the brass knocker. Tytian clung to the dark out of sight.

Sounds of shuffling feet preceded the door swinging open, and the old shop keep peered out into the night. "Yeah?" he asked, adjusting his glasses for a better look.

"Uhm, good evening, sir!" She had expected Callum's associate to open the door, not this small, old man, so Fenella worked up a lie on the spot. "I'm friends with Six. Just rode in tonight and wanted to surprise her! To say hello and... stuff. But I cannot for the life of me remember which house she said was hers. She mentioned that she worked here, so I thought maybe you could help me out." She attempted a kind of flirty smile, but the elder squinted so hard at her that she wasn't even sure if he could see her properly.

"Six's friend, eh?" His question sounded almost suspicious. "Wasn't aware Six even had any friends. That's wonderful!" His smile deepened the wrinkles of his face, and Fenella could almost hear the skin groan like leather. "She's in the loft above the shop there. Just take the stairs in the alley. But miss? Do me a favor, would ya? Take her out for a nice day tomorrow. She never takes any time for herself and always works so hard, it'd be good for her to have a little fun. Please, tell her I've given her... no no-" He tapped a finger to his nose, searching for a more forceful word. "*Insisted* she take the day off. Will you tell her that for me?"

Fenella nodded. "I sure will."

After giving the old man her thanks, Fenella trotted down the long shop porch, Tytian sweeping into her shadow. The two of them moved down the alley with light steps, climbing the stairs to the loft entrance. The curtains in the double pane window had been drawn, but the lights were on. Fenella was thankful that at least they wouldn't be waking her up. As she raised her hand to the door, her confidence wavered, wondering if maybe they would just make things worse.

"What if she yells at us like she did Callum?"

Tytian had no such apprehension, and struck the door for her, loudly so it would be heard over the rain. The pause that followed was taut with tension, intensifying the second they heard a bolt being disengaged. Light enveloped them, and Six stood in the threshold. She was in a short night shift and an open robe, the fabric thin, acting as a second skin around her full curves. Unbound hair framed her stern face: a look no doubt curated just for Callum. But when she saw that the pair at her door had no redheaded pickpocket in their presence, her expression softened.

"What do you want?"

Fenella felt a blush in her cheeks, attempting to catch her words before they stumbled. "Hello. We met earlier."

"I remember," Six cut in, coldly, tying closed her robe.

All at once, Fenella felt as sheepish as Callum did in the alley. "We would like to talk with you about exactly why we're here."

"I'm not interested." She started to close the door in their face, but Tytian stepped across the threshold and grabbed it, halting it in place. He kept his head bowed, hiding his unusual eyes.

This action sparked a change in Six's demeanor, and Fenella was quick to dampen her hostility. "We don't want any trouble. We just need you to hear us out, please."

"I have already told you people no."

"Well, if you've already made up your mind then what will it hurt to just sit and listen?" Fenella reasoned.

Six's teeth flashed with every word. "Get off of my porch."

"No." Fenella stood her ground. "We're not going anywhere until you hear us out. This isn't a job. We told you before, we're not with those Den folks and this has nothing to do with that. What's happening now is far bigger." She stepped forward, urgency in her eyes. "A lot of people are going to get killed."

"People are always getting killed," challenged Six. Reluctantly, she took her hand off of the door and allowed them to enter. "Come on then, let's get this over with."

The living room was modest. A few cabinets, a single couch, two chairs and a center table. The large rug in the middle of it all was the most exotic and out of place item in the room, and Fenella wondered if perhaps it was a gift.

She and Tytian took a seat on the plush couch as Six shut and bolted the door, then moved over to a desk directly across from them, leaning against its edge.

"Alright, speak."

Fenella decided to start from the beginning, covering everything. Callum's eavesdropping, then the market, their conversation in her kitchen and then finding Tytian. Six listened patiently, the furrow in her brow slowly changing from one of anger to confusion.

"The High Father is summoning a demon?"

Fenella nodded. "Malice in physical form, according to him." She made a small gesture toward Tytian beside her.

"There are nine ritual stones in total," he stated. "They already have four of them, and Welling is arriving with the fifth in a month. If we can intercept the transport or find another slab ourselves and destroy it, we could render this whole plot void."

"Why do they want to summon this thing?"

Fenella shrugged. "We don't know, but I'm sure it's not for wholesome purposes."

Six let this information steep, choking on the irony. "The most powerful man in the entire region is plotting to call on a demon, with the help of the king's own brother, and the man to overhear this and take action is Callum. The Divine really has a sense of humor." She rubbed the bridge of her nose, addressing them directly with judgement. "And you two just hopped on board? Never so much as a question?"

A warmth rushed Fenella's skin at being so blatantly shamed. "I did ask questions, and ultimately I believe him."

"Typical," Six muttered under her breath, then turned to Tytian. "And you. You're really a J'harenmar?"

He nodded.

"Wouldn't you be an old man? That place burned decades ago."

Fenella touched her elbow to his side. "Show her."

He pulled back the hood, white hair and unnatural eyes on full display.

Six's lips parted a little and she instinctively leaned back, eyes widening before falling into narrowed disgust. "Oh."

In the space between them, there was a shift. The air itself had an itch of friction, and it made Fenella tremble. She noticed how Tytian's hand had curled into a fist, how his shoulders rose like hackles. Six had slid a hand behind her, gripping something sharp and silver in her palm.

Acting quickly to dispel the tension, Fenella rose and stepped in front of Tytian. "It's fine! He's fine, I promise," she told Six, scrambling for anything that could ease the other woman's mind. "You have nothing to worry about." *He snapped a guy's neck a few days ago, but it's okay.* "H-he likes roasted chicken!" Both Six and Tytian looked at her after that last hastily blurted statement and she felt embarrassed, wondering why in the hell her brain told her to throw in that bit of useless information.

Again, she pleaded their case. "Look, Callum came here because he said that we needed you. That he needed to gather his team, so we'd actually stand a chance. He won't leave until you agree to come with us."

Six's interest grew sharper than a blade. "Gather his team? Who else did he mention?"

Fenella racked her brain and realized he'd only said two names. "Uhm, just you and someone else. Oh, what was it? Something with an A. Alvin? No... Aldan! Pretty sure he said Aldan, but he told us there'd be seven of us in all." Her shoulders shrugged.

"Must be one hell of a team you guys make. All impressive fighters, I'm guessing?"

Six adjusted her weight. "Not much of a brawler these days."

Tytian looked down to her knee, motioning with his fingers. "Callum have anything to do with that?"

"Wow, fifty saphs for the obvious guess. You must be the brains of the operation." With a scoff she pulled away from them, tossing the letter opener back on the desk. She stopped in the dark hallway, addressing them from over her shoulder. "I've heard enough and it's late," and then, with a voice almost too low to hear, "Take him and go."

Fenella understood she wasn't referring to Tytian. "He came after you for a reason. He thinks you're someone who can help. Was he wrong?" A warm hand slid around her forearm, Tytian leading her to the front door. As he ducked out into the rainy night, Fenella took one last look at Six, "Please... just think it over." She closed the door and headed down the stairs. When she met up with Tytian he sighed.

"Not sure we were very convincing."

"Guess we'll see." Looking up at the window, Fenella tried to let intuition give her a read on the situation, yet she felt nothing. Her words from before echoed in her mind about the group being destined, but she began to wonder if maybe that wasn't true for everyone. Doubt is a heavy thing to carry within you and Fenella could feel its weight sink from her head to her shoes.

Shoulder to shoulder, the pair retraced their steps back to the inn. Once inside they went their separate ways, Tytian stopping for a moment to listen outside of Callum's door. When he heard the faint sounds of snoring he went into his own room.

The narrow space was furnished with only a single mattress and mirrored vanity. There wasn't even a window, making the air stale and the walls closer than they were. This lack of, well, everything, reminded him of his coffin. Under his skin the feeling of cold granite permeated.

He flipped the switch on the wall, taking some comfort in the soft hiss emitting from the single, overhead globe. Tytian had always been a quiet man, preferring to observe people and their actions, rather just taking them at their word, but now he wished he would have spoken up more. Perhaps he could have persuaded the others to leave town, forget the one with the cold eyes, and just moved on. Savignos was still too close. Francesca was still too close, although he couldn't say for certain how far would be far enough with her. Even death didn't feel like a safe distance.

After kicking off his muddy boots, he hung his cloak from a peg on the door, placing the empty basin beneath it to catch the drips of rainwater. He sat down on the mattress, letting the day play over through his mind, picking apart every little thing.

"Oh." Tytian could see the woman, Six, clear in his mind. How unsettled she was by him. He knew that she knew exactly what he was, and that threatened to change everything.

Tytian considered leaving right then on his own. Slip out the front, grab Outstrider and be gone into the night. It wasn't a lingering thought, just one he considered long enough to talk himself out of it. Callum and his already crumbling former party he could leave, but his stomach soured at the thought of abandoning Fenella. And she was so sure about their flimsy mission, that she would follow her 'gut' rather than his logic, and remain with the bastard thief.

If that woman tells them what I am, they'll leave anyway.

Suddenly exhausted, Tytian laid down, the mattress a few inches too short for his frame. His feet dangled off the end, damp socks turning his soles cold, but he wouldn't cover them. The blankets were too heavy in the cramped space.

He would reluctantly sleep, fighting off nightmares without anything on top of him, the ceiling even too low for comfort.

There was a tapping at the door that stirred Callum from painful, liquor-soaked dreams. He cracked open his eyes and very gingerly sat up. Hungover, his brain felt like it was sloshing around in his skull, not so much as a vein to tether it in place. He groaned and fought off a surge of nausea.

"Yeah?"

Fenella came into the room and apologized heavily as the light from the hallway came with her, causing him to reel away. She shut the door quickly, sending the room back into shadow.

Callum blinked the stars from his eyes and carefully swung his legs off the side of the mattress. "What is it?" he asked her, rubbing his pulsing temple.

"It's morning," she said in a hush.

His head hung in his hands and again his stomach rolled over itself, but it wasn't entirely due to the alcohol. Fenella sat down beside him as softly as she could, offering a cup of water and a flat biscuit.

"Here."

He groaned into his palms and then rubbed his face before taking the cup. The water hit his soured stomach like a punch and his throat tightened to keep it down. Once he was sure he wasn't going to vomit, he took the biscuit and nibbled at it.

"Better?" asked Fenella.

"Room warm water and a stale piece of bread? I'm healed," Callum retorted playfully.

She rolled her eyes. "Just eat the damn biscuit." Then, "How are you feeling?"

He knew she didn't mean physically, so he took his time with the last bite of food. "I'll be fine." He tried to assure her after seeing the worried look on her face, but what he actually meant was that he'd cope. Callum had lived with Six's hurt and anger for the last few years but he'd stayed away. Even with cities between them he could feel her scorn. Now, seeing her again and seeing those emotions still as strong as the day he dropped her off in Rodenburg, he was struggling to keep his own feelings in check. He was never one to wear his heart on his sleeve, always trying to keep his current mood a mystery to everyone around him, even sometimes to himself. Callum had been taught early in life that keeping people at arm's length was what kept him safe. Six though, she was different.

Fenella rubbed his back. "C'mon, get washed up and let's go get some breakfast."

Callum grinned and slid her a suggestive look beneath his scandalous brow. "Or... we could stay here."

The way her nose scrunched when she tightly smiled was a forewarning. "Oh, hoping for a little QUICKIE IN THE MORNING, ARE WE?" she shouted into his sensitive ear, making him recoil. She then flicked him hard in the side of the head with her knuckle and he felt as though his eyes were going to explode. "Wash up. Now."

"Yes ma'am," Callum chuckled just as she closed the door.

Clean as a basin bath could get him, Callum lumbered into the hallway, donning his satchel and coat. The sight of his red eyes and ashen skin caused a waiting Tytian to grin.

"How are you feeling?!" he asked with a loud voice.

Callum flashed his middle finger in reply.

"C'mon boys, let's get breakfast," said Fenella, and then to Tytian, "And maybe some supplies? Food, some extra clothing?" Implying that he'd need to pay for them.

He obliged with a nod.

The rain had eased through the night, although not completely gone, making the walk from the inn to a little dining hall just up the road a dreary one. Once they climbed the tall porch and entered the eatery, some of the cold in their bones beginning to fade.

This place was made in the same practical fashion as everywhere else, albeit cleaner than the tavern. No fancy embellishments, meager tables and a massive fireplace that roared. In the front window perched a cat, cleaning her tabby paws. At the front counter, a woman of middle age greeted them with a thin smile, then pointed to a placard on the wall, listing a menu of items. They all surveyed the options and then made their choices. Fenella paid with the few coins she had on her while the men claimed a table near the fireplace.

It was quiet, only a few other tables occupied by locals who looked the group over with blank expressions. Tytian shifted in his seat, feeling their gaze on his back. There was sparse chit chat among the trio, no one wanting to bring up the possibility of leaving town without Six just yet, so they kept things at surface level.

The food was nothing too fancy; eggs and link sausage for both Fenella and Tytian, a stack of fruit sweetened flatbread topped with honey for Callum, and coffee for all three. They ate at a comfortable pace, nothing but the sound of cutlery on porcelain plates echoed between them. Once breakfast was gone and the coffee mugs emptied, they left, Fenella thanking their hostess on her way out. Further up town there were more shops and their first stop was a seamstress. From her they each purchased a few articles of clothing, each piece suited for long travel. From there they moved on to a butcher for dried meats, salt and vegetables, then to the apothecary for spices, honey and a few medical supplies. They took their time, carefully gathering things they thought they may need along the way and that would also travel well. Bo had provided bedrolls and leather saddle bags with the horse's tack, and while they were spacious the group still had to be mindful of how limited they were.

Around midday they headed back to the dining hall, ordered a quick lunch and then it was off to the inn. Fenella noticed how quiet Callum had been all morning, only speaking when spoken to and searching the faces of each person they passed on the street. She wondered if he was expecting to run into Six. And whether or not he was hopeful, or feared the very idea.

Once they arrived at the inn, they went straight to the paddock for the horses who were happily munching on hay. Dry and content, unlike their owners. Their tack was still piled nearby and Fenella remarked on how surprised she was to find it all still there, to which Callum replied, "Pretty sure the only thief in this town is me." When the supplies were safely packed away there came a long moment of silence, a question of *Now What?* looming heavily between them.

"So," started Fenella, breaking the awkward tension. "Do we stay?"

Tytian leaned his back against the corral. "We shouldn't linger in one place for too long."

"Yeah, I know." Callum rubbed at the bridge of his nose, frustrated and anxious. "But we can't leave town without her."

Fenella tapped a finger to her lips, thinking. "Do you think we could just... take her? Just snatch her right up and ride out of town. If we got far enough away, then she'd have to come with us!"

Tytian grimaced. "Fenella, I don't think kidnapping that one is a good idea."

"He's right, it's a terrible idea," spoke another voice, causing all three of them to jump.

Standing just under the eave of the corral roof was Six, dressed in dark traveling clothes and a long leather coat. Behind her stood a champagne colored horse in full tack, short and thick in build, much like Six herself.

"Lucia..." muttered Callum, his body tense.

She looked at him, opened her mouth then abandoned whatever hateful word had sprinted up her throat. Instead, she composed herself, and nodded towards Tytian and Fenella. "They told me what you're doing. What's happening back home."

Callum turned his confusion on the others.

"Last night," said Tytian. "After checking in."

Six continued. "I'll come, and I'll help. But Callum, I'm not doing this for you. I'm doing this for Popp. And Marlia. And Aldan and Duncan. I will do this for them, then we're done, understand?"

There was a slight tremor to his lips as Callum whispered, "Okay."

"Also, if this turns out to just be more Den bullshit, each one of you will wish you were fucking dead."

Callum's hand clutched his satchel, subtly pushing it a little further into the fall of his jacket. "It's not, I swear."

There was a loaded pause then finally, she nodded. "Well, let's get going."

EIGHT

The road out of Rodenburg was a mess. Hazy sheets of rain and vocal winds hounded them with every step. Both men rode ahead of the women, their horses being taller and longer of leg, but also because Six intentionally kept her distance from Callum. Fenella could see her rein in her mount every so often if he got more than a few yards from Red. She didn't want the other woman to feel cut off from the group, so she kept Apple at the same pace and while they rode for a while without a word between them, Fenella enjoying the quiet company.

She took the long stretch of silence to study as much about Six as possible. She had a good riding seat and posture, much better than Fenella who had only ridden one snarky pony at her grandmother's estate when she was ten. Six's tack was rugged and well used, and the saddlebags were roomy, designed for long travels. Obviously this was not her first cross-country trek.

Trying not to be too obvious, Fenella studied her face and hands next, noting the scars dotted along her light brown skin. A thin, old scar laid over the bridge of her strong nose, and another was etched at the corner of her mouth. There was a particularly jagged-edged blemish along her jawline and Fenella wondered if it came from some gut-clenching battle.

Feeling the inquisitive attention, Six turned somewhat awkwardly towards Fenella, who realized too late that she had been caught.

"Oh- I was just, uh..." she quickly motioned toward the two long handles that breached the mouth of the saddlebag, "wondering what those are."

Six reached back, flipped the latch and drew one of her twin war axes from the leather, passing it over to Fenella who took it gingerly in her hands. The handle was made of a darkly stained wood, smooth from use and wrapped in supple leather along the shaft. At the end was a cap of steel, intricately etched with an elaborate design. The head of the weapon was doubled. While one side bore an axe blade with a wicked curve to its end, the other side was a tapered spike: thick and brutal. Fenella examined it in awe.

"Are you proficient with any weaponry?" asked Six.

Fenella shook her head as she handed the axe back to its owner. "No. I have a dagger on me but I'm not entirely sure I could ever use it."

"You should learn. You're probably going to need it at some point."

Fenella's stomach sank. "Could you teach me?"

Six's nod was accompanied by the flash of a smile. "Sure."

Fenella felt a little victorious. "So, you're a fighter."

Another nod. "Yeah, when I have to be."

"Where'd you learn?"

"From the streets mostly. The world is unforgiving for orphaned children, particularly little girls. I had to learn at an early age how to defend myself."

"You're self taught?"

Six shook her head. "Not entirely. There was a mercenary that frequented the local tavern and he took a shine to me. Said he had a daughter my age back home, so he taught me how to use a sword. We had training sessions when he was in town until, eventually, he never came back around. I kept at it and practiced every chance I could. Then, when I joined with the city guard, I discovered how much I liked the axe."

"You're a member of the city guard?" Fenella asked with interest.

"I was."

"Huh." Fenella glanced at the men ahead of them. "Is that where you met Callum?" She tested the waters, hoping not to wade too deep.

Leather creaked as Six adjusted her position. "No. Callum and I grew up together at the orphanage in Savhignos."

Fenella huffed, slightly amused. "So, you went the path of city guard, and he went the path of a thief? That must have made for some awkward run-ins." She was surprised when she saw Six crack a smile.

"I covered for his ass a lot." But then, that smile faded almost as quickly as it had appeared. "Some things never change."

Immediately, Six withdrew and Fenella knew she had lost her. She wanted to ask her something else, anything else, but eventually she decided to just leave her be. Whatever history they had together ran deep, almost too deep.

She hoped that if she befriended this walking, talking thunderstorm then maybe she could help heal the rift between them. Six just felt so far away. Completely lost, as if she was forgotten in a forest somewhere, with no one to look for her. Callum certainly didn't seem like someone who would intentionally have caused her harm, yet the way Six acted towards him anyone on the outside would think he was her nemesis. And the way Callum shied from her gaze proved to Fenella that he felt guilty. She desperately wanted to get to the bottom of their tangled past, but she knew that this was going to take some time.

Luckily for Fenella, she was a patient woman.

When the group made it back to the crossroads, Callum took an unexpected turn and began heading southeast towards what the road signs indicated as being Talonwood.

"Wait, we're going to Talonwood?" asked Tytian, halting Outstrider, her dark nose pointed west.

"Yep." Callum kept it brief, with an air of dismissal.

"But that would curve back towards the city. We'd almost be doubling back on ourselves." Tytian shook his head, like the thought was a bee in his ear. "Why the hell are we going to Talonwood?"

"Aldan lives there," explained Six, who seemed just as confused as the others.

Tytian called out to their rogue-ish guide, who had yet to change course. "Callum! Why didn't we stop there first? We can't backtrack, not when Francesca could already be heading this way." There was no reply. "Hey!" Tytian barked, gravel roughing the edges in his deep voice.

When Callum turned to face them he looked pale, and determined. "We had to get Six first, alright? It was unavoidable, just like this is. Now, let's stop arguing, go fetch Aldan and get our asses to Riverport." He didn't wait for a retort, instead urging Red to pick up his gait.

Tytian looked over to the women, Six looking just as confused. "Why did we have to have you on board first?"

She met his frustration, her reply given just as roughly. "How the hell should I know?"

Fenella stepped in as mediator. "Maybe he thought you could help him talk the others into joining us?" Animosity was something she knew well, thanks to growing up in an unstable household, and these two ripped each other to shreds whenever their eyes met. It was an all too familiar feeling for Fenella. As was the urge to de-escalate the situation.

Tytian growled under his breath, and then urged Outsrider into a gallop after Callum.

"Who's Francesca?" asked Six.

"That's a good question," said Fenella as she stared down the road to Talonwood, a knot twisting in her chest. "C'mon, I'll tell you along the way."

When Tytian caught up with Callum, Red had slowed to a shambling walk, steam rising up from his wet coat.

"Okay," Tytian started with a dark tone, trying to keep his anger somewhat controlled. "I'm going to need you to explain a few things to me."

Always theatrical, and looking for an out, Callum turned and held his hands in wiggling explanation. "Alright. You see, when a mommy and a daddy really love each other, or when the daddy *really* loves the local whore, they do this sort of... dance-"

Tytian reached out with ungodly speed, snatching up him by the jacket. Red danced a little, but Callum kept his seat, laughing in surrender.

"Calm down, old man." He gently pried the fingers from his collar. "What do you want to know?"

Tytian shoved him away with a snarl. "I want to know why we didn't come this way first. Why go to Rodenburg just to turn around and go back the other way?"

"I told you, we had to get Six first."

"You said that, but I want to know why." Tytian flicked his chin over his shoulder at the woman behind them. "Who is she to you? If you did this because you wanted to pick up an old girlfriend.."

Callum cut him off, suddenly serious. "It's not like that. She's family."

"She's your sister?"

"No." He sighed, trying to find the right words. "She isn't my blood, she's just... my family. And she is a damn good fighter, which makes her essential to this group."

"That woman could barely get on her horse, and you're going to ask her to fight?" Tytian sighed with a shake of his head. "Never took you for a cruel man."

Callum turned on him and spoke with haste, "She's a lot stronger than you know."

There was a fire in his eyes that told Tytian he had found an exposed nerve. One he decided to explore. "So, we went out of our way, possibly putting all of us in serious danger, to gain the allegiance of a cripple with anger issues because 'she's family' and supposedly a 'good fighter'." He touched the tip of his tongue to his sharp teeth. "Can you feel the breeze that's blowing through the holes in that story?"

"Okay!" snapped Callum, wiping a hand down his face. "And don't call her a cripple."

Tytian raised a hand in frustrated compliance.

"I beg of you, this stays between us, alright? Can you promise me that?"

"What is going-"

"Promise me!"

Tytian weighed this vow of silence against just beating the truth out of Callum on the side of the road. As fun as one might be, he settled on non-violence. "Okay, you have my word."

Behind them, the women rode some length away. Fenella had explained Tytian's fears about Francesca but to her surprise, Six didn't appear to be too concerned.

"She's probably tough but shouldn't be impossible to take off the board."

Fenella was open to ideas. "Wouldn't happen to have a handbook on how to kill demons, would you?"

"No, but Duncan might. That man is a library of knowledge. And once we find out how, we'll take the bitch out."

Fenella was both impressed and a little frightened by her certainty. It was interesting, the energy difference between Callum and Six. One was chaotic; romanticizing uncertainty like a favored lover. Then there was the other. Self-assured and comfortable in her hardened rationality. Fenella tried to picture what this pair might have looked like in their youth. In her mind she could see them running the streets together, Callum gleefully picking pockets and Six having his back when he picked the wrong one. Climbing to the tops of every roof in Savhignos, crowing like little roosters at the rising sun. Sharing bread together in between jobs.

These made-up scenarios warmed her, putting a faint smile on her face. Fenella never had siblings, nor did she have many friends when she was young, so she never got to have those kinds of experiences. Sometimes, she would fantasize about what it would be like having a sibling, and every time it made her ache.

Lulled into a calm by her thoughts and the smooth stride of her horse, Fenella jumped when she spotted Tytian ahead move sharply in his saddle. He stared over his shoulder at Six for a few seconds and then gradually turned away after Callum's subtle request.

She turned to Six, brows raised. "What do you think that was about?"

But Six didn't answer, her expression souring from suspicion.

Fenella saw her hand slide down her thigh, and come to rest on the damaged knee.

Because they had left Rodenburg so late into the day, they were forced to set up a roadside camp. A situation no one was particularly happy about. Adjacent to the road they came across an assembly of large boulders. At their heart, someone had set up logs for seating around a river rock fire pit and cleared spaces for bedrolls. It was a traveler's meager oasis, and where the group was forced to stop for the night.

"This place is a stroke of good luck," remarked Fenella happily. The rain had finally stopped, the hill and boulders blocked the wind, making this spot perfect. No one else seemed to share in her enthusiasm.

Haggard, the other three were as mute as the dead. Not one word was spoken as they worked on stripping their horses of the rain-soaked tack. They didn't even look at each other.

"Plague rats would be more lively travel companions," Fenella muttered to Apple as she loosened his cinch. The gelding gave a snort in agreement.

Tytian was the first to finish his task, and after he had secured Outsrider's hobbles he announced his departure to find some dry firewood.

"I'll help you." Six's offer wasn't an offer at all but a declaration, and she led the charge as the two of them followed the fall of the sun, chasing the edge of night as it crawled the knolls.

Like a seasoned card player Callum was sometimes hard to read. In this moment though, as he watched their forms disappear, that mask of nonchalance was gone. Worry was left in its stead, hanging heavy on his face in a scowl.

"I'm sure they'll be fine." Fenella tried to offer some comfort with a kind word and soft hand on his shoulder.

Callum's sarcastic demeanor was restored at her touch. "Oh yeah, sure. Because he likes roasted chicken!" He cracked her a grin.

Horrified, she glared at him. "He told you about that?" His laugh made her fists curl. "I'm never defending either of you ever again."

"I like blackberry pie if you want to add that to your argument options."

Over the hill, Tytian and Six walked in an edged silence, trying to find anything that would burn. The only trees along the knolls were skinny saplings, still green and wet, with the exception of one. A half-grown ironwood had been struck by lightning, probably in the previous spring, and was cleaved in two. One split of the decaying husk lay flat against the ground, while the remaining half tilted precariously northward, its roots half emerged from the dirt. Scattered about were broken limbs and shattered branches, and Tytian started collecting the best pieces into his arms, keeping Six just on the edge of his vision.

What was her reason for tagging along? Was she just seeking refuge from Callum, or was this some kind of ill-planned trap? Would she try to attack him? She had her axes strapped in holsters on either thigh, but Tytian didn't fear their sharp edges. Steel was useless against things like him.

"Do they know what you are?" Six asked suddenly, with a tone that belied the danger beneath her inquisition.

And there it is.

Tytian abandoned the few pieces of wood he'd gathered and faced her. She stared, hard, one hand hanging at her side while the other sat on the butt of an axe.

"Do *you* know what I am?" he asked carefully.

Six inclined her head. "You know that I do, demon."

The way she pronounced it made his insides crawl. "Callum has his suspicions. But Fenella doesn't know."

"When were you going to tell them?"

"Eventually."

"Eventually?" A challenge.

"This has nothing to do with you." Only three days out of the coffin and already he was missing his slumber. Tytian had never been great with people, but between Callum's secrecy and this woman's harsh nature his patience was growing thinner by the minute.

"How do we know you're not working with the High Father?" She motioned back towards camp. "You could be leading that idiot straight into a trap."

"I'm not-" he tried to assure her, but she cut him off.

"Likely story. For your kind."

Tytian scoffed at her and her baiting insults. "You know, it isn't very smart to follow a demon out into the dark to confront them on their supposed 'plans'. Help is so very far away."

Six, eerily calm, "Are you threatening me?"

Habit rolled his tongue over sharpened teeth. "Not yet."

She arrogantly inclined her head, her lips twitching softly at the corners. "You should be more careful with your words, beast."

The heat that swelled within Tytian was familiar. Animal, raw. Before he could conjure his logic, rein in even an ounce of control, that fire in his veins sent him charging. He closed the gap in the span of a heartbeat, and wrapped his hand around her throat. Narrow fingernails dug into skin, stroked by the steady pulse of her arteries.

On occasions of extreme duress, his anger took over like a possession, and all composure would be lost. He wondered if it was the demon side of him but there was never any proof. This rage, it just as easily could have been his own. Although, in this moment, he felt his actions were justified.

Six stared up at him, steely and victorious. It was then he realized that her axe blade was pressed against his jugular, the razor edge cutting into his skin.

She's fast.

He flicked his eyes down to the axe. "You know, that won't hurt me."

"No, it won't kill you," she corrected. "But it will hurt. A lot."

The seconds ticked away, until finally he dropped his hand and eased a step back, attempting to hide the fact that his body was trembling. "Believe me or not, but I'm not an ally of the church. Aolfrun is no friend of mine."

Six lowered her axe. "And the woman? Draven? Fenella told me about her. Sounds like you two have a history."

There was a twinge in his chest, then one in his nose as he recalled the scent of burning flesh. "It's complicated."

"That's the usual old line, isn't it?"

He tried to deflect her interest. "Care to explain how you know so much about demons?"

"Personal experience," she countered.

"Oh, fraternize with the damned often? Called up a demon yourself, have you?" It had been a long time since Tytian had felt as though he was playing a game of verbal chess, and he was pushing for a checkmate.

"My father did. He was too drunk to read the instructions. I read them for him, and collected the ingredients. It took more than one attempt, with more than one spell. So, I'm familiar enough."

That was unexpected. "Your father performed a Carmine Ritual? Why?"

"My mother had died, he wanted her back." For the first time her voice softened, although it wasn't by much.

"Was the deal successful?" He was genuinely intrigued by this. It wasn't every day that you met someone who had an experience with the dark arts in a casual sort of way. The average citizen could go their entire life and never even meet anyone else who had done a demon deal. Things like that was the work of Carmine Priests and the desperate.

Six shook her head. "No, it wasn't."

"Where's your father now?"

"Dead."

"From the demon?"

"Tavern brawl."

"How old were you?"

"Eight. And, I know what you're doing."

"What am I doing?"

"You're hoping that if you keep asking personal questions then you'll finally come to one that I won't answer, and you can use that as an excuse to dodge the original subject. That tactic is one I know well, and it isn't going to work, I'm not like Callum. I'm not ashamed of my past." She took a step forward. "Why didn't Francesca kill you?"

For a moment, just worth a fleeting breath, Tytian looked down at her right leg and contemplated asking about it. It was a messy, knee-jerk tactic, and he was lucky enough to catch the words before they left his mouth. Instead, he tried to plead with her. "Can't you just leave it alone?"

Her silence was akin to a battering ram.

Tytian exhaled sharply through his nose. *To hell with it...* "Francesca won't kill me. Ever. Even if the High Father demanded it, she will not end my life."

"Why?"

"She's not allowed."

"Not allowed?"

The words left a bitter taste on his tongue. "She and I, we're both children of Khaladhuun."

Six couldn't have looked more affronted if he had slapped her. "You're a child of the demonic abomination that requires horrendous ritualistic sacrifice to summon into the world?"

"Yes." He tried to choose his explanation with care. "However, it isn't quite how it sounds. I was imbued with some of his power as a kid, but the gift didn't take fully, so I'm still partially human."

Her eyes roamed him, and Tytian felt exposed. "Why didn't it take?"

"I rejected him. In the middle of the ceremony."

Anger and suspicion fought for control of her face. "Why the hell would you willingly partake in something like that?"

"What makes you think I was willing?" This slipped from him before he could stop himself, and the feeling of vulnerability left him gut-punched. As did the memory of hands holding him down, the sting of a leather belt trying to force him into submission.

Six's expression softened so much that Tytian almost didn't recognize her. "It was *Mal Intent*," she whispered.

Simply hearing the ritual named made his skin crawl. "Now you know."

Finally, someone knew. Understood what he was, what this meant to him. There was a strange release with telling her the truth. Like a mountain had been picked up off of his shoulders. He wasn't sure what would come next. If she would try and get the others to leave him, or if she'd wedge that axe blade deep in his skull in a vain, and useless, attempt to rid them of him. Would she be an ally now? Or remain a threat? He couldn't tell. Her body language gave nothing away, and her eyes were hard to read.

"Who performed the Mal Intent?"

"My mother was a Carmine Priest."

"You're own..." A mixture of shock and disgust pulled her taut, and he watched her grapple with something at her surface, wrangling it with some difficulty back into stoic control. "Do you still serve him?"

"Khaladhuun? Never. His name wasn't spoken again in my house after she died."

"How do I know you're not lying?"

"I'm not. But, I'd think forty years in the ground would be proof enough."

Six stood there with her thoughts for some time, keeping Tytian on a thin edge until finally, she took a deep breath and dropped the axe into its holster. "When we get back to camp, tell them."

"It'll just scare them."

"It'll scare them more if you wait."

He considered Six's words then, reluctantly, agreed. "Alright."

A truce was born between them. Fragile, but it existed.

They gathered stray limbs and manageable chunks of wood, then headed back to camp. Tytian kept his pace slow, to match her uneven gait. Along the way, Six asked him a few more questions about his condition and he answered in earnest, the tension between them somewhat eased.

"So, Francesca won't kill you because you're a 'Son of Khaladhuun'."

"Mhm."

"Because, since you're a Son, Khaladhuun doesn't want you harmed."

"Yes."

"Can you kill her?"

"I plan to."

"Why haven't you done it yet?"

Tytian adjusted the load in his arms, although it wasn't the weight of the wood that made him uncomfortable. "I never had a reason to. Until I did. But the thing with Ches is that she's strong. She fully accepted Khaladhuun during her ritual, and received all of his blessings." He took a minute to set up his explanation in the simplest way possible, doubling as practice for when he told the others. "Due to my rejection, I only received the basics of his gifts; increased speed and strength, adaptable vision, halted aging." He hesitated a little before listing the last gift. "And, siphoning."

She raised her brow, clearly worried that it was exactly what it sounded like. "Siphoning?"

"If I drink blood- animal or man, doesn't matter- then I absorb their energy. The more of their life I drain, the stronger I become."

A genuine grin crossed her lips. "That explains the bullshit vampire story you told Fenella."

"It was better than the truth."

Six's next question carried a weight with it that sank them both. "If you can do these things at only half gifted, what can Francesca do at full power?"

"Much more." Heat flushed his skin and the pungent scent of burning hair invaded his memories. He could hear the beams in the main hall splinter, crumbling down the staircase. The family dog screamed from behind the kitchen door, trapped inside the inferno. Hydrangeas on the foyer table smelled almost rotten while they burned, the sweet perfume mixing poorly with the ash in the air-

"Earlier on the road, when you and Callum were speaking." Six's voice cleaved through the scene in his mind, forcing Tytian out of the blistering past. "You turned around and looked at me. Why? What did he say?"

"Uh. He just said that... you're the best fighter he's ever seen. And I found that hard to believe given your, uhm... state." He motioned up and down at her and hoped to every deity known to man that she would buy the lie.

The look on her face had settled somewhere in between bewilderment and insulted. "Wow, that's rude."

"Yes," he agreed, realizing there were about a thousand other things he could have said. "However, my opinion on you has since changed." That part wasn't a lie. She wasn't quite as defenseless as he'd previously thought.

"An axe to the throat will do that," she said, jokingly.

"Is that a sense of humor I detect?"

Six grinned a little to fight the frown that appeared first. "Not much of one."

Over the hill, back at camp, Callum and Fenella had set out everyone's bedrolls and portioned a helping each of dried meats, cuts of bread and some cheese.

Fenella made a face at her fiber-lacking dinner and sighed. "Probably should have grabbed more vegetables, huh?" While Fenella was digging into her little roadside meal, she noticed that Callum merely picked at his, constantly looking over his shoulder into the dark. Just under his breath he hummed a comforting tune on loop, soothing his own fears while they waited for the others to return. Any time she tried to reassure him that everything was probably, it never seemed to convince him.

Please don't have killed each other, she thought to herself.

Just as the sky finally lost its last wash of light, Tytian and Six wandered back into camp, juggling firewood, neither one murdered.

"Took you two long enough," said Callum sternly as he stood.

Tytian started arranging limbs in the pit. "This isn't exactly a forest out here. It took a while to find a tree that wasn't green."

With some effort, and a few choice expletives, they got the fire going. Once the flames were high enough to sustain themselves, Tytian sat amongst the others, accepting his meager rations from Fenella. Six had taken up the spot opposite from him and through the flames he could feel her expectant gaze.

"There's something that I need to share with you," he told Callum and Fenella, whose conversation had fallen silent. "I've just shared this with Six. Now it's your turn." Carefully, he explained his origin, taking great measures to ensure that they understood that he was in no way a spy or affiliate of the church, or even Khaladhuun.

As Tytian told his story, Fenella sat in conflicted silence, staring into the palms of her hands. A lot of what he was saying she didn't quite grasp and she was trying desperately to understand, but having a very limited knowledge of the demonic world, she couldn't quite wrap her mind around what he was saying. One phrase stuck out to her though, and it was more his tone than the words themselves.

"You said your powers came from a ceremony in your childhood. Something called Mal Intent? What is that?"

"Mal Intent is a ritualistic magic and as a rule among practitioners, it's forbidden."

"Why?" she wondered.

Callum was the one who answered. There was a strange look on his face and his eyes were downcast to the flames. "Because it's horrific. It requires mutilation and a level of brutality that most people aren't bred for. You don't just will the magic into being with your physical actions..." Callum wiped both hands down his face, scratching absentmindedly at the stubble along his jaw. "You have to damn your very soul for it to work."

Her eyes widened. "How does one damn their soul?"

"What do you know of magic?" Tytian asked her.

She shrugged. "I know its use was banned, like, what? A century ago? My father used to talk about how some towns would burn suspected practitioners, but that he hadn't heard of one since he was a kid."

"But you don't know anything about its application?"

She shook her head.

"In order for magic to work, not only does the wielder need to have a predisposition to use it, they must also put their intention behind the craft. You can train someone to say the words, but if they don't truly mean it, it won't work. Magic is a neutral, natural flow of energy, radiating off of everything. When you can channel it with evocation and intent, it manifests. Like the wind or the push and pull of the sea; you cannot see it, but if using the right tools you can harness it. A spell is only as strong as the intent put into it."

"So, Mal Intent is... mean magic?" asked Fenella.

Callum chuckled. "That's a simple way to put it, yeah. Mal-malicious. You use your own evil to warp the magic you're wielding so that it'll bend and conform. You put your soul into your intent, and whatever you feed it is what it becomes." A shiver ran through him. "Duncan told me about Mal Intent one time, and I nearly shit myself."

Fenella rubbed at her arms. "That's terrifying. Is that why it was banned?"

"No." Tytian shook his head. "It was banned by the royal family due to pressure from the church. They had deemed magic unnatural before the eyes of the Divine, and once they discovered that people were using it to make deals with demons, that was all the push they needed to issue a nationwide ban on its practice. In all honesty however, it was because a rebellion was building to overthrow the tyrannical marriage of the kingdom and the church, who had begun taxing all of the townships into poverty. They feared the magic users coming together for the cause."

"Why go to a healer for your sickness when you can pay the priest to pray it away?" chimed Callum.

Fenella bristled. "There are plenty of things that prayer can heal."

Her subtle change caught his attention and Callum's brow lifted. "Vanilla, are you a follower of the Divine?"

She sat a little straighter. "Yes." Three sets of eyes were on her then and she shifted awkwardly. "Are you not?"

Callum flicked a finger up toward the sky. "We're not exactly on speaking terms. But, maybe if I save the world from a demonic force he'll reconsider the copious amounts of shit he has dumped on my life."

"Most of the shit dumping you did yourself," Six countered quietly, almost as if she'd accidentally spoken a thought out loud. When Callum's shoulders rose and his jaw started to clench, Fenella tried to break the building tension.

"What about you Six?"

The other woman tore her attention from Callum. "Not particularly."

"And you, Tytian?" Fenella was especially interested in his answer.

"I believe in balance. And I've seen the hells so that means the heavens must exist too, but the Divine won't get an ounce of worship out of me."

"How are you a devotee, Vanilla?" questioned Callum. "You've seen how the church works, how greed fuels that work. Hell, you're at the mercy of the Beacon Sect yourself. Why remain one of the faithful sheep when the watch dogs are eating the flock?"

"I am devout to the Divine, not the church. Man made the cathedral-" she looked up to the stars, "but the Divine made this. Made us." Her hand settled against her stomach, stroking at the fabric of her shirt with some affection. "Besides, who's to say what we're doing isn't Divine work? Stopping the rise of his most hated enemy, taking out a corrupt regime that hides behind the holy cloth? That sounds predestined to me."

Callum began to laugh.

"What?" asked Tytian.

"If that's true, then this is just turning out to be more of a comedy than I would've imagined. The nation's hope against possible demonic reign is a primp, a half demon and a couple of orphans." He laughed again. "Who knew?"

"Don't forget a blacksmith, a mage and a healer," mumbled Six.

Fenella's face lit with excitement. "A mage? We're picking up a mage?"

Callum nodded. "Yeah, Duncan. He was in Riverport last I heard, lying low and selling books. He's very careful about keeping his head down and practicing in secret, but he's an accomplished magic user and we're going to need him."

Tytian sighed and leaned forward, resting his elbows on his knees. "I think we're going to need everyone we can get."

But Callum disagreed. "Nah, this'll be enough, you'll see. Once we're all together again, we'll be damn nigh unstoppable. There's nothing this group can't do."

Six stood abruptly, and marched out into the night towards the horses.

Tytian waited until she was out of earshot before he quietly asked Callum, "Is there anything you can do to fix that?"

His eyes fluttered for a second and he looked down to his hands, his thumb tracing the lines of his palm. Deep in his chest, unbidden but unstoppable, Callum hummed a soft, familiar tune.

NINE

Throughout the night Six stayed with the horses, giving each one of them a thorough brushing until their coats gleamed in the moonlight. When that was finished she retrieved a wet stone from her bag, found a comfortable place to sit among the boulders and started sharpening her axes. From one task to another she moved, trying to keep both her hands and her mind occupied while her emotions slowly eased their riot.

Sssshhhhiiiii. Sssshhhhiiiii. The methodical drag of stone against steel, over and over and over again, lulled her into an empty peace. Behind the wet slicks her thoughts could wander into more neutral territory, away from this hurt that ate up the air in her lungs. It had become such a comfort over the years, honing the blades. So much so that she had ruined a few good axe heads with over sharpening.

She recalled an instance from her first month with the city guard, sitting alone at the foot of her bed inside the barracks, dousing a wet stone in oil while absentmindedly humming an old lullaby. The door opened and closed quietly behind her.

"Psst, Six." Callum flopped down on her bed. "Ooo, springy," he remarked mischievously, bouncing up and down on the mattress.

"Civilians aren't allowed in here, you cow," she warned, shoving him only a little.

Callum protested with theatrics. "I am no civilian."

Six's eyes narrowed as she poked him in the chest. "No. You are a self-glorified vagrant. Now, what do you want? Quickly, before my captain comes back."

Callum rolled up onto his elbow. "What time does your shift start?"

"At dusk, why?"

"Oh nice, two hours is plenty of time."

"Plenty of time for what?" Six asked with mild dread as he dragged her up to her feet and under his arm.

"Time for-" skinny fingers danced in front of him like a magician, "A little adventure, with a dash of danger and a whole heap of fun."

Six rolled her eyes dramatically and smiled, despite her obvious sigh. "You know, you're going to have to learn how to fight one of these days."

He hugged her closer as they headed out the door. "Why? All of this is far more fun with my bodyguard tagging along."

The memory trailed away and Six was back, sitting on the damp ground, the stone and axe still in her hands. She blinked away tears and pinched the bridge of her nose between her fingers. The inky sky above her, twinkling with bright stars and drifting clouds, drew her attention and for a long time she sat within the stillness of the world around her, nothing but the sound of a breeze through the tall grasses.

Her eyes had just started to drift close when there was the sudden warmth of a hand on her good knee, followed by the gentle squeeze of fingers. Six leaned up quickly, axe raised in defense. Tytian was crouched in front of her, hands held aloft to block any possible incoming swings.

His tone was soft. "Easy." A gentle word to a wild animal. "It's morning."

The moon and stars were gone. Sunlight was starting to bleed through the dark blue skyline to the east, and the sight made her stomach turn. She didn't even remember falling asleep.

Six leaned back into the boulder, breathing in deeply through her nose to settle her pounding heart. Tytian offered her his hand, displaying an older brand of chivalry that she wasn't accustomed to. Briefly, she considered declining but the ache in her right knee was persistent, so with his aid she was soon on her feet. Through the low light she was able to see Callum and Fenella still in their bedrolls at camp.

"You were humming in your sleep," Tytian told her as he headed for the horses, two of which were already tacked up, a third in the process. "But then you started mumbling and it didn't sound like a good dream, so I thought I'd wake you."

Six collected her axes and stored them away. "I don't remember dreaming, " she replied. "Don't even remember going to sleep actually."

Tytian cinched Red's saddle. "Does that happen often?"

"Sometimes." She worked a palm against her temple, loosening the oncoming headache.

Once Red was bridled, Tytian stepped around him and rummaged through the saddlebags on Outstrider, pulling out two apples. He offered Six the fruit, which she accepted without a word, and together they ate breakfast. Tytian watched the sunrise, she stared at the glittering of dew around their feet.

Eventually, Fenella stirred, rubbing her eyes and yawning broadly. Spotting the others, she gave a little wave. Her good morning greeting came out in a croak when she brought over her bedroll for storing. Tytian offered her half of his apple, which she accepted with a mumble of thanks. This subtle commotion woke Callum soon after, and when he rolled over to see the camp bare of his comrades he sat up with haste, a panicked look on his face. When he finally found them, he placed a hand on his chest in relief.

"Shit. Thought you'd been picked off by bandits or something."

"Why would bandits take us but leave you?" asked Fenella with a mouthful of fruit.

Callum grunted as he pulled on his boots, the leather now tightened after being waterlogged the day before. "Because bandits know a vicious scoundrel when they see one." He winked.

"Ah yes," she said, flatly. "You're a real danger."

One more grunt and his foot slipped into the boot.

Out on the road to Talonwood, birds chirped and swooped through the early morning air. Big, white clouds dotted the cerulean sky, pushed along by a sleepy breeze. The scenery was beautiful out here, early spring in full effect.

"Apple, stop being so fidgety," Fenella whispered, the horse longing to stretch his legs down the straight cut of roadway.

Beside them, Six cocked her head. "Did you just call him Apple?" When Fenella nodded, she grinned. "Kind of a strange name."

"Thank you!" Callum called from the front of the pack.

Fenella rolled her eyes at him, motioning toward Six's own golden mount. "What's his name?"

"Sunrise."

She admired the thick fall of mane and his gentle, green hued eyes. "He's beautiful. And so well mannered."

Six reached out, stroking a hand down the stallion's broad neck. "For now. Might have my hands full when the moon changes and Outstrider goes into season." Sunrise's head bobbed as if confirming her words and then snorted, chewing restlessly at his bit.

Fenella, amused and thankful, ruffled Apple's mane. "I'm glad this guy here is gelded. No worries with him."

"The perfect man."

Laughter sparked between them, neither one aware of how closely Callum listened in from afar.

Around midday they shared a riding lunch and cooled the horses in a little slice of creek that banked against the road. When an airship buzzed overhead, they slunk into the tree line and waited for its shadow to disappear. Beyond the creek cut was a long drag through the valley, finally ending at the mouth of Talonwood's city gates by late afternoon.

Ribbons tied to mahogany poles waved them through the archway. Overhead it was lined with discarded fin poles from an airship, each curved to look like the talons of a cat. The markets here were extensive and numerous, nearly half of all Savhignos's imports from places like Crown's Cross or Mar passed through Talonwood, making the local trade business a profitable one. Vendor stands marked the streets with higher end boutiques, exotic grocers and tradesmen stations worked out of brick-and-mortar spaces. Their doors were open, perfuming the air with a distinct, if not a bit heavy, scent. Live animals, butchered meats, fabrics, vegetables, fruits, jewelry, homewares, clothing, fine liquor, art from across the seas. Just about anything to want for was available, a patron only needed to turn their head to find the next treasure.

Beneath a web work of strung lights and soft fabric banners, the four of them waded deeper into this thrumming heart.

Frequently, they dodged both chicken and child, each overly confident in their own existence, unaware or uncaring about the heavy hoof of a horse. Beyond the market was the residential area, houses here just as decorated as the vendor stalls up the street, but far quieter. Among the boarding houses and narrow apartments was a long, one-story house with a cobblestone front yard. Flower boxes hung along the fence line, full of blue and yellow trumpets. Behind the house was a lot, well maintained with short grasses that fed a sturdy, aged horse. Under the western wing of the extended porch there was a smithy station, where a man swung a hammer against steel.

Callum led them inside the yard, tying Red off to a hitching post. Everyone else did the same and followed him up the steps to the small armory. He leaned against a supportive pillar and crossed his arms, watching the man shape the steel to his liking. He was meticulous in his swings, bringing life to his creation little by little.

Out of the house emerged a little girl, carrying a tankard and a rag to the smith, careful not to spill her cargo. She spotted the strangers gathered on her porch and paused, searching their faces.

"Uncle Callum!" She set down the tankard and rag, then sprinted into his open arms.

"Genny!" Callum scooped her up in a swinging hug before putting her back down. "You're still so short," he told her, and she gave a little crumble, annoyed.

"I know! I'm going to be small forever." She pouted.

"Could always melt you down and stretch you out," said the smith as he tossed the horseshoe into a bucket of water, a warm grin on his face.

"No, daddy!" Genny cried with amusement, stamping her foot.

"That's actually not a bad idea," said Callum, with a thoughtful tap on his chin. "He could make you as tall as a house, and give you swords for arms!"

Genny giggled loudly while swatting at him.

The smith picked up the rag and wiped his face, smoothing away loose strands of long, rose-gold hair. "Been a while since I've seen you."

"I've been meaning to visit but-"

"Something always pops up."

Callum rubbed the back of his neck. "Yeah." He turned to Fenella and Tytian. "Guys, this is Aldan Franks. Best blacksmith in the region."

Taller even than Tytian, and thick through the body from decades of swinging a hammer, Aldan was a force. Despite his intimidating stature, his tone and mannerisms revealed a kind nature, amplified by the smile lines near his dark eyes.

"Hello!" He greeted them with a handshake for each, but when he spotted Six at the back of the pack, his expression turned to one of shock. He threw a glance at Callum, who simply looked down at the floor.

"Six?" Aldan asked.

She gave a little smile of her own in response. "Hi Al."

Aldan stepped down the line and gave her a gentle hug, treating her carefully, as though she may break apart in his arms. When he pulled away he placed a calloused hand on her cheek. "How've you been?"

Six replied behind a well rehearsed response. "Fine."

In the instant, Aldan's brow wrinkled with worry and he looked back to the others, studying Callum's face for answers. "Something's wrong, isn't it?"

Callum stuffed his hands into his jacket pockets, his previous light extinguished. "What makes you say that?"

"Well for one, you're both here together, and there's no blood-shed."

"Yeah, I suppose that does seem suspect." He took a deep breath. "We need to talk. Somewhere private."

Aldan nodded slowly, scratching at his beard. "Alright."

Genny was given the important task of picking fresh flowers for the dinner table, Aldan insisting on the blue ones her mother liked best. Once she was off the porch, flitting around the yard, he opened the front door and invited them inside.

"Coffee?" he asked and everyone accepted.

They strolled into a clean kitchen, where the smell of morning bacon was faint in the air. At the heart of a dining table sat a misshapen glass vase, the odd rise and fall of the rim suggesting a failed venture into glass blowing. Ugly, but it did its job, housing the wilted remains of old flowers. Aldan made sure to dump them in the bin, making room for Genny's incoming bounty. He then set to work on the coffee, and once steamy cups were settled in everyone's hands Aldan took up the seat at the head of the table. He gestured for everyone to sit.

Callum pulled himself closer to the table, elbows anchored to the hardwood, his hands just as expressive as his words. "Okay-"

Immediately, Aldan interrupted, hoping to save them both some time. "Listen, if you're going to try and sell me on a job, don't. I'm done with all of that."

"It isn't a job," Six told him, her tone level but insistent.

Aldan's demeanor shifted. "Really?" His eyes flicked across the table to Callum.

"It's the High Father. And the Beacon Sect." He counted on his fingers. "And Duke Welling, plus some demon woman."

"A what?"

"Demon woman," Callum repeated. "But, we'll get to her in a minute." Starting from the beginning, Callum broke down his encounter at the cathedral and every step taken after. Aldan listened intently, soon abandoning his coffee mug to lean in closer, drawn in by the information being laid before him. Callum's story led from Fenella's house to the J'harenmar estate, and once the dots connected and the reveal made about who Tytian was, Aldan had too many questions to wrangle at once.

He held up his hands, pausing Callum's recant. "Wait a minute." Aldan pointed a finger at Tytian, "You're Tytian J'harenmar?"

Still hooded and cloaked, he nodded slowly. "Yes."

A tight suspicion stickied his voice, and Aldan tilted his head to look deeper into the shadows that obscured Tytian's face. "You don't seem like you're north of eighty."

Nervously, Callum scoffed. "Duncan doesn't either, ya know?" It wasn't enough to break Aldan's interest, and he started blathering the moment that the blacksmith stood up. "Uh, big man?"

"Take off the hood," Aldan demanded with a steady, dangerous tone.

The tension in the room rose as he did and now everyone was on edge.

Fenella tried to aid him, but Tytian stopped her. "It's fine." He slipped a hand under the hood hem and let the fabric fall away, watching the predictable shock and confusion play out on the other man's face.

"What the hells happened to you?" Aldan asked, studying those pupilless, yellow eyes. In the moment that everything Callum had told him clicked into place, he realized with sickening clarity what sat at his table, drinking coffee from his daughter's favorite mug, polluting his home with its very presence.

"A demon," Aldan whispered.

Callum waved his hand, trying to pull him away from his rage. "Hey, listen-"

"A demon?!" Granting his wish, Aldan swung around on Callum, making him sink into his chair. "You brought a fucking demon into my home?! Where my children sleep?!"

"Just a little one." The nervous chuckle that escaped Callum's throat was involuntary, strangled by the almost non-existent good sense he possessed.

Interjecting, Fenella motioned toward Tytian. "It's not his fault!" But it wasn't enough, information had turned him hostile, and Aldan Franks was now a juggernaut in human skin.

Mugs rattled as he pushed away from the table, closing the short gap between him and the thing in his kitchen. Tytian stood as well, freeing his right hand from the folds of his cloak, long nails ready for the slice.

In between them, swallowed instantly by Aldan's shadow was Six, a small but effective blockade. She spoke Aldan's name, the inflection sharp, commanding his attention. He looked down at her, bewildered and teetering on the edge of betrayal.

"I would never bring down any harm on you, Shara or the kids," Six assured him. "You know that."

"Yeah, come on buddy. You trust us, don't ya?" Callum's attempt at an assist only splashed fuel on Aldan's fire.

"Six has my trust, but you?" His lip curled in a sneer. "Trusting you is a death sentence. I'd be better off with a snake in the dark."

Eyes wide, mouth hung ajar, Callum was clearly stung. "What the hells have I ever done to you?"

"Should I read from the list?!"

"You wrote a list?!"

Slamming her hands on the table, Fenella stood up with a shout. "Okay!" The room fell silent and the longer they stared the more nervous she became. "Oh. I didn't think you'd actually... never mind." She gestured toward Tytian, pleading for some grace from the blacksmith. "Please, just listen to his story. And if you want to kick us out after, you can. Although, I think that would be pretty stupid, and you don't seem like a stupid man."

Callum huffed and whispered, "Opinions vary on that."

When Fenella tried to slap the side of his head Callum countered, batting her away.

After a long pause, Aldan consented. He righted his toppled seat and sat down, clasping his hands together to keep them from seeking a neck or two.

With some extra encouragement from Fenella, Tytian retold the story of his making. They all listened intently. Fenella with her usual look of pity, and Callum's hard stare, his thoughts more concerned with convincing Aldan that there was no threat. Six listened for a different reason and he could tell in the times when he couldn't help himself and his eyes would jump to her. She held him in study, making sure that his story, now thrice told, still held up. That he was as true as he said he was. She was watchful. Careful. But she didn't need to be. Tytian told them nothing but the brutal truth of it.

In his stomach, that familiar knot pulled itself tighter.

Tracing a thumb over his brow, Aldan exhaled heavily through his nose. "Mal Intent, huh? That's nasty work right there."

Tytian agreed, taking a deep swig of his chilled coffee.

"Son of a bitch..." Aldan whispered under his breath. "You've really gotten us into some shit now, Callum."

Callum threw up his arms in listless celebration. "It's one of my many gifts."

Burdened with choice, the smith stood and went over to the window. Just outside, Genny, tiny fists full of wildflowers, bounded about with carefree joy, laughing at the small yellow butterflies who followed her.

"Do you have a plan?" asked Aldan, full of some small, cautious hope.

Callum hated to disappoint him. "So far, the plan was to get all of us together again and then go from there. We do have options though. Either keep the Duke from ever reaching Savhignos, or letting that ritual slab slip by while we try to find another and destroy it. Or at least put it somewhere that no one will ever find it."

"Where are these slabs coming from?"

"Havnul? That's where the one that Welling is transporting was found."

Aldan turned around, jabbing a finger at Tytian. "Don't you know where they are?" When Tytian shook his, Aldan became annoyed. "Why not? You went through that summoning thing, said your ma was a Carmine."

"Communicating and receiving a gift of power from Khaladhuun is very different from actually allowing him to physically enter the world," Tytian explained. "The ceremony performed on me was like cracking a window. What they're planning on doing is not only opening the door for him but taking it completely off the hinges. He would be manifested on our soil. No demon prince has ever done that."

This information wasn't what he'd hoped for. "How does someone even know how to do something like this? What bastard made these ritual stones?"

"The heads of Khaladhuun's worship. I guess he figured out how to break his seals and relayed the instructions through his most loyal of Carmine Priests. My mother never spoke of it often; her focus was solely on my ceremony."

Aldan dropped back into his chair and rested his elbows on the tabletop, rummaging through all of this new information and trying to make sense of it. "Just when you think the corrupt system is at its worst with increased taxation, they decide to top themselves with demon deals."

"You can say no," Six said with understanding. "Not a soul here would blame you if you wanted no part in this."

The door opened and in bound Genny, a mix matched bouquet in hand. "Here daddy! I found some good ones." Marching over to the counter she had to stand on tiptoes to grab the vase. Fenella offered to help but the child shook her head. "I got it." With some effort she managed to squeeze all of the flowers into the glass, pulled out a free chair and climbed into the seat, propping her dirty knees against the side of the table as she positioned the vase in the middle. "There. Isn't that pretty, daddy?"

Aldan was staring at her, tented fingers pressed against his mouth. "Yes, little one, they're perfect." He reached out then, scooped her into his arms. One hand hugged her to him while the other traced the stitch work on the table runner, made by his wife with needle and thread. Near the door were his son's house slippers, the tiny embroidered bees dancing along the calfskin edges. All around him were reasons to say no to Callum, but they were also reasons to say yes.

Tears sprang to his eyes, heavy with grief and regret, and Aldan quietly wished he had never met Callum.

"Okay," he said with defeat. "I'm in."

TEN

Callum gave him a weak smile that rose and fell in a flash, devoid of anything close to joy or triumph. "Welcome aboard."

After finishing their coffees, they all returned to the porch, Aldan leaving Genny to her toys in the living room. As they headed down the steps a tall, dark-haired woman was crossing the yard, twin boys about four years of age gripping the pockets on her apron. In one hand she carried a basket of vegetables, and in the other a folded bundle of fabrics. She gave the strangers on her porch a concerned look until she found a face she knew.

"Callum!"

"Shara!" Callum called with forced excitement and then gave her a hug.

"Haven't seen you in ages." When she pulled away from him, she looked over the others. The sight of one in particular made her smile droop. "Six is here?"

"She is?!" Callum said with theatrical shock.

Six shot him a little look, clearly not amused, and then gave a wave. "Hi Shara."

"Uh, hi." A little flustered by the sight of them both there together, for a second all she could do was look back and forth between them, until she found Aldan and saw the state of his face. A light came on in her mind and all of her previous confusion faded. "Where's Genny?" she asked of her husband.

Aldan jabbed a thumb over his shoulder. "Inside, playing."

Shara nodded slowly. "Boys?" The twins looked up to her with eyes the same deep shade as her own. "Go inside with your sister. Take these with you, okay?" She handed off her purchased goods to her sons, watching carefully as they climbed the steps and tottered inside the house. Once they were out of earshot, Shara snapped on Callum, all of her previous hospitality gone.

"No." Was all she had to say, with enough force to make him take a step back. She then looked up to Aldan, almost pleading with him. "You told him no, right?"

Aldan stammered for a second, so Callum took up the lead. "It's not like that, Shara. This isn't like the other jobs-"

"That's what you said the last time. And the time before that." Angrily she closed in on him, waving a finger around in his face. "I told you, did I not? I told you not to slink into this house with another one of your schemes. He barely came back alive from the last one!" She threw a hand out toward the others. "I mean for gods' sake Callum, look at what happened to Six!"

He was trying to get a word in, unable to dance past Shara's hostility. Aldan came to his rescue, taking her gently by the wrists and pulling her out of Callum's face.

"Hey." He put his hands on either side of her neck, forcing her to look into his eyes. "Honey, please." Worrisome, his expression told her that something was very wrong. Aldan swallowed hard and stroked her cheek with his thumb as he turned to the others. "Give us some time to talk. There's a great bar here in town, with good food and a place to water the horses. Wait for me there. I'll find you all later."

They did as they were bid, collecting the horses and heading out of the yard as Aldan and Shara settled in for a long discussion on the porch.

"You really have a way with women," snarked Tytian.

Callum had no response.

Wandering back through town, with the sun beginning to set, the crowds hadn't thinned much but the shops were all being packed up for the night. Through the masses they waded until finally the bar came into view, and once the horses were hitched, the four of them started inside. Just as Callum crossed the threshold, he heard her call his name. Six stared at him from the yard, arms crossed tightly over her chest. Flicking her chin, she gave the other two the go-ahead to wait inside.

"What is it?" Callum asked in a hush once he was by her side.

Something was on her mind. Something that was accompanied by the familiar pang of guilt.

Six shook her head. "We shouldn't have dragged him into this. He has a family, Callum. Children. This isn't right."

"It wouldn't be right not to tell him. We're giving him the chance to fight for his family. Even if he-" Callum took a quick pause, uncomfortable with even saying the word, "*Dies*, hell even if we all die... if we're able to succeed and stop this, then he'll have won. His wife and children would live." He bent down a little to catch her downcast eyes. "But if we were to fail, he'd never forgive us for not giving him the chance to at least fight for his family's lives." Taking a risk, he reached out to put his fingers to her arm. She recoiled from his touch.

"You always find some way to justify the shit you put us through," Six whispered bitterly, striding ahead of him into the bar.

Her vitriol might as well have been a fist to the gut.

Callum shoved his hands into the safety of a jacket pockets.

"Everything okay?" inquired Fenella by the door and Six replied with a quick, dismissive nod.

In the usual fashion, they were greeted by a perky barmaid and escorted to a table, where she took their food and drink order and disappeared into the crowd. Almost the entire establishment spilled over with people. Their table was tucked away in a far corner so the overcrowding wasn't too intense, but they couldn't carry on a conversation without shouting. The maid returned to them after a half hour, bearing a large tray laden with tankards of house-made beer and bowls of seasoned rice, thinly sliced beef and buttery cabbage soup. Once they had all eaten, the table was cleared away and another round of drinks passed between them. Each one kept an eye on the door, waiting for Aldan to show. Night came slowly, darkening the frosted window panes.

It had been a little more than two hours and still no sign of the smith.

"Think he's going to show?" asked Fenella, but neither Callum nor Six had a definitive answer.

Tankards were empty and tensions were high, so Fenella volunteered to go apprehend more spirits, their barmaid having disappeared somewhere in the bustle.

"I'll come with you," said Six, looking for any excuse to get up and move. A full day of riding had left her damaged knee swollen.

Squeezing her way between two passed out regulars, Fenella caught the attention of the busy barkeep behind the bar. "Hi!" she shouted warmly, hoping her voice carried over the sound of a party singing off key somewhere across the room. "Can I get four more beers please?" Fenella turned to Six while the keep busied himself with their order. "I feel like I'm in a beehive," she laughed.

Six smiled in return. "Really? Because I feel like I'm in hell!"

Fenella chuckled and gave a playful roll of her eyes.

A group of men stood just the other side of Fenella and one in particular leered with a slimy kind of attention. Over the edge of his cup he dragged his eyes up her body, taking a long, messy drink. Fingers tipped in dirty nails tapped her shoulder and when she turned around he stepped into her space, deep set eyes staring noticeably at her breasts.

"Hello there." His breath was stale.

Fenella's lip curled and she made a pinched sort of face. "Can I help you?"

He traced his teeth with his tongue. "You sure can, little lamb." The man reached out to touch her hair. When she tried to pull away he grabbed her wrist with force, nearly snatching her off of her feet. "Come on. Just a little taste of that porcelain skin."

Six stepped between them, shoving him away. "Do not touch her again."

The man scoffed. "Oh, I get it. You're jealous. You want a piece of me too, huh?"

"I'd say a piece of your spine, but I don't think you have one," spat Six. Her hand slid down to the holster on her thigh, freeing up the axe.

He gave a pungent sort of smirk, eyes lighting up. "I do love it when you bitches got some fire in you. Makes it all the sweeter when I pin you down."

Two things happened at once, and they happened fast.

Six drooped low, her weapon now in hand, the head of it scraping the floor as she prepared to carve upward, flaying him where he stood. Breaking her mad-dog attention on this target was a hand, gripping so tightly around the drunk's throat that the knuckles rolled white under the copper skin.

Tytian lifted this man into the air, slamming him down on the bar top. People scrambled away from them, glasses and tankards clattered to the floor. Beneath Tytian's vice grip the man writhed like a bug.

Callum sauntered over, amused at how quickly his demonic comrade worked. "Well, that was probably the dumbest thing you have ever done in your entire life," he told the aggressor, now gasping for air. Spindly legs kicked and thrashed as gurgled cries escaped past his lips. "Perhaps, in the future, you keep your hands to yourself. Then you won't be in a room with all of your friends, pissing your pants while getting the shit strangled out of you by a stranger"

Just as his bulging eyes started to roll backward Tytian released his grip. The man gasped in a ragged breath of air and spun onto his side, coughing violently. Behind him stood the shocked barkeep, two tankards in his hands.

Callum raised his eyebrows in question. "Those ours? Perfect, thanks so much." He took the drinks before the keep could even protest.

As they all started for their table Callum spun on his heel. "And by the way, you should thank him," he advised, pointing towards Tytian. "Because had he not intervened that woman would've cleaved you in two. And you would've deserved it."

Humiliated, reeking of piss and spilled ale, the drunk slid off of the bar top like a slug and slumped into the floor, his buddies slowly coming over to help him to his feet. Voices were growing in strength around the room and soon people had resumed their conversations, although now more eyes than ever were watching the group as they headed for the door.

"Perhaps we should step outside," offered Fenella, and the rest agreed. In the shallow yard they occupied a free ring of stone benches, keeping watch for the strangled man or one of his friends to stumble out of the door.

Fenella and Callum started up a quiet conversation that soon turned boisterous, both making jokes at the expense of the battered man inside. Six took the opportunity to speak with Tytian.

"Thank you for stepping in back there," she told him with sincerity. "You saved me a murder charge."

He nodded with a small smile. "Thank you for earlier, at the blacksmith's. You took a risk, siding with me, and I appreciate it."

Without another word, Six passed him her drink.

Leaning back against the stone wall, Fenella marveled at the sights, warmed by the company and the alcohol in her system. "Can't believe I've never come here before. Aside from the leering asshole, Talonwood is nice. Everything is so colorful."

Six quirked a brow. "How have you lived in Savhignos your whole life and never stepped foot in Talon?"

Fenella lazily flicked a hand. "I'm not native to Savhignos. Only been there about two years."

"Where were you before?"

"Ravenloch."

"The 'loch?" asked Callum with a whistle. "Well damn, Vanilla I didn't know I was in the presence of royalty. Should I bow? Or do you prefer I curtsy?"

She hit him with a glare. "I can't help it my family is wealthy. Can you help it that you were an orphan?"

He chuckled. "Alright alright, I concede, no need to start boxing below the belt. However, I am proud that you went straight for the traumatic childhood. Well done."

Fenella started to apologize, then decided to stand by what she said and thanked him instead, raising her cup in toast.

They carried on for several more minutes, tossing quips back and forth, until Six cut the merriment short. She nodded behind them and Callum turned to see Aldan approaching, wearing a rocky expression. Once within range he forced a smile.

"Passed a buddy of mine on the way here. Says there was some sort of fight earlier. I swear, I can't trust you two not to make a scene."

Callum bristled. "How do you know it was us?"

"Was it?"

"Well, yeah, you know it was. But it was totally justified. And no one died."

"This time," Aldan said pointedly at Six, who simply shrugged and took a sip of her beer. As well rehearsed as it was, the nonchalance began to fade, leaving Aldan nowhere else to go. "I know you're all wondering... and, yes. I'm still on board. But if we're successful and pull this thing off, Shara has requested that we never see you again, Cal. You're my friend, and you were my family when I didn't have one. But I agree with her. This has to be it."

Callum expected as much. Shara had never been his biggest fan, especially not when her husband always came home with more scars than he left with. "Okay then. One last adventure for the books."

"Alright," Aldan said, relieved. "Let's go back to the house. You all can stay with us for the night, save some saph. Come on."

They traveled the streets back to Aldan's where they untacked the horses and stalled them in his barn. Walking across the porch, they were startled when Shara opened the door, hugging a shawl around her shoulders.

She passed a look between her husband and Callum. "Did you tell him?"

Aldan placed a hand to her cheek, then a kiss on her temple. "Yes baby, I told him." He tried to usher them inside but Shara held up her hand, looking towards Tytian.

"Not you," she declared. "The rest are welcome but, I cannot sleep with you in my house."

Tytian swallowed his retorts and ignored the burn of shame in his cheeks. "Very well."

Six spoke up in his defense. "You can't have him sleep out on the porch like a dog."

Her hands tightened around her shawl, fear smashing the words between her teeth. "This isn't your house. It isn't your family." This decision was final, and Shara would not move.

"Alright." Callum played mediator. "The man said he'll sleep on the porch, so he'll sleep on the porch."

"We'll all sleep on the porch," Fenella stated with a firm tone.

Callum slumped. "But my back-"

"Will be fine, you baby. Come on."

They retrieved their bedrolls from the barn and Aldan supplied them with a few extra quilts and pillows, only slightly apologetic. As comfortable as they could make it, the far corner of the smith station was cozy in its own way. They settled in close, making a neat little line.

"Anyone want to cuddle for warmth?" Callum asked with mischief.

"Tytian's your closest option," Fenella suggested coyly.

A tone of disgust could be heard in Tytian's rebuttal. "I'd rather let him freeze to death."

Callum protested, and together the three of them lobbed petty insults and humorous jabs back and forth like cannon fire.

Six turned her back to the banter and stared into the dark.

ELEVEN

Francesca sat atop her mare at a crossroads, trying to detect any sign that may indicate where her prey had gone from here. The heavy rain washed out the roads, leaving nothing behind but a mess, and she couldn't detect a scent through the downpour.

"What are you thinking?" asked one of her soldiers. "Could they have just kept moving west?"

"Tytian could push through but not the other two. They would need rest. Supplies." She put her nose to the wind again, inhaling deeply. Nothing.

Tytian's affinity for humans was something that always puzzled Francesca, but she guessed it was due in part to him being impure. That human side of him made him weak, and it was such a pity. She often thought about what Tytian J'harenmar could have been had he just accepted his gift, and that thought always sent a shiver throughout her body. He could have been glorious. A true force of nature. Then he went and spat in the face of their creator. Their shared father. The fact that Tytian never came into his real power was a travesty. However, compared to her usual targets, he made one hell of an adversary.

Her body flushed with heat.

Francesca pointed the mare down the rocky pathway to Rodenberg, calling instructions over her shoulder to her squad captain. "Take twelve, go to Talonwood. If you find J'harenmar, apprehend him. Kill the rest."

The soldier grinned, adjusting the warhammer strapped to his back. "Yes ma'am. How discreet should we be?"

Francesca rolled her shoulders. "Makes no difference, just be back here at dawn." Then, to the remainder of her squad, "The rest of you are with me."

The trek from the crossroads into town was hell on the horses and by the time they rode past Roden's front gates, each animal was heaving and quivering beneath their rider. People were openly staring, not bothering to hide their curiosity and confusion as to why there were armored strangers roaming the streets like a pack of strays. Pointing, Francesca signaled for her men to break apart and search the town in pairs, each one taking a different alleyway or side road. They studied every face they passed, stopping locals to ask them a few questions. Everyone in Rodenburg seemed as tight lipped as a clam.

Francesca headed for the bar. The Tossed Tankard had proven to be lucrative, so she was eager to see what secrets she could pry out of this one. Inside, there were only a few patrons lined around the bar. Most of them were either already passed out against the counter top or sagging into their drinks.

A barmaid, brandishing a tray on one hip, greeted her. She was pretty and professional. "Would you like a table, miss?"

"No table necessary. But perhaps you would be kind enough to help me?" Her voice was sweet as sugar, and there was a light in the eyes that drew the maid in.

"What can I do?"

Francesca stepped in a little closer, subtly drinking in the other woman's smell. "I'm an investigator from Savhignos, looking for a party of three; two men and one woman. One of the men would be tall, with white hair. The other is a redhead."

The barmaid shrugged. "Can't say that I have. It's hard sometimes to keep up with those coming and going. You could try the inn though. It's right across the street."

Francesca leaned in, her smile curled with a hint of hunger. "Thank you, I'll do just that."

A slight blush reddened the maid's cheeks and the exposed peak of her breasts. She fumbled with a smile of her own, then swished away back to her duties.

Francesca fought the urge to lure the woman into the stockroom, eager to know what she tasted like. Particularly, her liver.

Just as the barmaid said, the quiet inn was close by. There were no horses stationed in the attached paddocks, and no fresh mud on the porch. Inside, the innkeeper offered a lazy greeting, not even bothering to look up from her book.

"How many rooms, how many nights?"

Francesca reached across the countertop, snatching the book from her listless grip. "I'm not here for a room."

Immediately the keep was enraged, rising from her seat. All of her bravado fled when their eyes met, and slowly the woman eased back down. "What do you want?"

Faintly, the scent of Tytian clung to the wet air, and Francesca pulled it down into her lungs as if it gave her life. "There was a man here, traveling with another, and a woman. Tell me everything you know about them."

The keep's breath quickened, and she tried to swallow her nerves, all former nonchalance now replaced by a professionalism that didn't suit her. "I'm sorry miss, but I don't talk about my clientele."

Faster than she could dodge, Francesca reached out, grabbed the woman's braided hair and snatched forward. Her forehead slammed into the counter, opening a cut that sent a stream of red down her twisted expression. When she instinctively recoiled, Francesca's hand was already wrapped around her mouth like a muzzle.

"Try again," she sneered.

Muffled by the palm that threatened to break her jaw, the keep's words came out sloppy. "They were here! The night before last. Stayed one night, left the next day."

"What time did they leave?"

"Midday." The talon-like fingers on her face grew hot and she searched her panicked brain for anything else she could remember. "T-they left with another woman, a local! I've seen her around but I don't know her name."

Francesca tilted her head. "Well, that doesn't give me much to go on, now does it?"

The keep whimpered. "I-I don't know what to tell you! Uhm ... she's brunette! Walks with a limp. I think she works at Popp's, just up the street."

Another bird to his flock. Francesca ran this information through her brain, trying to see if there was something to this that she was missing.

"That's all I know, I swear." Pink tears slid across the woman's grimaced cheeks. "Please, let me go."

"Alright," Francesca obliged, and closed her hand into a fist, crushing the keep's skull. The body fell to the floor without so much as a twitch.

Flipping off the lights and locking the doors behind her, Francesca moved on. She was licking the last bit of gore from her fingers when her soldiers regrouped, all reporting the same information: Two men and two women were seen riding out of

Rodenburg recently, and one of the men fit the church thief's description.

Francesca told them to return to the horses and wait for her. "I have one last shop to visit."

The store was easy to locate, stationed not far from the main gates. It would have constituted as prime real estate, had anything in this washed-out town been worth something. Popp's Exotic Imports might as well have been an oasis in the desert compared to the dull establishments that flanked it.

In the second Francesca stepped over the threshold, an old man waved her in.

"Hello," he said brightly from his perch on top of a step ladder near the assortment of pots along the wall. "Welcome, welcome. Please, have a look around and take your time! I'm not going anywhere." He smiled kindly, and then with shaky hands, began the steep, three step descent off of the ladder. When he felt a hand on his elbow and another on his back, Popp turned to Francesca, who had come to his aid. "Oh, heh heh, my hero! Thank you, my dear." With her help, Popp's feet finally found the floor.

"You're quite welcome," she purred and then looked around. "This is an impressive collection."

Popp beamed with pride. "Yep!" He started for the front counter at a slow shuffle. "Been in business a long time. Made some good friends along the way who can get me just about anything anyone could ever need." He climbed into a stool near the register, wiping his brow with a rag.

Francesca browsed his herbs and jarred remedies, plucking up a bottle of crushed mustard seed. "You work this whole shop by yourself?"

Popp raised a hand and shook his head. "No, not entirely! My help did recently take a leave, but she'll be back." He smiled proudly. "Best damn help this old man could ask for too."

"Oh? Why did she leave?"

"She didn't really say, come to think of it." He gave a chuckle. "Probably should've asked but, she'd earned some time off. That woman hadn't taken a day for herself in almost five years!"

Francesca turned with a smile. "She sounds like a model employee!"

"She's just the best."

"What's her name?" she asked innocently, sniffing at a small bag of dried dandelions.

"Six! Bit of a weird name. Though, even the most common moniker will sound strange to someone somewhere."

"I think it's nice," she lied. "What is she doing on this overdue vacation, hmm? Hitting up the coast with friends?"

Popp shrugged. "Well, she was with friends, but I don't think it was the coast they were headed for. Think she said something about heading west. Might be Bravenya! At least, that's where I'd go." He gave her a wink.

Francesca slunk up to the counter and leaned her elbows on its top. "I'd go to Bravenya too." A girlish chuckle made his cheeks flush. "These friends of hers, any of them men? Does this Six have a sweetheart?"

Popp's face wrinkled in thought. "Hmm, don't know! She was in a bad mood after talking to the one fella. Blood red hair he had! Ooph, she gave him a tongue wallopin' out there in the alley. Must've made up though! Rode out with him the next morning."

"Must have." She tapped at her teeth in thought. "How did she come to work here at the shop?"

Popp grinned, looking at her out of one eye. "Why? You want her job?"

Francesca giggled and bowed her head, hands raised. "You caught me! Truth be told, I'm just a sucker for stories."

"Me too." The wrinkles on his face deepened when his nose scrunched. "Six came into town years ago from Savhignos. Poor thing was beat all to hell and back. Bruised and bloodied from head to toe. Spent a few days up at the doc's house. I was there visiting my uh, lady friend." He winked, before his humor turned somber. "She was passin' from a fever, and I wanted to hold her hand as she went. Doc rushed in with Six and put her in the bed across from Greta. After my lady left this world, I just didn't feel like going home yet so, I sat with Six for a while. Poor thing didn't have anyone. I figured at least she could have the company of a sad, old man. Came to see her every day until eventually she was well enough to leave, and by that point we were friends." He laughed. "Well, as much as one could be friends with an angry cat! She eventually warmed up to me though. When she did, I offered her a job and a place to stay." Popp smiled fondly, a little twinkle of a tear in his eyes. "Best decision I ever made."

"That's quite a tale! Why was she battered?"

"I don't know," Popp admitted. "She was near death, according to doc, and it's a miracle she was even able to walk again! Praise the Divine."

Francesca's smile tightened. "Yes, praise the Divine." Across the counter, she slid the bag of dandelions. "I'll take this."

"Good choice." Popp rang her up.

Transaction made and information gathered, Francesca bid him farewell and headed for the door.

Popp called out to her, "Be sure to come back and see me!"

"Oh, I plan to."

Out on the street this nugget of information rolled around in her brain like a marble in a jug. A new player to their little game. One with a trackable trait. Cloaks could hide hair and eyes that weren't quite human, but a limp would be an easy spot.

Francesca tossed the sack of flowers into the mud and called in her men, heading the charge out of town. By the time they made the rocky trek back to the crossroads, it was close to an hour before sunrise. The rains had stopped and the sky opened her dark arms to the stars. The horses stood shivering in a cluster as the soldiers and their mistress took the time to rest and wait for the arrival of the second team.

Perhaps they'll come back empty handed, she hoped. It would be a travesty to end the hunt now.

The burning sun crawled up from behind the mountains. It brought with it warmth and busy songbirds, however what it didn't bring was Francesca's secondary team. Two hours ticked away and still there was no sign of them. The other men began to get restless.

"Should we send some to Talonwood?" one man asked.

She gave a little pop of her teeth, thinking. If the men she sent were killed in Talon, or along the way, then Tytian and his growing band of misfits would be heading out of town in an instant. She would still be dragging behind, when what she needed was to jump ahead.

One of her soldiers spoke up beside her, pointing a finger eastward, down the highway.

A lone rider was closing in on them, quickly.

Francesca stepped out in front of her small squad, the hell blade sword materializing in her hand, only to crumble away once she could see the banners on the horse's breast collar.

He was from the church.

The young man reined in his sweaty horse, then hopped down. He gave a quick bow, followed by handing her a sealed parchment. "Draven? From Jonhas. He said it's urgent."

The Beacon Sect. She snarled and snatched the paper from his hands. *How dare he think he can just-* She tore past the seal and scanned the page, rage giving way to curiosity.

Draven,
We've uncovered some information about who J'harenmar
is traveling with. Also, I've sent a gift. Check in when you
can. -Jonhas

Francesca stared at the words until the edges of the note began to blacken and curl inwards, the parchment slowly burning down to ash in her grip. She had no love for that council of men, and the fact that any one of them would have the audacity to speak to her directly filled her with raw hatred.

They saw her as a pet in the beginning. Something to be controlled, to be turned loose and then called home at the sound of a whistle from their lips. Not Aolfrun. He treated her with the same level of respect that he held for her maker, proving he was a smarter man than the rest. His Beacons might be the wolves mingling in his flock, but Francesca was the dragon's shadow circling the field. One wrong move and both shepherd and wolves alike would be smelted.

The Beacons had learned their place quickly though. A few of them even wearing their new found respect as scars. Jonhas, however, had always been the least problematic of the group, his loyalty to the High Father being far stronger than his own lust for power. He knew where the best place to be was, and if he couldn't sit the throne himself then he could at least be seated at its right hand. The man also had an impressive array of connections that spanned the entire region. If one needed information on anyone, Jonhas could get it within the week, given his patron had the right connections themself. He never did anything for nothing, every action came with a price tag.

She motioned toward a nearby field, ordering her men to rest. "Take the horses and let them graze. We won't get anywhere on their carcasses."

Her soldiers moved out.

"Will that be all, ma'am?" asked the messenger. There was a cocky sort of way about him, bred from cushy life that was easy to read. Young, good looking, trusted by a Beacon to do his bidding. He had the air of a man who'd been handed so many blessings in life. Who knew he had a bright future ahead of him.

What a pity.

Brandishing that weaponized smile, Francesca flicked her chin toward a swath of forest that cut into the valley. "Actually, come with me." Under the canopy, she caught the smell of still water and ventured deeper into the woods, following her nose until she and the messenger came upon a large, man-made pond left behind by a mining endeavor some generation ago. "Perfect."

The messenger looked around, confused but obedient.

Francesca started unbuckling the shin guards and thigh plates of armor, stacking them each in a neat little pile. "Would you?" she asked him as she dropped the cloak from her collar and slid her hair over her shoulder, giving him access to the clasps on the underside of her spaulders. He didn't hesitate and with skilled hands, unbuckled her remaining armor with ease.

"Talented fingers," she complimented, sly as a fox.

Her intention wasn't lost on him, and his response came back just as coy. "Thank you, ma'am, I practice when I can."

"I bet you do." Down to nothing but her pants and a thin tunic, Francesca stretched her arms above her head, relishing in the freedom of her body.

The messenger continued speaking, beaming with arrogant pride. "I'd hoped to be a squire but Beacon Jonhas has picked me up as his personal steward."

"Did he now?" she asked with fake interest, sliding off her shoes. "How long have you been employed by Jonhas?"

"Just this week. This was my first big task, ma'am. I hope my promptness was *satisfactory*?" There was a cheeky tweak of his lips.

With all the ease of a recoiling snake she stood, and gave him a dreamy sort of look, her lashes suddenly very heavy. "You performed exceptionally well." Her words were met with a confident bounce of his head. All of his prepared self-praise faltered when she took up the hem of her shirt and slid the garment off her body.

He turned his gaze away, although not too quickly. "Should I go wait with the others, ma'am?"

Francesca stepped free of her pants, closing the gap between them. When she reached out and slid her hand under his chin, angling his face towards her, she could feel his racing pulse. "Now why would I bring you all the way out here, just to have you go right back?"

His weak chivalry faded, and he looked her up and down, taking his time. He never asked before running his hands up her sides, cupping the full breasts in his palms while his thumbs rounded her nipples. He never asked before setting his open mouth against her neck, lapping at her skin with an eager greed that turned him sloppy. He never asked if he could have her body.

And she never asked if she could have his heart.

Bone popped and wet meat squelched as she drove her hand into his chest cavity. Her fingers busted through his air sack, gripping around the fluttering heart. He rasped in a breath as shock took his senses. Recoiling, he tried to pry her off of him, but she was affixed. In her eyes he finally noticed the vertical pupils, outlined in a faint orange and contracting into thin slits. Blood started to seep past his lips.

"Ah," she whispered, feral delight carved into her face, changing her beauty into something inhuman. "You had so much hope. And I have taken it from you."

Twitching, his system was falling into chaos as Francesca pulled his heart through his shattered sternum. He was dead before he hit the ground.

Heart in hand, she moved to the pond bank, and using the blood from the inner chambers of the thrifted organ, she painted symbols down her arms, across her clavicle and in the center of her forehead. Under her breath she spoke a fetid language, giving life to each drawn character. The final word slipped from her tongue, and she tapped two fingers to the symbol between her brows. From the waist down her body grew rigid, anchoring her feet to the ground. Her abdomen slumped backward, exposing her open eyes to the sky, allowing the sun to witness her emptying flesh.

There was a rush in her vision as she traveled across the dread astral, flying faster than a falcon over the rooftops of Savhignos. Where trees and stagnant water once was, there was now a study. The Beacon was sitting at his desk, signing papers with a golden tipped quill, unaware of the specter that watched him from an outside plane.

"Jonhas," she spoke, her disembodied voice causing him to sit up abruptly.

Smoothing his robes, the Beacon regained his composure with nervous hands. "Francesca. I'm assuming my errand boy found you?"

"Yes. He delivered your message not too long ago."

"Good. Dare I ask, where is the boy?"

"He's nearby. Congealing."

Jonhas grinned. "I figured as much. Well, I hope you enjoy him. He wasn't cheap."

"You said you had information?"

"Ah, yes." He wagged the quill and stepped around the desk, moving to an armchair in front of his fireplace. From the seat he picked up a stack of papers. "The man who broke into the church, the redhead. I have a name, and a little history." He shuffled the parchment until he found the page he wanted. "His name is Callum. No surname, no known aliases. My associate who runs the orphanage, Bruznik, says he grew up there. Showed an affinity for picking pockets and once he aged out of the home, he fell in with The Den, a thief syndicate out of Crown's Cross. Chances are, he was probably here on their orders."

"For what?"

Jonhas shook his head. "Trinkets, it would seem. We did a catalog of the store room. The only things missing were a damaged holy item, and a decades old scroll."

"What did it contain?"

"It was a deed, for a homestead foreclosure." He huffed a wheeze of air. "I'd love to be there when he breaks the seal and realizes all he got was a piece of bureaucratic garbage."

"Does he have any connection to Tytian?"

"Not that I am aware of. Seems he simply pieced together a theory from Trebor running his mouth during the meeting."

"They're both traveling with two women. One is a blonde, who was with them at a tavern outside of the city. She was spotted with them again, just the day before last. The other they picked up while in Rodenburg. Seems she knows the thief."

"What can you tell me about that one?" asked Jonhas.

"Her employer said that she came into town on death's door. Brunette, and walks with a limp."

"Hmm," Jonhas mulled over this news. "If she knows this Callum fellow then maybe she's native to Savhignos. I'll go speak with Bruznik again, see what he knows. That man is a well of social knowledge, especially with the gutter rats." Back at his desk, he contemplated their situation over a cup of hot tea. "Where are they going? Could J'harenmar just be running away?"

"Tytian is a fool, but he isn't a coward. He isn't running. They're planning something."

Jonhas sighed into the steam clouds. "This needs to be over with. You have my permission to do whatever it takes. Raze the entire countryside if you must, just handle this."

Born in an instant was a severe pressure inside his nose, the meat hot and begging to pop. Porcelain shattered at his feet, the cup abandoned in favor of pawing at his face.

Francesca's cold voice broke through in a hiss. "I don't need your permission to do a fucking thing."

Jonhas stammered, his nose beginning to bleed. "Please, I spoke out of line. My sincerest apology."

The pressure increased dramatically, then faded away, just as Francesca did.

Her eyes rolled over in their sockets and she blinked in the sunlight, returned to the forest. The pond was still as glass. No birds stirred in the trees, no breeze swept the grassy bank. It was as though the world had stopped just for her.

The messenger boy's body laid in wait, but he was still a little too fresh. With a lazy flick of her wrist, she discarded his heart over her shoulder and waded out into the pond. The water around her started to steam and then roll over itself, boiling around her body like a kettle-bound stew. With one push of channeled power, she sent a ripple through the pond. Fish, turtles and snakes started to bob to the roiling surface, cooked in an instant. Francesca swam through the bodies, washing the bloody markings from her skin.

She thought of Tytian and his collected hoard, dreaming of all the ways she would peel them from their bones.

TWELVE

T alonwood's residents seemed to all rise and work as one once the sun was visible on the horizon. Shop keeps steadily unpacked their wares and hung them out for display, butchers began to slice the day's ration of meats, and the bar owner started his preparations for the usual crowd to flood in through his doors that coming evening. He and the maids worked tirelessly to clean and organize the place throughout the morning, sweeping floors and wiping down table tops. A few regulars had shuffled in as soon as the door was unlocked. They took up their usual stools, bowed their heads and drowned their sorrows in a freshly poured drink.

Irregular to this depressive scene was a man in armor, strolling through the door. Against his back sat a warhammer, polished to perfection, embossed with a grinning mask. Outside in the yard stood a dozen more men in identical dress, each one spaced evenly from the next, hands clasped behind their backs.

The barman looked up from his duties, set on edge by this unfamiliar, domineering patron. "Can I help you?"

"You can help the High Father." Authority clung to him like grease. "I'm looking for a trio. Outlaws, from Savhignos."

Before the keep could answer, another voice cut in from a customer nearby, who stroked his thumb over the bruises on his neck. "One of those men have blood colored hair? And a blonde little bitch with him?"

"You've seen them?"

"Yeah, they were here. Last night."

The armored man tightened with anticipation. "Are they still in town?"

"Should be," burped the battered drunk. "Haven't seen 'em leave, and I've been watchin' too." He flashed a dagger on his side. "Got a little parting gift for them."

Across town Aldan readied a one-horse wagon, loading it down with general supplies and anything else they may need along the way. Callum suggested just bringing the horse, citing how much slower they would be with the burden of a wagon. Aldan countered with how long of a journey they had ahead of them, and how both supplies and taverns would be far and few in between some nights. They would need supplies at the ready, or this half-cocked plan of theirs could crumble.

"If the church is on our ass, then we shouldn't even bother with cities at all," Aldan advised.

Callum, used to his comforts, didn't care for the thought. "You know how much I hate camping."

Chuckling, Aldan hefted a sack into the waiting cart. "You'll hate being at the mercy of the Beacon Sect even more. We all have to make sacrifices."

To this, Callum groaned.

Crates of dry goods and medicinals were stored beneath the bench seats, while furs and extra blankets were in a trunk strapped under the tail end of the wagon. Fenella worked with Shara to ensure their rations were balanced, while Tytian and Six readied the other horses for travel. When the last saddle was cinched, a skinny man came jogging into the yard, throwing a look over his shoulder.

"Aldan," he said between panted breaths. "There're soldiers in town. Say they're looking for some folks matchin' your friends' descriptions."

Tytian instantly grew tense. "Is there a woman with them? Tall, with copper colored hair?"

"I didn't see a woman. Just about a dozen men or so, all in dark colors, and not a banner among them. But at the inn one of them flashed a pin under his collar. He's a Beacon Sect sentry."

"Oh that's perfect," chimed Callum. It was only midday and already he was exasperated.

The man gave a pleading look. "Aldan, they're turning the streets upside down. People are scared."

"Can we just leave?" asked Fenella of the others. "They don't even know we're here."

He shook his head. "They know you're here. Brant said he heard that some fellow at the bar gave you up."

Aldan looked over the group, a questioning look on his face.

Callum turned his nose up to the sky, closing his eyes in agitation. "I'm taking bets now. Who thinks it was our tiny peckered friend from last night? Show of hands."

Pulling her axes from the saddle bag, Six removed her coat and tossed it over Sunrise's saddle, heading across the yard for the gate.

With a grimace, well-educated on the way she operates, Callum called out to her. "Maybe we should just haul ass?"

"I don't like being hunted," she snarled over her shoulder, disappearing around the bend.

"Wait, are we fighting?" asked Fenella, her stomach doing flips.

"We are, you're not." Aldan rushed up the porch and into his home, reappearing soon after equipped with a bow and full quiver. In his left hand he carried a sword, which he tossed to Callum. Shara followed out behind him, a butcher's knife in her grip.

"Fenella? Stay here with Shara and the kids," advised Aldan. When she started to protest, he put a hand on her shoulder, halting her attempt to follow. "Keep them safe. I'm trusting you with that, alright?"

Despite her disappointment, she gave him a quick nod. "Okay."

Callum gently squeezed her arm. "We'll be right back." With Tytian close behind, all of them were through the gate and jogging up the street towards the center of town.

Aldan caught up with Six and strung his bow. "I don't mean to sound insensitive but, are you up for this?" he questioned gently, watching as she limped along, haggard as an old dog.

She never gave him an answer, just kept her eyes trained ahead, because truth be told she really didn't know. It had been a long time since she'd seen a proper battle and that was against run of the mill bandits, not highly trained soldiers. But she'd kept her body in shape and practiced her combat maneuvers almost every night, tweaking them to fit her limitations. As long as they kept the combat in close quarters, she was confident that she could still fell a foe. Long-range weaponry however could prove lethal, her dodging abilities almost nonexistent.

"Where exactly is this inn?" Tytian asked of the fellow who had come to fetch them.

He pointed to the right. "It's just around this corner."

Six threw a look to Callum beside her. Her eyes never made it past his collar. "You should have stayed at the house."

He grinned a little. "And miss all the fun? I don't think so."

"You don't know how to fight, Callum. You're going to slow us down."

"Give me some credit. Might just surprise you. Dare I say, even make you proud."

"What will surprise me is if you don't get yourself killed," she growled.

The crowds grew thinner as they made their way up the street, folks unsettled by the appearance of the soldiers. Many had closed up their shops and windows, peeking out from behind drawn curtains. When the five of them rounded the corner they came across the pack of sentries exiting the inn, their lead man wiping blood from his hammer head with a cloth. Six's pace picked up and she drew her axes.

"Oi!" she barked at them, and the man snapped his head in their direction.

"Okay, guess a stealthy approach isn't what we're going for," muttered Callum to Aldan, but the smith was no longer beside him. Instead, he had slipped into the sparse crowd, readied bow kept low.

"And who are you?" The man with the bloodied hammer inspected Six as she approached, wearing a shit eating sort of grin. Through the inn doors behind him, a child was crying for a father who would never wake up.

She ignored his question, eyes flitting between each man, counting and calculating. "So few of you. That isn't exactly impressive, I expected more."

The soldier scoffed with amusement at her brazenness, but once he spotted Callum, noting the color of his hair, and then

Tytian who had lowered his hood, he stiffened. "J'harenmar." His voice curdled the ends of the name. "Where's the little blonde bitch? I'd like to give her to Draven alive."

Tytian stepped closer. "Where is Francesca? Why didn't she come herself?"

The armored man sneered. "That's none of your business."

Callum, in a sing-song tone built for taunting, "Why does she send her lessers to do her bidding? Gettin' weak in her old age?"

A cold laugh shook his shoulders, the soldier gesturing with his blood-smattered weapon. "I am going to enjoy forcing my hammer down your throat."

Callum made a face. "Eh, I've had bigger."

"Enough!"

Six agreed, "You're absolutely right," and hurled one of her axes as hard as she could. The blade pierced through the breast-plate of the lead man's armor, making him stagger. It never touched his flesh, but it was an effective distraction from the arrow that whistled past his face. It found its mark with accuracy, lodging deep within the throat of the soldier next to him.

"Why didn't you aim for his head?!" cried Callum.

Six snarled. "I did! I'm just a little rusty."

Unable to control himself, "Hi little rusty, I'm Callum-"

"Shut the hell up!"

The crowd scattered as Callum, Six and Tytian met Draven's group, blades singing their war songs in clash. Aldan knocked another arrow and let it fly into the fray, piercing a soldier's shoulder. As he started to draw again, he noticed three of them step to the back of the pack, each one armed with crossbows.

Panicked, Aldan called out to the others. "Long range!"

Tytian heard his warning and swept through the chaos, using dagger-sharp nails to slash at any exposed limb or face in his path. These men were well outfitted, their armor an aid in keeping all of their vitals shielded while maintaining exceptional mobility. While designed to protect them from a rogue blade, it might as well have been paper compared to Tytian's enhanced speed and the vicious use of his clawed hands. More than once, he managed to rend tender flesh, digging deep into the few open spaces he could find.

His intent was on the ranged soldiers, targeting the one closest, dodging their loosed bolts. With his left hand, Tytian ripped away the horned helm as his right gripped the first man's face, lifting him high into the air, smashing his victim into the cobblestone street until the skull cave. Another bolt was fired, close range, lodging itself into his rib cage. The pain was nothing more than a pin prick in the demon blood that vibrated his veins. Reaching around, Tytian retrieved the bolt, brandished it like a blade, and drove it through the archer's padded sternum.

Nearby, Callum parried a blow, laughing in the face of his attacker. "How are you so slow?" The broadsword cleaved the air in song as it swung toward his face. "Are you someone's overly pampered cousin that they had to let on the team so your mother wouldn't pitch a fit?" The man yelled, frustrated at the quick feet and even quicker tongue Callum possessed. "Ooooh, you are," he teased. "Well damn, buddy, now I just feel bad." Gracefully, he danced away from another swing.

Six ripped one axe from the crown of a fallen soldier's head while retrieving the other from where it laid in the street. Blood smattered her face, and her right knee was throbbing, making the move from one opponent to another messy. At her back Aldan had given her as much aid as he could, using arrows to weaken or distract as she hacked the life out of their skin.

Not only was she focused on her own kills, but she also kept a side-eye track of Callum, who was now backed into a vegetable stand. Dumb was luck the only thing keeping a claymore from caving in his face.

"Aldan," she called over her shoulder, "Get Callum!"

"On it!"

Whoosh.

The head of a warhammer skimmed just past her nose, reflex saving her from eating her own teeth. The lead man hefted his weapon, swung it overhead and brought it down again, steel cracking against the street with a thunderclap as she outmaneuvered his strike. Six darted at him, putting herself in close combat, ducking under his next swing to drive an axe spike into his weakened breastplate. She was rewarded with a sudden exhale of air, then a ragged gasp. He began to lose his balance, reaching out for an anchor. His fist curled around her collar, snatching her right into a headbutt. The rim of his helmet struck just above her right brow, and she hissed, staggering backwards with blood running into her eye. He kicked her then, smashing his boot against her hip, sending her down on her bad knee. As he widened his stance to prepare for another swing, Six struck, fast as a viper. She buried the axe blade into his inner thigh where the armor was weakest. A gush of blood poured from the wound; determination working the blade deeper.

"You bitch!" he cried out in a furious roar and faltered in his stance, the injured limb already beginning to quake.

Six found her feet again, parrying to the side as he took a frantic swing. With his arms straight, she hacked into the back of his elbow and twisted it skyward, ripping the bone from its socket. A howl climbed its way up his throat, only to die at the tip of his tongue when the world went white, the spike of her left axe catching under the lip of his helm, ripping it from his head. Next came the other axe, blade first across his face in a vicious uppercut. He fell away, collapsing against the cobblestones. Only one eye had any vision and he started to panic. With a flick of her hand, Six spun an axe around and drove the spike right between his eyes.

When Aldan reached Callum, his shirt was torn and bloodied at the bicep, and he had a bruise beginning to blossom around his eye. Beneath the damage, he wore a feral grin, poking and slashing at the soldiers who had him perched on top of the cabbage cart.

"Ah, Aldan," he called with merriment. "Come dance with us, will ya? These shit for brains have two left feet!"

Aldan advanced with a leveled shoulder and big hands educated in the art of brawling. Although he was a large man, the smith's movements were studied and smooth; a bull executing a well-aimed gore. As he knocked one man out of his battle stance, he twisted the claymore from his grip, using the base of the blade to cut open his exposed throat.

Callum jumped backwards, avoiding the swing of a mace and then took a jab towards his attacker's shoulder. The soldier raised his own weapon in defense, giving Callum the chance to grab hold of his wrist and, with all of his strength, jerk him off of his feet into the cart. The stand toppled, sending them both to the street with a herd of rolling cabbages. Twisting, Callum managed to drag himself out of the wreckage, kicking at the man who held fast to his leg.

A bellow rang deep inside his skull as Aldan brought down the won claymore against the soldier's neck, cleaving head from shoulders. Callum was sprayed with hot blood, the grip on his calf falling slack.

He wiped a hand down his face. "Gross."

Aldan retrieved Callum's lost weapon and tossed it into his lap. "You have to kill them, or they'll kill you."

"Yeah, yeah."

On his feet, Callum took a brief pause to check in with the others. Six was prying a war axe from a dead man's throat. Tytian had one hand pierced through the rib cage of the last archer, his other hand forcing the man's jaw upward until there came a wet *pop.* When his limbs started to twitch, Tytian dropped him in a heap on the ground.

All around them lay broken bodies, the smell of blood hanging thick in the air. No moans came from the soldiers, each one of them as silent as the graves they would never fill. And for some time not a word came from the on-lookers who had stayed to watch the battle.

The group slowly came together, covered in red splatters and dust. Callum was relieved to see that everyone only had minor injuries. "Well," he said with an upbeat tone. "That's one way to solve a problem."

Among the faces was the man who had sold them out, blood-shot eyes wide with fear. Six spotted him, gaping in disbelief at the carnage in the street. In his trembling grip was his dagger, small and ineffective. Six cleared herself a path through the locals, who scuttled away, leaving the backstabber exposed. He raised his hands, stammering some weak apology that did him no good. With vicious force, Six swung her axe upward, the blade catching right at the top of his belt and slicing a path up to his crown. He screeched and stumbled away, hands flying up to his face, his dagger clattering about his boot heel. From groin to brow there was a deep-set laceration. The tip of his nose, his lips and the cleft of his chin split open. It wasn't a life ending wound, but it was certainly a disfiguring one. A reminder of his heavy mistake.

Not a soul came to his aid.

People began to murmur, and suddenly Six was aware of how many eyes were on them.

"Burn the bodies," she advised with a raised voice. "Don't scavenge them, not even a single saph from their pockets. Wash the cobblestones clean. What happened here, needs to stay here... for all of your sake. These men, they were not good men, and they deserve no protection from you."

A woman of middle years stepped out from the herd. "We won't tell a soul," she promised them, looking around at her fellow townsmen. "Talonwood has never been an ally to the Beacon Sect. Plus, Aldan is a pillar of our community. If he sides with you, so do we." There was a wave of nods and spoken agreements flowing through the crowd. Slowly, people started to band together and clean away the dead in the street.

Aldan looked around until he spotted the willowy man who'd come to fetch them. He motioned him over. "Bertie, can you do me a favor?"

"Anything. What do you need?"

"I need you to take Shara and the kids to her sister's place over in Vinerock. I hate to ask but-"

The old man held up a hand. "I'd be happy to. Tell them to pack and we'll head out tonight."

"Thanks, Bert."

Tytian slid up beside Aldan, glancing around. "I think now might be a good time for us to leave."

He nodded in agreement and all four of them headed back to the house.

Fenella sat at the kitchen table, nervously chewing at her thumbnail. They had been gone for some time and a sinking feeling had settled in the back of her head, but she tried to hold on to hope. *They're fine*, she repeated over and over again. *They have to be.*

On the porch there came the sound of heavy footfalls and then a knock at the door. Shara stood ready, butcher knife in hand. When she heard Aldan's voice call out, she had to catch her breath. With haste, she lifted the oak bar and flung open the door, ushering in the group.

Fenella rushed around the table, relieved to see all four of them had returned. That relief was short-lived when she saw their injuries. "You're hurt."

Shara sighed and went to the sink. "I'll prepare some needles, you'll need stitches-"

"Afraid there isn't time for that," Callum told her gently. "We need to leave. Now, before anymore show up."

Aldan stepped up to his wife, placing his hands on her shoulders. "Bertie is coming by tonight to take you and the children over to Vinerock. I don't want you staying here while I'm gone."

Shara's lips trembled, more so with anger than fear. "I hate it when you leave."

His big hands came up to rest on her face and he kissed her deeply. "I always come back, don't I?"

"You better." Shara pressed her forehead to his.

Aldan said his goodbyes to the children on the porch. The twins, being too young to understand, hugged their father before heading back inside to gather their toys. It was Genny who stared at him from under a furrowed brow, her lips set in a pout.

"But I don't want you to go."

"I'm afraid that I have to. I'll be back before you know it. And I'll bring you a present," he promised her, but she wasn't satisfied with that answer.

"One present isn't going to cut it," she scowled.

Aldan laughed. "Are you extorting your old man?"

She tried to hide a smile. "Uncle Callum said it's called '*haggling*'."

Aldan looked over his shoulder at Callum, who was giving Genny an enthusiastic thumbs up. "Oh, did he? Well, I suppose I could bring you a whole MOUNTAIN OF PRESENTS." He then snatched her up and swung her around, causing her to giggle in delight. When he hugged her, Genny hugged him back, snuggling her face into his hair.

"I'll miss you daddy."

There was a stab in his chest, and he tried desperately to keep his voice even. "I'll miss you too."

Shara covered her face with her hand to hide her tears. Aldan reached out and pulled her into the hug as well and together they shared one last farewell. Reluctantly, he handed Genny over to his wife and fled the porch to the waiting wagon.

As quickly as possible they were all mounted and headed for the gate. Clusters of onlookers made way for them without a word, this once bubbling hub now silent as a corpse. When they reached the inn, all of the bodies were gone, however the street was still sticky with blood.

Fenella looked at the scene in awe, suppressing the chill that shook her spine.

THIRTEEN

When Aldan steered his cart off of the road and down a barely there path that cut across the valley, Callum halted and raised an eyebrow, gesturing broadly towards the crossroads in the west.

"Uhh, Aldan? The road goes this way.?"

"Uhh, Callum? Weren't we just attacked by mercenaries? Who followed you from the main road? Whose murderous demon leader is still out there somewhere?" He asked sarcastically over his shoulder.

Callum's mouth hung a gape for a moment as he tried to rally a retort, then conceded. "Yeah, okay."

Aldan was victorious. "We'll cut through the trapper's pass. Gonna warn you though, it can get a bit rough."

"I actually don't mind it rough." Callum smirked, finding his own joke hilarious.

Tytian glared at him from beneath his hood. "How has no one murdered you yet?"

"That one, murdered? Ha!" Aldan laughed. "Callum is a damn cat. He's got nine lives, if not more." He then jabbed a thumb at himself. "It's the rest of us that nearly die when we throw in with him."

"What!?" cawed Callum. "That's a bit over dramatic, don't you think?"

Turning to face them, Aldan raised his brow. "I was nearly eaten by cannibals on that last venture. CANNIBALS, Callum. Still have the scars from all the fork holes they poked into me!"

Callum's face pinched and he waved a hand in front of him, trying to downplay the severity of the tale. "They weren't- well... yeah okay, they were cannibals. But, you got paid, didn't you?"

"Cannibals."

"You got paid-"

"CANN-IB-ALS."

He threw his arms in the air. "How the hell was I supposed to know they were cannibalistic?"

Aldan gaped at him. "The artifact we were stealing was made from human flesh. It literally had teeth marks in it!"

Back and forth they bickered, making Fenella's sides hurt with laughter on more than one occasion. Even Tytian was mildly entertained. Trailing behind, Six kept her distance, surveying their surroundings. Fenella felt as though they were the pups and Six was their den mother, on high alert for eagles and bears while they romped in the sun without a care. She had been silent since leaving Talonwood and Fenella wondered if maybe she was more injured than everyone thought. No one's wounds had been addressed, putting as much space between themselves and the bloodbath they'd left behind. Not all was lost, as Callum's arm had ceased its bleeding and Tytian was already healed.

Fenella dropped back to ride beside Six. "See anything out there?"

She shook her head. "Nothing so far."

"Maybe we got lucky and that was the only group of them in the area." She studied the other woman for a moment, noting the dried blood and dirt smears on her face. She reached out and swept back Six's hair, grimacing at the nasty cut above her eye. "We should stop soon. I think you all need a good clean up."

Six flashed her an appreciative smile. "We should save the medical supplies for when things get worse."

"It's going to get worse?"

Six was staring at Callum's back when she whispered, "It always does." There was a shift, her attention turning to Fenella. "You can go home at any time, you know that, right? If this gets to be too much there's no shame in saving yourself and going back to your life. I know how infectious Callum and his crusades can be, but if you ever want to walk away, you are free to. Leave the suicide missions to those of us who are old hands at nearly getting ourselves killed."

"You think this is a suicide mission." Fenella was disheartened, and it wasn't because she believed her. It was the pain she could see on her face.

"I think we're getting ourselves into something that's over our heads," Six admitted. "We've made powerful enemies before, but this is different, and I'm not sure you can challenge someone like the High Father and come out unscathed."

"If you think we're all going to die, then why did you come with us?" Fenella kept her tone easy.

"Because Callum was going after the others, and I wanted to make sure that if things got hairy and they were walking into a pitfall, I could be there to pull them back from the edge. Callum often doesn't see past his own desires, and that can make a slippery road for those who follow him."

Fenella cast her eyes ahead to the men. "You sound as though you hate him."

For a moment, Six considered her next words. It was clear what she chose to speak wasn't the first thing on her tongue. "I just... *know* him. I know his drive, and his ideals. And I know how sometimes he thinks what he's doing is harmless, when in fact it's detrimental. The man can barely wield a sword and yet, somehow, he's the most dangerous person I know."

With the way she was describing him, one would think that Callum was some sort of criminal mastermind, hell bent on chaos and glory. Fenella's intuition told her a completely different story. And it wasn't his good looks or his charm blinding her to his truth. She wasn't one to be so easily swayed by a nice smile. It was the look in his eye when all was quiet, and he thought no one was watching him. Beneath the confidence and quip there was a haunted man who was searching for something, and potentially laying his name in the history books as the savior of mankind wasn't it. She felt deep in her heart of hearts that Callum truly was trying to do what he thought was right.

"Perhaps he's changed," Fenella offered carefully. "It's been a while. Maybe he's no longer the man you once knew." And then very carefully, "Won't know unless you talk to him."

Fenella bumped Apple into a trot and caught up with the others, leaving Six with her advice, praying to the Divine that she didn't just make things worse.

The trapper's trail they followed proved Aldan right, and after they crossed the field and made it into the forest, the worn road started to become a little trickier to navigate. It was wide enough for the cart and horses, but just barely. Grasses had grown up in the center and the bushes hung their branches over the path, causing most of them to either have to duck or swat leaves from their face. The sunlight through the thick foliage speckled the pathway and birds chirped in chorus all around them. Even though it wasn't the most comfortable road to take, it certainly proved to be far prettier than the barren expanse of the main highway.

Callum took in a deep breath through his nose. "Mmm, the honeysuckle is blooming."

"Aye," chimed Aldan. "That'll make for good hunting in these hills."

"What's our next destination?" asked Tytian.

"Riverport!" Callum had a gleam in his eye. "Going to pick up our man with the magic touch."

Aldan grinned. "I haven't spoken to Duncan in two years. It'll be good to see him. Although, I'm not sure he'll tag along with us this time, Callum."

"Why wouldn't he?"

"Because he's an old man now, that's why. He's what, seventy six? Seventy seven? This isn't just a quick little smash and grab in Crown's Cross."

"True," Callum agreed. "But, if he can't come with us then he'll at least be able to provide some sort of aid, whether that be literal fire power or information. I'm hoping he'll know a little something about these demon slabs."

Behind him, Fenella could barely contain her excitement. "I can't believe I'm going to meet a mage. What's he like?"

Fondly, Callum and Aldan took turns building Duncan's story. From the time the two of them met him during a job, to some of their more harrowing adventures. Every mission with Duncan, there wasn't a single soul lost, his magic used more for mischief and distraction rather than murder. That's what they had Six for.

"Now, don't let the sweet old man act fool you," Callum advised. "He's powerful. I've met a few other magic tuners in my time, and none compare to Dunc."

"I can't wait to meet him," said Fenella with a smile.

"You're gonna love him. He's far better company than the rest of us."

Aldan laughed in agreement. "No arguing with that."

Beneath the high sun, the warm morning turned into a sweltering afternoon. Sweat slicked the horse's necks and beaded across their rider's brows. A unanimous decision was made to seek shelter in the next patch of shade, under the thick foliage of an oak grove. They took the opportunity to pass around a lunch of dry goods, and Fenella insisted on dressing wounds.

"I hink I'll eed shum shtitshes," Callum said with a wad of cheese in his mouth. When he removed his shirt, sure enough, he was right. He had taken a mace strike to his bicep and while it wasn't too terribly deep, the lacerations were open and long. Fenella hissed at the sight of it and began to rummage through the boxes in the cart while Callum poured some water on the wound.

Six approached with Sunrise, tying him off to the cart. Aldan tapped her on the shoulder and when she turned, he nodded towards her brow, then cupped her chin in his large hand and examined the injury.

"Hey Fenella?"

"Yeah?" she asked as she hopped off of the cart, her arms loaded with bandages and a small tin sewing kit.

"Put a stitch or two in this one."

Six rolled her eyes. "It's just a small cut, Aldan. Don't worry with it."

"Oh really?" He poked it with his thumb and she recoiled. "Yeah, hurt didn't it? That's because I can see bone, hard ass. Get it taken care of. Won't have you dragging us down because it got infected and you're filled with fever."

Six relented. "Fine."

Fenella patted the back of the cart next to where Callum sat, a coy little grin on her face. "Step right up to my hospital, miss. Nurse?" She addressed Tytian with haughtiness, who simply squinted his eyes in return. "Disinfect that patient's wound. If she fights you, use brute force. She can't punch you if she's unconscious!"

Aldan's laugh echoed around them and he gave her shoulders a squeeze as he passed by her. "I like you."

Fenella used a dark liquor to clean up Callum's arm and then passed the bottle to Tytian, who soaked the corner of a rag and began dabbing at Six's brow. His fingers were gentle, turning her chin up for better access to the cut.

"I'll be quick."

She grimaced at the sting.

Once the tattered bicep was drawn back together in neat little seams, Fenella put three stitches in Six's head, trying to take extra care not to add to the array of small scars that were already faded across her face. "If it doesn't get infected, that should heal up nicely," she told her as she snipped the end of the final horsehair suture.

Callum gingerly stretched his bandaged arm, taking a long sniff of his armpit. "When we get to Riverport, I am jumping head first into a wash tub. Pretty sure you can smell me from Savhignos." He grinned at Tytian. "Your friend Draven doesn't have scent hounds does she? They'd have me treed in no time."

Tytian shook his head. "She doesn't need hounds. She can do that on her own."

Callum nodded in agreement. "Probably, because I am rank."

"No, I mean she has a heightened sense of smell. She could pick out someone's scent from a whole crowd of people, and if she's been anywhere that we have, she'll already have your scent stored to her memory."

Callum and the others stared at him. "Huh?"

Tytian saw their horror. "Just another part of the Khaladhuun gift."

Fenella looked thoughtful. "Can you smell us like that?"

He nodded after a brief pause.

"Oh man. I do not envy you right now." Callum's grimace was apologetic.

"Wait, I want to know what humans smell like," inquired Fenella, curious and eager to learn.

"Everyone smells different," Tytian explained. "Even your blood won't smell like someone else's. But the scent of your skin or your hair or your clothing, that's what's trackable. Each person's personal aroma is made up of things in their day to day surroundings."

"So you just smell us like, all of the time." Callum nodded. "That's not the least bit unsettling."

"I find it fascinating!" admitted Fenella, countering his sarcasm. "What do I smell like?" she asked with anticipation, but then dimmed. "Oh no, do I smell bad?"

Six cut into the conversation, like a machete through a stick of butter. "Is this something we should be worried about? Can that woman follow us all over the country?"

Tytian shook his head. "No, it's not that strong. Just something to keep in mind that if you're ever in close quarters with her, she'll be able to sniff you out."

This knowledge made Six uneasy. She'd never been one for impossible odds, and things were quickly stacking against them. A man was far easier to avoid or kill compared to the monster Francesca Draven was shaping up to be.

All around her, the forest suddenly had eyes, and Six shivered.

Once their lunch was eaten and the horses had been watered, they started on, the trail carrying them up into the mountains. This haggard, off the map path would take them the long way around to Riverport, but it was safer, especially with a guide. Aldan knew these woods like he knew his own home. In places where the trail seemed to just disappear, he would guide them through the entangled brush and wind up back on track without a single hiccup. They maneuvered through the forest for most of the afternoon until the trees opened to a quaint clearing, a single fallen tree at its heart.

Aldan stopped the cart horse in a bed of wildflowers, and climbed from his seat into the back, fishing out his bow and quiver.

Callum was tense, bunched tightly as an offended cat in the saddle. "What's wrong?"

He slid his quiver over his head. "Nothing, this is where we're making camp tonight."

"It's still a few hours before sundown?"

"Which gives me a few hours to hunt us up some fresh meat, and to rest the horses. Look at them. This isn't the sort of terrain they're used to. All of these long pull hills have them exhausted."

Callum patted Red's sweaty shoulder. "I know how you feel, pal. My ass hurts too." The horse gave a snort.

Quiet as a field mouse, Aldan disappeared into the forest, dissolving into the emerald shadows. The rest untacked their mounts and strapped hobbles to their ankles, the horses happily dropping their head in the grass. After that they set up bed rolls and stripped a few branches from the dead tree. The remnants of a stone ring campfire were discovered by Fenella. She ripped free the stray weeds, then Six helped her build a flame.

Callum sat down on the back of the cart, gently massaging his battered arm. He watched as Six and Fenella chatted back and forth about something he couldn't quite hear. Fenella nodded enthusiastically and jogged his way, while Six took her axes from their holsters. She threw her riding cloak in the back of the cart, then rummaged through her pack until she found something to tie back her hair.

Callum leaned over on his good elbow. "Whatcha doin'?"

Her fingers wrapped and cinched the velvet ribbon with precision. "Six is going to teach me some moves."

He gave her a toothy, lupine grin. "Ya know, I could-" but she cut him off, holding a finger up to his face.

"If you say that you could show me some moves, I'm going to poison your food." A jovial threat, but it ensured his surrender, and Fenella walked back to Six with a bit more swing in her step.

At the cart, Tytian joined Callum with crossed arms. They watched the women start their lesson Six instructed Fenella on how to stand first and judging by her hand gestures, explained how to balance her weight throughout her legs. Then, she put an axe in her hand. Six demonstrated different strikes, slowly so her student could mimic the motions. Fenella was shaky at first, but with a little tweaking, she started to add more confidence to her movements. They worked through a slow strike and parry dance, Six stopping her every so often to lift or lower her elbow or give a slight turn to her wrist. Back and forth they practiced various moves, and Callum could tell that Fenella was getting ahead of herself, wanting to try more and more intense maneuvers. There was a quick little exchange of words, a nod from Fenella and then a shrug from Six.

Callum's back straightened. "Uh oh."

The pair parted a few steps and took up a battle stance. After a deep breath, Fenella advanced on Six, axe swinging with effort in front of her. Steel bit steel, and with a flick of her wrist Six had torn the other woman's weapon clean out of her hand. Fenella stared at her in shock for a moment and then laughed. She retrieved the axe and started again.

"Fenella's tenacious, I'll give her that," remarked Tytian, amused. He started studying Six. How she observed her opponent and moved herself through footwork with precision. Even with her injury, she found ways to compensate, driven by her limitations to work faster, strike harder, think steps ahead.

"Six," he said to Callum, "She's impressive."

"Always has been, the showoff."

There was something he'd been wanting to ask, that seemed best brought up when the hostile pair were separate. "Back in Rodenburg, you called her Lucia."

Callum glanced at him and nodded. "Yeah, it's her name. Not a lot of folks know that though. She's gone by Six since we were kids."

"Why 'Six'?"

Nostalgia tweaked the corners of his mouth. "After her old man died, she got signed over to the orphanage. The dean, Bruznik, is a callous old shit bird and the ink wasn't even dry on her papers before he put her to work. He sent her out, alone, to collect donation boxes he had at different shops. She had only managed to empty one before three older boys cornered her in an alley and tried to take it from her. I had been slinking around on a roof top when I spotted them. And she was a tiny thing. Those boys had her backed into a corner. When one of them reached for the purse, she grabbed up an empty vegetable tray and smacked the shit out of that kid." Callum laughed at the memory. "She then lunged at the rest of them, purse completely forgotten, her fingers curled into fists and her teeth bared. She punched and kicked and bit and head butted those little assholes until they were black and blue. They might as well have thrown water on a cat. Once they had been thoroughly flogged they ran off, little Lucia standing victorious. I slid down a gutter and she nearly jumped me too, but I talked my way around it. *They didn't last six seconds,*

I told her. *Think that's what I'll call you. C'mon little Six, let's go collect the rest.*"

"And thus began your friendship," concluded Tytian.

Callum chuckled, scratching at the budding stubble along his jaw. "I don't know why but when I saw her, I knew we would be thick as thieves."

Tytian turned to him then, a firm set to his gaze. "What happened between you two? What was so bad that you went from childhood friends to her barely even looking at you?"

A quick flash of bile burned the back of his throat, and Callum dropped his eyes down to the ground. "I just, uh... messed up. I messed up pretty badly and Six paid the price." Memory laid fat snowflakes against his skin, filled his nose with the smell of blood, burned his lungs with frigid air.

"Do you love her?" Tytian asked.

Callum's eyes fluttered and he rubbed the bridge of his nose where a pressure started to build. "Of course I love her."

"No, I mean do you *love* her?"

"No, no not like that. She always deserved someone much better than someone like me." He watched her as she ducked and swerved, showing Fenella how to execute a proper block. "I don't know how to explain it. Six just feels like she's the other half of me."

"The other half of you that wants to put an axe in your face," quipped Tytian.

Callum cracked a grin. "Given the day, that's both halves, bud."

"You should make amends."

"Not so sure she wants that," Callum muttered.

"If she truly didn't, then she wouldn't have come." Tytian moved off to the fire pit, leaving his words to saturate Callum's mind like a wet blanket.

It was a half hour before sundown when Aldan returned, a couple of fat rabbits and three squirrels laid over his back. "Let's get to skinnin'!"

Sprawled out in the grass, legs and arms like jelly after the sparring lesson, Fenella groaned. "Someone help me up, please."

Callum gripped her wrist and got her to her feet, only to catch her when she crumbled.

"Hey, easy there noodle knees."

She grimaced at her sore joints. "I'm going to be so sore tomorrow."

"Yeah, and it's a long ride," he teased.

Another long groan propelled Fenella into action. With Callum's help, she pulled an iron cooking pot from the wagon and buried it in the fire coals. Carrots, celery, onions and small, red potatoes were finely chopped into the pot when the water started to roll. Shara had been kind enough to let her raid the spice cabinet and Fenella unwrapped her bundles of herbs with care. A few sprigs of thyme, a helping of salt and a sprinkle of red pepper just to give it a little warmth. She was stirring it all together when Tytian brought over the first cuts of meat.

Simmering, the camp stew radiated a flavorful smell, luring in the group. Everyone sat down around the fire and stretched their legs. Nearby, the horses stood together quietly, dozing in and out of slumber. It was peaceful, under the waking stars, and in some sort of unspoken unity they all knew that nights like this were going to be rare in the coming weeks.

The meadow had been taken by the night when Fenella announced the stew ready. She passed around bowls and stiff bread rolls from the grocer at Rodenburg. It was a meager meal by Fenella's standards, but the others ate with gumption, reminding her that simplicity wasn't always a bad thing.

Callum savored a bite of broth-soaked bread. "This is delicious." He then shook his spoon at Fenella. "See, this is why we keep you."

"And here I was thinking it was due to my quick wits."

"Your wits are average at best, but this... slightly above. Good job."

She lowered the spoon from her mouth, face pinched in a glare. "Average at best, huh?"

Aldan looked over his utensil with dark intent, then at Callum. "I've never gutted a man with a spoon but I imagine it wouldn't be that hard."

"A soup spoon might take a while. You'd need a thin edged sugar spoon. Cuts right through." Tytian's tone was very matter of fact, which acquired him some strange looks.

"You killed a man with a spoon?" Callum inquired.

"It didn't kill him. It just maimed him."

When Tytian didn't elaborate further, Fenella rolled her hand in the air, indicating he should continue. "Well, go on."

"It isn't some epic story," he explained. "There was a young man and his family at our house for a dinner party, and he said something rude to my sister, so I stabbed him in the arm with a spoon."

All of Fenella's former amusement faded. "You have a sister?"

"I had two."

"Are they still...?" Fenella stopped short, not wanting to pry too deeply.

"Alive? No." Tytian pushed the contents of his food around in the bowl, suddenly no longer hungry. "Francesca was very thorough."

Fenella stared at him from across the flames, the waves of heat distorting her look of heartache. "I'm so sorry, Tytian."

"So am I."

Although she hadn't said a word, Tytian could feel Six's attention on him, but he couldn't bring himself to look her way.

After a pause Callum spoke up, "Well, I'm sad now. Someone pass me more bread."

Tytian handed off his untouched dinner and left the circle. By the time he reached the wagon, his chest was so tight he could barely draw breath. His heart felt like a stone, weighing him down, drowning him inside his own head. Gripping at his shirt, trying to catch his panicked breath, Tytian's fingers slipped past the fabric, dragging a touch over the scar left behind by Francesca's blade. He used it to claw his way back to shore, settling his thoughts that swallowed him so quickly. The smell of ash faded away to the smell of forest air, and the screams of his family were replaced by the gentle conversation of strangers nearby.

When he looked their way, one of them was standing just outside the edge of the firelight, facing him. Arms crossed, weight shifted to the left. She kept watch while he fought the plunge, and oddly enough, he felt better knowing she was there.

FOURTEEN

Curled against the chilly air in their bedrolls, camp was all quiet. The fire had burned down to embers, bugs had ceased their trilling songs, and the nightbirds had finally gone to roost. Just before sunrise their world, for a singular moment, was at peace.

"Tytian..." Warm fingers spread round his face, the palm pressed into his teeth. "I found you."

Violent, orange light erupted beneath his lids, heat scorching the skin from his bones. He rose up from the ground, sucking in the crisp air with a gasp. All around him, the others were still sleeping, undisturbed. The nightmare faded once his brain realized it was safe, out in the meadow, under a soft fold of bedroll, but his skin could still feel the ghost of Francesca's grip.

A shiver rolled over him, and Tytian knew that sleep wouldn't come again.

Without waking anyone else, he peeled himself from the bedroll and bundled it neatly, storing it in the wagon. His heart was still racing, and he stroked the scar on his breast, while deciding on what needed to be done.

Through Fenella's pack he rummaged until he found her little dagger. Palming it, he waded out into the dew-slick field, to where the horses gathered in a protective herd. The animals were content and calm, heads drooping while they dosed in and out of slumber. At his approach, Outstrider raised her head and nickered gently. Tytian stroked a hand down her face, comforted by the contact.

"Good morning, pretty girl," he said, gently.

"Good morning."

Startled, he turned towards the source of the voice, dagger poised to strike. His shoulders eased their tension when he recognized there was no threat. "I didn't even notice you weren't at camp."

Six stifled her grin. "You should work on those observation skills."

He didn't disagree. "Why are you out here?"

She held up an oval brush and gave it a shake. Tytian then noticed that all of the horses were clean, groomed to polished perfection. They looked like creatures from a fairy tale beneath the last light of the moon. He recalled this behavior when they camped outside of Talonwood, and was beginning to see a pattern.

"Seems you groom the horses whenever you're upset."

Six ran the brush down Sunrise's broad back, flicking away dried sweat and collected dust. "Yeah. Calms me down, clears my head. Plus, cold mornings make me ache. The movement helps." She regarded him over her shoulder. "Why are you out here?"

It occurred to him that he could simply lie. Tell her some bullshit story to keep her pushed away. But he thought of her injury, how she too was branded by something from her past. If anyone would understand what he was feeling it would be her, so he opted for honesty instead.

Hooking a finger into the V of his collar, he pulled the tunic down enough to show Six the vertical, white strip of flesh down his sternum. The dagger flashed as it danced between his fingers. "I'm tired of carrying her signature on my skin."

Gray eyes narrowed when she realized his intention. "You're going to cut it off? That's going to be one hell of a wound to travel with."

Tytian took the blade and made an incision along his forearm, showing her how the skin gathered back together, closing the cut. Only a thin trail of blood remained.

"Oh, right." Six's tone was steady, despite the way her pulse quickened.

Tytian could hear this shift in heart rate, and he started to regret his decision of honesty.

Stuffing the brush into her back pocket, she dusted her hands clean of the horse grime and closed the space between them. "Want some help?"

What? That wasn't what he was expecting. His mouth opened, ready to decline. But instead, he accepted her offer, handing her the dagger pommel first. "Sure. This way."

Further into the clearing were a few dead stumps, dotted in a row like earthly headstones. Tytian picked the shortest one and sat down, removing his shirt. He noted the hole in the flank from the archer back in Talonwood, and wiggled a finger through it. *Should probably ask Fenella for a patch.*

Six leaned around and looked at his back, finding not so much as a bruise on his skin. "Must be strange, not carrying around your stories." She then eased down on the stump in front of him.

"I still have some scars. Ones I had before Khaladhuun." He took her on a brief tour. "There's one on my kneecap, the inside of my left foot and this one-" a faded line across the outside of his right wrist, "Courtesy of a stray harbor cat when I was a boy. I wanted a friend, but it did not."

The tip of the blade was cold when it touched his skin, Six pausing to allow him time enough to rethink what was about to happen. When he didn't protest, she started to cut.

"How old were you when you were, ya know ..." Her eyes flashed up to his, "Gifted."

"Thirteen is the common age."

"Is the Mal Intent required, or was that only the option because you didn't want to be involved?"

Tytian's face pinched a little as she started to make the long, even incision. "Both, actually."

She had to work quickly to avoid his healing process, but the dagger blade was razor sharp. "Why such harsh workings? My father's demon was summoned without his damnation."

"Well, Khaladhuun isn't a run of the mill deal maker." He hissed a little as she drew the last line and started to skin the flesh away with quick, precise strokes. "If you want his attention, you need something loud, and nothing is quite as loud as Mal Intent."

"Why were you chosen?" Her fingers stopped, and Six regarded him with something he read as remorseful. "You don't have to talk about this if you don't want to."

He shook his head, loosening the tight clench of his jaw. "Not talking about it doesn't change it." She resumed cutting. "My family had been loyalists of Khaladhuun for generations. It's how my great grandfather made his riches. He started out just sacrificing people in Khaladhuun's name in exchange for favorable fortune and his son took over for him when he died, and then my mother after that. Leanor J'harenmar's ambitions were greater than just money. She wanted real power, but she didn't meet Khaladhuun's tastes. When she asked him who would, he told her that he'd gift her first born."

"Which was you."

"I rejected his blessing and managed to tear away from the ritual before it was completed. My mother was mortified, offered to sacrifice me in his name, but Khaladhuun forbade her from killing me. Haven't quite figured out why."

"Your mother sounds like a bitch." Six was blunt in her delivery.

Tytian agreed. "She definitely was."

Down to the last bit of flesh, Six had kept a steady hand, the edges of the slowly closing wound precise. "What happened to your mother?"

Tytian admired her handiwork. "She ruptured a vein in child-birth, both her and the baby didn't survive. Which, as grim as it sounds, was a mercy for the boy."

"And your father?"

"My mother never took a husband. All of her children were conceived at... *ceremonies*."

Immediately, Six picked up his meaning. "Orgies."

"Please don't tell Callum."

Six made a locking motion over her lips, then asked about Francesca.

"Her parents were Carmine Priests within Khaladhuun's church." His skin felt fevered. "They were close with my mother."

"You and Francesca were friends?"

"She was my only friend." A fact that now sickened him. "When we were young, Ches and I would talk for hours, reading books or playing table games. Back then she was bed bound with a birth defect of the legs, so sickly that they weren't too sure she'd live to see her next birthday. After my botched ritual, I didn't see her again for some time, until one summer solstice, when we received an invitation from the Dravens. Mother suspected it was to attend her funeral, but it was a celebration. She'd accepted his blessing, Khaladhuun finally had his scion. Tall and perfect, with the devil in her eyes... my Ches was gone." He didn't hide his disappointment. "The gentle girl I'd known was now cruel, an animal. She thought I'd be happy for her, but I was horrified, and we didn't speak again until-" Tytian's words trailed on their end, his expression growing distant as the images overtook him.

Six studied him closely, carving out the last stretch of scarred skin. "What happened that night?"

Her question surprised him, and the feeling it brought surprised him even more. It was never something that he wanted to share with anyone, but he felt oddly comforted by her presence. By the isolation of the dark field, with only the horses and the moon for company.

When he spoke, his somber tale poured out of him like water from a glass.

"It was nearing dinner time, and there was a knock at the door. My niece answered as I came around the corner. I asked her who it was, but before she could answer she was just swallowed up by fire.

"Brigitte came down the stairs, saw her daughter and started screaming. I scooped her up in my arms and tried to run for the kitchen, but there was a flush of heat at my back that sent us both flying. Francesca set her alight then too. I don't remember standing or even rushing in, I was just on her, trying my hardest to just rip Francesca's throat out. She was fast. Faster than anything should be, and she dodged every punch I threw.

"My boy, Gabriol, was in the kitchen doorway. His little hands in fists at his sides, face red and he was screaming at her to stop." Tytian could feel the stinging of his eyes, but couldn't blink away the tears, lost in the trance of memory. "Coming in to grab him was my wife, Elonya, and I told her to take him and run, but it didn't do any good. Francesca opened her right hand, then everything went black. When I came to, their bodies were nothing more than ash. Elonya... she had wrapped Gabriol in her arms, tried to shield him. I left them where they lay and sought out Francesca. The whole house was on fire. In the foyer I found my other sister, Adeline, halfway down the stairs, her husband and both of their boys dead beside her.

"Francesca was sitting at the head of my dining table, waiting. We fought for some time but she was just toying with me, like a hound with a rabbit. Pushing me, trying to see how far I could go before she pulled that dagger out of the air and shoved it into my chest." He shuddered a breath. "Her dark magic kept me suspended in that bleak in between. A waking sort of slumber. I knew my family was gone, spent decades with that horrid knowledge, unable to sleep the time away." Tears spilled down his face, his teeth rattling as he kept his rage on a delicate, short leash. "I wish I'd gone crazy. Crazy would be better than this."

Around them, a breeze whispered through the tall grass, the chill to his exposed torso bringing him back. Although it was painful to relive, there was a kind of peace within it. A release. When Tytian turned his attention to Six, she was staring at him, and not with pity or accusation but with genuine sorrow. And anger.

She slid the sleeve of her shirt down over her palm and used it to wipe away the blood on his chest, showing the clear, freshly healed skin beneath. "Her mark on you is gone now." With a whirl of her arm, she threw the scarred skin out into the dark. "Let the crows take it."

Tytian's fingertips touched his chest and he examined the new skin, flawless and tight. "Thank you."

She wiped the dagger blade over her thigh, offering him a gentle tweak of the lips. "Anytime."

After sliding his shirt over his head, Tytian helped Six to her feet and together they headed into camp, where he returned the small blade to Fenella's pack. The sky was beginning to gray around them, sunlight spilling over the eastern mountain range, running gold through the craggy seams.

FIFTEEN

After everyone was awake and stirring about, they ate a modest breakfast, packed up their things and caught the horses. They were tacking up when a sound started to rise from the west. It was faint at first and sounded like nothing more than a strong wind, but as it grew closer there was a distinct choppiness to its pattern and Callum threw a concerned glance among them.

"Airship," he warned and with haste they all cinched down their saddles, bitted the horses and headed for the cover of the trees.

The gentle *thud thud thud* of the airship's engine became a thunder in the wispy, overhanging clouds and soon the nose of the bow and the inflated balloon top came into view. At its altitude Callum was certain the occupants wouldn't see the group hiding in the forest, but surely, they would notice the well-used camp site, with its smoldering fire pit and trampled grasses. When the entire ship came into view, Callum spotted an emblem on its sails and squinted.

"Tytian? Can you tell me what that symbol is?"

Golden eyes narrowed in study. "It's a triangle, with a rabbit wearing a crown of roses."

Callum's shoulders loosened and he led Red from the safety of the overhanging canopy. "Oh good. We don't have to hide from them."

"Who are they?" asked Fenella, who was peeking between two low hanging dogwood branches, white petals decorating her hair.

"The Derrion's, a socialite family from Crown's Cross. Local celebrity type. New money from selling their cattle farm after they found it was a hotbed for light stones." He waved a finger skyward. "Nothing happens in Crown's Cross without them knowing about it. The entire city gossips about their lavish parties and galas. And hey, don't get me wrong, they seem like nice enough people, although that one kid is kind of secretive. But all of the old money can't stand them, yet they always show up at the Derrion manor with bells on when that invitation arrives." He gave a pompous little shake of his head before mounting up.

Fenella wrinkled her nose. "All of that money and power, and they throw it away on trivial things."

"Not everyone has such a charitable heart, Vanilla," remarked Callum. "Some of us are just scoundrels who like the touch of silk and the smell of aged wine wafting through their halls."

Once seated in the saddle, she leveled her gaze at him beneath her brows. "So, if you just suddenly came into wealth, you wouldn't do some good with it? You'd be just like those Derrion people and squander it on parties and collecting other wealthy friends?"

Callum thought it over for a beat before nodding. "Probably, yeah." He was rewarded with a scoff.

"Horrible," Fenella muttered under her breath.

Callum challenged her. "Alright then. Say a bag of gold bars and diamonds with your name on it falls from the sky, landing at your feet. What do you do with it?"

Wearing a confident smile, Fenella proceeded to explain her well thought out plan of buying an old monastery and turning it into a self-sustaining homestead for the poor. There would be acres of gardens with vegetables, orchards for apples and pears, and plenty of grazing lands for meat animals. A school would be built within two years of the garden's establishment and whatever food stocks they didn't use at the homestead would be sold to the cities so they would have a constant revenue to keep the wheels greased for many years to come.

Callum whistled. "After I blow all of my money on fine clothes, hookers and booze, can I come live at your vagabond sanctuary?"

Fenella tried to hide her amusement. "Oh, I expect you'll be the first take-in."

Aldan chimed in. "If I had that kind of money I'd turn Talonwood into the largest import station in the country. The rarest of rare would be sold in those streets and people would come from every corner of the globe to shop there." He looked over his shoulder, "I'd also make a donation to your homestead, Fenella."

She gave a bow of her head. "Well thank you." She turned to Tytian, roping him into their road game of hypotheticals. "What about you?"

As he opened his mouth to answer, Callum cut him off with a wave of his hand. "Uh uh, no. You're already rich and we already know what you did with your money."

Tytian surrendered with a shrug. "That's fair."

"What about you, Six?" asked Fenella. "Any lofty ambitions with this theoretical bag of money from the sky?"

Six glanced at them all with halfhearted interest. "I don't know. Haven't really thought about it."

"That's not what you said when we were kids," Callum reminded her. "You said, if we were to ever find ourselves rich, you would buy Haffin's and we'd live in the back room."

"The candy shop downtown," she recalled, fondly.

"Mhmm. You wanted to eat orange taffy for breakfast and lunch, then make pasta out of the licorice for dinner."

"With chocolate drizzle for the sauce."

"It was better than that over cooked fish and boiled red cabbage at the orphanage."

"Not sure how that man was able to make cabbage taste stale, but he was gifted at it."

They both chuckled but the rest of the group was in a sort of unified tension, afraid that the slightest outside word would cause this rare moment of civility to shatter and fall back into distress.

Callum shared that same fear, so he let the conversation end on a good note, Six's smile still lingering in a hint around the corners of her mouth. It was good to have her talking to him again, even if for this short interval and the all too familiar ache in his chest reminded Callum just how much he had missed her.

Reluctantly, he pulled his gaze from her and planted it firmly on the road ahead.

Travel went smoothly the rest of the morning, the forest trail rising and falling throughout the hills with an almost rhythmic ease. The afternoon brought with it a misting rain that came and went, cooling the air just enough to remind them it was only early spring. They raised cloak hoods and popped collars against the weak bursts of deluge.

One last winding hill to pull, then they topped the rise. In the open sweep of valley below, the Paratooke River cut through with a serpentine twist. Tucked into one of its bends was the town of Riverport. The bay was visible from their perch, people working both the cargo crates and the ships in dock. Nearby rolled a yellow waterwheel, just outside the mill warehouse and large flour silo.

Callum had a smile on his face, the sight of the town filling his chilled bones with warmth. "C'mon, let's get our man with the magic."

Down the hillside and across a patch of wildflowers, they found the main road and followed it into Riverport. They were immediately greeted by the clanging sounds of bells and raised voices. From the paperboys to the dockhands, everyone here seemed to have only one octave to communicate. All the buildings were stacked at least three stories high and every one of the cobblestone streets were narrow, giving those who weren't used to such tight quarters a slight touch of claustrophobia. The alleyways were barely big enough for the cats that wandered through their shadows. There were laundry lines drawn between almost every open window and the smell of the water mixed heavily with the scent of burning wood. Overall, it was a busy and bustling city, with no room for lollygaggers or tourists.

Familiar with the setup, Callum instructed them to leave the horses along the outer wall, just beneath one of the guard towers. The man on post looked down from his roost and gave them a nod of his head, indicating that he'd keep an eye on their stock.

They followed Callum through the throng of busy people, Fenella apologizing every few minutes after accidentally bumping into someone. Some would flash her an angry look, as if that two second little interaction had made them a day late for tea with the queen, while others were so tied up in their own thoughts they didn't even seem to notice her.

"Don't worry about apologizing," Aldan told her. "Being polite in this place is wasted."

The main thoroughfare through town forked in its center, and then either street forked again, those tines swung out towards the mill and docks and then encircling the town before meeting back up again at the city gates, giving Riverport an almost heart-shaped curve to her roadways. In the very center of that main fork, sat a long row of quiet shops, and in its core was a brick storefront, blue paint chipped and peeling from the weather. The glass windows and door were hazed from a lack of cleaning, and the sign above the entryway, depicting an open book, had fallen askew.

The group stood outside of this ramshackle looking business and Callum crossed his arms; face twisted in a confused squint. "Huh. Guess Duncan decided *'to hell with outward appearance, just come in and get your damn books.'*"

Aldan scratched at his beard. "Think he closed up? Maybe moved out?"

There was a flick of light from the windows then, a few lamps glowing in the gloom beyond the foggy windows.

Without a word Callum opened the door and walked in, the others falling in behind him.

Inside had that beautiful scent of dry parchment, leather and damp wood. The main storeroom was wall to wall bookshelves and curio cabinets, displaying all sorts of biographies, cookbooks, different knowledge-based tomes, crystal balls, inkwells, quills, writing satchels and jars of paints and ink. A spiral staircase corkscrewed up to the second floor, which resembled a library, ceiling high bookshelves disappearing into deep shadows. It was dark and uninviting for the most part, but there was also a certain charm that held appeal to those who sought literature and an atmosphere that scholars always sought to achieve.

The floorboards creaked beneath their boots as the others spread out around the room, investigating whatever caught their eye. Callum however, had a goal in mind and marched across the room, up the short stairs to the register. He noted the bell on the desk and the purchase logbook. He turned his head and inspected the sales; the last one having been made almost a month prior. He looked around and spotted the door to the stock room was closed, but the other door just behind the desk, the one that led back into the attached apartment where Duncan resided, was ajar.

With a quick flick of his fingers, he tapped the bell twice, sending a *ting ting!* through the stale air.

Up on the second floor, something tumbled over. All of them turned in sharp unison, hands landing on their weapons.

"Ow, ow- coming! One moment please!" shouted a voice from the abyss. More sounds of books scattering to the floor, then a young man peered over the top railing. He knocked the dust from his oversized robes and adjusted the glasses on his face. "Hello!" He greeted them cheerfully, but his light started to quell when he noticed their weapons. "Can I help you? Would you like to make a purchase?"

Callum moved in front of his knife-happy crew, motioning for them to stand down. "We're actually looking for someone."

"Ah, I see," he stammered, trying to keep a smile on his face. "One moment." He wagged a finger and then hurriedly made his way down the spiral staircase. His auburn hair was tossed about on his head, a few thin wisps of cobwebs blanketing the locks that curled around his ears. When he reached him, the young man shook Callum's hand with vigor. "How can I help you?"

"We're here for Duncan. Old man, sweepy robes? Can't grow a beard to save his life?"

Looking at the others, the youngster's demeanor slowly drifted into a state of dismay. "Oh..."

Callum shared a nervous glance with Six. "Oh?"

He put his eyes to the floor, pushing his glasses further up his nose. "I'm sorry to have to tell you this but, mister Duncan is dead."

SIXTEEN

A hush settled over the room and Callum had to take a second to absorb what the boy had said, hoping that maybe he had just heard him wrong but knowing he didn't.

"He-" Callum stopped as his voice wavered and cleared his throat. "He died?"

A nod. "Three months ago this midweek." The young man looked between them all apologetically. "I'm sorry you're just now finding out. Mister Duncan didn't get the chance to write a list of kin or friends to contact about his passing."

Aldan reached out, set a hand on Callum's shoulder and gave it a gentle squeeze before addressing the boy. "How did he die, lad?"

"A canker of the stomach. Came on quickly and then he was just... gone."

Fenella spoke up. "What is your name?"

"I'm Warwick, miss. But you can call me Wick. Everyone does." They shook hands and he gestured towards the heavens. "I'm- I mean, I *was*, mister Duncan's apprentice."

Their exchange fell on deaf ears, the knowledge of Duncan's death coating Callum's brain in a fog. That old man had felt more like a father to him than anyone else in his life. Not even his real father came close, and Callum could remember his parents with excruciating clarity.

A pressure was building in his head, and his throat was clenched to stop the sob that had formed all at once. Callum realized he needed something, anything, to hold on to before the grief could overtake him. He looked for the one thing that could settle his heart and found her staring back at him.

Six was standing on the other side of Fenella. There was a stern set to her face, but when Callum's distressed gaze found her, she softened.

He could breathe again.

"Wait, Callum? You're Callum?" asked Wick, bringing him back to a conversation that had continued without him.

"Uhm..." Callum tripped over his words, trying to replay the last few seconds of chat between Wick and the others. "Yes?"

The young apprentice had a look of astonishment, and he gave a toothy smile. "Oh wow!" Wick looked among the others and pointed to each as he named them. "You must be Aldan? And you're Six!" When they both nodded, he put a hand to his head. "Mister Duncan told me all about your adventures! This is so exciting, I never thought I'd get to meet you! What brings you to Riverport?"

His energy was exhausting but Six calmed herself with a long inhale. "We came here to speak with Duncan. About a- time sensitive matter. But it appears that our arrival has come too late."

"Right," said Wick with a fall to his voice. "Well, is there anything I can help you with? I was his apprentice after all, and you're his friends." He smiled somberly. "He always spoke about you with such affection, I feel like it would be disrespectful to his memory not to offer you my aid."

The group all passed around an apprehensive look.

"When you say apprentice, do you mean at selling books or..." Aldan wiggled his fingers like snakes, trying to seem mystical. "Something more of the crafty nature?"

Wick's eyes narrowed in confusion. "Am I good at... making things? Like, arts and crafts?"

Aldan squinted as well. "I don't know?" he asked with an arched brow and more wiggling of his fingers.

Wick's confusion persisted until Tytian broke through the code talk. "He means *the* craft. Were you a magical apprentice? Oh, calm down, no one is coming in here," he told Aldan, who threw a concerned look towards the door.

There was a chuckle, and Wick rubbed the back of his head, smiling. "Heh, yeah! Mister Duncan started teaching me the ways of magic when I first came under his care. I had actually progressed into advanced offensive spells when he first became sick."

"Offensive spells?" asked Callum. "Duncan never liked the violent magics, why would he teach you this?"

Wick gave a small shrug. "He'd never really say. Just woke me up one morning and handed me a book about it. When I asked him why I'd need to know such things he said that to understand the peace of magic I'd need to understand its violence too. Although, he also spoke of troubling things near the end."

"What sort of things?" asked Fenella.

"That he'd had been having these dreams. About a mirror framed in blood and bone. He said it was broken into nine pieces, each one slowly being pulled back into their place, to make the mirror whole again."

"Nine pieces?" asked Tytian of Wick, while looking at Callum who had paled a shade. "This Duncan of yours a seer as well?"

Callum shook his head. "No. That's more Marlia's territory."

Wick eyed their interaction with interest. "He told me to go visit Marlia, to tell her of what he saw. I haven't had a chance to see her yet." Reading their faces made him outwardly uneasy, and he opened his mouth again, but his inquiry was cut short.

"Wick," Callum said with such abruptness that he made the boy jump. "Could we pop into the apartment for some coffee? Maybe sit by a fire, warm our bones a little?"

He nodded briskly, his deep interest replaced by natural politeness and an obvious need to please. "Oh yes, of course! Absolutely." He spun on his heels and hurried to the front door, giving the stiff lock a turn and flipping the Open sign over to Closed. "So we won't be disturbed," he explained with a smile as he quickly passed through the group.

"That was a concern?" muttered Tytian sarcastically under his breath while looking around the empty store. Fenella replied with a slight elbowing to his ribs.

Wick walked them through the door behind the counter, into a narrow stairwell, followed by another spiral staircase that twisted in a short rise to a higher floor. Single file they climbed the creaky steps until they reached an open archway.

"Please, make yourselves comfortable." With a flourish of his hand, Wick motioned to the sitting area. Shiplap walls were painted in a deep navy, with more shelves and curios lining the walls. From the ceiling hung a variety of articulated animal skeletons and air ship models, with strands of crystals dotting the spaces between. At the heart of the room was a roaring fire pit, inset into the floor, allowing for comfortable seating. There were no logs or anything combustible to keep fed the flames that shimmered in a colorful haze. When Fenella noticed this, she became entranced and rushed to the fireside.

"Is this made with magic?" she asked. Wick nodded and she smiled brightly, warming her hands in its prismed light.

"I'll go get started on that coffee." The apprentice dusted his hands on his robes. "Think I'll make us all some lunch as well.

Feel free to look around!" Hiding a small slip of the foot behind an obvious cough, he disappeared through an archway.

But none of them took his advice, instead they all clustered together, a shared question hanging heavy between them.

Tytian kept his voice low. "So, no mage."

"No mage," mirrored Six.

Fenella's face scrunched. "What about Wick? He's a mage."

"Apprentice mage," Six corrected. "We don't even know what he can and can't do."

Callum shrugged. "We could ask for a demonstration. Take him outside of town, see what he can do with those offensive spells he learned."

Aldan nodded. "That might work."

"Or that might get us caught and jailed," opposed Six. "Plus, he's a kid. Can't be more than eighteen or nineteen years old."

"How old were you when you joined the city guard?" asked Tytian.

"Sixteen," Callum answered for her, and Six shot them both an irritated look.

"Are we seriously considering this?" she asked swiftly. "You're really talking about dragging this kid, who's as green as fucking grass, into something that could very well end his life before it's even begun?"

Callum shook his head. "No, we won't be dragging him. We'll just be giving him the option. If he doesn't want to come, then he doesn't have to."

"I got a good feeling about him," Fenella offered gently, a hand settled against her stomach. "There's no harm in asking, especially if it turns out he's got the skills for it,"

"There's plenty of harm," Six hissed, jabbing a thumb at Callum. "Especially if this one does the talking."

He crossed his arms across his chest, offended. "Now what's that supposed to mean?"

"You know exactly what I mean. Your honeyed words and promise of grandeur will have that boy packing his things before you even finish with the details, and he'll wind up either hurt or-" She cut herself off, clenching her jaw shut in a rage to keep the words from spilling out.

Callum raised his brow. "No, say it."

"Or wind up pulled apart, face down in a gutter."

There was a quick flutter of his lashes, his tongue tracing over his teeth. "You're gonna bring that up? Is that really what you're comparing this to? This is nothing like that." There was a controlled fury in his tone that the others had yet to hear, and both Tytian and Fenella exchanged a look.

Aldan stepped in then, laying a hand on either one's shoulder. "That's enough. This isn't helping." He threw a glance towards the next room. "This is a strange situation that we've been put in, and turning on each other isn't the way to solve it."

Callum pulled away from him, soothing his nerves with a hand through his hair. "Okay. We'll do this the old fashioned way; we vote. Those in favor of giving the kid a chance, raise your hand."

Four hands raised in unison.

A strangled laugh rose out of her chest. "Unbelievable. You really are the best con man I've ever met."

Callum stared at her, his lips moving over every conceivable retort until he found one that didn't hurt so badly. "I can't keep doing this with you. I finally make it one step forward and then fall three steps back. Are you ever going to forgive me? Or have you settled on hate? Because I'm getting a little sick of waiting to see which way this falls, Lucia."

The tension that filled the space between them was slowly becoming electric, and Six's affronted glare actually made Fenella take a small step back.

"You really expect me to forgive? Pretend like none of it happened?" she asked, struggling to keep her anger from spilling over them all.

Callum shook his head. "You need to choose; heal or hate. You can't do both. You can't keep throwing my failures in my face one day and then give me hope in the next. I understand you want to hurt me, but this needs to stop. I need it to stop."

Breaking through the pending storm was Wick, brandishing an oval tray with a carafe of coffee and cups. "Here we are!" He sat the tray down on a stack of books piled high atop a reading desk. "Piping hot and fresh. I have cream, sugar and a little bit of honey. Oh, and some dandelion petals, as well as-" He turned to them and read their expressions, mild dismay wiping away his cheery mood.

Callum stepped up, plastering a phony expression on his face. "Don't mind us, just having a bit of a debate."

"About what?"

"Well, it's about what we had originally come here for. We wanted to involve Duncan but he's no longer here. However, since you were his pupil, perhaps you could fill the position."

Instantly, Wick beamed. "One of your adventures?"

Callum stammered a little. "Sort of!" There was the sound of a scoff behind him, and he flashed Wick a reassuring smile. "Have a seat, and we'll explain everything." He told his tale, leaving nothing out and with aid from the others here and there. Wick's facial expressions were almost comedic at times, ranging from shocked to appalled, then astonished and inquisitive. He asked a lot of questions about Tytian, and he even asked Fenella if she was a magic worker. When she told him no but wondered why he would assume she was, he told her that there was something in her aura.

"You should try light working! You might be well suited for it," he said as he poured himself another cup of coffee.

Fenella shrugged. "I don't know what that is."

"Wanna learn? There are loads of books on it in mister Duncan's private arcane collection. I can go get them and then we can see if you have a predisposition for-" Wick's enthusiasm was apparent, but Callum reined him in with a smile and a wave of his hand.

"You two can delve into that later. Right now, we kind of need to know if you can help us. What is your skill level?"

Wick's shoulders squared with pride. "Well, I'm quite adept at elemental work. Ice and earth are my strongest channels. Mister Duncan said it's because ice is the easiest to form and earth came to me naturally because I was born under an earth star, therefore I am attuned to it. My weakest form is fire but, what do you expect? It's hard for a rock to hold a flame."

"Have you ever seen battle?" asked Aldan.

Wick shook his head. "Not much war happening here in Riverport. But, mister Duncan had me practice battle forms in the last year and I've mastered them all."

"Have you ever killed someone?" asked Tytian, bluntly.

"Gosh, not to my knowledge, no," Wick answered without hesitation. "But in the event of either saving my life or my comrades, I have no issue sending a man born of the earth back to her soil. Although the thought doesn't bring me joy."

Callum was content enough with this, and he was glad to see that, although Duncan was a man who sought nothing more than peace in his time on this earth, his pupil had a slightly sharper edge to his laurels. "Well, if you're confident that you can be of assistance to us, then welcome aboard! We have no lifeboats, there's a few leaks and a serious possibility of mutiny... But, if all goes according to plan, we're going to put a halt to an upcoming reign of terror."

"You can say no," Six told the young mage, stepping alongside Callum as an alternate choice. "This is a monumental undertaking and you are in no way obligated to join us."

There was no second thought to be had, Wick's mind made up. "I understand that. Honestly though, I'd be a fool to turn this down." He grew somber, his body slumping down into his seat, fingers tracing the chipped edge of his mug. "This morning I woke up in a bed that I will soon be evicted from, with no family to care for and no real career to my name. These last few months have been difficult and I wasn't sure how I'd get by without Mister Duncan. I was finding myself with no purpose to my life, no meaning and nothing of note to carry me through to the end." An enthusiasm blossomed within and he smiled with gratitude. "And then you five walked through the door, three of which I have heard such epic tellings of!" He sat forward and pointed at Aldan. "Your stealth killing of twenty seven bandits in the Daulorag Hills." Then Six. "The story of when you took out an entire group of hired thugs by dropping a chandelier on them in that crooked constable's cabin." And finally Callum. "And don't even get me started on the heist that you and Duncan pulled on the stage actress Vivalyn Rabeaux in Crown's Cross." Wick moved to the edge of his seat and addressed Fenella and Tytian. "They walked in, pretending to be her newly hired hair and makeup artists, then walked out with well over twenty pounds worth of jewelry from her home." He laughed. "She didn't even know it was a swindle until she found the real artists in nothing but their skivvies tied up in her downstairs broom closet!"

Callum chuckled. "I'm surprised we got away with that one. The hair stylist's clothes didn't even fit Duncan."

Amused, Fenella tried to picture the scenario in her head. "Wait, so *you* did her makeup? And she still didn't put it together?"

"Of course not, her makeup was flawless." Callum laid a hand to his chest. "I am an artiste, Vanilla. That woman was a goddess once I was done."

Tytian was skeptical. "Was she really?"

Over his shoulder he gave a grimaced chuckle. "No. Her eyebrows looked like this." He placed one finger on his brow and then the other finger near his hairline.

Wick laughed loudly, motioning with enthusiasm. "See, that's what I want! To go on harrowing adventures and build stories, build a legacy. I want to leave behind something worth telling once I am dead and gone."

Six tried to reason with him, damn near pleading. "It's not all dashing tales and happy endings, kid. Sometimes these aren't heroic stories. Sometimes they're a tragedy."

"I know that death is a possibility," Wick told her gently before rising to his feet and pacing the floor, his hand gestures punctuating his speech. "But staying means something worse, at least for me. I grew up on your tales! Duncan would spend hours almost every day regaling me with all of the details of your adventures, sparing very little details. And believe me, I know why you're warning me. Mister Duncan always said that you were severe, but he also told me that you were fierce and brave and headstrong, and I appreciate that you're trying to make sure that I understand how dangerous this all could be. But I couldn't live with myself if I were to turn down the opportunity to fight alongside you all." With a tight smile he tried to hide his quivering lip, but the tears in his eyes gave away his emotions. "Ever since I was small, I wanted to grow up to be the kind of man that Mister Duncan was. The kind of man that he would be proud of." He turned to Callum. "So, yes. I would be honored to join your party and help in your quest."

"Glad to have you," Callum told him with sincerity as he stood and shook the younger man's hand. "Dunc would be proud."

Wick wore an expression mixed with professionalism and bottled-up excitement. "Thank you-Oh, the pie!" He then spun around and rushed through the doorway into the kitchen, a chorus of bangs and scattering dishes ringing out across the apartment.

Callum slowly spun around to the others and gave an uncertain grin. "I'm sure he'll be a uh, true asset to the team."

BANG!

After some time, and a few muffled curse words, Wick returned with a cast iron pot clutched carefully between two gloved hands and under each arm was a stack of plates, silverware was jingling in his robe pockets. "Careful, it's still hot." He set the turkey pie down on a small side table and then handed out the wooden saucers. "Fork or spoon?" He asked the group as he plucked the utensils from his robes.

Once everyone had a helping of food in hand, they all sat around the fire and ate.

Wick fell in with them faster than anyone would have guessed, happy to finally have someone to talk to who had known his teacher. When the food was gone and the eatery cleared away, Callum asked a question that had been sitting on his mind most of the morning.

"Hey kid, where is Duncan buried?"

Wick pointed to the east. "Cemetery, next to the chapel. I thought perhaps he'd want a pyre instead, but for some reason he heavily insisted on an in-ground burial."

"Huh," said Callum. "Always pegged him for a pyre man myself."

Wick shrugged. "He was pretty adamant and detailed about how he wanted his funeral handled. In ground burial with a few sealed letters, some sort of etching, he didn't want shoes or socks-"

"Wait-" Callum interrupted. "An etching?"

"Mhm." Wick flicked his chin at the window. "It had come to him in the post a few weeks before he died. Said it was from a cartographer friend of his in Kartheos?" His brow furrowed. "I don't know, he wouldn't really talk about it."

Callum rolled the name over and over on his tongue, trying to see if it tasted familiar. He turned to Tytian. "Kartheos... do you know where that is?"

He thought it over, a hint of dread settling across his face. "It's a dead city, northwest of Havnul."

"A dead city? What's that?" asked Fenella.

"Few hundred years ago it was owned by a necromancy order, until Mar sent its army to their doorstep and slaughtered every last man, woman and child within the walls. Since they were using black magics, the church deemed the land inhospitable and declared it a dead city. No one is allowed to rebuild on its soil."

Callum started walking through this new information. "So, Duncan was having dreams about some broken mirror with nine pieces, then a map maker from a dead city sends him an etching of a slab with strange writing, which he had buried with him upon his death." He huffed a small chuckle in disbelief. "Dunc, you son of a bitch."

"Did he know something?" asked Fenella.

"There's only one way to find out."

SEVENTEEN

"Hold on, are you suggesting grave robbing?" questioned Wick.

Callum patted his shoulder. "With respect, of course. And since it's us, I don't think he'd mind."

The young mage didn't disagree. "No, he wouldn't, but the city would. You can't just stroll out there and start rifling through coffins, there's a stationed guard. They'll lock you up. Grave robbers don't fare well in Riverport."

"How many guards?" asked Six, in a way that made him obviously nervous.

"Two, usually."

Tytian motioned towards her. "We can easily handle two guards."

Quickly, Callum held up an objecting hand. "Let's leave these alive this time, okay pal?"

"Alive?" repeated Wick, apprehensively.

Tytian simply shrugged.

Clapping his hands together, Callum was eager to get to work. "Alright! At sun down we hit the cemetery and see what we can find."

After mapping out their plans for later that night, the group spread out through the apartment and browsed through Duncan's collection of tomes, looking for anything that may be of additional use. Wick even brought the old man's personal collection into the living room, though none held anything close to what kind of information they were looking for. Outside, the rain had eased up throughout the afternoon and finally stopped a quarter after four o'clock as Tytian and Aldan headed back for the horses and cart. There was a small barn near the flour silos and, for a small fee, they were able to station the animals there for the night.

Dinner was a joint task between Fenella and Wick, and it filled the apartment with a delectable scent. Thick cut potatoes fried in shallow oil with sea salt and green onions. A whole chicken was broiled in the oven, butter and rosemary stuffed beneath its browning skin. A golden broth filled with carrots, cut celery stalks, onions, parsley and collards was boiling on the stove top. A pan of freshly baked rolls was stationed nearby, and fat tomatoes were waiting in a wooden bowl to be sliced.

Wick and Fenella worked well together, both exchanging recipes and cooking tips they had picked up from either trial and error, or reading about them in books. When everything was almost ready, Fenella popped back into the living room and asked Tytian quietly if he would set the table.

"Why me?" he asked with a low tone when he noticed Fenella doing the same.

She threw a quick glance at the others. "You're used to formal dinner parties. You know where everything is meant to go and how to arrange a handsome table. Wick and I worked hard on this meal, and I want it to be nice. Have a touch of class."

Tytian gave her a sly grin. "Are you saying the others lack class?"

She pursed her lips. "No. They just lack... raising." Quickly, she added, "Which is not their fault."

"Mhmm. Fine. Where is the silverware?"

Working with a schooled ease, Tytian set the table. It had a high societal flare, despite what little he had to work with.

"It needs flowers," Elonya would say. *"Flowers make a space feel special."*

Tytian thought back to the times when his wife would set up their dining room for a family banquet. She'd spend hours in town trying to piece together the perfect arrangement for the centerpiece. All of the napkins were imported from some of the best seamstresses in the country, and the dinner sets were made by masterful artisans. Tytian had often thought such obsessiveness about the presentation kind of silly, but she was always so proud once everything was just as she'd pictured.

He remembered the lilies she brought home for that final dinner. Light pink, like a blush. Then, they wilted, the petals boiling as black curled along the edges-

"You alright?" asked Callum before casually pointing. "You're kind of stranglin' the silverware."

Tytian blinked and released his grip on the utensil. He hadn't realized that he'd been standing in place for some time, lost inside his head. "I'm fine. Just finishing up," he said with an absentminded tone as he organized the last few plates.

Callum was skeptical, but he relented. "Alright, if you say so."

Fenella and Wick emerged from the kitchen, one with the pot of broth and the other with the still sizzling chicken. They scattered the dishes down the table, Fenella delighted with Tytian's handiwork.

"Dinner is ready!"

Everyone took a seat at the long table, filling their plates. Callum dipped the vegetable soup into everyone's bowls while

Tytian passed out rolls. Wick walked the table and divvied out the tomato slices and Aldan carved up the chicken. Six retrieved a bottle of wine from the cabinet near the archway, and Fenella scooped heaps of seared potatoes onto each plate.

The group ate with collective mirth, and passed around stories while they did. Those who knew him spoke of Duncan, and told tales of his humor and wit. Wick absorbed every word of it, seemingly happy that finally, even if in a roundabout way, his teacher was getting the kind of funeral he deserved.

Callum groaned as he took a bite out of a roll, shaking it at Fenella. "I think you do know some magic, Vanilla. This bread is outstanding."

Aldan agreed. "What got you into cooking?"

Fenella wiped her mouth on a napkin. "I cooked a lot with my mother when I was younger. Her mother had taught her how to bake, so she continued the tradition. We would start early in the morning and make all kinds of things; bread loafs, biscuits, tarts, pies, cookies...whatever we had the ingredients for is what we made that day." She smiled fondly after taking a sip of wine. "My mother makes these small, custard filled puffs just for afternoon tea. I've never been able to make them as fluffy as she does."

Callum smiled dreamily at her, propping his elbow on the table and resting his chin in his hand. "Must be nice."

Fenella tilted her head. "What?"

"Having parents."

Aldan choked on his laughter, and Fenella simply shook her head before throwing a carrot at Callum's face, which he dodged.

He spoke through a chuckle. "Oh come on, as the only one among us that still has their dear old ma and pa, you're going to get picked on. Odd man out sort of thing."

Fenella scoffed with humor. "This really is a tragic bunch."

Later, when dinner was finished and the plates were stacked in the kitchen, the light that streamed in through the windows grew more and more opaque. In well timed unison, the street lamps began to click on one by one, signaling it was time to move.

Callum donned his jacket. "Let's go."

Out on the street, fewer people roamed the narrow streets, many fleeing to the comfort of their homes or the local tavern. The sound of bells came rolling in from the river, signaling the end of the dayshift, calling in those who worked through the night.

Wick led the group through the unwinding clutter, to the eastern edge of town. The graveyard was larger than expected, dotted with thick, old trees. Moss swung from their branches like the tattered clothes of a specter, adding a sense of whimsical serenity. Encasing the grounds was a well made rock fence, and near the gates a shack, whose windows glowed with light.

The six of them stopped in the shadows of an empty house nearby. They could see one watchman pacing steadily behind the closed gates, hands shoved into his pockets.

"Alright," spoke Callum right before he reached out and placed his hand over Tytian's mouth. "Who has a plan?" He then grimaced as his wrist was painfully bent backwards.

Wick studied the watchman's methodical patrol. "I have one, but I'll need a volunteer." Both Callum and Fenella's hands went up, but he only chose one. "Fenella, perfect. Come on." Together they slipped out of the shadows.

Aldan looked at Callum, amused. "Your feelings are a little hurt."

And Callum agreed. "My feelings are a little hurt."

Quickly, Wick and Fenella jogged across the street. He instructed Fenella to approach the gate as he hid behind one of its vine-crawled pillars. When in position, he gave her a thumbs up.

Fenella waited until the watchman was within ear shot, then called him over.

"Yes, miss?"

Fenella stammered for a moment, fishing for a believable lie. "Hi. Uhm, I was wondering if perhaps, maybe...you've seen...a cat come by? He's a gray tabby, little white snip on his nose? Uhm, bob tailed! Yeah, yeah, bob tailed. With a bell on his collar."

The man scratched at the corner of his mustache, thinking hard. "I don't think so. Let me ask Percy, maybe he did-" Suddenly, he was cut short as Wick appeared beside him, reaching through the bars to tap his fingers to the man's temple. Out cold, the watchman folded into the soft grass.

He motioned for the others while Fenella fished the keys free of the other man's belt and opened the gate.

"Wow kid," said Aldan, nudging the watchman with the toe of his boot. "What did you do?"

Wick shrugged. "Just a sleeping spell. He'll wake up fine in the morning."

Peeking through the shack window, they could see the other guard sitting at a desk, a cup of coffee next to him and a book in his hands. He was facing the door, and was well armed.

"Got any magic for that?" asked Callum and Wick began to mutter out scenarios.

"Well, I could use a fog spell to carry in a sleep charm, but it won't be effective if he holds his breath. Or we could use his coffee as a distraction. Make it bubble over and when he turns I could slip in and-"

Knock, knock, knock.

Tytian banged on the shack door, luring the man out into the night. One hand on his weapon, a question on his lips. He began to question Tytian's presence when Six slipped up behind him and struck the back of his head. This sent him to the ground with a thud.

"Or...we could just do that," Wick cringed.

They gathered up both men and laid them comfortably inside their station, then slipped into the maze of headstones.

Once again Wick led the charge, one hand held out in front of him, producing a small ball of light. The cemetery rolled twice with long, dragging knolls. Raised plots required some climbing, and a few family mausoleums caused a serpentine twist in the trails. Duncan's grave was set along the backside of the final rise. His tombstone was modest, decorated with day-old flowers and an empty teacup.

Duncan McCreeve

Aged 77

Adventurer - Mentor - Friend

No one spoke. It felt wrong to, in this solemn place of rest, staring at the marker of a man who four of them considered family. Callum read the carved words over and over, as a heavy dread at what they were about to do settled on his chest.

"Okay," he whispered, "Let's get this over with."

Wick planted the little orb of conjured light on a nearby tree, then raised his hands out in front of him and closed his eyes. With a few mumbled words, he rolled his palms skyward and then held his hands aloft. The grave dirt rumbled, then broke and lifted up in one solid, rectangular slab. Wick set the soil down away from the opening and as the spell was released, the slab crumbled apart in a neat pile.

"Kid, you're handier than a shirt pocket," Aldan told Wick, impressed at his skill.

There were no immediate volunteers, but eventually it was Callum who hopped down into the freshly made hole.

The top of the coffin had already cracked from the weight of the dirt and he apologized under his breath as he peeled back the damp planks, revealing the corpse within. He tried desperately not to linger on the body and to ignore the smell that wafted up into the night air.

It was silly, but a part of Callum had hoped that when they opened the casket, they would find nobody. Just a note saying that Duncan had faked it all and he was living peacefully on some tropical island somewhere, getting piss drunk on the beach while working on his tan. But of course, that wasn't the case. He was here. Here, and gone.

Overlooking the black flesh, sunken cheeks and gaping mouth, Callum sifted through the old man's robes with shaky hands.

"Breast pocket, on his left. And under the pillow beneath his head," instructed Wick.

Callum found the two-page letter, wax sealed with a stamp from Duncan's office in the robes and with as much gentleness as he could muster, he slid his fingers under the pillow and pulled out a bundle of rough spun fabric. It was tied closed with blue string, dried lavender and mugwort bound inside the weave. Callum tossed them both up to Aldan's waiting hands. Carefully, he pieced the coffin top back together.

"I'm sorry, old man. I should've come by sooner," he whispered to the quiet corpse. "Should've done a lot of things." With the final piece in place, he left his goodbye and wiped the biting tears from his eyes. He reached up for assistance, and Tytian grabbed his hand, easily lifting him from the grave.

Six and Aldan took turns planting their soft farewells into the earth, to keep their friend company. Wick allowed them their moments of solace, then, ever so gently, returned the soil to the grave. It was neat and tidy work. They fled from the scene then, following their tracks back to the gates and out into the misty streets.

As soon as they were all back at the apartment, they gathered in the dining room. Callum unfurled the fabric and spread out the parchment etching that was bundled inside. At the center of the paper there was a faint, triangular outline of the ritual stone's edges, and within the lines were crookedly carved runes. Crude, jagged, the script often crossed each other like the scratches of a cat.

At Callum's shoulder, Tytian grew stiff. "I've seen these before." He reached out to the etching, but never touched the cloth. "

"Can you read it?" asked Wick.

"Not exactly." He traced the markings in the air with his fingers, trying to decipher a meaning. "A few of these look like they could be from a standard demonic alphabet, but the others don't quite fit."

"Hmm, perhaps a sub dialect? Dedicated solely to Khaladhuun?" offered the young apprentice.

Across the table Six opened the letter, scanning the pages. Her eyes narrowed against the handwritten words, prompting Aldan to sweep in behind her, reading it aloud.

"*Duncan,*

I hope this finds you well. My apologies for the short notice but I've only just been able to slip outside of the excavation site.

Two months ago I was hired by Duke Welling to assist on a dig that he was doing in Kartheos. At first I asked what kind of artifacts we would be searching for, but he always dodged the question and when I refused initially, he added a few more pounds of saphs to my payment and eventually the number had grown so greatly that I would have been a fool to say 'no'.

By the Divine, I wish I would have followed my head instead of my coin purse.

When I arrived, the dig had already begun and for some time I was simply here to sit on my backside and make money, but then, one night, there was a discovery deep within the long-buried ruins of the old library. A stone had been found, one with a language written on the surface that I hadn't seen in many years.

As well as my expertise, Welling had enlisted the help of another ancient literature scholar. A woman, whose name nor face was ever revealed to me, but I swear to you Duncan, I think she is a Carmine Priest. She didn't stay long, and the Duke mentioned that she had moved on, to another dig. He pointed it out on a map, but I didn't have my glasses and couldn't see it clearly. He keeps that map on his person, but if I can sneak into his quarters and take a peek at it, I will.

I am enclosing an etching of the ritual stone. Perhaps you can decipher more, but from what I can gather it's but a piece of a much bigger plaque.

From the writing itself I've been able to determine a few words. On the second parchment I've included with this letter is a rough translation. Welling's men have been checking all of the outgoing post but I have a friend who frequents a nearby town for supplies, and I trust him to make sure this letter reaches you.

Something is afoot here Duncan, and I fear it may be some-thing sinister.

The dig site will be packed up within a few weeks and as soon as I have my money in hand, I'll come to you. Maybe we can figure this out together.

Signed,
Jeriah"

Aldan looked at Callum. "Duncan knew."

The room felt hot, at least that's what he thought as Callum pulled off his jacket, his skin crawling. But it wasn't the room, it was him, and a realization that made him want to vomit.

He turned to Wick. "Did this Jeriah ever show?"

Wick shook his head. "No, never did."

"He ever send any more letters?"

"Not that I'm aware of."

"Did Duncan get mail from anyone else?"

"No, but he didn't get much to begin with. Some out of city bills here and there, Marlia's usual care packages, a parcel of books and ink from Cloud Haven." He pointed toward the etching. "This was the only thing out of routine in the four years I've apprenticed."

"Do you know if he told anyone?"

The boy seemed paler than usual. "I don't know, it's possible. He was in and out of the shop a lot, and when he was here, he was almost paranoid. Then he got sick and-" A light clicked on inside his head and Wick's eyes widened. "Do you think someone killed him?"

Callum gripped the edge of the table, pushing his palms into the polished top until the pain was enough. "Yeah kid, I think someone did."

"Godsdamnit," Aldan muttered, beginning a slow pace about the room.

Shuffling aside the top page of the letter, Six produced the second and laid it on top of the etching. On the face was a crude drawing of the ritual slab, and in a few, seemingly random, spaces there were words written.

Widow, betrayal, quarter a babe and flesh offering.

"Quartering a babe..." Just saying the words made her sick. "This is from the one they already have."

Callum rubbed a nervous hand across his forehead. "Shit."

"This map he mentioned, could be worth a look." Tytian took the letter from Six, poring over the contents.

Slowly formulating something that could be considered a course of action, Callum ran through what they knew. "Welling will be in Savhignos in three weeks. But that leaves us with a few decisions to make. Do we go after him before he reaches the city, or do we intercept him along the way? Do we steal the ritual slab he's carrying, or the map to the others?"

Aldan offered up a point. "I have a feeling the stones may be more heavily guarded than he is. Picking his pocket may be the safer option. We know his air caravan will have to make fueling stops, so if we hit him at one of those, quickly and quietly, then maybe we can be halfway to the next dig by the time he hands over the latest piece to the High Father. Before anyone knows it, we've stormed the excavation, hopefully located a ritual slab of our own, and then we're gone like bandits in the night."

"There are a lot of holes in that plan, Aldan," Six told him, sounding on the edge of defeat.

He shrugged his broad shoulders. "All of our plans are going to be as holey as cheese until we know for certain what's going on. We're going into this shit blind."

Wick frowned. "You know, there's no guarantee that any of those other places marked on that map will hold a slab."

"That's true," said Callum. "But the map is the easier route. If we try to steal the slab from Welling before he gets to Savhignos, we run the risk of bringing the royal forces down on our heads. Can't stop shit if we're dead or imprisoned." He gestured towards Tytian, "And we're already in a tight spot with your pal Franny on our heels."

"If we get spotted stealing from the Duke, we'll be on every Wanted poster in the region," Fenella remarked as she stared at the etching with worry.

Callum laid a hand on her shoulder. "I'm already on Wanted posters, sweetheart, it's not that bad."

"Okay, so we steal the map. How are we going to get to it?" Tytian asked.

Scratching at his beard, Aldan offered a destination. "He'd have to refuel on the way. And the biggest fueling station between Havnul and Savhignos is-" Cautiously, he looked to Six and found her staring daggers into Callum across the table.

"Crown's Cross." Her delivery was calm, but the white roll of her knuckles as she gripped the back of a chair portrayed something else.

Callum cleared his throat, swallowing the lump that threatened to strangle him. "Yeah."

Oblivious to the tension that cloaked the air between them, Wick was excited to have a plan of action. "Okay then, let's go to Crown's Cross!"

"First, we go see Marlia," Callum corrected. "And then we go to Crown's and get that map."

"Right. I'm going to go pack!" And with a rush, Wick was gone to the other end of the apartment.

Slowly, the others started to clear away the etching and letters, Aldan pulling the other two into a quiet conversation while Callum moved in closer to Six, risking her wrath.

"Hey," he said softly. "Look, I think you should stay at Marlia's while we go to Crown's Cross."

"I don't want to stay at Marlia's," she said in a hush. "I want to go home."

Callum's heart slammed against his ribs, beating at the bars of its cage. "Six... you can't leave. Not now. If we abandon this, we'll all die."

"If we keep at it, we'll die," she challenged. "I mean hell Callum, who knows, maybe the High Father will croak from old age before they ever even find the rest of the ritual stones."

"That isn't a chance we can take. We can't just hope this goes away."

"Duncan is dead. He's dead, and we have a fully gifted demon hunting us, now you want to rob the brother of the king in Crown's Cross of all places. This plan hinges on nothing more than probability. Do you see how ridiculous this all is? It's dangerous enough for those of us who actually know what they're doing, but to drag Fenella and Wick along too? We can't do this, Callum. Not this time."

His panic and anger fled out of mouth faster than he could trap it behind his teeth. "When did you become such a coward?"

Six flinched away from him.

Regret nearly toppled him. "Lucia, I didn't mean that."

Pushing past him, she left him where he stood, sweeping into the living room without another word.

Nauseous, Callum ran his hands down his face, sighing audibly into his palms. "Shit."

"What was that about?" asked Fenella gently as she walked up behind him. Her eyes were still trailing after Six.

Callum could have knocked his own teeth out. He was surprised Six didn't do it for him. "Just furthering the divide."

Her arms were hugged around herself when Fenella moved in front of him. The worry on her face was apparent. "Does any of this feel weird to you?"

"What do you mean?"

She shrugged off a chill, rubbing at her arms to bring herself a little comfort. "I don't know. I can't put a name to it."

"What's that gut of yours saying?"

"Nothing. And that's what scares me."

Callum reached out and gently brushed the end of her nose with his knuckle. "You don't have anything to be scared of," he lied with a smile. "Just think of it as a fun little heist with friends. Once it's all done, we'll take a trip to the coast or something. Get Wick drunk off his ass."

But Fenella didn't seem so sure, despite the fleeting smile.

After packing up his things, and the items of Duncan's that he wished to keep, Wick grabbed some spare blankets and throw pillows from around the apartment, setting up sleeping areas for everyone around the fire pit. There wasn't a whole lot of chit chat between them, everyone deep within their own thoughts and the grim information they'd learned through the day. Over time, the magic fire started to dwindle and in the early hours of the morning, it fizzled out.

The only one still awake to notice was Callum.

EIGHTEEN

"Alright, I think I'm ready!" Wick stuffed full everything he had that resembled a bag. Books, trinkets, scrolls of paper, tins of charcoal sticks and pens, all tucked neatly into an old saddle bag and two pillowcases with mismatched patterns. He set his collected things in a neat pile by the door, cleaning his dusty glasses on the long sleeve of his tunic.

Aldan looked around at the bags and scratched the back of his head. "Uhm, son, did you bring any clothes?"

Realization dawned on Wick's face and he waggled a finger, fleeing into the back rooms. "Oh yeah. I'll be right back."

With a chuckle and shake of his head Aldan told Callum, "It's like having a new puppy. There's more air in that head right now than sense."

"Oh leave him alone," countered Fenella humorously. "He's just excited." She then handed a mug of coffee to a tired-eyed Callum. He took two big gulps, sagging deeper into the chair. His body felt soured, and his jaw was aching up into his temples from clenching his teeth through the night. Luckily, the coffee was loosening him up.

Cautiously, he ventured a glance at Six. She stood near the window, steaming mug of coffee in her hands, looking out to the street below. It gave her an excuse to put her back to the room, denying Callum the opportunity to read her. But he didn't need to see her face to know she was still upset, and he didn't blame her. He'd be upset too if someone called him a coward.

You are a coward, Callum.

All around him, the room was flush with a fresh snowfall, the smell of coffee overpowered by the metallic reek of blood.

"Alright, now I'm ready." Wick returned with a satchel bearing Duncan's initials, a fine layer of dust covering the leather flap. He took one last look around the room then dipped his head, and ducked through the archway to the stairwell.

Filing downstairs, they made their way across the store, slowing as Wick did. He came to a halt in the middle aisle, cataloging everything he could in his memories, and they allowed him this moment of farewell. He stroked a hand down the shelving, touching the parchment stacks with care. "I'm going to miss this place," he told the others, a solemn smile on his face.

Fenella put a hand on his shoulder. "You're coming back, Wick. This isn't goodbye."

He patted her fingers, taking one final look around the room. "I'm two months behind on the rent. The city will take her as soon as I step out of the gate." He huffed a bit of air, readying himself for the final push out the door. "But, it's alright. It isn't my home anymore without Mister Duncan."

There was a thin sheet of fog drifting through the streets off of the river. It twirled and danced about their boots as they weaved into the rising day. Work hard already started for most, the roadways flooded with carts, animals and dockhands. Slipping through the crowd, they made their way towards the flour mill, stopping at the barn where the horses were stored. The shadow of a tall silo loomed over them, and around its skirts they could see the docks, a boat pulling up to one of the piers, bells ringing its arrival.

"Do you think maybe we could get a better look at the water wheel before we leave?" asked Fenella, craning her neck to get a better view, but the wheel was enveloped by fog. "I've never seen one that big before."

"That's what all the ladies say," commented Callum, smoothly.

Wick answered her, completely oblivious to the crude joke. "If we take the north street out of town, we'll pass right by it!"

Aldan hefted two of Wick's bags into the back of the cart. "Works for me. Marlia's is north of here anyways."

"Yes." Fenella gave a little pump of her fist at the news.

In one of the cart's storage trunks, Callum snatched his satchel out from under some medical supplies, checked the contents for his stolen treasure, and slipped it over his head. He'd considered leaving the sword Aldan gifted him mixed with the spare blankets, but he grabbed it anyway, tying it off to his belt. When he tacked up Red, he tried his best to stay clear of Six as she brushed down Sunrise beside him, but Callum was never good at holding his tongue, especially not when it came to her. Always preferring to settle the dust, he tried to run through icebreakers in his mind, to have somewhat of a script prepared for when he approached her.

Faking confidence, he turned around. "Hey, Six?" She didn't acknowledge him, only patted out her saddle pad before tossing it onto Sunshine's broad back. He repeated himself, "Six."

"What?" she snapped with a masterful coolness.

Every single word of his well crafted, well articulated and perfectly leveled script disappeared right out of his head, and for a second he just stood there in abject terror, trying to force himself to say something. Anything at all. "Uhm...Look, what I said last night-"

"I'm not a coward for wanting to go home, Callum."

"I know."

"And I am sure as shit not a coward for worrying about them," she argued, throwing a glance to the others to make sure they hadn't overheard her.

Callum felt about two inches tall. "I know."

She took a breath to steady herself. "I'm still in this, but not for you or your half-assed schemes." Six nodded towards the others. "I'm staying for them, to make sure they don't get themselves killed."

"Okay." *As long as you're here.*

"Hey guys." Fenella sounded worried as she cut in, her face pinched somewhere between confusion and discomfort. She looked around, although she didn't know what she was searching for. "Something doesn't feel right."

Tytian, buckling Outstrider's bridle, stopped immediately. "What do you mean?"

Shaking her head, Fenella's fingers latched onto her belt where it rested against her midline. "I don't know. I just..." Her voice trailed, eyes cutting to her left, out into the street, seconds before the crowds fell into a strange hush.

Their toppled-anthill-like activity slowed, the people of River-port staring at a group of armored men who moved in a pack up the city street, studying every face they saw. Outfitted and aired like those from Talonwood, these were, without a doubt, Francesca Draven's thugs.

Callum groaned with a slump. "Shit."

"Friends of yours?" Wick asked nervously.

Calmly, Aldan slid the cart horse's tie rope free from the hitch post, angling the gelding out of the open barn front. "Think they've spotted us?" Growing closer, broadsword in hand, the head man laid eyes on Callum as the last syllable left Aldan's lips. He pointed his blade, and the foul grouping corrected course.

"You tell me," Callum snarked. He then turned to Tytian and Six. "Feel like getting your hands dirty?" But Tytian had already freed himself from the constraints of his cloak and Six had eased to the front of the pack, axes at the ready in each hand. She pumped her right knee three times, stretching the damage in an attempt to loosen the built-up inflammation.

"Stop right there!" called the broadsword, the man to his right shouldering a crossbow. All around, the locals slowly bled away into buildings and alleyways, keeping their heads down and noses poked into business that didn't concern them.

Callum raised his hands and stepped out from under the barn eave. "Hi there fellas. If you're looking for 'Gerry's Stick-From-Ass-Removal Clinic', you've come about a block too far."

The broadsword sneered, "That's them." He then raised his fingers to his mouth, whistling sharply. Seven more foot soldiers filed in from around the corner, accompanied by two spearmen on horseback. "We will accept the surrender of Tytian J'haren-mar," barked the lead man, eyeing Tytian as he stepped out from under the eave. "You should comply, for everyone's sake."

Six flicked her eyes to Callum, caught his attention and redirected it toward Fenella, who had been tucked carefully behind Aldan. His nod of understanding was almost undetectable.

Callum tried as discreetly as possible to speak to Aldan over his shoulder. "Take Fenella, take the horses, and run."

Ting... ting...

The twinkling of riding spurs heralded a new figure's approach, her voice rising above the tumbling fog. "Yes, please run," begged Francesca, as she weaved her way through the gathered soldiers. "And when I catch you, I want you to scream." *Ting.* "And I want you to plead." *Ting.* "And to cry." *Ting.* "Can you do that for me, Fenella?"

Tytian's ears were ringing, the blood in his skull rolling in and out as a thunderous wave. His body shook, fists clamped so tightly blood ran to the end of his knuckles, dripping into the street. "Ches." Her name slipped from him, lost in the space between them, bringing her hellfire eyes to his own.

Francesca smiled; perfect, deadly teeth on display. "I found you."

Drawing breath was damn near impossible. He might as well have been anchored to the deepest ocean pit.

Her head tilted, a shimmer running through her hair even in the overcast. "You're so quiet, Tytian. Nothing like the last time we saw each other," she crooned. "I can fix that." Fingers spread, palm open, Francesca raised her hand and pointed it at their grouping, orange light seeping free of the skin as it opened, unleashing licking tongues of flame.

Tytian's own mind betrayed him, prompting him not to act, but to recall the slow creak of door hinges, and the screams of his youngest niece as she boiled alive inside her own skin.

Sweeping in front of them all, Wick pushed his palms together and then pulled them apart, forming daggers of solid earth in the air. He maintained the power channel, holding the shards aloft at the ready. "You should leave, hellhag! Before you're put down in the street."

Francesca regarded him briefly, clearly entertained by his vigor. She laughed, the sound smooth as still waters, then addressed her men. "If you're smart, you'll kill that one first."

There was no time to react after that. She never gave them the opportunity to. Francesca Draven crossed the gap almost faster than a blink, sweeping Tytian into her grip, driving him backwards into the butcher shop. Glass exploded in a glimmering rain across the cobblestones, screams from the staff inside sending the area residents into a panic.

Callum swung around to Aldan, waving a frantic hand. "Run! You know where to go!"

Fenella was scooped up and plopped on Apple's back before she even knew what happened, following Aldan's orders while he released the other horses and steered his own down the roadway, heading north for the city exit. They rode out of the reach of danger, with Red, Outstrider and Sunrise herding on their heels.

Watching them disappear into the chaos, Callum was given just enough time to draw his sword before there was a spiked club whistling past his head. He swung to the side and hacked at the soldier, only to have the man parry the blow and go in for another swing. With effort, he lurched backwards out of the way, brought his blade down against the club and gave it a twist, trying to ream it from the man's hand. To his right, another soldier charged in, his sword arced for the slice and as Callum attempted to kick him in the gut, he wrung his body out of dodge, positioning himself shoulder to shoulder with the club wielder. Callum leapt backwards and grabbed a small crate filled with tomatoes that was stacked against the storefront behind him and flung it in their faces.

Wick released his summoned artillery, striking a footman in the thigh, the earthen daggers harder to control with the adrenaline shaking his hands. Wick managed to dodge an incoming crossbow bolt, and then another, and another. But what he didn't realize was that with each dodge, he was being herded into the fray until he was struck in the shoulder by a horse. Wick hit the cobblestones, hard. Hard enough to knock stars into his vision, obscuring the mounted soldier as he dismounted, sword and disposition eager for blood. Wick rolled on to his back, raised his hands and tried to conjure a shield of stone when suddenly Six was there, hacking one of her axes into the man's ribs. She bellowed as she struck him, withdrew her axe and then struck again. Against the cloudy sky Wick could see a spray of red erupt from the soldier's mouth as he stumbled away, Six surging against his retreat, hammering her axe down against his skull.

Callum's attackers had him backed into the mouth of an alley, both men well educated in vastly different combat styles, causing Callum to have to think on his feet and use whatever was around him. A vase, a bucket of rainwater, some fruit crates, clothing strung out to dry. Whatever he could grab, he used to his advantage. Deeper and deeper they forced him down the alley, the narrow space working in Callum's favor somewhat, keeping the soldier's movements restricted. When he finally backed into a back road, Callum reached out with his sword and cut a laundry line, bringing down a pile of heavy blankets on the men. They fought their way free from the fabric while Callum took off down the row, hoping desperately for an escape.

Merging, another cut of back street carried him past a few shops, all of the doors were locked tight. Behind him the soldiers were closing in, jumping over the trash bins and boxes Callum would pull down to slow their chase.

One more sharp turn led him down a roadway that funneled him into a food district, noted by the scent of kitchens at work. Languishing by a back door, a grease-smattered cook rolled a joint of tobacco between his teeth, folding the edge of thin paper down with a flick of his tongue. Callum nearly crashed into him as he cut through the door and across the kitchen, swerving to miss a woman carrying a platter of eggs. Another doorway led out into the dining hall, and Callum skittered to a halt, catching his breath and locating the front entrance. Behind him, there was a crash of plates and angry yells, followed by screams. "Shit." He sprinted across the patron-packed room and out the front door, tumbling out to main street.

At the other end of town, Tytian struggled under Francesca's crushing grip and his own, shattered body. His bones were gritty underneath his skin, shivering with friction as they bound themselves together again. He spat the pooling blood in his mouth across her face as he pawed and pulled at her locked wrists. She sneered down at him through the spray, her hand wrapped so tightly around his throat he could feel the arteries beginning to rupture. Around them, debris lay scattered. Once a butcher shop, now the broken stage of their inevitable reunion.

Very fitting.

"You're still as weak as I remember." Francesca's grip tightened, unmoving against his attempts at freedom. With a flick of her left hand, an ashen dagger formed within her curling fingers, poised to strike and send him back into deep slumber. "Perhaps I'll wake you long enough to watch me eat your newly collected friends." She slid in closer, her breath hot against his bloodied lips. "Or perhaps, I'll do worse." Her smile was wicked, the light in her eyes building. "You know how I like it. Defile, and devour."

Tytian summoned every bite of his returning strength and locked his fists in her hair. When she recoiled, he pulled her to him, until his forehead smashed against her nose. There was a wet crunch, then she flailed, giving him enough relief to rise and wrench, ripping her off of him by her roots. She roared, her voice splitting the unsettled air like a cleaver, and grappled against his hold, gaining leverage through her strength and vicious resolve.

Standing, free from her strangle, Tytian tried dragging her closer to a fallen rack of meat cutting blades, but she planted her feet and drove her palm upward, into his jaw. Once more his neck bones snapped in rhythm, heat flooding him almost as quickly as it left him, his body panicking at the severed connection. His arms dropped, feet staggered, Tytian was open to her next attack until his body could regain control again.

Francesca leveled her shoulder and charged, striking him in the chest, toppling him through the shattered window and back into the street.

When it came to the militia, Six was faster than they expected. Hit harder. Fought with a fervor they had only even seen in cornered animals. It gave her an advantage, as they soon learned not to get too close, but these men were trained killers, skilled at adaptation. In the time they were at her mercy, they learned her, and moved accordingly.

Six ripped her axe from the body of a soldier and moved on to the next, gritting her teeth against the burning pain of her right leg. He scrambled backward from her oncoming assault, and she thought it a wise decision. Then she heard the clapping of steel shoes and realized it wasn't her that pushed him, it was the horse charging at her back.

Turning slower than she would have liked, Six saw the animal just long enough to distinguish its color, just as its rider kicked her hard in the face, sending her spiraling into the dirt.

 Coughing against the blood that pooled in the back of her throat, Six rolled, gathered herself up to her hands and knees, hands searching for the axes lost from her grip. The footman advanced, his comrade spinning the horse with a rough hand, spurring it into action once again. She had only seconds to reclaim her weapons, one leg taking all of her weight as she rose onto her left knee, face twisted in a snarl. Six bellowed as she threw one axe over her shoulder, striking the footman in the collar, folding him fast. For the next, she would need to roll and find her footing, the timing a dangerous and uncertain thing.

Above her, glistening and singing in its sail, a shard of ice blew by. It hit the horseman square in the chest, sending him careening out of the saddle with an explosion of fine ice. He hit the street with a groan, lungs now deflated in his caved chest.

The horse skittered, flanked Six and fled up the thoroughfare.

Behind her, triumphant in his attack, Wick was beaded with sweat. "I did it!" he exclaimed, helping her up to her feet. He had managed to remain mostly unscathed, the cut to his arm just enough to spread a red stain across the sleeve of his robes. "And I didn't hit you! My aim's always been a little dodgy. Almost killed a cat once trying to knock a flowerpot off of a stool-" He was cut short when Six grabbed his robes and snatched him out of the way of an oncoming attack, throwing up her axe to meet the soldier's sword.

Wick stumbled, righted himself and moved in, pulling the water he needed from the damp air. Lighter and easier to weaponize than his first choice of stone, the ice shards sailed from his grasp as quickly as he could form them, only a few hitting shy of their marks.

Together, ice and steel collected the unfortunate souls of those who remained, Wick unable to contain the smile on his face. It was exactly how he had imagined it would be, fighting alongside Mister Duncan's infamous party. And now, he was a part of their lore.

Six looked around at the still bodies, hunting for any sign of life. Satisfied, she retrieved her stray axe and gave Wick a swift nod of approval. "You did good. Real good."

He kept his composure as much as he could on the outside, but inside, he felt as though he was going to burst. "Thanks!"

Crashing into their scene of carnage was Tytian, slammed into a stack of vegetables crates. Covered in open claw marks and grime, there wasn't a bit of visible flesh that wasn't bruised or bloodied. Francesca emerged around a corner, stepping over the bodies of her men as if they were simply garbage in the street.

When Tytian was on his feet she charged him again, seeking to flay him open with the tip of a hell-summoned sword. He maneuvered through her footwork, keeping himself just out of reach while searching for a weapon of his own. He was pretty sure there was a rib puncturing his lung, but he was healing quickly enough from her hand-to-hand attacks, it was the wounds caused by her sword that were taking much longer to close.

"You could have been this, Tytian." She whipped the blade at his chest, the flourish cutting through the air in metallic song. "Stronger, better, more capable-"

"Damned, befouled, a fucking bitch," he snarled, capturing her wrist as it fell past, twisting enough to feel a squelch that forced her to drop the sword.

It clattered against the street, then crumbled into sand.

Francesca took a step back, holding onto the crushed wrist until the pieces slipped back into place. "You were always such a pretentious prick." Rolling the joint, pleased to see it healed anew. "Perhaps that's what makes this so much fun."

The words had barely escaped her lips when she turned on her heels, throwing up her right arm to block the shard of ice that threatened to crush her skull.

Brazen amongst his kills, Wick worked up another barrage of shards, turning them tail over crown to build momentum before the launch. He called out to her when his first shot landed, repeating her earlier sentiments. "Hey! If you were smart, you would've killed me first yourself!" With a turn of his hand Wick sent another earth dagger at Francesca, only this one never hit home. Instead she swung her arm and a force came from her body that knocked the dagger away.

He had her attention now, that predatory focus locked on his hands, and Francesca started her advance.

Wick paled and started backing away, delivering shard after shard only to have it knocked away. Though a fraction slower to conjure, he swapped back to the earthen daggers, forming bigger arsenal in the vain hope they might be harder to deflect.

"Wick!" Tytian shouted, "Just go!" A quick scan of the street told him it was empty of the others, and he sickly hoped that if they weren't gone then perhaps, mercifully, they were dead. Because dead meant better than what Francesca would do to them.

Scrambling over the debris, Tytian scooped up a splinter of oak column and charged. He knew he couldn't kill her, but maybe a stake through the heart would slow her down enough for him to grab the kid and run. Another sweep of channeled force was directed behind her, striking Tytian in the gut, bringing him to his knees with a cough that tasted of blood.

Backing deeper into the street, Wick tried his best to keep his barrage steady and accurate, but he was tiring and she was closing in, not a single nick to the skin to show for his efforts. With a cry, he gathered as much stone into the air as he could, razored the edges and hurled it at her core. This one, his last chance, wasn't so easily deflected. Francesca was forced to dip, calling on her energy in both hands to career the dagger off course.

Her howl of frustration echoed through the streets as she hefted the earthen shard and directed it away. She sent it sailing over the rooftops, whistling through the air before striking the flour silo with thunderous force.

The tin groaned, split open and spilled its contents in a wave of white. Flour cascaded, crushing and rolling from roofs, collapsing the barns, uprooting streetlamps. A gust spewed the powdery fog out into the streets, forcing all in its path to brace for the suffocating impact.

Wick had thrown his robe sleeve over his face, turning his back against the cloud as it rolled over him, closing his eyes tight against the sting. It was only a minute, barely even two, but it felt like an eternity, knowing that Francesca was still only paces away.

Cautiously, he mumbled a gentle spell, churning the air around him just enough to breathe while calling on the stone for one last hit.

Tytian spat a wad of pink foam into the dust, climbing to his feet, squinting against the unsettled atmosphere. To his left, he could see Francesca's silhouette forming, waving the air in front of her for a better view. Just beyond her, readying himself for another round of attack was Wick, flipping a stone dagger over and over. He walked backwards, issuing an insult, drawing in Francesca like a moth to flame, and suddenly, Tytian understood.

He's herding her.

One step. Then another. And another. Wick trailed backwards, pulling Francesca in with the promise of brutality should she catch him. His energy was waning, his conjurations nowhere near as powerful as before, but he persisted. And weakened. And she was very much aware.

"You're getting tired, little mage." Her voice rang through the air, spurs jingling as she creeped closer. "Why not surrender?"

He took another step.

"I could use someone like you."

Another.

"If the wrong people knew of your skill, you'd be hunted."

Another.

"And slaughtered."

Another.

"But I will give you the chance to not only live, but live and thrive."

One more.

"All you have to do, is say-"

"Now!"

At Wick's cry, a shadow emerged from the narrow alley just behind Francesca, dull light gleaming as it raced along the swinging axe blade. The frosted air swirled in the currents, breaking and parting around Six, who brought her weapon down in a sweep. She was too fast, even for Francesca, and the honed blade cut through the base of her neck, sliding through muscle and bone, breaching her throat in a spray of hot, dark blood.

Francesca's severed head hit the cobblestones, spiraling away into the settling flour.

"Yes!" With his arms raised in victory, Wick laughed in disbelief. "It worked! It actually worked!"

His breath was hitched, Tytian's body and mind locked in a state of shock at what he'd just seen. Ches, toppled at last, cut out of the world like a blight. Could it have been that easy? Was it that easy? He waited with anticipation for the body to fall to the ground, to confirm that the bitch was dead.

It never did.

Francesca's headless body remained standing, arms limp at her sides, knees flexed just a little against the legs that anchored her firmly in position, torso leaned to the left. It never faltered, because it wasn't empty.

"Six..." Tytian whispered, fear pulling her name out of his lungs with sharp fingers. "Six, move!"

Just as he called her name, Francesca's hand swung upwards. Six raised her arm against the assault, her flesh laid open by the vicious claws just before her throat was locked in Francesca's grip. The headless torso rose and straightened, lifting Six off of the ground and throwing her down the street.

Tytian intercepted her trajectory, managing to catch her against his chest as the force slammed them into the brick siding of the general goods store. He took most of the impact, one arm wrapped around her core while the other covered her head, minimalizing the whiplash. Pain erupted throughout his body, the brick bursting in a rocky shower around them.

"No!" Wick arced around Francesca's body and raced up the street. "Please be alive," he begged them, pulling loose stone free from the pair.

Six coughed roughly as she slid out of Tytian's arms onto her hands and knees. She gulped down ragged breaths, bloodshot eyes focusing on the shadowy form. The body was still standing there, fingers twitching, control slowly finding purchase in meat that didn't have a brain. Six's hand slid down to her holster, felt the other axe still locked in the leather, and devised a new plan. A stupid, desperate, last act kind of plan.

Behind her, Tytian pushed himself out of the bricks, straightening his arm until his shoulder could reset itself in the heal. "Wick," he said past clamped teeth. "Get out of town. Now."

But the mage shook his head. "No, not without you."

It was Six who shoved him, climbing up to her feet. "If you want to be a part of this group, you take orders. Now, move!"

Wick hesitated, then ripped himself away, sprinting down north street, heading for the town exit. Once he was gone, Tytian rose up, shrugging free the tension from his newly realigned shoulder blades.

"What do you plan to do?" he asked her. Her arm was bleeding badly, the claw marks laying open the deep meat and he worried how long her strength would last.

Francesca's body jerked, the torso bending back, then snapping erect, her arms now rigid with control. The legs shifted, took a step, then another, until the movement was fluid enough not to topple her. She walked like a marionette through the dusty street, bent and collected her head from the small dunes of flour. Palms to temple, she lofted the slack jawed skull and set it on top of her neck stump.

Disgust, disbelief, fear. All were wrestling for dominance inside of Six and she felt every option she could concoct dribble out of her mind.

Marrow, bone, fluids, muscles, nerves and skin all melted back together, and once she was whole again, Francesca worked her jaw until it was set in place. "You're fast," she told Six with a smile. "But are you fast enough?" Her right hand started to open, slender fingers splayed.

Tytian ran cold. All around them were heaps of spilled flour, the air still polluted with the mist of it. It might as well have been black powder in a keg.

With no time to think, Tytian wrapped an arm around Six's waist, and with all the strength he had left, dragged her down the neighboring side street, towards the docks. He could smell the water, hear the gentle ring of bells in the air. It was close. Salvation mere yards away.

Francesca watched their desperate attempt with amusement, then raised her destructive hand. A spark of light in the palm was all it took, and she set the flour-filled air ablaze. Like breath from a dragon's jaws, it swept through the city with a deafening roar, and once it hit the open silo, Riverport was lost in a concussive blast of flame.

NINETEEN

There was a numbing, high pitched ring in his ears, as if the world itself was wailing. The air was fragrant with both the pleasant scent of burnt wood and the pungent sting of charred flesh. As his eyes fluttered open, Callum stared up at a gray sky. Thick and rolling, the cloud cover looked peaceful. For a while he sunk into it, his mind gloriously empty of thought. Then there came a shadow sailing across through the murk. Then another. And another. The vultures arched their wing tips and circled, quietly ominous.

For a moment there was only the ringing and the sky and the birds. Slowly came the pain and with it, the memories. Then, the panic.

Callum rose with a gnarled inhale, his vision swirling in kaleidoscope patterns. Smoldering pieces of debris were scattered about him as he lay in the tall grass just outside of the main gate. For a second, he couldn't even make out what he was seeing, the roiling black smoke making it difficult to see. He coughed roughly, managed to stand. He was injured, although he had no idea how badly, but he could move and he could think, and that was enough for him.

The last thing he remembered was running out of the restaurant, out onto main street, crashing into a citizen. The two soldiers were quick on his heels and the three of them resumed their sparring. He recalled a strike to his ribs and felt of his shirt, finding it damp with blood. As they fought, the two pushed him further and further down the street until a constable came to his aid, requesting the two soldiers to stand down. They killed him without hesitation. Three of his comrades came sprinting around the corner and soon it was Callum and the local law against the two soldiers, but a town like Riverport isn't going to have highly trained town constables and while they did their best, eventually both soldiers took them off the board.

Injured and separated from the others, Callum retreated again, trying to make it back to the town gates so he could use the watchtower to gain access to the roof tops. When he turned the last corner and the tower was in sight, he mentally mapped out his route back to the others, trying to count how many short-gapped alleyways were between here and there. His sparring skills may have been less than useful, but no one alive could out-cat Callum. Rooftops and narrow escapes were his specialty.

Near the gates is where he heard the loud boom and saw the white cloud rise over the back end of town. That's when he took the club to the ribs.

His saving grace came in the stampede of locals down the street, seeking refuge from the chaos, many dusted in flour, leaving white footprints in their fleeing shadows. It was enough distraction to free Callum from his attackers, and he'd limped into the herd. They were almost beneath the gate arch when a bright light swept over them, blotting out the sky.

The mill, he remembered in a panic.

Gritting his teeth he shambled towards what was left of town, fumbling numb fingers through his satchel for a handkerchief. He found it beneath the scroll from Savignos, offered the document a sneer, then tied the handkerchief around his face. He made it as far as the first row of burning houses before he spotted a figure walking out of the destruction, her stride easy and controlled.

"Shit, shit, shit." Callum ducked behind what was left of a thatch roof.

Francesca materialized out of the smog like a nightmare, not a scratch on her pallor skin. She stopped here and there, lifting heavy articles of debris as if they were nothing, searching for something in the destruction. Behind her, two bodies were bound in ropes, neither one familiar to him.

With steady movements Callum rolled away from his hiding spot and started following along the fallen rim of the town wall, morbidly thankful for the sounds of burning wood and crumbling structures to hide his escape. She had heard his whisper of retreat to Aldan, so his boots through the grass would have given him away had it not been for Riverport's collapse.

Near the back end of the town, where the silos once stood, there was so much damage spilling out into the surrounding field. Wood splinters, food, clothing, bodies. All of it piled in rows of ash and flames, revealed in glimpses as the black smoke rolled through on the wind. He limped through the settled destruction as quickly as possible, grimly surveying each corpse he passed.

"They made it out," he told himself over and over again with weak hope, laying a woman back into the grass. He used her apron to cover her face, smoothing down her blonde hair.

Climbing through the wreckage, Callum found the shattered remains of the waterwheel. Planks once painted bright yellow were now singed black, streaked in dull shades of red.

Fenella had been so excited to see it.

A shuddered breath turned into a coughing fit, his lungs itching. "Son of a bitch." He hacked, snatching the handkerchief from his face just before he threw up. With his hands balled into fists on his knees Callum clamped his eyes shut, trying to think of what to do while simultaneously not giving into his thoughts.

All your fault-

I can't find them even if they are in there-

Go back and kill the bitch-

Six knows to go to Marlia-

Cut her open in the street-

Aldan will go for Marlia's too-

Bleed her dry. If she kills me, I'll take her with me straight back to hell-

Marlia will be able to help, maybe she can See them and know for sure-

Six-

You don't deserve them-

Six-

You betrayed her again, Callum-

Six-

Callum roared into his palms, his throat growing tight with grief. "Shut up, shut up, shut up." He wiped his hands down his face, noticing the flares of pain as his fingers grazed over bruises and cuts. "Stick to the plan," he panted. "Go to Marlia."

Moving on felt like its own kind of death. It threatened to buckle him, but Callum knew when he was beat. And right here, standing in the ruin of the city, he was beat worse than he could imagine. Onward he pushed, feeling his way through the wreckage until he found the riverbank. The waves were unsettled, crashing over cuts of roof and capsized boats. The tumbling surface was speckled by fresh drops of rain that started gentle at first, then turned into a downpour. It was a typical spring deluge, but Callum saw it as a blessing. Under this, it wouldn't take long to smother the remaining fires across town.

Callum followed the river for a half mile, to a one-horse bridge that arced over the thinnest curve in the Paratooke. He had hoped to see some kind of tracks in the mud. Boots, horse hooves, anything, but the rain had beaten the path into soupy mud. With one arm gripping his damaged side, he made his way across the bridge, trying to keep his mind on placing one foot in front of the other and nothing else. On the other side, he followed the road up into a gentle, long slope. His wounds slowed him, air now a painful, precious commodity. Wheezing, he pushed onward to the crest. It was here that he finally allowed himself to look back.

Riverport looked like a bonfire in the distance, the smoke billowing from her bones starting to shift from black to gray beneath the heavy beat of the rain.

"Holy shit." As terrible as the scene was, Callum was thankful that the explosion hadn't reached the lightstone chamber under the city. If that had blown, they'd all be pink mist, simply floating right out of existence.

He left the pyre behind, following the roadway up another climb, into the thickening mountain forest. Marlia's home wasn't too far from Riverport, if traveling by horseback. For the most part it was a relatively easy journey to make. On this day though, battered and exhausted, fighting against storms that raged both inside and out, the trek was pure hell.

It took him all day to walk that trail, stopping only when his vision swirled and the ache in his head nearly put him on his ass. All the while, he surveyed the gravel and lanes of overgrown grasses. Still, no signs of previous travelers.

Someone, please have made it out.

When daylight started to fade around him, Callum rounded a sharp turn, spotting the marker he was searching for. "There you are." Eager, he sped up his pace, fighting against the pain and nausea until he could place a hand against the trunk of an old birch. It stood tall, out of place among the pines and oaks that surrounded it. From its branches hung bottles, chimes and ribbons. Most important among the adornments was a ward, created out of carefully shaped limbs and rough-cut crystals that glimmered, even in the low light. He planted a swift, grateful kiss against the bark, then moved around its base, weaving inside the wall of honeysuckle, to the narrow path beyond. It was well kept, but not too much, making it easy to lose if the one who climbed it didn't know the way. The footing was sandier than the road, with well positioned roots that often acted as a stairway. It led him up the mountain face, twisting here and there through small dips and gentle, high rolling peaks.

As he hiked the trail, a shiver started to take over, wind-whipped rain and shock turning existence into a hellscape. "If I never encounter another storm after this, I'll be a happy man," he muttered, a quick flash of lightning adding emphasis to his words. "Exactly." The sky rumbled gently in response.

The sun sank quickly, her light consumed by cloud cover, forcing Callum to decide if he should risk following the path in the dark, or huddle under a tree and wait for morning. He paused with consideration, upturning his face to the top of the mountain.

A tiny, neon light blinked in the gloom, gone as quickly as it was born. He squinted, wondering if maybe he had reached delirium. It happened again, then again, luring him closer. Stepping between a twin set of pines, there was a cluster of fireflies, seemingly unaffected by the downpour. They beamed their yellow lights and bobbed in front of him, urging him to follow their ascent.

Callum reached out, tried to touch one, but the tiny beetle fluttered just out of range, and up the pathway. "Okay, I'm listening. Flare those tiny butt beacons. Show your pal Callum the way." And show him the way they did, blinking through the trees, bright as any star.

Across the wet winds rose the smell of chimney smoke and Callum knew he was close.

Pushing through the numbing pain he topped the final rise, greeted by the glow of lit windows in the distance. The cabin was just a shape in the dark, but for him, it might as well have been a paradise. Feeling some crumb of safety, Callum dragged his half-dead carcass across the open yard. Exhaustion pursued, caught him at the steps and collapsed him. His knees hit the bottom rung, both arms flying out to brace himself against the fall. The light that enveloped his vision was blinding, too blinding, and for a brief moment he had the silly thought that perhaps he had died.

"Callum?" There was a sweet voice spoken over the rain, then the rushed sound of bare feet and tinkling bells across the porch. A warm hand grabbed him, eased him out of the dark. "Come on now. You're not dying on my porch."

TWENTY

His heart fluttered at the sound of her, then again as his eyes adjusted to the light.

Marlia looked down at him, curly hair wrapped in a halo of golden light, dark brown skin complimented by the sunset hues of her embroidered shawl. She looked like a goddess. A saving grace.

All at once, Callum choked on his words, tears blurring the sight of her. "Please, tell me she's here."

"Callum?!" Someone stormed out of the cabin and knelt beside him. "Are you alright?" Fenella placed her hands on his face, turning him toward the light enough for her to see. Over her shoulder, she called back inside the house, "It's Callum!"

Aldan was in the doorway then, big as an eclipse, his eyes brimming with concern. He gripped a dagger.

"Is he hurt?" asked Wick as he peeked around the blacksmith's wide frame.

There was a rushing sensation in his skull and suddenly Callum felt as though he was going to black out. He swayed a little, but Fenella caught him, letting him prop on her shoulder. "Easy," she whispered. "Let's get you inside."

Aldan helped him to his feet. Together, he and Fenella drug him into the cabin, where Wick rushed ahead, grabbed a saddle bag from an armchair in front of the fireplace and cast it in the floor. The others eased Callum down into the seat.

"I'll get you some tea," Fenella said as she disappeared from his line of sight.

Wick pulled over an ottoman and slid it under Callum's feet while Aldan unfurled a patchwork blanket over his lap.

Callum looked around the room, the details messy to his tired eyes. He didn't see anyone else. "Where-" he asked Marlia as she hovered at his side, examining his wounds.

"Six and the other aren't here." Her reassurance was accompanied by a stroke of his cheek, "But that doesn't mean they won't be."

"Can you See them?" he asked, hopefully, but she shook her head.

"It doesn't work like that, Cal. You know this."

Fenella crouched down next to his chair and handed him a warm mug of tea, which he accepted with trembling hands. "What happened?"

He took a long drink and let its heat wash through him. "I was separated from the others. Two soldiers chased me through town, and I was trying to make it back to the gates when I heard the silo open. They caught up to me, we fought and then..." He stared into the fireplace. "Boom." Another gulp of tea. "When I woke up everything was burning. And then I saw that woman, Draven, come out of the smoke. She walked out without a scratch." The scene replayed in his mind and he shivered, but not from the cold.

In the armchair across from him, Aldan sat down, fluffing a pillow against his lower back. "When we hauled ass, we were just to the first knob in the road here when we heard the explosion."

"I've never seen anything like that," remarked Fenella. "The whole sky was black."

Wick sat down on the floor in front of the fireplace and Callum had a chance to notice that he wasn't wearing his robes, stripped down to a thin under shirt and dark colored trousers. His arms were wrapped in bandages and there was a red flush to the side of his face where he'd been burned.

"You were that close, kid?" Callum grimaced, moving to the edge of his seat. "What did you see?"

There was a look in Wick's eyes- terror maybe. And he looked down at his feet, pushing his glasses up his nose. "We had killed the soldiers, Six and I, all while Tytian was fighting with that demon woman. Six told me she had an idea and said to offer as much distraction as much as I could while she circled around to get behind the demon using the alleys. I tried to pin her down with the daggers, but she just swatted them away like they were nothing." His jaw clenched then, and he shuddered a breath, guilt turning him green. "She hit one and it pierced the silo, spilling the flour, which is highly combustible. I should have thought about that, but I was so wrapped up in the moment that I didn't realize how much danger we were all in.

"Six finally got in close and she managed to cut the demon's head off, and I mean clean off." He used his hands for emphasis. "I watched her head tumble down the street. Thought for a moment that it was over, and we had won." Horror widened his eyes. "Her body moved on its own. She grabbed up Six, threw her at Tytian. He caught her, but they were pretty hurt when they hit the storefront. Six told me to run then, so I did." He pointed at the scorch of his face. "Guess I just didn't move fast enough. After that, I jumped into the river and let the current take me down to the bridge, then I ran here as fast as I could."

The small amount of tea in his gut clotted, rolled over and spoiled in the instant. Callum was sick. And not from his injuries or the long trek to safety. The last person in the room to see Six alive, and his story was painting her survival in a grim light.

"We gotta go back," he said with strain, pulling himself up to stand. Marlia was quick to stop him, offering him some reason in the face of his blind determination.

"You won't even make it out of the yard. Not in this condition."

He shook his head, his voice calm despite the plea in his eyes. "Marlia, if Francesca gets her hands on her..."

"Have some trust in Six," said Aldan. "And Tytian. He fights like a mad dog. Between the two of them, I'm sure they made it out okay."

All of their stupid logic was making his head swim. Defeated, Callum sat back down, rubbing at the vein in his forehead.

From her perch on the floor beside him, Fenella gave his hand a gentle squeeze. "They'll be okay."

"Yeah." He was thankful for her attempts, but he still felt sick.

Ribbons of small, golden bells chimed when Marlia left the room, and they chimed again when she returned a few moments later. She had a bundle of clothes in her arms. "Come on, Callum. You should get cleaned up."

With Fenella's assistance, he was on his feet and followed their hostess down the hall at a shuffle, his body starting to grow stiff with exhaustion. She led him into a bathing room and flicked on the lights, dropping the clothes on the vanity. She then turned the taps on a deep, stone tub. Spring water gurgled up the piping, running over her slender fingers as she placed the stopper. Duncan and Callum had helped put in the plumbing system to the cabin many years ago, mostly through magical means, but the sound of the pipes beneath the floorboards brought back a host of memories to an already raw mind.

"Wick?" called Marlia.

There were footsteps and then he popped his head in the room. "Yes ma'am?"

"Could you heat the water again please?"

"Oh yeah, absolutely." He placed his hands above the water and murmured a spell, which made a small orb of molten light drip from his palm and sizzle into the water.

Marlia smiled and patted his hand. "Thank you, baby."

Wick gave Callum a remorseful look and wiped at the end of his own nose. "I'm going to go sit on the porch, keep watch for the others. Maybe send out a few more fireflies."

"Those were yours?" asked Callum and Wick nodded in return. He grinned. "Smart."

Wick bounced away, eager for any chance to help.

There were various types of wooden boxes, and multicolored jars lined on shelves behind the tub. Marlia chose a few of them with care. A sprinkle of this, a drop or two of that, and some crushed herbs went into the steamy water, sending a clean smell around the room. "There, you should feel much better after a bath. You just shout if you need anything, okay? When you're finished, I'll get that side of yours wrapped up." Dusting her hands, she stood up and headed for the door.

"Marlia?" The tone of his voice stopped her short of leaving. "Do you know why we're here?"

Gravely, she nodded, clasping her hands in front of herself. "Aldan told me."

"Everything?"

"Yes."

"*Everything?*"

Her back straightened a little. "All of it."

Callum's tired eyes started to sting. "I can't let them get her, Marlia." Grief found its way into his throat, clotting up his airway with a sob.

Reaching up, she swept the hair from his eyes, her fingers gentle against the bruised skin as she cradled his face. "Have a little faith. Six is tough. She's the second best at getting out of a pinch."

He huffed an unexpected laugh, dabbing at his nose. "Second best, huh? Who's the first?"

She grinned. "Duncan."

This made him laugh in full, the action earning him a painful twinge of the ribs. "Dunc's dead."

"Exactly. He got out of the biggest pinch of all."

Another chortle, another grimace. Callum looked at her with a twisted sort of smile, genuinely grateful for the moment of peace, even if it did hurt. "Thanks for that."

"Anytime, baby." She brushed his face with the touch of her hand and left him alone, the door falling shut behind her with a light click.

Callum leaned against the vanity, looking up to his reflection in the mirror with a flinch. The dark circles under his eyes were stark against the ashen shade of his skin. The bruise on his cheek looked like an ink blot, and he had cuts on his nose, forehead, lip and jawline. His hair was plastered to his head like a dead animal.

"You look like shit," he told his mirror-self.

Slipping a finger under the strap, he took off the satchel and dropped it on the floor next to the toilet. It plopped on the floor, stiff as a wet piece of meat and sagged into itself, the soaked leather losing all rigidity. The end of the stolen scroll peaked out from behind the top flap, its sea glass handle glinting in the light.

"Don't look at me like that," Callum told the scroll. "You're the one who got us into this mess."

It sat there, as silent as the inanimate object that it was.

"That's not true," he sighed. "I got us into this. All of us." He shook his head and turned to the scroll. "But what was I supposed to do? What do I do now? Huh?"

The scroll was still silent.

"Oh, some help you are," he sneered in anger, but then it faded, and his shoulders slumped in tired defeat. "Sorry. It's been a long day." He rubbed at his brow. "But you know that."

Realization sprang open the eyes that now rolled in his skull. "I'm talking to a scroll. I have officially lost my damn mind."

Turning away from his own special brand of insanity, he removed his shirt, hissing like a snake as he raised his arms. In the mirror, the wounds were on full, gruesome display. Along his back were bruises and scrapes. There was a lengthy scratch running across his collarbone, and his side looked like raw meat, the skin puckered and angry. A flourish of deep purple went from his waist to his under his arm and the punctures from the mace spikes had clotted with dark blood. When his pants were off, he spotted a few more abrasions to his right thigh and a dark blue knot on the side of his left knee. Nothing too life threatening at the moment, but the next few weeks would hurt like hell.

Callum climbed over into the tub, holding back the grunt that tightened his throat. The bath water felt like lava against his cold skin, lapping the exposed meat on his side with waves of pain. He took in several deep breaths through his nose and tried to calm his screaming body. Concentrating, he was able to regain some composure and the water began to lose its bite.

With rag in hand, Callum started the tedious process of bathing his battered body, the previously clear water slowly turning a murky shade of red.

Sometime later, in the living room, the others had gathered around with a somber silence between them, each clutching a warm mug in their hands. Rain pattered against the tin roof, mixing in harmony with the soft crackle of the fireplace.

"They cut off her head," said Fenella, breaking through the silence. She stroked the cup with her thumb, seeking comfort in the small action. "And yet, she just kept coming. How was that not enough to stop her? How does something function without a head?"

Marlia was using a thin, glass file to pull the dried blood from under her nails, dressing Callum's wounds had been messier than she anticipated. "Demons are out of balance with the natural world and her laws. They do not abide by bodily rule."

Fenella glared into the flames. "Does that mean we'll have to come up with an unnatural way to kill her?"

"Maybe, maybe not." Using a cut of soft fabric, Marlia buffed her nails to a shine. "I'll speak within the Current in the morning, see if they can offer up any insight."

"The what?" asked Fenella.

"The Current. Spirits and energies that sometimes offer insight from their place in the void."

Fenella perched on the edge of her seat. "You mean like ghosts?"

Marlia laughed softly, deepening the age lines around her eyes. "Not exactly."

Without even realizing it, Fenella touched her hand to her core.

The front door creaked open and in walked Wick, rubbing some warmth into his arms. "It's kind of chilly out there. Anyone have a jacket I can borrow?"

Aldan grabbed the blanket that was draped over the arm of his chair and tossed it to Wick. "Here, warm up some, son. I'll take over for you."

"That's alright, I'll do it." Callum stepped out of the hall, drying his hair with a towel. "I'll sit watch for a while."

Fenella eyed him, particularly the wind of bandages she could see where his shirt hem rode too high. "You really should be resting."

"Nah, I'm perfectly fine," he lied. "There isn't a horse alive in better health than me." He stifled a cough, his body clearly trying to humor itself with its timing.

"Uh huh." Her delivery was flat. "At least eat something." In the kitchen she poured him a bowl of stew and handed it over before she stuffed a fat piece of buttered bread into his mouth. She also handed him another cup of tea just before tossing the blanket over his shoulders, fluffing it up around his neck. "Comfy?"

He nodded. "Yeth. 'hank yoo," he said around the bread, then shuffled for the door and stepped out into the night.

Marlia's porch was covered from one end to the other in potted plants of various species, size, color and smell. She had bags of mulch and barrels of rain water lining the walls. Birdhouses hung from the edge of the roof just out of the reach of the weather. Wind chimes clinked together in a calming chorus and hand woven warding symbols spun in the wind. There was a sitting area set up and Callum took up a seat on a patchwork cushioned bench. Once he was settled in, he started to eat, keeping his eyes trained on the dark yard for any kind of movement or sound. The only sign of life was Wick's conjured fireflies.

"Where are you, Lucia?" A quick streak of lightning was the only answer he received.

Warmed by both bath and stew, Callum reclined and prepared himself for the long watch ahead. Mug in hand, he worked on the tea, sipping regularly as a means of engagement, keeping his thoughts centered around the act so they didn't stray too far into absolute panic.

Light poured across the porch as Fenella opened the door, swinging around the frame with a teapot and a question. "Hey, want some more?"

He raised his cup a little and shook his head. "Still working on this one. Thank you though."

"Oh, okay." She turned to go back inside, then paused. "Want some company instead?"

Callum cocked a grin. "I'm not sure if Aldan and I can both fit on the bench, but I'm willing to try if he is." When she laughed there was a fuzzy feeling in his chest. "Actually, I'd love some company."

Gingerly lifting his arm, he made room for her under the cover and she slid in beside him, closing up the fabric around them. Callum noticed she smelled like the rose soap from Marlia's collection.

"She's okay, you know." Fenella's tone sat somewhere between hope and confidence. "They both are."

Callum stared at her, both admiring her certainty and fearing it. "Yeah," he agreed weakly. "I mean, if ol Franny can survive getting her melon lopped off, then maybe Tytian can survive an explosion."

"And Six is too stubborn to let anyone else kill her."

Callum chuckled. "True."

"What was she like when you two were younger?"

He took in a deep breath, wincing at the act, his chest tightened by more than just the damage done. "Well, still a hard ass, but not quite as much of one as she is now. Surprisingly funny, once she's comfortable. Strict morals, although a little muddy now. Always had high walls around herself."

"So, the opposite of you?"

Callum tweaked a brow. "You sayin' I got shallow walls?"

Fenella laughed. "I'm saying you would carry on a conversation with your own executioner." She bounced a fist gently against his knee. "You're chatty, my friend."

"I just enjoy the social aspects of living is all," he countered. "Everyone you meet has a story to tell. Or a pocket to pick."

Fenella rolled her eyes. "Is that all you ever think about? Stealing?" In response, he gave her a look that made her blush.

"It's not all I think about."

She stared at his mouth long enough for him to notice, then turned her attention to the forest, fidgeting in her seat. "So... were you always inclined to thievery?"

It hurt to shrug. "Just doing what I can with what I have. It's what I'm good at. A that the cosmos, or the divines or even hell itself dealt to me at birth. I didn't get a proper family and a silver spoon. Instead, I got a network of criminal misfits and a talent for burglary work."

"If you had roughly the same upbringings, how on earth did you and Six wind up so vastly different?"

"Me and her may have eventually been orphans together but didn't grow up the same. My parents were thieves themselves, although their moral compass was a little broken. They'd steal from anyone, didn't matter if it was a nobleman or a pauper, they took whatever they wanted. Six's father however, he might have been a drunk, but he wasn't a bad man. He actually did love his kid, even though the drink made it hard to do right by her."

"Your parents didn't love you?" Fenella asked with a touch of sorrow.

Callum's nose wrinkled. "Nah. A kid just weighed 'em down. They used me for as long as they could but eventually everyone in the city became wise to our schemes and no one fell for the acts anymore, so they sold me to the orphanage and skipped town." Talking about his parents was always something that he had hoped would make him feel better and help him move on from the pain of it, but no matter who he talked to he could never erase the deep seeded feeling of being left behind. Especially being left behind by those who were supposed to take care of him. All throughout his childhood Callum would see other kids with their parents and it would make him sad, and for a long time he didn't really know why. It's hard to piece together your traumas when you're too young to understand them and there's no one around who gives two shits about you to explain it.

Fenella looked at him apologetically. "That's horrible."

He simply smiled. "That's life."

"Do you know where they are now?"

"Why? You want to hunt them down for me and exact some revenge?"

A tiny shrug. "Maybe."

Callum appreciated the sentiment. "Thank you for the pre-meditated acts of violence but they won't be necessary. I haven't the faintest idea as to where they are." Once, at the risk of a beating, he broke into the office at the orphanage when he was fourteen and read through the in-take documents. His only had 'Callum' under the child information section and an X on the signature line, nothing else was filled in. They had made damn sure that neither their pup nor anyone else would ever be able to find them.

"Well, it's their loss," Fenella said with simmering anger. "I couldn't imagine dumping my child at an orphanage like that."

"That's because you're not a shitty person." Callum was thankful for her anger because he couldn't manifest within him-self- something that Six had often told him he was entitled to. Even though they abused him and abandoned him and spoke to him as though he was garbage, Callum had loved them, as children always do. Hoping against hope that maybe one day they'd love him back. They were his parents, and no matter how mean they were to him, like a beaten dog, he'd always crawl right back, thinking that maybe they'd give him a scrap of a kind word.

They sat in silence after that; both lost to their own thoughts as together they kept watch on the night. Both of them waited desperately for Six or Tytian to emerge from the black, unharmed and just a little weathered from the storm. Only the winds stirred the undergrowth.

Sleep was the furthest thing from Callum's mind, but it overtook Fenella in the early hours of the morning and slowly her head settled against his shoulder. He wrapped the blanket around them both a little tighter.

Somewhere out in the dying storm, an owl cried.

TWENTY ONE

Six felt the heat at her back and then there was the rough push, and she was suddenly airborne. Tytian had tried to get them to safety, but the blast was too strong. Both of them hit the docks first before getting flung into the unsteady waters. Six was fortunate, snagging a pile of fishing nets. Tytian however, struck a pile of wooden cargo crates, shattering them. Both were taken under by the river.

The water converged over her. A hungry, swallowing mouth, pushing her down beneath the currents and then raising her back to the top. As her head broke the surface another wave came crashing down and repeated the process, turning her over and over in its grip.

Don't panic, don't panic. Look for light, find the sky.

Six inhaled deeply as she breached the turbulent break once more, bobbing up and down like a fishing lure. Debris was scattered around her along with a few limp bodies rocking in the surf. Behind her the city was nothing but a wall of flames, heat from the structures making her skin feel unbearable. With effort she managed to wade through the broken planks, barrels, food, ship parts and corpses, heading for the far shore away from Riverport and her horrors. Six longed to call out, to see if anyone was alive out there with her, but the fear of Francesca kept her voice within her throat.

With aching fingers she felt of her holsters. One axe was still in its place but the other had been lost when she was thrown into Tytian. Injured, down to one weapon and without backup. The odds were steadily stacking themselves against her, anger and fear mixing like a bad cocktail in her stomach.

As she swam, Six made sure to check the bodies one by one for life, yet no one seemed to have made it through the blast. "Shit..." she muttered as she gently pushed a singed corpse out of her way, the features too far gone for recognition. One by one she flipped those in her path, until finally, "Tytian?"

Face down in the sloshing waves, snowy hair stuck out like a pharos in the murky green waters.

"Oh no." She swam to him as fast as she could, her right leg's lack of dexterity making her stride uneven. Quickly, she threw a glance towards town for any sign of Francesca. If she survived a beheading then certainly she would have survived the blast. Six hoped that maybe she was in a few pieces at least.

When she reached Tytian she rolled him over with dread. Although still mostly intact, he wasn't breathing, and she wasn't sure if that was always the case.

He breathes, right? I've seen him breathe?

It would seem anything was possible with the demonic sort.

Six grabbed a handful of his shirt and rolled, dragging him close to her chest as she used one arm to backstroke. "You can't die because of her, Tytian," she whispered, teeth grit tightly as she worked her way towards the shore. "She doesn't get to win, alright?"

The bank was a little steep, and there was no shelf of sand to stand on. Roughly, she climbed out of the river, grunting as she pulled Tytian with her. Pure spite hoisted them up the sloughing sands. Shoulders, elbows, hips and heels. Every inch of her worked them both free of the waves, all while she silently cursed their size difference. Once she had her knees on dry land, she was able to heft him little by little into the high grass. Immediately, she placed her palms on his chest, her hands shaking violently from nerves and the building shock in her system. Her left arm throbbed with every beat of her heart, blood pooling between her hands. The lacerations made by Francesca's nails were both wide and deep, in need of stitches. But she pushed through the pain with a toothy sneer and started pumping on his chest in rhythmic beats.

One, two, three, four, five... "Come on Tytian. Please wake up." *Ten, eleven, twelve, thirteen...* "Wake up." *Fifteen, sixteen, seventeen...* "Wake up, you asshole." She raised her right hand above her head and brought it down hard in the center of his chest, grunting with the impact.

Water spewed from his mouth, his lungs choking up the river from inside. Six quickly turned him on his side and started patting her fist between his shoulder blades. There came a series of wet gurgles and finally, a ragged gasp for air.

"There," she muttered. "Just breathe."

Tytian's eyes snapped open, adrenaline permeating every fiber, and he turned on her violently. Teeth bared like a feral animal, claws at the ready, he gripped her shirt, forced her to the ground and pinned her there. Her arm was thrown across his clavicle in an attempt to keep his fangs from her throat.

"It's me!" she cried out to him, "You're safe!"

In the instant she spoke, his mind cleared, all hostility draining away. Tytian eased off of her with a whispered apology. Wheezing breaths were rattling from his lungs and there was a large cut on his face, but he seemed to be no worse for wear. At least he was alive.

Six sat up, trying to subtly catch her breath. "Are you okay?"

He nodded and turned towards Riverport, coughing gently every few breaths. "Wick?"

"I don't know," she sighed.

He scanned over the destruction, deciding on a cold conclusion that turned his stomach. "We can't stay."

"We can't leave. We have to find the others."

As she sat beside him, half drowned, caked in blood and grime, Tytian knew their fight ended here. And it wasn't a draw, or a victory. They'd lost, and lost big time. "Look, if I can get you somewhere safe, then I can come back and search for everyone else. But right now-" There settled a stern fix to his eyes. "Six, we cannot stay."

Timed perfectly, as if to prove his point, a blast of flames pushed up through the rubble.

"Come on," Tytian said with urgency as he helped Six get to her feet. Together, they made for a cluster of boulders at the foot of the hillside. He helped her climb over, both settling in behind the stones, well hidden from town. Another ball of fire bellowed and plumed, dropping bits of shingle into the river. When the next one sounded further away, Tytian carefully peered over the stones, seeing no sign of their huntress.

"She's gone." Next to him, Six was holding her arm, trying to stem the blood flow from the gashes that ran wrist to elbow. Her color was soured and Tytian's worry grew.

"I cut off her head," she said to no one in particular, the scene playing over and over behind her eyes. The automatic drive to stay alive was beginning to wane, now reason was taking over and it gave her time to reflect on this new, frightening enemy. "Her fucking head. And she just...just put it back on. Like a hat. Did you know she could do that?"

"No. That was definitely outside of what I thought was possible."

"What are the chances any of them survived?" She looked up at him. "I lost track of Callum, Wick was barely out of sight and what if Aldan and Fenella never made it out of town?"

He couldn't tell whether the shake in her voice was due to fear or her injuries. He figured probably a bit of both. "I don't have an answer for you. But if they were in that-" He took another look at the smoldering remains, "Their chances of survival are slim. Slimmer with that snake slithering the flame."

A numbers game. That's all they had. Chances and statistics, neither one in their favor. Still, she held out a little hope, no matter how illogical it made her feel. "We survived."

His sigh was edged. "Yes. And now, we're going to your friend Marlia, which is what the others would do too. Which way?"

To their left was an open expanse of valley that was hugged tightly by a wall of steep hills that rose into the forest covered mountains. Six pointed to a little knoll up the ways from a bridge that was a mere dot in the distance.

"See that knob?"

"Yes."

"That's the old Paratooke Pass. Follow it, and it'll lead to the trail up to Marlia's cabin. She lives high in the mountains."

There wasn't any cover between their hiding spot and the barely-there road Six had pointed out and it made Tytian nervous. "That's a lot of open land."

"Yep," Six said bluntly, throwing a glance over the boulder to Riverport.

"We can't go that way."

"Wouldn't advise it."

Tytian rested his elbows on his raised knees and held his head, his fingers kneading at his temples as he tried to formulate an alternate plan. Had he been on his own he probably could have slipped away across the field unnoticed with some ease, but Six was injured, in more ways than one, so he couldn't take any chances. "Could we go around that way? Over the hills and up into the mountains?" Tytian pointed to a row of tree-topped rises to their right.

Six squinted at the tree line, judging the distance. "Maybe? Her place is at the very top of an overlook. There is no back way, but we could go around this forest here," she pointed to the trees in front of them, "And make our way to the trail. It'll be the long way around and one hell of a hike..."

"It's better than sitting here."

Tytian looked over the top of the rocks again, then studied the quarter mile stretch of valley they would have to traverse before they could make it to the tree line. It was a long run from their hiding spot to the forest wall and he wasn't too sure they wouldn't be spotted by Francesca.

Kneeling forward, he offered to let her climb on. "Here, get on my back. It'll faster if we-"

"No. I will not be carried," she told him with a bit of stung pride.

Tytian tossed another glance towards town. "Don't be so stubborn."

"I said no." There was a finality to her tone that told him not to push the topic further, not unless he wanted a bloody nose.

Defeated, he stood down, offering instead his hand to get her on her feet. "Fine. Let's go."

Together they left the cover of the rocks, cautiously at first but when there was no sudden flash of flames they broke into a run. Tytian kept his pace slower than his body was capable of, making sure not to leave Six behind. He might have admitted to being impressed with how well she was able to keep up, had he not also been so exacerbated by her. She had developed her gait to accommodate for the bad knee, causing a kind of skip to her step. It was painful, a fact she didn't try to hide, but it worked.

As if to put more wind in their sails there came another blast from town. Six flinched and grit her teeth, pushing herself to pick up speed even though she was at her limit. Hope and relief came in the form of overgrown ferns and dogwood branches, the two of them crashing through leaves into the forest as though it were an ocean wave. There was nothing more than a thin cover of trees between them and Riverport, but those tall pines and oaks might as well have been the vast walls of a fortress. Being back under the green canopy gave Six a feeling of comfort and she laid a palm against a nearby tree trunk, silently thanking the earth for its existence.

"Think she saw us?" she asked him.

Tytian shook his head. "We would know if she did." He then eyeballed the high rising forest floor, tracing the seams of sandstone and rock. It was steep, damn near vertical, even the trees had to adapt to the slope, their root systems spreading out for any nook to take their hold. This facing stretched on in either direction, forcing him to decide; up, or around.

He turned to Six, opened his mouth to ask her opinion, then stopped short. She was catching her breath, lacerated arm held tightly against her stomach. Soaking wet, coated in river mud, blood smeared just about everywhere- she looked like hell. "How's the arm?" He wasn't a big fan of the sickly tone to her skin.

Slowly, she rolled the limb over and examined all of the cuts, happy to find that only one of them was still bleeding freely. "Well, it's still attached." Six clamped her hand over the offending wound.

Tytian ripped a sleeve from his shirt and wrung it out as much as he could. "Come here." With skilled fingers he tore the fabric and laced its pieces around her arm, tying them off just below her elbow joint.

The pressure of the cold bindings felt nice, and she flexed to test the hold. "Thank you."

It wasn't a permanent solution, it wasn't even a good one, but it was better than nothing.

"Alright, looks like up is our fastest option," Tytian told her as he craned his neck, pointing out the top ridge.

In the distance thunder rumbled, low and urgent.

Clumsily, they made their way through the trees and up the rise, using saplings, rocks and exposed roots as footholds. There were a few times when Tytian would have to help Six with reaching a branch or two, but for the most part she did well enough with only one arm and a less than helpful right leg. The last outcropping of rocks proved to be an almost impossible obstacle, barren of trees and bushes, only glimmering sandstone staring them in the face.

Tytian revisited his offer. "Either you grow some wings and fly up there, or you let me help you."

Sweating, injured and overall unpleasant, Six regarded him with a glare. "I don't really appreciate your tone."

"I don't really appreciate your pride slowing us down."

Another roll of thunder forced her hand, and after realizing there was no way for her to make it over without aid, she relented.

Tytian maneuvered to her thin shelf, sliding himself between her and the wall just enough for her to wrap herself around his back. He adjusted her arms around his neck, then took hold on a crag, following the chips and seam paths up the steep facing. With her chest against his shoulder blades he could feel Six's heart pounding in its cage, despite her calm and even breathing.

"Almost there," he assured her.

"Feel free to take your time," she muttered sarcastically, swallowing hard.

"Don't like heights?"

"Heights are fine. Just don't like being carried."

Her torture was over within a quarter hour, Tytian's gifted strength an asset. Once they topped the cliff and were on solid ground again, he eased her off of his back, noting, but not mentioning, the strange look on her face.

Honeysuckle scented the air, carrying over them with the warm breeze. Overhead, the canopy shivered, speckling them in dull light as they weaved in and out of the underbrush. Deeper into the trees, where the sweet scent of wild vines hung thickest, they found a narrow trail. In the soft dirt, hooves had left imprints winding around the white oak grove. It was easy, following the deer's cloven road, and Tytian's worry was beginning to ease.

He called over his shoulder, "Seems we're due for a bit of luck," but his words were almost cut short by the sudden snap of thunder. A grand herald to the arrival of a downpour. With dripping hair and an expression that read defeat, he turned around. "And to think, we were almost dry."

Six blinked into the falling rain. "At least this will put a damper on Draven as well. Unless she's somehow aquatic? Like some hellish, fiery polliwog?"

"Not that I am aware of. But the functioning decapitation has me questioning things."

The hunting trail was becoming a sloppy mess the further they traveled. For the first hour of their trek the storm was mostly just heavy rains and gusty winds. Soon the energy shifted, making the air tingle. Tytian eyed the towering trees around them. They swayed like dancers in the ripping gales.

"I think it's time to take shelter."

Six pointed ahead of them. "We're almost to the pass. Maybe another hour or-"

Everything went white. Completely silent for only a heartbeat. Even the rain seemed to have fallen into a hush as the lightning strike arced across the sky just above the tops of the trees. The crack of thunder that followed was felt deep in the meat, making Tytian's teeth hurt.

Both of them flinched downward, hands instinctively covering their ears.

"You were saying?" he asked over the fading rumble.

Six was rattled into compliance. "Shelter it is."

Hastened, they traveled down the ridge, into the mild safety of lichen covered boulders. Two mammoth stones had toppled together in some ancient tumble down the hillside, kissing their crowns to form a shallow cave. Tytian pulled back the thin draping of vines that covered the mouth, and ushered Six inside. Scattered about were small rocks and Six chose one for seating, eager to rest. She leaned back against the mossy wall, rubbing her knee with fingers that were shaking from more than the cold. Deeper in the crevasse she could hear the rhythmic drip of water.

Tytian stood nearby, watching the storm. Thick cloud cover made it difficult to determine what time of day it was, but he had a feeling they were sitting around late afternoon.

Lightning crawled the sky.

"We might be stuck here for the night." There was no response. "Six?"

The ashy pallor to her skin had gotten worse and she was shivering. That concerned him most, but he could hear her pulse, and it was still strong. They just needed to get to Marlia's and get there fast.

Again, he tried to reason with her. "Look, I know you don't want to be carried-" When she made a face he held up a hand to stop her pending argument. "But at least let me help you get to the Paratooke Pass. If the storm lets up, we need to move, and I'm not sure you can make it off this mountain on your own."

Her nose wrinkled at the bridge as she looked down to her feet with annoyance, tenderly rubbing her bandaged arm. "We've made it this far. Save the piggyback rides for cliff faces."

Tytian rubbed a hand down his face, trying not to shout. He crossed his arms, staring out into the rain. "It isn't from a place of pity, you know. I'm not offering to help because I feel sorry for you, or because I feel superior. Carrying you through this mess would still be faster even if you were at the peak of physical health."

A small pause. "I know that."

"Then stop fighting me on it!" He could feel her glare on his back and turned around to meet it. Sure enough, her gaze was as sharp as a blade, accentuated by another flash of lightning.

"You're not used to folks saying no, are you?" she asked, calling him out with a tilt of her head.

"Just like you're not used to people not backing down from you?" he dished out in return.

Six rubbed at the space between her eyebrows and shook her head, finding a splinter of humor in the situation. "You know, you can be a bit of an asshole sometimes."

"Well, we are often identified by our own kind."

She chuckled, then grimaced, her whole body sore. Looking down to her arm, she lightly traced her thumb over a spot of blood and for a moment she was lost in the sight.

"Okay," she conceded softly. "We'll do it your way."

"You mean the right way?" This earned him a flick of her middle finger.

The lightning kept up its grand show, slowly moving it further down into the valley. Weakening, the gales no longer howled like lost souls through the leaves. This obstacle was finally moving out, but the forest was getting darker by the second, and soon the two of them would be swallowed by a stormy night.

Tytian steeled himself for the cold bite of the rain. "We should leave now. Put ourselves on the backside of this wind."

Stepping up beside him, shoulders high with tension, face set in a grim mask, Six watched the rain with dismay. "I keep thinking that maybe the others out here just like we are. Or safely tucked away in Marlia's living room. Then again, what if they're still in Riverport? Pinned down somewhere in the rubble with that abomination trying to sniff them out, and I've just left them."

A familiar ache unfurled in his chest. "Can't help anyone if you're dead. And she would have killed you if you stayed." It wasn't reassurance, but Tytian didn't want to patronize her with something as useless as false hope. The look on her face suggested that his answer wasn't what she was expecting to hear and he worried for a moment that it may have been too blunt. "For now let's focus on tonight's plan. We'll get you to your friend and then I'll look for everyone else."

Before she could have second thoughts, he crouched down in front of her. "Hop on."

Six exhaled heavily, then slid her arms around his neck and offered him her right leg. He kept his grip gentle on this one in particular, cupping the back of her knee inside his palm, ensuring his fingers were spread evenly for comfort. One extra hoist for the perfect fit, and then they were ready for the descent. Both of them hissed from the stinging pelt of fat droplets, cool air now sweeping out the warm. Tytian picked through the ever darkening trail with precision and ease, losing his footing only once in the slick mud. The lightning seemed to head their path. It wasn't as aggressive as its arrival, but it was still present. Every time there was a particularly impressive streak through the sky Tytian would feel Six's grip around him tighten as she anticipated the impending explosion of thunder. He often found himself giving her a reassuring squeeze of his fingers every time she flinched, to remind her that she wasn't out there alone.

"Not fond of lightning I take it?"

"Not really, no."

"Why not?"

"Because it's faster than I am."

"And dodging isn't exactly your area of expertise."

He felt her chuckle a little. "You're pushing your luck, pal."

Night had fallen in full when the forest thinned, an opening in the underbrush revealing their destination. Just as she'd said, they reached the pass after a little more than an hour, the tall grasses beaten down from the deluge. Tytian peered out from the cover of the trees, checking the road for any signs of Francesca or her men.

"Looks clear," he told Six as he stepped out into the open. "So, which way?"

Six slid off of his back, waiting for another lightning flash to help her situate herself. Once the area was briefly lit silver, she pointed to their right. "That way. It'll be pretty straight forward until we get to the pathway. Look for a thick birch tree, there will be a hand crafted warding symbol hanging from its branches. It'll look like this." Using her fingers she mimicked the rune.

He nodded, burning the symbol to memory.

The Paratooke was lengthy but comfortable terrain and didn't have too many rises to drain what was left of Six's stamina, which she was thankful for. Her feet were beginning to blister in her boots, and her calves felt as though they would never regain any feeling. But it was the pressure in her head that was driving her mad, and every step just seemed to make it worse.

*If I ever get my hands on that Draven bitch, I'm going to rip
her to pieces. Can't put your head back on if your hands are locked
in boxes at the bottom of a trench, you slag-faced whore-*

"Six?" Tytian's voice broke through her homicidal thoughts,
"You're mumbling."

"Oh. Just thinking happy thoughts."

"Alright," he nodded in a whatever-you-say kind of way as she
fell back into muttering angrily under her breath.

Step after step, their pace slowed, Six struggling to keep up.
When Tytian offered to carry her this time, there was no refusal,
and as she laid across his back, he could feel how cold her body
had become.

A few more miles down the pass there came a bend in the road,
and in its middle sat a fat birch tree, its white bark illuminated in
a flash of lightning. He rushed to its side, trying not to bounce
Six around too much and sure enough, tied to a low branch was
the wooden warding symbol. He described it to her, let her feel
of the tree. She confirmed that was what they were looking for,
and behind its large trunk Tytian found the barely-there trail.
He started up the mountain side, adjusting his passenger every so
often.

The climb was a little steeper than he anticipated. Loose stones
would betray his footing, winding roots sought his boot toes.
Every pool of mud was a quagmire, and finally, he went down
to his knees.

Nearly bucked off, Six slid down to her aching feet. "I can
climb the rest of the way."

He wanted to fight her on it, knew he should. Instead, he
agreed, although a bit reluctantly. "Okay. But keep hold of my
shirt. Last thing we need is for you to get lost up here."

She grinned a little. "Yes, mama hen."

They worked their way up the trail carefully, Tytian calling out a warning of an exposed root or slick stone that needed to be avoided. Through the gloom and soaking rain, faint flashes of light caught their eye. The fireflies were beckoning, dancing in time with the distant twinkle of chimes.

"Well that's suspicious." Tytian's eyes narrowed. "Is this your friend Marlia's doing?"

Six was just as confused as he was. "I'm not sure." Raising her nose to the air, she took a long sniff, noting the hint of woodsmoke. "We should be getting close. Maybe she asked for their aid."

"She speaks to bugs?" Tytian asked with skepticism.

Laughing, Six used his arm to stabilize her next step, climbing over a jut of stone. "Marlia can speak to a lot of things. Come on."

The fireflies lazily weaved through the tree trunks, flashing like tiny lighthouses in the inky black as the pair topped one last knob. When they reached the open yardscape, Six could see the illuminated windows of the cabin and released a weak puff. "Finally."

Next to her, Tytian was staring at the homestead, a funny expression on his face.

"What is it?"

"That son of a bitch," he said with humor, keen eyes staring in disbelief at who was waiting for them on the porch. "Aldan was right. He really is a cat."

TWENTY TWO

Between the sound of the rain against the tin roof, and his companion's soft snoring, Callum was fighting off sleep. Changing the curve of the earth seemed like a more achievable feat than staying awake, but he was determined, and worry aided his endeavor, while also souring the food in his belly. Every minor snap of a waterlogged tree limb made him jump and he would stare into the night with hopeful expectancy, only to find there was no one there. Sitting in this horrible in between of emotions, he had made up a plan to head back down to Riverport and sift through what remained. Wick could take him to where he last left the others, and from there Callum would begin his search. He tried to keep the image of finding Six alive and well in his mind, all the while knowing there was a high chance all he would find was a body. If he found anything at all.

"Never worry until it's time to worry." He played Duncan's favorite bit of advice on a whispered loop, trying to solidify the concept within him. He was worried though. Hurt, scared and without the one person who always seemed to make it better, even when she was the one doing the hurting and scaring.

His left arm had gone numb while wrapped around Fenella, fingers not responding to his commands of movement. Gently, he slid his arm from around her and winced as the heat returned, bringing with it a tingling rush. The wound to his ribs flared in protest and as he eased to the edge of the bench, lying Fenella down on a cluster of cushions. He could barely seem to move his stiff legs.

His spirit might have had the will to fly back to Riverport, but his body sure didn't.

He stood up, shaking, his back popping like corn kernels in hot oil. "Oh. Oh, that hurts." Risking a stretch, he was rewarded with cramps running up both calves and on either side of his spine. "Nope, no. We're not doing that." Callum took a few steps across the porch, working the cold muscles and easing their tension. He made two passes by the stairs but on the third he paused, and he looked out across the yard.

At first, he only saw one tall silhouette, barely visible, their outline cut from the dark by the light from the cabin windows. *Francesca?* A flash of lightning illuminated Tytian's white hair and Callum grabbed at his chest, releasing a heavy sigh of relief. "Ty." His voice faded as he spotted Six limping along beside him, a sudden rush pounding in his ears. He took a step back, eyes fluttering to combat the spinning in his head. Before he knew it, he was jogging down the steps and across the yard, working against the ache in his joints.

She was alive. She was alive and she was here. Safe from Francesca. Safe from the church.

"Lucia." He sounded far away, even inside his own skin.

"I'm fine," she said quickly, and it was then that Callum noticed how she held her arm. The deeper she moved into the light, the more damage he saw.

Fenella was sitting up and rubbing her eyes when the three of them climbed the steps. The instant she saw them her previously sleepy expression was wiped away. "You're alright!" Her light was short-lived once she saw Six. "Eugh...-sorry." Tossing the blanket aside she jumped for the front door, flinging it open on well-oiled hinges.

Aldan and Marlia were in the kitchen, teacups in hand when Fenella ushered the others in, Callum trailing behind, a sick look on his face.

"You made it!" Aldan said, relieved. "Gods Six, you look like shit."

Her mouth settled into a thin, frog-like frown, brow furrowing under his inspection. Aldan returned to his tea, looking everywhere but her.

Wick had fallen asleep on a blanket in front of the fire, woken up by all the ruckus. He rolled over, hair a mess, a stream of drool drying on his chin. "Whasgoinon?" he muttered, trying to blink the sleep from his eyes.

Fenella handed him his glasses off the mantle, speaking quickly as she worked to make room for the wary. "Ty and Six."

"Titan sticks?" Wick asked, confused.

Callum narrowed his gaze at the boy and tilted his head. "Try it again."

Wick put on his glasses, his blinks big and purposeful. He then pointed with enthusiasm. "Tytian and Six!"

"There ya go." Callum patted his shoulder. "Now get up, we need this blanket."

Six looked around the room and counted the faces, happy to find that everyone was accounted for and mostly in one piece. Wick was bandaged and burned, but seemed in good spirits. Callum however was moving very carefully while favoring his right side. When he locked eyes with her, Six raised her brows and gave a small dip of her head towards his ribs. She was expecting some sort of sly retort of 'you should see the other guy'. Instead, he gave her a weak smile of reassurance. One that never made it past his cheekbones.

There was a soft touch to her face and Six was pulled away.

"My precious girl." Marlia caressed her temple with motherly affection. "Let's take a look at you, okay?" She steered Six to the round dining table and sat her down, untying the bindings on her arm. The skin beneath was shriveled from the rain, the edges of the lacerations raised and red.

"This is one hell of a wound," Marlia told her, tracing them with a feather-soft touch. "You must have really made this woman angry."

Six grinned. "Well, I did cut off her head."

"I heard about that." Her tone was one that Six was familiar with.

"Don't approve?"

Marlia moved to the tall cabinet behind them, pulling out a tin box and a few jars of healing ointments. When she sat back down, she pursed her lips, sorting through the tin. "Just getting a little tired of patching you up is all. Last time you were here I was stitching up the back of your head." She dabbed at the cuts with a clean cloth. "Seems like you're the only one getting really hurt out there."

It was hard to disagree. "If I don't charge in head first those idiots are going to get killed."

Marlia held up a finger with a stern glower. "That bravery of yours is what's going to get you killed one of these days. And we can't have that."

But it wasn't bravery. In reality Six was no braver than the next person. She didn't like snow or lightning, or the yip of coyotes. However, when faced with a fight or flight situation, fight was the strongest instinct. Like the belief system of a stray dog. If she were to die, she would do so with a snarl on her face. Oftentimes, it was a mindset that threw her into the frying pan. But if death was coming to take her, she wouldn't go in a whimper.

"I'll be more careful next time." She tried to assure Marlia. The grunt and shake of the head she received told her that this declaration wasn't taken seriously.

Across the room, standing by the fireplace, Tytian watched the two of them, eager to see Six patched up. And to meet the woman who offered them sanctuary. The symbols on her birch tree down the trail had sparked something deep inside his memories, he just couldn't recall what.

"How did you two make it out of town?" asked Wick from one of the armchairs.

Callum occupied the other. "Yeah, I'd like to hear this story too."

Tytian pried his eyes away from the pair. "Well, when Francesca put her head back on-"

"That is an uncomfortable sentence," mumbled Callum.

He continued, "It was clear we needed to get out of there. We headed for the docks, then boom. My memory gets a little hazy after that. The next thing I knew I was on the shore with Six. She wanted to stay and look for the rest of you, but she was bleeding pretty badly and Francesca was still in town so we decided to head here."

Fenella handed him a hot mug of tea and then hugged an arm around his waist. "I'm glad you both made it out alive." Tytian rested his arm over her shoulders, giving her a gentle squeeze.

"What do you think that Francesca woman will do now?" asked Aldan.

Wick spoke up, "Maybe she'll think we all died in the blast."

Tytian knew better. "No, she'll figure it out soon enough. Especially now that she has collected most of our scents."

"Our scents?" Wick's question was dripping with horrified disgust.

"You know those dogs they train to sniff out folks who have gone missing?" asked Fenella. "She's like those. But, from hell."

Wick paled and slumped back into his chair. "Oh."

"Oh indeed." Callum stared into the fire, watching the logs collapse in on themselves, sending a spray of embers up into the chimney.

Aldan paced behind the chairs, one arm across his middle while the other held a fist to his mouth. "Now we know that we can't kill her. And she's seen all of our faces and caught our scent. It's not an ideal obstacle to overcome, but I think if we keep a low profile, especially through the more populated townships, we can stay out of her reach."

"Keeping a low profile is when you make sure no one knows you're there," Fenella told Callum jokingly with a grin but he never acknowledged her words, he just kept staring into the fire, one hand under his chin. "Callum?"

"Hmm?" He drug his far away gaze over to her, brows high in question.

"Nothing." Ever since the other two had returned Fenella noticed a sudden distance in Callum, one that seemed to come and go like a tide. It was the same kind of mood he fell into their first night in Rodenburg. She didn't need her gut to know that he was lost in some distant memory.

Pulling away from Tytian she made her way over to him and crouched down next to his chair as the others picked up their conversation.

"What is it?" she asked him with a hushed tone. He looked so tired in the warm light. The dark circles under his eyes, the cuts and bruises, the ashy cast to his flesh. Callum looked like a living corpse.

"I'm fine." This lie was punctuated with a brief tweak of his lips.

Fenella took a stab in the dark at what might have been bothering him. "This wasn't a loss, you know. We took a hit, but we're still standing. Everyone is alive and now we've met the enemy. We can plan this whole thing better."

There were missing factors in her statement that Callum chose not to point out. A lot of people died yesterday, a lot of good people. A home he'd slept many nights in was now ash. The final resting place of his friend was blown into the wind. He knew that Fenella had these things on her mind as well but was choosing to find the positive in the situation. When faced with a battlefield, Fenella was the kind who sought out the sight of the wildflowers instead of the broken bodies in the grass.

"You're right, Vanilla. We survived, and now we can be more prepared for the future." He squeezed her shoulder. "What would we do without your sunny optimism?"

She wrinkled her nose. "Probably spiral into deep despair."

"We need to discuss what we're going to do once we're in Crown's Cross," offered Aldan but Marlia cut in as she pulled tight a suture on Six's arm.

"What you all need right now, is rest." Marlia's tone was firm. "These two need a hot bath and some food in them, Callum needs some sleep before he falls over, Wick needs at least two days of salve on his burns, and those horses out there in the barn need fed." With an educated flourish she tied off the last suture and snipped free the excess.

Aldan threw a look out of the kitchen window towards the barn and nodded, the truth in her words hitting home. "Okay M, you win. No plan making for now." He grabbed his coat from its peg by the door and stepped outside, heading to the barn to give the horses their grain.

Her honey-gold eyes flicked around to the faces in the room. "I know how much some folks in this group like to go charging off with little regard for their bodies, but you all need to rest. Stay for a few days, make up a foolproof plan and then start again." Marlia wrapped clean bandages around Six's arm and packed away her kit.

"Yes ma'am." Wick agreed almost immediately, which made Callum grin.

"Good. Now, I'm going to find you two some dry clothes," she told Tytian and Six, moving across the room and down the hall. "The bath is free! And I suggest you use it."

Fenella moved into the kitchen with a goal on her mind. "I'll get started on some breakfast. Wick, will you get the tub ready?"

"Sure thing." He bounced up from his seat on the floor and disappeared around the corner.

With everyone else off to their duties, the other three were left in mutual silence. Six flexed her arm gently and tested the hold of the bandages. The pain was still there, but it was duller than before, and the pounding in her head started to subside. Almost all at once she felt incredibly tired and wanted nothing more than to curl up in a corner somewhere and go to sleep.

Tenting her fingers she rested her forehead on her knuckles and let the tension she'd been carrying in her core to loosen.

Tytian stared at her, his jaw set and his arms crossed over his chest. Six had come awfully close to losing her life, they all did, and it was too close of a call. He ran over his fight with Francesca in his mind, breaking down each blow and each misstep he took. Ches was strong, almost stronger than he had remembered, and it was painfully clear that when it came down to hand-to-hand, she would best him every time. He hadn't picked up a blade since his early twenties and was out of practice. When he was well oiled, Tytian was an animal with a glaive, and right now, he could kick his own ass for not being ready. Not that steel was going to help him out very much if completely cutting off Francesca's head did little more than annoy her.

"Alright! Tub is hot and ready to go," Wick declared as he returned to the living room.

Fenella waved him over. "Want to help me cook?" She smiled as he nodded, then tossed him a tomato.

Six hadn't moved from her seat and when Tytian gave her a concerned look Callum turned in his chair. He called out to her, "Hey, woman."

She jumped a little, coming out of a light slumber. "What?"

He nodded towards the hall. "Go get cleaned up." As she started to stand, he saw the shake in her legs and got up to help her. He moved a little too quickly, the pain in his side anchoring him to the chair.

"Not sure either one of you would be much help to the other right now." Marlia came back holding a bundle of fabric and disengaged Callum with just a flick of her fingers. After getting Six to her feet, she handed her a set of clothes and then the other to Tytian. "I don't know if they'll fit, but it's better than nothing."

Six made her way to the bathroom, waving a dismissal over her shoulder as Marlia offered her help. Once safely behind the bathroom door, she slumped against the vanity, avoiding her reflection in the mirror, its edges fogged with steam. The room was warm and smelled like a meadow. It would have been easy to just lay down on the floor and drift off. Tempting as it was, Six grit her teeth and started the taxing process of peeling herself out of her wet clothes. Her inner thighs were chafed, her right knee was puffy, blisters reddened her heels, bruises crawled her skin like a mold. It hurt, stripping down to her skin, but once the warm water lapped over her body, there was no better feeling. Even through the sting, this tub was her own little pool of relief, and she sunk deep into its depth.

From beneath the calming surface, Six watched the ceiling, trying to block out the invasive image of flames slithering across the rafters.

TWENTY THREE

Pans sizzled and knives struck a chopping block with an educated rhythm, Fenella lost in her craft. Marlia's food selection wasn't fancy but it was plentiful, almost all of it coming from her homestead. Fat strips of bacon were frying while Wick stirred eggs in a bowl, readying them for the scramble. Thin tomato slices were placed in the cold box beneath the floorboards to chill and Tytian had been given the task of squeezing oranges for their juice.

Marlia was across the counter from him, washing a bundle of spinach. "So, you're the half demon, huh?"

Tytian waited.

"No judgment from me, honey," she told him with a smile, noting the way body stiffened. "We can't help what we're destined to be." Once the spinach was sorted, she fished a tin of coffee out of the cabinet. "You did good, getting her here. I want you to know that I appreciate you taking care of something so precious to me. Six, well, she and him are like my own children." She looked over her shoulder at Callum who had fallen to sleep in the armchair. "I took those two little heathens into my heart a long time ago, and I'd be devastated if anything happened to them. So, thank you."

He felt a little awkward under her praise, but Tytian accepted it with grace and a small smile.

Fenella flipped the bacon strips over, tossing a plat of butter into a waiting pan. "Do you have any biological children, Marlia?" She waved a spatula toward the back of the cabin. "I noticed some height scales carved into the doorframes."

Pride warmed her expression. "Yes, two. They're grown now, both living in Mar."

"Really?" Fenella was surprised. "That's so far away. What do they do there?"

Marlia pulled a percolator for the coffee off of a high shelf. "My daughter, Oonlai is a doctor, and my son Ederyk is a professor of botanical studies at the capitol academy."

"That's impressive! You must be so proud."

"Oh, I am."

Wick poured the beaten eggs into the pan, stirring them quickly to trap the steam, adding fluff to their texture. "And your husband? I've never really heard you mention him."

Marlia gave a kind of mischievous grin. "Never took one. Didn't like the idea of some fellow in my own house trying to tell me what to do because he thought he was entitled to do so. I wanted children, so I went out and made it happen. Remember, Wick love, men are only good for one thing."

"Yeah," Fenella agreed, nudging his shoulder then pointing at his pan, "And that's scrambling eggs."

Panicked, he stirred faster, trying not to burn his dish.

The front door opened, letting in the early morning light. Aldan dusted hay off his jacket, hanging it up. "It sure smells good in here!"

"It's almost finished so wash up!" Fenella commanded. Wiping her hands on her borrowed apron, she swept out of the kitchen, a pep in her step. Early morning was when she felt the most alive, an active kitchen bringing her more peace than a day of rest. At the fireplace, she laid a hand on Callum's arm and gave it a soft shake while saying his name. When he rose from his nap, she told him about breakfast and once she was satisfied he wouldn't drift back to sleep, she went to the bathroom and knocked on the door.

"Six-"

The door swung open, and both women gave a little exhale of a startled sigh. Fenella laughed. "Oh! You scared me."

Six chuckled. "Sorry."

She smelled like lavender and sage grass, dressed in a simple shirt and dark pants that had been sewn with a man's build in mind. The seams were tight around her full hips, and the legs were rolled up to her knees. Although clean, with color returning to her cheeks, her eyes were bloodshot with exhaustion.

Fenella motioned over her shoulder. "Uhm, breakfast is almost done if you'd like to claim a seat at the table."

"Actually, I think I'm just going to lay down for a bit." Six nodded across the hall and stepped around her. "I drained and refilled the tub for Tytian. Will you tell him please?" She gave Fenella no chance to argue and moved quietly into the guest room.

The urge to follow after her was strong, but she decided to give her some space and let her rest instead. "I'll just have to make her a really good lunch," she told herself and started to mentally plan the menu as she joined the others in the kitchen.

When she returned alone, Callum gave her a questioning look and she told him that Six just wanted to get some sleep. Setting his plate down on the counter he slipped away from the group, heading to the guest room. He hesitated, gathered his strength, then gently rapped his knuckles against the door. After a pause he heard Six speak.

"Yeah, come in." Her voice sounded strained.

Callum entered the room, closing the cozy space off from the chatter and sound of clanking dishes. Six was sitting on the bed, one hand rubbing at the nape of her neck. He cleared his throat and for a second, she froze.

"What?" Her tone was flat.

Nervously, his fists bumped against his thighs as he crossed the room and sat on the other side of the mattress. It took longer than he thought to speak. "I thought you were dead."

"That wouldn't be the first time."

Stung, he grit her name between his teeth. "Six-"

She hung her head, a little disappointed with her choice of words. "I'm just- tired."

"Yeah, I know the feeling."

"What happened?"

"Got separated and pushed out. Made for the front gates so I could roof hop back to you guys, took a mace to the side and then woke up singed in the grass."

"How many soldiers did you have after you?"

Would she believe him if he'd said a dozen? Because he really wanted it to be something impressive like a dozen. "Uh, it was two." He felt her turn around.

"Two?" she asked with dismay. "You let two soldiers chase you away from the group?"

Callum turned to face her as well, a finger raised in defense of his story. "Hey, listen." But he didn't have a valid reason that didn't make him sound completely incompetent.

She pressed her lips together and raised her brows, waiting for his answer.

He had nothing. "Look, all of this fighting highly trained, demon-run private militia is a little new to me so I'm not quite as skilled as you are."

"I'm not sure fighting against highly trained, demon-run private militia is in anyone's skill set right now." She swung inward and positioned herself at the top of the bed, resting her back against the headboard. "Still, if they're going to be a problem then we need to work on your battle defense. Fenella's too. It'll take us roughly two weeks to get to Crown's Cross, and that isn't a lot of time so we'll have to really perfect what we can with you both."

Callum mirrored her position, setting his back against the shallow foot board. It was uncomfortable but he was happy just being beside her. "Actually, I've been thinking."

"Didn't know you were capable."

He made a face that rolled his upper lip, showing his teeth in a mocking display. "Uh huh, you're so funny." What he was about to suggest made him sick to his stomach. "I think you should stay here, with Marlia." That got her attention but he wasn't sure that was a good thing.

She pondered his words for a minute, trying to map out exactly what he meant by them. "If this is about going to Crown's, I'll be fine."

"I don't just mean for that. I mean, *stay* here. If, in a few months, one of the others or myself show back up then you'll know that everything is over, and the High Father has been stopped. If no one shows, then grab Marlia, jump on the first airship you find and sail as far south as possible."

She leveled her gaze on him. "Where is this coming from? Is it because of this?" Her mangled arm raised. "This is nothing, I've had worse."

"I know you have." He tried to keep his eyes off of her leg and failed.

The silence that followed was heavy, neither one eager to cross old waters.

Finally, Six declined his suggestion. "Tytian told me what that woman did to his family. And after seeing her in the flesh and experiencing what she can do, I can't just walk away. Our chances of finishing this are better if we don't split up."

"Yeah, but-"

"No."

He picked at a scab on the back of his hand, reopening the shallow wound. "Okay." Simmering in his stew of defeat, Callum searched for stable ground. "Got any idea how to kill something that can withstand explosions and decapitation?"

Six's smile was slow to come, and it was vicious, bringing malevolence to her eyes. "Not exactly, but I'm going to have fun figuring it out."

Out in the kitchen everyone grabbed a plate and divvied out breakfast. Aldan wanted coffee but Fenella insisted he stick to the orange juice, since Tytian had worked so hard on it. It really made no difference to Tytian if anyone drank it at all. He only made it so Fenella would stop pestering him. They sat around the table and enjoyed their meal, talking back and forth in easy conversation. Recipes were discussed, leading to food preferences, which eventually turned to smoking meats. Fenella found this particular subject fascinating, questioning Aldan on all the different types of wood one would use to get certain flavors. When there was an appropriate opening, Tytian changed the subject, knowing full well that if someone didn't intervene they'd be stuck on the debate between hickory wood and pecan for hours.

"So, Marlia. Six mentioned you could speak to bugs?" Tytian asked over his glass of juice. The laugh that followed suggested that maybe she had been pulling his leg.

"Bugs? Honey, unless it's complimenting a bee on her stripes or a month on its coloring, I don't have anything to say to bugs."

"We saw fireflies out in the storm. Six figured you had asked them to meet us."

Wick swiftly chewed a mouth full of scrambled eggs. "That was me! Just left a little spell at the top of the hill to help escort you guys to the cabin."

"Oh." Tytian turned back to Marlia as Wick coughed on some inhaled egg. "Six said something else about you being able to speak to things. What did she mean by that?"

Marlia rested her elbows on the table and laced her fingers. "Why don't you just ask the real question you want answered?"

Tytian stared at her, not comfortable with how easily she saw through him. From the moment he spotted the ward symbol there was something humming in his bones, and when he finally laid eyes on the woman, he was aware of an energy that radiated about her. Something that was hard to pin down unless you knew exactly what it was you were sensing.

Tytian met her challenge. "Fine. What are you?"

Aldan scratched at his beard and cast his eyes down to his plate, suddenly very interested in the texture of the bacon. Fenella and Wick exchanged confused glances but neither one of them interrupted. Marlia simply smiled.

"I was wondering if you'd be able to sense it." She sprinkled a pinch of red pepper over her tomatoes. "*Astareos Prima.*"

Tytian's yellow eyes widened, and he leaned back a little, surprised. "No wonder Callum wanted to come see you."

"The boy isn't as dumb as you think he is."

Fenella looked between them with confusion. "What's going on?"

"So," Wick turned to her, using his hands to punctuate his explanation. "You know how the Divine has the High Father?

And the demonic church has Carmine Priests? Well, the earth mother has the *Astareos Prima;* Priestess of the Star. Exclusively women and, unfortunately, almost extinct. At least, that's what I've read."

"There's a few sisters left in the northern region," Marlia chimed in, though her eyes never left the demon sitting at the end of her table.

"Six wasn't joking when she said you could talk to more than just bugs," Tytian concluded.

"No, she wasn't. Although, like I said, bugs aren't really my thing." Her eyes crawled him in evaluation. "I'll be doing a ceremony today, calling on the Current for information. You should join me."

"I've been to enough seances in my life."

"With demons maybe, but not like this. I want you there. You too, Fenella. I think your energy might help stir the void a little." She took a bite of tomato. "Never know, half-son, might learn something."

He would be lying if he said that he wasn't intrigued, but the thought of opening himself to the earth's Current made him a little hesitant. Carmine's were taught that demons are not a welcomed creature to the Mother, much like the arch seraphim. Instead, they were seen as invasive, and if given the chance to destroy one, the Current wouldn't hesitate.

Are you trying to kill me, Marlia?

Aldan finished off the last bite of food on his plate and drained his juice. "I'm going to get spoiled by all of this cooking, Fenella. Is there any left?"

"Just Callum's portion." She looked around the room, a frown tugging at her mouth. "Where is he anyway?"

Wick cleared away his dishes and Fenella's as well. "I saw him go down the hall. Think he went to check on Six? That was a while ago though."

Fenella frowned. "Oh God, what if she killed him?"

"If she did, I call his grub," declared Aldan, happily accepting what was left of Tytian's juice.

Rolling her eyes, Fenella pushed away from the table and went down the hallway. She stopped abruptly and put her ear against the door, trying to see if she could hear chit chatty banter or a full-on, rage-fueled argument. There was only silence. Careful not to squeak the hinges, she engaged the handle and peered inside.

Both of them were fast asleep, Six laying in one direction while Callum laid in another, each one snoring peacefully. Fenella leaned against the door frame and watched them with a smile, until she realized that spying on people while they were sleeping probably qualified as creepy.

Awkwardly, she left them to their rest.

She was happy, seeing them content in each other's presence, even if it were still at a fragile stage. And all it took was the mass destruction of an entire town to bring them just a little closer together.

In the kitchen, she handed over Callum's breakfast to Aldan, who accepted it without a single question and a gleam in his eye.

TWENTY FOUR

On the first day of Riverport's destruction Francesca took her
time picking through the remains in search of Tytian or his
companions, hoping that maybe she could find one of them with
just enough life left in them to call out for him as she broke their
bones. Instead, all she found was disappointment. On the winds,
their scent had faded, leaving behind no trail in the ashes. They
were gone.

"Shit." A puff of flame slipped through her fingers, and she
watched as they extinguished themselves back into the opening of
her palm. Streaks of red still marred her skin, some hers but the
rest was what was left after her attack on the brunette.

Qucik bitch, she thought with venom, neck still sore. *I didn't
even feel you coming.*

Intrigued, Francesca raised her hand to her lips and licked
her fingers clean. The taste of that woman's blood was different.
Burning with a strange chill, sweet and intoxicating. It tingled as
it slipped down her gullet, the sensation making her shiver. "Who
the hell are you?"

She needed answers. And for that, she needed a heart.

The remaining fires across town were slowly being extinguished by the heavy, northern downpour. Above the hiss of steam and rain patter, the muffled screams of those trapped under the rubble began to surface. Convenient for the predator who lurked outside.

Somewhere in the husk of what had once been a shop, echoed a cry for help.

"I hear you!" Francesca's words were sweet with false concern as she studied her nails, noting their grimy state.

"Please! Please help," a survivor shouted, the voice belonging to a young woman. "My leg is caught. I can't move!"

"I'm coming to help you, sweetie. Just try and stay calm." Stretching her arms over her head Francesca took her time climbing the collapsed roof, kicking loose shingles from her path. She could hear the breathy panic, the struggles and whimpers beneath the remains. Once she had the position pinpointed, she started ripping back beams and rubble, opening a decent sized hole at her feet.

Trapped near the store entrance, a young woman pulled and wiggled against the large cabinet that pinned her leg. Jars of preserves were scattered about, the shards of glass cutting her palms.

"There you are." Halo'd in murky light, Francesca's silhouette appeared almost angelic. A blasphemous comparison.

"Oh, thank the Divine!" The victim sobbed, reaching a bloodied hand up towards her savior.

With ease Francesca dropped down through the hole, taking a moment to look around the destruction for anyone else. "This is quite the pickle you've gotten yourself into," she said with a cluck of the tongue.

Tears sparkled in her doe eyes. "D-do you think you can lift it?" she asked hopefully of a rescuer who didn't seem to be listening. Instead, she was staring at her with a strange expression. One that made her own begin to wilt.

Francesca was in no hurry as she crossed the gap, crouching down to study the young woman in closer detail. "You're a pretty one." Affectionately, she pulled a finger down her plump cheek. "Bet all the boys chase after your skirts."

"M-miss... please." The young woman pleaded softly, tears streaming down her face.

Shushing her pitiful attempts, Francesca stood and rolled her neck, cracking the bones that were still trying to find their proper alignment. She then stepped up onto the toppled cabinet, making its pinned victim squeal in pain, blood rushing out from the seam. Francesca browsed through the mixed jars still pooled within the toppled shelving, picking them up one by one and tossing them over her shoulder until she found what she was looking for.

Sharp teeth gnawed on her lip as she gave one jar a little shake, watching the fruit slices slide around in the honeyed water. "Peaches. I used to eat these all the time when I was a girl." She flicked a finger to the young woman, "Do you like them?" and then rose, dropping down from the cabinet while cracking open the jar lid.

Stifling a sob, she shook her head, too afraid not to play along. "Not really, miss."

Using her pinkie, Francesca stirred the water and then slid her finger into her mouth, savoring the taste. "Mmm. That's too bad." She crouched in front of her again, and pushed the tangled hair from her face. Delicately, she pinched a peach slice between her nails and held it in front of the young woman's mouth, wetting her lips with it. "Eat." The word was spoken in such a way that refusal was not an option.

Her jaws trembled as they parted, a weak sob escaping from her throat. She tried not to gag as Francesca slid the slimy fruit onto her tongue, and watched in amusement while she choked it down. One by one she fed her every single piece of peach in that jar and once it was all gone, she had her drink the juice that was left. When the jar was empty Francesca tossed it aside and wiped the spilled liquid from the woman's chin, licking it clean from her thumb. "Do you know anything about pigs?"

Confusion mingled with the fear in her eyes. "No, miss."

With an almost kind smile Francesca laid her hands on the other's shoulders and gripped them tightly. She then planted her feet and heaved, ripping her free from the cabinet. Her shriek echoed around them as her knee dislodged from its socket, skin and muscle tearing away from itself like wet paper. Once she had been completely freed, Francesca dropped her on the floor, inhaling the fresh scent of blood through the ashy air.

"You see, with pigs, the farmers will feed them things like corn and fruit to make the meat sweeter." If her victim heard her, there was no telling, the girl wailed as she dragged herself across the floor, tattered leg weaving a river of red through the grime. "They'll also make sure to kill the pig when it's comfortable. Because fear, at its most chemical level, taints the meat. Bitters it." Using the toe of her boot, she flipped her onto her back, hoisting her up and settling her down against the back of a cashier counter. Francesca dropped straddle of her legs, easily dodging the ineffective fists swinging towards her face. She captured her wrists and pinned them above her head, continuing her macabre description. "And I've found this to be true. Particularly with men. You make a man happy, or even aroused, and the cuts you'll get from him are as buttery soft as one can hope for. It's easy. Sometimes, too easy. Women, however-" With her free hand Francesca trailed her fingers down the girl's lips, then her chin, and her throat, where she gathered a handful of her blouse. In a swift motion she ripped open the shirt and underdress, exposing her chest. "Women are usually always afraid." Her touch trailed the shivering skin, goose bumps rising in the wake. "Even in moments of pure happiness, there is still that little collection of fear in their core. Makes them tough and bitter."

Shrinking but with nowhere to go, the young woman tried one last time. "Let me go. Please."

"This is why I prefer men, you see. Their arrogance and their stupidity- their simplicity, it makes them delicious." Hot as a branding iron, her palm pressed into the space between the woman's breasts. "But the peaches, as *they* rot inside *your* rot, should do their job well enough."

Francesca burst her way into the chest cavity, splintering the wet bone. She had to weave through, effortlessly keeping the other woman pinned as she thrashed about. The commotion ebbed slowly once she clutched the fluttering heart and pulled, popping the connective veins and arteries free, blood spreading from the breach.

One final gasp of air and then, silence.

Wasting no time, Francesca moved a little deeper into the shop, far away from the rain that spilled in through the hole she carved in the roof. Slipping out of her top armor and tunic, she covered her skin in bloody calling symbols, spoke the words, and fell across the void.

Her disconnected energy landed in the center of Jonhas's study.

"Beacon."

Jonhas flinched, spilling his tea across his robes. "Ahh- Francesca." He dabbed at the setting stains. "It is *good* to hear your voice. Any luck with J'harenmar?"

His question was ignored. "What did the orphanage owner say about the brunette?"

Her voice was like grinding rough steel in his mind. "I haven't had the chance to speak with him yet," he told her with apprehension, readying himself for one of her attacks.

"Why not?" she asked in a sing-song tone.

"One of the orphan boys said he was out of town for a few days. Something about bringing in a new shipment of kids. He should be back first thing in the morning."

She grew silent for some time and had it not been for the chill still crawling up and down his spine he would have thought she was gone.

"I need a fleet of at least three airships, each stocked with capable soldiers."

This surprised him. "A fleet? What happened to your militia?"

"All dead."

"Really?" He stood from his armchair by the fire and moved to his desk, fishing a log book from a drawer. "J'harenmar did this?" But he received no response. In the small leather-bound book, he traced his finger down the list of airship names and picked out three. "Where are you? It'll take a day or two to stockpile supplies and ready the men, but your order should be no problem to fill."

"I tracked Tytian and his little posse to Riverport."

"Riverport?" He wrinkled his bulbous nose in disgust. "That place always smelled like fish."

"Well now it smells like ash."

This made him pause. "You burned it down?"

"Yes." The word was spoken with immense disinterest, as if he had asked the simple question of whether or not the sky was blue.

Jonhas swallowed roughly. "Oh."

"Beacon."

"Y-yes?"

"Have the information on the brunette by morning when I contact you again. And have my fleet in the sky no later than the morning after that."

He licked his lips. "Of course. The church is at your service."

Francesca left him to his scrambling. Once the color came back to her eyes, she dressed in full and moved back to her fresh kill. Gripping the dead girl by the arm, she threw her through the hole in the roof. The body tumbled down slick shingles, landing with a wet plop on the street. Francesca then followed, emerging out of the fallen shop into thick sheets of rain.

"Oh gods, is she dead?" asked a male voice.

Along the street there were no more than a dozen survivors clustered in a ball, holding wet bandages to various wounds.

Francesca put on that politician's smile and stepped off of the roof. "Unfortunately, yes." She motioned to the corpse at her feet. "This young woman is now within the Heavenly halls of her Father. May the Divine bless-"

"Wait a minute..." A man of middle years stepped out of the crowd, shrewd eyes glued to her face, a fat finger wagging at her. "You're one of them. One of those armored folks that came into town before the explosion. You caused this!" He gave a gurgled cry when she struck him in the leg with a sword that seemed to appear out of thin air. The man fell to the ground, blood pouring down his calf.

"Harold!" The remaining survivors all huddled together, the women grabbing up what few children they had as the men stepped in front of them.

"We should rush her, no way she can fight us all off," one of them muttered, wielding a pitchfork in both hands.

Their little show amused her. "So eager to fight." Her right hand raised, palm slicing open with wagging tongues of hell. "So easy to kill."

Roaring, the stream of fire became a swallowing wave as it hit the air, not even the rain was able to weaken its bite. Their herd mentality pulled them together, melting each one quick as thin metal. When she closed her fist, there was nothing left but a heap of blackened bones, sizzling in the downpour.

The injured man at her feet, Harold, watched in horror. "You..." he stammered, "You're a devil."

Francesca turned her gaze down to him and smiled, lightning webbing through the clouds above her head.

Using a strand of dry line, she lashed the injured man to the body of peach girl and dragged them out of town, the man alternating between crying out versus from the holy books and begging for her to release him. If she didn't need him for another calling ritual, she would have left his carcass hanging from what was left of the town gate.

There was no escaping the storm, the outlying fields in front of town vast enough to resurrect at least two more. Instead of the forest, she picked a spot in the middle of the green and tossed her victims into wind-whipped grass. Harold had started to sob. The sound of his thick sniffing and quiet prayers making Francesca's head hurt.

A hiss rose up from the back of her throat and she turned on him. "Enough!" Bringing down her boot heel against the wide laceration on his leg, she was rewarded with a gasping scream.

Trembling, Harold fumbled a pendant from under his shirt, the bronze monolith swinging wildly on its cheap chain. He held it before him like a shield, with a prayer from his lips. It was sloppy at first, spoken with a fearful speed that made him stumble. Eventually, in the face of her sadistic grin, his voice grew until he was shouting the holy words, hoping against hope that his conviction and strength would call down a lightning bolt to smite her where she stood.

It never came. No avenging hand reached from the sky to aid him. He tried again, repeating the prayer with even more force than before, trying to ignore the fluttering of his heart in his throat when she laughed at his paltry attempts.

"Open your gates, o lord! Send down your seraphim to cast this wretch back into the darkest corners of hell!" he screamed into the rain. "Strike down the whore where she stands, Father!" But there was nothing. Only grumbling rolls of thunder.

Francesca turned her gaze skyward, searching for feathers or spiraling rings of heaven flame. Disappointed, she let her eyes fall to meet his. There was a light within them, coming from just behind the vertical pupils, and he stared into them, transfixed by the burning illumination.

Laughing, the sound rising up from deep within her chest, Francesca lofted her fist high above her, then brought it down against the crown of his head, sending his vision spiraling into dark unconsciousness.

On the second day the rains had left the valley, and the smell of smoke had been washed away. Every so often there were subtle booms and cracks coming from town as the shattered debris shifted, settling under its own weight.

Harold opened his eyes to the hazy sky, his head pounding with a headache. For a moment he didn't want to sit up. A heavy weight sat on his chest, numbing his arms and legs to the cold earth beneath him, but the croak of a bird sent a buzz down his spine, and he was reminded.

His offending leg ached and when he rose to examine it, puffy and raw to the touch. The knot on his head was tender, but he was relieved to find the skin unbroken.

Around him the grass was too high to see properly, and he wondered if the demon woman had left him be. With clumsy effort he managed to stand, one hand gripped across his wound. The field was bare in either direction, but there was movement a few hundred yards away. Black silhouettes bouncing here and there through the green. Curiosity was always a weakness of Harold's. Too often he found himself wandering into places he knew he shouldn't or peeking through keyholes in doors that didn't belong to him. Sometimes he was rewarded. That dark alley taken might lead to a nice bar, and those open keyholes might reveal a young woman bathing on the other side. You never know if you just walk away. And besides, there was nowhere left to walk away to. His home was gone, the whole damn town nothing more than ruined firewood in the mud, so out into the damp grasses he went, dragging one foot behind him.

A series of vocal clicks broke across the silence, echoed by a ragged screech. Tall vultures were gathered together in a single mass, staring at something that lay in a circle of crumpled reeds. Their vocalizations were kept short, as if they didn't dare disturb the scene before them. Powerful beaks clacked with impatience while dusty black feathers bristled and flattened at his approach.

He thought it strange, to see these creatures, wing to wing like this out in the field. Perhaps there was a coyote with a fawn and the birds were merely waiting their turn. Or maybe it was someone from town, having dragged themselves as far as they could until their injuries got the better of them. Could it be the demon woman? Did the Divine strike her down after all? Yes that must be it. Why else would such creatures be so afraid to approach whatever it was that lay sprawled in the grass?

He'd sped up his pace, hoping to lay eyes on the charred body of that ghastly thing, but when he finally reached the ring of carrion birds Harold felt his spirit slip out of him like smoke.

The young woman, who had been dragged out of Riverport with him, lay on her back in the trampled blades of switch, not a scrap of clothing on her. Only one dry eye gazed up into the clouds as the other was gone. Her lips were tattered as if they had been chewed and there were deep teeth marks scattered across her neck and breasts. All of the flesh, meat and organs from the last rib to her knee caps, was gone, only pink bones remained in their stead, summer flies eating a feast.

Clicking their calls again, the vultures scuttled together, dark eyes greedily watching the corpse in anticipation. Harold however didn't share in their delight. The moment his mind recognized the red in the green, he heaved stomach bile at his own feet, coughing in disgust. His retching made the birds restless, and they opened their large wings, croaking and cawing at him as though he had committed a crime.

The body, the birds, the one staring eye- all of it overwhelmed his mind and Harold threw his hands up to his face, spittle flying from his lips as he groaned. "Shut up! Shut up!"

The vultures fell into a hush.

Harold spun away from the scene, eager to flee into the valley, to find some salvation in the hills. There was nothing to be found except the figure who now loomed above him. Her skin had turned to a dark shade of gray, and she was taller. Much taller than she had been. Along her naked body was a mapwork of illuminated veins, molten light carried throughout her system, pooling in her half-lidded eyes. Covered in filth, from the dirt on her knees to the dark, clumpy blood that smeared from thigh to cheekbone, she looked more like a corpse than the mess behind him. Each breath came from her breast in primal pants, fiery gaze traveling down her sharp nose to the trembling man before her.

He couldn't bring himself to run. Not when her lips pulled back in a wide snarl, not when that horrific sound broke from her throat. Not even when her damp hair began to rise around her like a twisted, unholy crown. No, all he could do was stand there in abject terror at the sight before him.

Francesca cut short her sickening scream, plunging her hand into his ample belly. She ripped past fat and weak muscle, snaking her limb up through his core until sharp fingers found his heart. Instinct had taken over now, and he flung his fists at her, dirty fingernails at the end of chubby fingers clawing at her skin. When his over-sized heart was free of his chest, Francesca tossed him away.

Broken open, Harold lay in the grass, gasping like a fish for air that would never reach his lungs. There was some kernel of useless hope alive in his quieting mind as he found himself staring into the cloudy eye of the pretty girl from town. When her head moved, his brain convinced him that perhaps she was alive, that maybe she had survived somehow and together they could make it out of this. But when she moved again, he saw the vulture slide its bald head out of her open eye socket and gulp down a string of flesh. The bird hummed deep in its throat, cocking its head to gaze down at Harold briefly. Once more, its face was buried in the red.

That was the last thing he would ever see.

Using the heart blood, Francesca drew the runes, called out the words and raced across the void into Jonhas's dining chamber. He was taking a bite of his lunch when her voice resonated within his mind.

"What news from the orphanage master, Beacon?"

Jonhas was startled as always, a reaction that never ceased to amuse her. He coughed roughly. "Oh, Draven. Good noon to you." When she didn't reply he continued. "I spoke to Bruznik soon after his arrival this morning." Dabbing the crumbs from his lips, Jonhas pulled a scrap of paper from the stack. "He had a bit of information on the woman. Surrendered at the age of eight after her father's death. Bruznik said that she and the redhead were joined at the hip, even after they aged out of the home. She got a job with the city guard, but she didn't stay long. Rumor has it she followed the Callum fellow out to Crown's Cross. Probably joined up with The Den as well."

"Does she have a name?"

Quickly, he scanned the parchment. "Yes. Lucia Morisydo."

Francesca paused. "What was her father's name?"

"Uhm..." Another scan. "Kenton Hyde."

"The mother?"

"Not on record."

"Death records?"

"If there are any, they're not here. The girl wasn't born in Savhignos."

"You're sure?"

"Yes." Jonhas began to take a sip of his tea when the pressure in his head started to increase. Knowing how this game is played, he set the cup back down on the saucer. "The only records I could pull were from her time at the orphanage, and the quick stint with the city guard."

For a moment, she considered rupturing an artery or two. Instead, she left him without a word.

Once back in the void, Francesca didn't return to her body, but followed the tether up, and found the High Father in his bathing chambers.

Aolfrun reclined in a large, marble tub, steam rolling about his slender body. He didn't experience the battering ram of intrusion as Jonhas did. For him, it was a gentle caress, traced up the back of his skull.

"Ahh, my dear," he sighed. "Such a pleasure."

"High Father." Her voice was heady, just how he liked it.

"What brings you to my mind? Do tell me that it's to regale me with the story of how you've dismembered J'harenmar and his friends."

Without a single hint of hesitation, "No. Tytian still breathes."

Currents churned as he leaned forward, lips pursed in a dreadful scowl. He caught his anger quickly, knowing better than to lash out, well-disciplined in her art. "That is unfortunate."

"It is," she agreed coolly. "However, I have some information."

Intrigued, he slunk back into the water. "I'm listening."

"Tytian is traveling with a woman. She and the thief are longtime friends. Grew up at the orphanage that Jonhas frequents, and today he spoke to the headmaster and got a name. Lucia Morisydo."

Aolfrun clambered to his bony knees, eyes wide. "Morisydo? You're sure?"

"Jonhas confirmed it only moments ago."

"That must be why J'harenmar is traveling with them." His liver spotted hands gripped the side of the tub with force. "Where are they now?"

"I'm not sure, but they cannot hide from me."

Leathery lips stretched in a smile. "No, I suppose not. Continue your hunt, do whatever is necessary. Jonhas told me of your call for a fleet. I'll see to it that they're in the air immediately-"

"High Father?" A maid slipped into the chamber and glanced around, nervously kneading at her apron front.

"What is it?!"

"Uhm, a messenger has arrived for you, sir. They represent Welling house."

"My morning just seems to get better." He turned his attention back towards the demon in his mind. "You'll get your fleet Draven, just keep an eye on the sky."

"High Father, I have a request."

Thin brows raised in surprise. "Of course my dear, anything for you."

"Tell Jonhas to send me something to eat."

Aolfrun laughed. "I will have him bring you a whole banquet."

A tingling wave of pleasured heat crashed over him, gifted to him from Francesca. His body reacted, giving him back the stamina that age had stolen. Envigored and ready, he turned his eyes to the maid. "Come join me, girl. I have some celebrating to do." As the woman started to untie her gown, eyes trained to the floor, Aolfrun stared in hunger. "You could stay and join us, Draven." He heard her bewitching laugh, followed by the connection slipping.

"She's not to my taste. Enjoy your spoils."

That night was spent in feral bliss. With rotting meat in her stomach and the smell of blood on her skin, Francesca stalked the field as an animal. The vultures had flown to roost but the other scavengers, they slithered out of the forest once the sun had taken her light behind the mountains. The foxes came quietly enough, snatching up what they could from what was left of the girl and then scurrying back to the trees, afraid of the shadow with the glowing eyes in the distance. When the coyotes spilled in, all bristled fur, thick of scent and loud of mouth, chaos erupted.

They converged on the skeletal remains without fuss, but the real fighting began when they started tearing into Harold, starting with the softest parts. Squeals and snarls, barks and snaps, they ripped each other apart over the bloated corpse. Soon, the tidy little murder scene was a smear of carnage. They were so focused on their bedlam that only one of them noticed Francesca approach. Still naked, still coated in dark matter and grime, but with eyes glowing brightly with hellfire. She drew in their thick smell through her nose and threw back her head, tasting the scent on her tongue. That wild animal musk had always been intoxicating.

Gracefully, she laid herself down into the grass next to the feeding frenzy. Harold's half-eaten face stared at her, and she stared right back, lulled into slumber by the wet sounds of teeth.

The third day passed her by unnoticed. She didn't stir until the early hours of the fourth morning. Dew glittered her human hide, rolling off of her hips as she sat up and stretched. The monster she harbored, only just a peek of it, was now gone.

Much like her victims.

Except for the disturbed ground, nothing remained of the bodies. Between herself and the animals, it was as if they had never existed at all.

Using the dew in the grasses she cleaned herself and got dressed. She was cinching the final buckle on her shin guards when there came a soft hum in the distance. Airships formed on the waking dawn. Out of the three, only one dipped its nose and headed towards her, the other two keeping a steady course to the west. The engines thrummed in her ears the closer the rig got to the ground, making her teeth grit. Steadily, the massive beast lowered out of the sky. Golden hued runners sunk only a little into the rain-soaked field, the operator keeping the balloon filled enough to hover.

She took her time crossing the gap, making sure to wipe clean the corners of her mouth, should there be a little Harold left in the creases.

From the ornate gondola door stepped a man dressed in military finery. His colors spoke of the royal army, but on his lapel was a pin marking him as a devotee of the church.

"Draven, I presume?" he called over the sound of the engine with a smooth smile. He removed his hat and tucked it beneath one arm, extending the other to shake her hand. "I'm Darwin Porter, head of the fleet and Captain of the city guard for Savhignos." He gave her an appraising look. "And for now, I belong to you."

Thick, dark hair, clean shaven face, bright eyes and fine frame. He was a handsome man. And his beauty enraged her. "Hello Captain." She smiled politely and took his hand in her own. "I appreciate the rescue."

There was a cocky tweak to his lips. "Oh, a thing like you? I'm sure you didn't need any rescuing." He withdrew his hand before she could set it on fire and pretended not to notice the glow in the center of her palm. "The High Father asked me to pass along some information to you. He's sent out word to his contacts in all the major cities about J'harenmar and his...*friends.*" He seemed to chew on the last word before spitting it out. "Should they be spotted, they'll be detained and their whereabouts reported."

Francesca's brow narrowed, the mask slipping just enough to reveal a glimpse of the hostility beneath. "That's an unnecessary move. I will find them."

Realizing his poor choice of words, Porter delivered a throaty, rich man's chuckle. The stilted cadence gave Francesca the impression this was something he practiced, and often. "Oh, you've got it all wrong, miss. He only put out the word because he's asked for you to do something else. Something more important."

"What could be more important than J'harenmar and the Morisydo woman?"

"You're to meet with Welling when he makes his stop to refuel. He sent news days ago. His dig site in Havnul? They unearthed the rest of the stones."

Francesca's shoulders rose as her eyes grew wide. Out of everything he could have said, she was not expecting that.

Deep within the corners of her mind she felt Khaladhuun stir.

"Welling is bringing them to Savhignos with his caravan?"

Porter nodded curtly. "Yes, and his scholars will be working on the translations along the way. It'll be close to three more weeks before they reach the church, but that should give them plenty of time."

"Where will he be refueling?"

"Crown's Cross."

Her skin prickled, the pieces of a plan sliding right into place.

Porter took a step back and motioned to the gondola door. "Your chariot awaits, madame. Oh, and Jonhas sends his regards. Says you'll find quite the feast in your quarters."

Every sharp tooth glistened as she smiled, the taste of peaches fading on her tongue. "Good. Because I'm starving."

See You Soon

in

Thiefman's Folly

ΔBOUT THE ΔUTHOR

Rachel Pendley is an American author with a love of all things horror and fantasy. Growing up in the rural south she often found herself lost in the beauty of nature, and the comforts of family cemeteries. She is an advocate for mental health awareness, and a huge animal lover, feeling the most at peace when in the company of her furbabies.

To stay up to date on all upcoming works, check out her socials and be sure to sign up for the monthly newsletter on her website!

www.rachelpendley.com
Insta: @author.rachelpendley

Made in the USA
Columbia, SC
31 March 2026

.

81155582R00215